TOM CLANCY

ACT OF DEFIANCE

TOM CLANCY

ACT OF DEFIANCE

★

ANDREWS & WILSON

G. P. PUTNAM'S SONS

NEW YORK

PUTNAM
— EST. 1838 —

G. P. PUTNAM'S SONS
Publishers Since 1838
An imprint of Penguin Random House LLC
penguinrandomhouse.com

LCCN: 2024932731
Hardcover ISBN: 9780593422878
Ebook ISBN: 9780593422885

Printed in the United States of America
1st Printing

Maps by Jeffrey L. Ward

This is a work of fiction. Names, characters, places, and incidents either are the product of the
author's imagination or are used fictitiously, and any resemblance to actual persons, living or dead,
businesses, companies, events, or locales is entirely coincidental.

PRINCIPAL CHARACTERS

THE RYAN FAMILY

Jack Ryan: President of the United States
Dr. Caroline "Cathy" Ryan: First Lady of the United States
Jack Ryan, Jr.: Campus operative
Dr. Olivia "Sally" Ryan: Ophthalmic surgeon
Kathleen "Katie" Ryan: Lieutenant Commander (Select), U.S. Navy
Kyle Ryan: Lieutenant, USN

WASHINGTON, D.C.

Scott Adler: Secretary of state
Arnold "Arnie" van Damm: White House chief of staff
Mary Pat Foley: Director of national intelligence
Robert Burgess: Secretary of defense
Admiral Lawrence Kent, USN: Chairman of the Joint Chiefs of Staff
Major General Bruce Kudryk, U.S. Army: Joint Chiefs of Staff

CIA TEAM

Ginnie
Tom
James
Spencer

THE CAMPUS

John Clark: Director of operations
Domingo "Ding" Chavez: Assistant director of operations
Adara Sherman: Operations officer
Bartosz "Midas" Jankowski: Operations officer

USS *GERALD R.FORD* CARRIER STRIKE GROUP

Rear Admiral Bentley Kiplinger, USN: Strike group commander
Captain Otis Mackenzie, USN: Commanding officer, USS
  Gerald R. Ford
Captain Sarah "Baby" Williams, USN: Executive officer, USS
  Gerald R. Ford
Commander MartinVasquez, USN: CAG Carrier Air Wing 8
Commander James "Spacecamp" Huddleston, USN: DCAG
  Carrier Air Wing 8
Commander Brian "Mr. Pibb" Hanson, USN: Executive officer
  VFA-31
LCDR Jaya Kumari, USN: Naval intelligence officer on the *Ford*
IS2 Caspar, USN: LPO of the intelligence shop, USS *Gerald R.*
  Ford

USS *WASHINGTON*

Commander Clint Houston, USN: Commanding officer
LCDR Dennis Knepper, USN: Executive officer
LCDR Jackie "Juggernaut" Guevara, USN: Weapons officer

USS *INDIANA*

Commander Bresnahan, USN: Commanding officer
LCDR Pifer, USN: Executive officer
Xavier Harris: Sonar Technician Second Class
Chief Schonauer: Sonar supervisor

K-329 *BELGOROD*

Captain First Rank Konstantin Gorov: Commanding officer
Captain Second Rank Yuri Stepanov: First officer
Captain Lieutenant Blok: Conning officer
Starshina First Class Fyodorov: Quartermaster
Captain Lieutenant Ivan Tarasov: Engineering officer

K-560 *SEVERODVINSK*

Captain First Rank Lev Denikin: Commanding officer
Captain Second Rank Mats Tamm: First officer

RUSSIA

Nikita Yermilov: President of Russia
Colonel General Oleg Andreyev: Director, National Defense
  Management Center
Admiral Ivan Boldyrev: Commander in chief, Russian Naval Fleet
General Aralovich: Director of the FSB
Colonel General Nikolai Ilyin: Former KGB, retired
Admiral Rodionov: Director of the GRU
Erik Dovzhenko

JSOC SEAL TEAM

SOCS Max Harden, USN: SEAL strike team leader
SOC Reed Johnson, USN: SEAL/Special operations combat
  medic
SOC Billy Harper, USN
SO1 Owen Delacorte, USN
SO1 Marty Rich, USN
SO2 Scott Todd, USN
SOCS Dwight Merrell, USN

OTHER CHARACTERS

Captain Russ Ferguson, USN: Commanding officer, Nimitz
Warfare Analysis Center

Intelligence Specialist Second Class "Bubba" Pettigrew, USN:
Office of Naval Intelligence

Dr. Ronald Jones

Captain Pete Miller, USN (retired): Undersea Weapons Program
manager at the Naval Research Lab

Matthew Reilly: Retired CIA case officer

PROLOGUE

Dimitri Gorov resisted the compulsion to shove his hands into his overcoat pockets.

It wasn't just the bitter cold making him tremble.

Fear was the true culprit.

Tonight's clandestine face-to-face meeting with his American CIA contact had been months in the planning. They had a simple brokered arrangement: information in exchange for freedom. In his coat's breast pocket, Dimitri carried a microfilm roll containing the schematics and engineering details of the *Red October*—the Soviet Union's most advanced and stealthy Typhoon-class ballistic missile submarine. With its revolutionary "caterpillar drive," the *Red October* would be able to slip undetected past the Americans' undersea hydrophone arrays, past their SH-60 Seahawk helicopters with dipping sonar, and past their Los Angeles–class fast-attack submarines patrolling the Atlantic like sea wolves. This new submarine had cost the Kremlin tens of billions of rubles and was the product of a decade of research and design collaboration between the country's greatest scientific minds. He took great pride in his contribution to the project, but pride didn't change his station in life. Pride didn't put quality food on the dinner table, buy his wife a fur coat, or give his son a chance to find greatness as a man.

Nyet . . . *Pride is a poor man's compensation for following the rules.*

Dimitri had grown weary of following the rules.

A blast of arctic air buffeted him as he trudged west toward the city center. The metaphor was not lost on him. Even at this late hour, the *rodina* bullied him, trying to turn him back. Jaw set, he undid the fur-lined earflaps on the top of his wool *ushanka* and knotted the ties under his chin. As if in response to his obstinance, a streetlight flickered and went dark as he made his way along Nevsky Prospekt. Leningrad's main promenade, and quite possibly the most famous of all streets in the motherland, was utterly abandoned. Only the desperate or deranged would be out at this hour and in this weather, and the thought brought a fatalistic smile to his face.

Which one am I? Probably both . . .

He'd lived in Russia his entire life, but this was his first visit to the city formerly known as St. Petersburg. Originally named after St. Peter, not Peter the Great, which was a common misconception, the city was the most western and cosmopolitan of all Russian cities. It was often compared to Venice, due to the city's many rivers and canals, but Dimitri had never traveled outside of the Iron Curtain, so who was he to validate this claim? Regardless, Leningrad was beautiful, even blanketed in snow. He'd arrived earlier in the day by train with his wife and son at Moskovsky station—named as such, he presumed, because in Russia all roads lead to Moscow. They'd taken a walk along Nevsky Prospekt while the sun had been up and the city had been bustling. The architecture bespoke a past age—an era of tsars and prosperity—when hotels, opera houses, and even apartment buildings were designed to compete with palaces.

A lifetime of conditioning under the tenets of communism at first made him scoff and resent such waste, but the beauty and possibility advertised by such design quickly crept into and excited his bitter heart. This bygone city, eclipsed and barely persevering in the shadow of communism, represented but a fraction of the wealth and opportunity he would find in the West. In America, the land of prosperity and dreams, he and his family would eat meat every night. They would buy Levi's blue jeans, wear comfortable shoes, and Alina could go to a salon to have her hair done every week. But the thing he looked forward to the most was living in a house with central heat.

In America, we will finally be warm . . .

Squinting into the wind, he spied the landmark he was looking for—grand equestrian statues flanking the eastern entrance to the Anichkov Bridge. As he approached, the Horse Tamers came into focus—four sculptures, depicting men in the various stages of breaking a stallion, had been commissioned by Emperor Nicholas I and sculpted by Pyotr Karlovich Klodt. On Dimitri's side of the street, a bare-chested, kneeling horse master pulled against the reins of a rearing stallion. Despite not being an actual sculptor himself, Dimitri did consider himself an artist. Where Klodt was a sculptor of bronze, Dimitri was a sculptor of iron and titanium. Where Klodt depicted man overcoming nature, Dimitri's art literally empowered his fellow man to tame the sea. At this very moment, Marko Ramius and his crew were traversing the depths of the cold and unforgiving North Atlantic. Inside the *Red October,* they were warm, provisioned, and immune to both wave and weather. But take away the metal and the machine, and they wouldn't last a day.

"I would have liked to have gone to sea on my creation," he murmured as he approached and stared up into the wild eyes of the rearing stallion, "if only for a day. It would have been enough."

He'd met the captain at the *Red October*'s christening ceremony. Handsome and self-assured, imposing in his naval officer's black and gold parade uniform, Ramius had almost been too intimidating to approach. But Dimitri had mustered his courage and introduced himself to the man. Ramius's handshake had been firm as iron, but it was the submarine captain's dark and penetrating eyes that had unnerved Dimitri—eyes that seemed to peer beneath the flesh and into the inner workings of Dimitri's soul. In that moment, he'd felt judged and stripped naked, as if Ramius had extracted his secret plan to betray the homeland with merely a look. Then something unexpected happened. Ramius had thanked him, acknowledging the engineer's attention to detail, his ingenuity, and the thousands of hours Dimitri had spent working tirelessly on the design of the *Red October*.

"It is the finest warship in the Soviet fleet," Ramius said with a stoic nod.

"Thank you, sir," Dimitri said, with a stoic nod of his own.

"Exceptionally quiet, plenty of power, and armed to the teeth." But then, with a wry smile, the sub driver added, "My only complaint is that she is so bloated she changes depth like a crippled whale. Maybe you can fix this flaw in the successor class, *da?*"

"That is good to know . . . I will make a note of this," Dimitri said, and that had been the last time they'd spoken.

I almost feel bad for him, Dimitri thought, imagining the intrepid sub captain patrolling the ocean depth with false confidence, believing his ship and crew to be immune to detection. *Once I give this data to the Americans, they will know how to find you, Marko.*

A dribble of snot from his nose ran onto his top lip—pulling him back from his romantic ruminations to the new journey he had planned for himself—and he wiped it away with a finger of his glove. He pulled back the cuff of his coat sleeve to check the time on his wristwatch, which read 10:42 p.m. The time for daydreaming about the future and reminiscing about the past was over. In three minutes, his contact would meet him under the southernmost arch of the bridge, where they could talk in shadow. Dimitri was no spy and no student of tradecraft. Nor was he a managed asset of the CIA, indentured to a life of espionage where he would be expected to supply a steady stream of information to the Americans. He'd refused that offer outright. His betrayal would be a one-time event. Reilly could either take it or leave it.

The CIA man had taken it, without a moment's hesitation.

Dimitri resisted the urge to look behind him. He'd not seen anyone following him, but that meant nothing. The KGB was an omnipresent threat. They could be watching him right now, from behind curtains in apartment buildings or through the windows of darkened parked cars. He'd taken great risks bringing his family with him to Leningrad. If he was caught, the price he and his loved ones would pay was too horrific to contemplate. Alina and Konstantin would be tortured and executed, but not Dimitri. Not right away. His penance would be to watch. Only after they'd murdered his heart would the KGB sadists go to work on the rest of him. He shuddered and pushed the grim thoughts from his mind. He was in the endgame now, which meant he'd had no choice but to bring them with him. After he handed over the schematics, the CIA would orchestrate their defection. Dimitri didn't know how they planned to get him and his family out of Leningrad, but Matthew Reilly had assured him that they had done it safely many times before.

He wiped his nose again.

Now that it had started running, it wouldn't stop until he got indoors and warmed up.

Annoyed, he turned south, crossed Nevsky Prospekt, and

walked down the Fontanka River Embankment road. After a hundred meters, he reached a set of stone steps leading down to the riverbank and boat dock. The Fontanka was completely frozen and the icy crust was covered in several centimeters of snow, marred by numerous tracks and footsteps going every which way. Apparently, walking the frozen river was a winter novelty enjoyed by both young and old, because Dimitri saw footsteps both small and large. The calculating engineer in him hesitated before putting a foot on the ice, questioning if it would bear his weight, but then he chided himself. The empirical evidence was right before him. Hundreds of people had taken a stroll on the frozen waterway and walked away dry and safe.

This is the least dangerous thing you'll do today, you fool, his inner voice said.

With a sniff, he stepped onto the frozen river and turned back to the north. The Anichkov Bridge had three shallow arches, each spanning an equal third of the river. He walked along the bank toward the easternmost arch, where Reilly would be waiting bathed in absolute shadow. Heart pounding, he shuffled his numb, booted feet over the ice. Not until he'd stepped under the arch and into the darkness could he make out the crouching figure in the center of the hollow with his back to the sloping wall of the bridge.

"I'm hungry and cold. Can you spare a ruble or two?" the figure said, turning his head to look at Dimitri.

This was the challenge-response phraseology that Dimitri had expected to hear. His own answer would dictate how the meeting went. In the event he suspected being compromised or had failed to recover the plans, he was supposed to say, "*Nyet*, I have none to spare, comrade," and keep on walking. However, that was not the case tonight, so he used the other option.

"Life is difficult, comrade, but tonight I am feeling generous."

The figure stood.

Dimitri walked over to greet him, but his heart sank the instant Reilly's features came into focus. Something was wrong.

"Do you have the item?" the CIA man asked in Russian. Dimitri's English was terrible, so all communication was conducted in his native tongue.

"*Da*," he said, but made no move to retrieve the canister from where it was hidden in a false pocket inside his coat. "Have you made all the necessary arrangements?"

The American hesitated a moment before delivering the most crushing news of Dimitri's life. "Go home," Reilly said, his weight betraying his own disappointment. "The deal is off."

The words hit Dimitri like a punch to the solar plexus, and he suddenly felt ill.

"What? I . . . I don't understand," he stammered.

"I know, and I'm sorry, but it's out of my hands. This came down from the highest level."

"Why? This information changes everything for your country."

"We don't need the schematics anymore."

"But of course you do. You will never find the *Red October* without these data . . . And without me."

"I probably shouldn't be telling you this, Dimitri, but with your clearance level I'm sure you're going to find out soon enough. Ramius defected. He's provided us with everything we need to know about the *Red October*," Reilly said, and from the look in the CIA man's eyes, Dimitri knew it was true.

His American dream shattered, the Russian engineer stood unmoving, as if his feet had become absorbed by the ice. "But I brought my family . . ."

"I know."

"I risked everything for you."

Reilly nodded solemnly. "For what it's worth, I want you to know that I lobbied for you, and so did the station chief, but we got overruled. The risk-reward calculus has changed, and the higher-ups don't want to risk our defection chain or you and your family's lives for information we already have. If we part ways now, you go back to your life and your job and everything will be fine. As far as we can tell, you're not compromised."

"American bastard," Dimitri said, his voice more growl than speech. "Fuck you and your lies and false promises. I should have known. I'm so stupid."

Reilly pressed his lips into a hard line.

What was that expression? Defeat? Shame?

Dimitri could see that the man's eyes had gone wet, but American pity meant nothing to him. If he had a pistol, he'd shoot the man. He turned and walked back the way he'd come without another word or a backward glance. Just like before, his hands trembled, but this time, instead of fear, anger was the driver. His son, Konstantin, didn't know the real reason they'd traveled to Leningrad, but his wife did. How could he face her like this?

Rage blind, he trudged back to the hotel where they were staying. With each step his fury grew.

This is Ramius's fault. How could such a man defect? He is a naval captain!

He stopped abruptly in his tracks.

The *Red October* was on patrol. It had left Polyarnyy on December 3 and was not due to return for months. How could the captain defect at sea? How was such a thing possible?

"Unless Ramius surrendered the *Red October*," he murmured, stunned instantly at even the possibility of such an act. "I offer them the plans, and he gives them the ship—this is the only thing that would make the Americans back out of our deal. How could he do such a thing to me? He's cheated me, and my wife, and my son of our future. And the Americans . . . They made me a promise!"

What happened next unfolded in a blur—his normally

analytical engineer's mind a tempest of rage, denial, and shattered hope. He arrived at the hotel and told Alina everything, oscillating between shouting and sobbing as he did. He was vaguely aware that his ten-year-old son was listening, vaguely aware that he should not be saying such things in front of the boy who idolized him, but Dimitri was not himself. Nor was he himself when he drank a half a bottle of vodka, stormed out of the hotel room, and wandered the streets of Leningrad in the middle of the night, mumbling about the injustice of life and God and country. And when he decided that he would find the American CIA man and broker a new deal, he mistakenly wandered out onto the Neva River . . . confusing it with the much smaller Fontanka.

When the ice cracked and gave way beneath his feet, Dimitri sobered instantly in surprise and dread.

The current took him, dragging him unseen and unforgivingly beneath the crust toward the Gulf of Kronstadt. As the cold, black nothing took him, Dimitri breathlessly cursed Marko Ramius, the American CIA, and his own rash stupidity.

PART I

By the grace of God, America won the Cold War.
—President George H. W. Bush

1

Jack Ryan shrugged on his most comfortable cardigan in the master bedroom while looking out the window at the Chesapeake. Despite being several weeks into spring, the temperature had stubbornly refused to crack forty degrees this weekend. The kids and Cathy would tease him mercilessly for wearing this particular sweater, but that was the point, wasn't it? Traditions, inside jokes, and making memories were the bedrock of a happy family, and the Ryans were a happy family. That was the reason he loved this house so much. He and Cathy had built a lifetime of memories here—some harrowing, but most precious and warm.

A savory mélange of odors wafted up from the kitchen below as the family prepared to celebrate their daughter Katie's selection for lieutenant commander, a step up in rank she would pin on in the coming months. He took the time to breathe in the moment—the warmth of this home, the sound of the wind on the bay, and the commotion downstairs.

For a moment, he was no longer President Ryan, leader of the free world.

For a moment, he was just Jack—husband, father, and a guy who loved his country.

His mind's eye watched a parade of memories march by: celebrating Christmas with their kids Sally and Jack Junior in the early years before twins Katie and Kyle had even been born. Holding hands with Cathy on the porch, staring out at the bay, Sally and Jack older now, pushing each other on the tire swing, while the toddler twins scampered at their feet. Then an unwanted memory intruded—the horrorific night when ULA terrorist Sean Miller had come for them, shattering the illusion of safety the house provided. But all the good and wonderful things the Ryans had lived through and experienced in this house overpowered the terror of that night. Graduations, new jobs and careers, a wedding, Christmases and Thanksgivings—always with so much to be grateful for—celebrated right here inside these walls, the Chesapeake Bay smiling up from below as if celebrating right along with them . . .

From downstairs, Cathy called, "Jack, are you coming? They'll be here any minute."

Ryan hurried out of the bedroom and descended the stairs, excited for the family dinner ahead. Upon entering the kitchen, he saw his wife furiously prepping dinner at the island, while their staff chef, Agatha, stood off to the side with her arms crossed, unable to hide her exasperation with the First Lady.

"She won't let me help her," Agatha said to Jack with a helpless, beseeching look.

"You're preaching to the choir," he said, shaking his head.

"I know it might not look like it, but I'm actually enjoying myself," Cathy Ryan said with a genuine smile. "Besides, I've been cooking for my kids for years. I know what they like and how they like it."

"Yes, ma'am," Agatha said, trying not to sound put out. "Just know I'm here if you need me."

But that was the point, wasn't it? Here in the Ryan family home, the Ryans wanted to do the meal prep, the cooking, and even the dishes. It wasn't theater, it was real, because the doing *made* it real. This wasn't the White House, it was their family home, and in a family home, the family does the work.

"You're making the poached salmon?" he asked, but the aroma of the kitchen gave him the answer.

"It's Katie's favorite."

He wrapped his arms around his bride from behind and kissed her on the cheek. "Is there anything *I* can do to help?"

Cathy let out a sigh, then turned, threw her arms around his neck, and gave him a proper kiss.

"You can check on the bread in the oven and put the salad on the table," she said, turning back to her work. "And then feel free to take off that ratty old sweater."

"Ratty? This is handwoven Scottish wool, thank you very much. You couldn't buy quality like this today if you tried."

"Mm-hmm," she said, but she was grinning, and this was the game they played.

Agatha made a move for the oven, but Ryan waved her off. "I've got it."

"Well, perhaps I can at least let a bottle of wine begin to breathe," Agatha said, grabbing a corkscrew and trying her damnedest to be helpful.

"That would be lovely, Agatha, thank you so much," Cathy said as Ryan pulled a flat pan with two loaves of bread from the lower oven and put the pan on a hot plate. The smell of butter and garlic made his stomach growl.

"Do you want me to slice it?" he asked, but the doorbell chimed, and he raised his eyebrows to ask if he should answer it.

"Go," she said. "I've got this."

It wasn't just his schedule that had kept him from seeing his youngest daughter for months, even though she worked just a short drive from where he sat most days in the Oval Office. After graduating from the Academy and completing her training at the intelligence school at Dam Neck in Virginia Beach, Katie had served a fleet tour in Norfolk, the three hours as distant as a continent with everyone's schedule. Now Katie had tackled her job as intelligence analyst with ONI the same way she did everything in life—with quiet focus and one hundred and ten percent effort. Like her older sister, Sally, who loved her work as a pediatric surgeon, but not as much as the work in the lab, where she searched for new knowledge at the cellular level to make her care for her patients even better, Katie was all about the details. It was no surprise that today they were celebrating her promotion to senior analyst for Russian threats, with that promotion to lieutenant commander soon to follow. She'd been at ONI for only a year and a half, after finishing an operational tour aboard the *Truman*, so her advancement to senior analyst was way ahead of the norm. Captain Russ Ferguson, CO of the Nimitz Warfare Analysis Center, had told Jack that she was a prodigy.

Not that he was checking up on her . . .

"Daddy!" his all-grown-up little girl hollered when he entered the foyer, and he wrapped her up in a big hug. In that moment, he wasn't the President and she wasn't a naval officer—they were just daddy and daughter. "I missed you so much, Dad."

"You too, kid," he said when she broke the embrace. "We've both been busy. I hear you're tearing it up over at ONI."

"Keeping tabs on me, eh?"

"Only a little," he said with a smile.

"Isn't that abuse of power or something?"

"Only if I tip the scales for you, which I don't," he protested. "And from what I hear, you don't need it."

"What can I say, I love my work," she said. Then, eyeing his sweater, added, "Really, Dad, I can't believe Mom hasn't thrown that thing out."

"Believe me, she's tried."

They both laughed at this, and he pulled her in for another hug. *Mission accomplished.*

The doorbell chimed. They turned together to watch Secret Service open the door and Katy's big sis, Sally, come through, hand in hand with her husband and fellow surgeon, Davi.

"Hi, sweetheart," Ryan said, giving Sally a hug and peck on the cheek.

"Missed you," Sally said, beaming at him. "Nice *dad* sweater, by the way."

He grinned and turned to Sally's husband. "Come on in, Davi."

"How are you, sir?" Dr. Davi Kartal said, extending his hand.

Ryan shook the firm grip. He liked Davi, a lot in fact. "When we're home with family, Davi, I'm Jack or Dad, okay?"

"Right," Davi said, properly chided. "Sorry. It's still so weird."

"Yeah, for me too, sometimes," Ryan said. "Cathy's in the kitchen. How about we help her out?"

"Is Jack coming?" Katie asked, referring to her older brother, Jack Junior.

"Not sure if he's going to make it," Ryan said as they passed through the dining room for the kitchen. "He was busy at work, but was hoping to come by. Haven't heard from him yet."

"Mom!" Katie said and ran to Cathy, who was still working at the kitchen island.

Ryan watched with affection as his two daughters hugged and greeted their mother. An upswell of pride tickled his throat at seeing how accomplished and confident his girls had grown up to be.

And every bit as beautiful as their mother.

After the requisite hugs and small talk were complete, Cathy announced, "Dinner is ready. We should probably get to the table before everything goes cold."

"Let me help you," Katie said, but Cathy shook her head.

"This is your dinner, Katie. No help from you."

"I gotcha, sis," Sally said, grabbing the salad bowl.

Minutes later they were around the large table, the bay window behind Ryan, who sat at the head, reflecting the sunlight from the bay into the room, where it danced color on the walls. He was about to lead the prayer, when the door chimed again.

"I can't believe you almost started without me," Jack Junior called from the foyer. He strode into the dining room, set a coyote-colored backpack on the floor, and slipped into the empty seat between Katie and his mom.

"I can't believe you made it," Katie said with a big smile. "If only Kyle was here, it'd be perfect."

"I barely made it from the Beltway. Kyle's in Bahrain," Jack said, dropping a napkin into his lap. "Besides, after four years at the Academy together, surely you guys need a break."

"Yeah, but that was years ago. This is the longest we've been apart. I miss him," Katie said.

"Use your twin powers. If you channel his thoughts, it'll be like he's here," Sally said, and everyone laughed.

"A little bird told me you're putting on O-4 ahead of him," Jack Junior said as Agatha slid a plate of poached salmon on a bed of saffron rice in front of him.

"Really? Congrats, sis, that's fantastic," Sally said. Then, with an impish grin, added, "Kyle was always the more competitive twin. Can't wait to see the look on his face when *he* has to salute *you.*"

"Yeah," Jack Junior said with a chuckle. "That oughtta cool the twin connection."

"Hey now, let's not pick on the only Ryan who isn't here," Ryan said, the familiar intimacy of this table of people, their easy, comfortable connection, filling him with warmth and making his eyes wet. "Let's say a blessing, and we can pray for your brother, who wasn't able to join us for this special day, and the important work he's doing with Task Force 59."

The table quieted, and Ryan led them all in prayer.

"Bless us, oh Lord, and these thy gifts, which we are about to receive . . ."

Cathy squeezed his hand.

Life was good.

2

Captain First Rank Konstantin Gorov stood on the bridge of the K-329 *Belgorod* as two tugboats eased the nuclear-powered submarine away from the pier. A brisk gust of wind chased away the cloud of noxious diesel exhaust from the tugs chugging and sputtering along his starboard beam. The western breeze smelled of salt and pine, prompting him to momentarily close his eyes and take a deep, cleansing breath.

This moment was one he wanted to remember.

The conning officer, Captain Lieutenant Blok, who was standing at Konstantin's right shoulder, ordered a backing bell to help back the massive submarine away from the pier.

"Captain, the ship is underway," Blok said a moment later.

"Very well. Sound three short blasts for operating astern propulsion."

Blok repeated the order, as was naval protocol, before speaking the command into the bridge handset microphone, which transmitted into the control room belowdecks. A moment later, the submarine's horn bellowed three times, echoing across the sound and informing all who were listening that the Russian Navy's biggest, deadliest, and most capable nuclear submarine was going to sea.

At one hundred eighty-four meters long, the *Belgorod* was the longest submarine ever built—nine meters longer than even the famed *Red October* Typhoon-class guided missile submarine (SSGN) of the Cold War era. Unlike the Typhoon class, the *Belgorod* was not a ballistic missile submarine. Nor was she an SSGN, designed to carry anti-ship and land-attack cruise missiles like the rest of the Oscar II–class submarines upon which she was based.

No, the *Belgorod* was conceived with an entirely different purpose in mind.

Konstantin adjusted his black winter visor cap to block the sun. Normally, at this time of year, heavy foul-weather gear would be required for the topside watch standers. But not today. The weather for the submarine's send-off was unseasonably pleasant—partly sunny, with light winds from the west, and a balmy eight degrees Celsius. On days like today, standing watch on the bridge was a privilege rather than the familiar trial for submariners assigned to Russia's Northern Fleet, homeported at a latitude above the Arctic Circle in Polyarnyy.

"Conning officer, secure the backing bell," Konstantin said, eyeing their progress.

"Aye, Captain," Blok said and ordered the engines to all stop.

"Inform the tug pilot I intend to cast them off once we are in the middle of the harbor," Konstantin said as K-329's massive hull repositioned away from the pier.

Blok hesitated a moment before saying, "But, Captain, the tugs are planning to assist us out into Dvina Bay. The release point is beyond the harbor entrance choke point and *after* the first turn."

Konstantin turned and looked down at his conning officer.

At one hundred eighty-seven centimeters tall, the Russian submarine captain towered ten centimeters above his average countryman. His height, along with his commanding, baritone voice, made him an intimidating figure—something he'd learned to leverage to his advantage at a very young age. Blok was Konstantin's most capable and intelligent junior officer, which is why the captain had assigned the man as his conning officer for this evolution. But like too many Russian submarine officers, Blok had spent far more time in port than at sea, which meant he needed much more time driving the boat and more time under pressure. This was one such opportunity.

"I am aware of that, Captain Lieutenant," Konstantin said, "but are you telling me you're afraid of making a single turn?"

Blok didn't answer, just wilted a little under Konstantin's gaze, looking up with his mouth open.

"It's a simple right turn and then we are in the White Sea, driving for hours in a straight line before turning again. It's the only decision you will make for hours. Would you not like to do it?"

Blok swallowed hard and said, "*Da*, Captain. I will inform the tug captain."

Konstantin resisted the urge to smile as his junior officer called the lead tugboat and informed the man of the change of plans. As expected, the tug captain questioned the decision, but yielded to the Northern Submarine Fleet's most senior commanding officer.

"As soon as they throw off the lines, order the topside watch belowdecks."

Blok nodded nervously. "*Da*, Captain."

Konstantin understood the young officer's trepidation. The harbor mouth at Severodvinsk was intimidatingly narrow because of a jetty that did double duty as a storm break and pier. The entrance was so narrow, in fact, that it was barely wider than the *Belgorod* was long. Celebrated for their silent running, deep diving, and

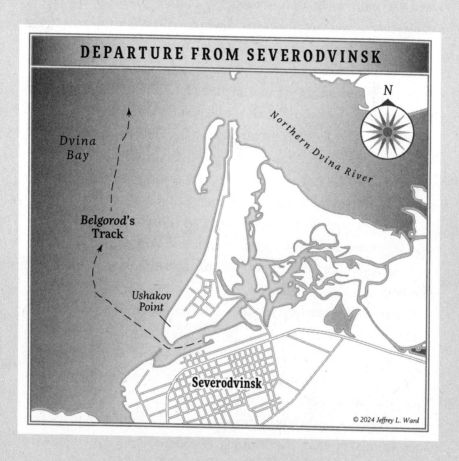

DEPARTURE FROM SEVERODVINSK

Dvina
Bay

Northern Dvina River

N

Belgorod's
Track

Ushakov
Point

Severodvinsk

© 2024 Jeffrey L. Ward

nuclear-powered propulsion, submarines like K-329 were not known for their maneuvering capability. The ninety-degree turn from the Severodvinsk harbor's main channel into the White Sea—a maneuver that would be child's play for a civilian motorboat—was a sphincter-clenching evolution for a vessel as long as two American football fields. Turn too late, and the *Belgorod* would crash into one of the two decommissioned Typhoon-class submarines that sat mothballed along the end of the pier. A collision like that would send the *Belgorod* back into the Sevmash Shipyard's dry dock for repairs, delay the underway for months, and result in him losing command of the boat. But Konstantin would not let that happen. A man who couldn't navigate his own ship out of the harbor had no business at the helm.

"The tugs are clear, Captain, and all topside personnel are reporting belowdecks with hatches shut and dogged," Blok said, repeating the report they'd both heard from the control room over the bridge's box speaker.

"Very well. Take us out, Captain Lieutenant," Konstantin said. "Turns for four knots."

"Turns for four knots, aye, Captain," Blok said, and then into his hand mic, gave the order, "Helm, Bridge, engines ahead slow, make turns for four knots."

The helm acknowledged the order over the bridge's box speaker and, an instant later, the *Belgorod* shuddered for a split second as her twin screws churned to life at the stern.

"Captain, the ship is making—" Blok started to say, but Konstantin cut him off.

"When are you going to order the rudder and how much rudder are you going to use?"

"The charted turn is based on Ushakov point, so I was going to order a full rudder when the navigator marks the turn," Blok said.

"Then we will crash . . . Try again."

"Um, well, I will order sooner."

"The charted turn was based on using our rudder to supplement the tugboats, which are pushing astern and pulling at the bow to rotate the boat. You cannot turn so late. It is always better to turn early than to turn late. You can always ease off the rudder, but you can't order more rudder than full. But let's say that you are not turning fast enough even with the full rudder. What else can you do?"

"I can reverse the starboard engine," Blok said as a bead of sweat ran down his left temple.

"*Da*, but this will slow us, and we are only making four knots. Without speed, the rudder is useless," Konstantin said as he eyed Ushakov point, which was rapidly approaching on their starboard bow.

The junior officer squinted with consternation.

"Ushakov point is thirty degrees off our starboard bow, conning officer," the lookout, Starshy Matros Ivanovych, the leading seaman, prompted. Ivanovych was the only other crew member on the bridge for the maneuvering watch and Konstantin had purposely written him onto the watch bill because the young man had leadership protential in the noncommissioned ranks.

Blok keyed his handheld mic. "Helm, right full rudder."

"Right full rudder, Helm, aye," the helmsman reported back. "Bridge, Helm, my rudder is right full."

"Very well, Helm. Navigator, mark the turn and confirm our track."

"Bridge, Navigator, aye," the navigator, Captain Third Rank Sokolov, said over the comms circuit.

As soon as we released the tugs, Sokolov should have plotted our new track and marked the turn. That's one strike, Sokolov, Konstantin thought, making a mental note.

"We are turning very slowly, Captain," Blok said, his voice a tight cord.

"*Da*, what did you expect? We are not driving a Ferrari."

"Should I reverse the starboard engine?"

The two decommissioned Typhoon-class SSGNs docked at the end of the jetty pier drew the sub captain's eye. The mothballed goliath submarines were an inauspicious and omnipresent reminder of the Cold War glory days when the Soviet submarine fleet numbered four hundred vessels strong. Konstantin's eyes crept over the long missile deck, which, unlike the American Ohio-class SSGN, was located forward of the Typhoon's iconic and bulbous sail design. His mind rarely drifted far from the Russian Navy's most infamous Typhoon—the *Red October*. The Kremlin had constructed a glorious fiction about this submarine and its vaunted captain. According to the history books, Marko Ramius and the senior officers on board had valiantly scuttled the *Red October* after a reactor accident to prevent the sub from falling into American hands. Ramius had received the Order of Lenin posthumously for his heroism.

But Konstantin knew the *real* truth.

Marko Ramius was not a hero to be celebrated, but a traitor.

Despite only being ten years old at the time, he remembered that fateful night like it had been yesterday. He'd listened while his father, Dimitri Gorov, had wept and shouted and cursed Ramius and the American CIA, before storming off into the night, never to be seen again. At the time, Konstantin had not understood, but his poor mother's deathbed confession had brought everything into focus. The authorities had never found his father's body, nor the roll of microfilm he planned to give to the Americans. Konstantin was certain of this fact because, had the KGB learned of the older Gorov's intention to defect, the younger Gorov would never have ascended in the Russian Navy. No son of a traitor would ever be given command of the Northern Fleet's submarine flagship.

Nyet, my legacy is still untarnished . . . As is that of Marko Ramius.

"Captain? Did you hear me?" Blok said, snapping Konstantin out of his rumination. "Should I reverse the starboard engine?"

"I told you, that will slow us and cause loss of steerage."

Panic washed over Blok's face as the situation deteriorated. "Then what do I do?"

"You are the conning officer, Captain Lieutenant. Give an order," Konstantin said, unwilling to bail out his junior officer by making the decision for him.

"Sir, I recommend—" the lookout said, trying to intervene, but the sub captain cut him off.

"*Nyet*, we give him ten more seconds, Seaman Ivanovych," Konstantin said, but he glanced back at the lookout and nodded—a captain's acknowledgment that the young seaman's intention to bail out the conning officer was both warranted and appreciated. A nuclear submarine could not function effectively if competent crew were cowed into keeping their mouths shut for fear of retribution. However, this was a teaching moment for Blok, and he would not have it ruined.

The sub captain counted the seconds down in his head.

With only two seconds left before he relieved Blok of the conn, the junior officer sprung into action.

"Helm, Bridge, turn the stern thruster to port zero-nine-zero and start the engine," Blok said, practically tripping over the words as he spoke into his mic.

"Bridge, Helm, stern thruster is turned to Port zero-nine-zero and running," the helm reported a beat later.

The bullet-shaped thruster, which was lowered from the keel at the stern of the ship, was designed for maneuvering situations when a tugboat was not present. Despite its small propeller and much lower horsepower than the main engines, the perpendicular thrust and long moment arm from the ship's axis of rotation meant it outperformed the ship's rudder at low speeds. With the thruster running, the *Belgorod*'s heading rapidly began to change, and the giant submarine's stern was finally coming around.

"Bridge, Navigator, ship is coming back onto track. Recommend securing the aft thruster," said Sokolov over the bridge's box speaker a few moments later.

"Look with your own eyes before you do as he says," Konstantin said, grabbing the conning officer's wrist before Blok could mindlessly parrot the navigator's order to the helm. "Check your lines. Feel the ship. Do *you* think we're on course?"

Blok looked at Ushakov point, then at the harbor mouth, then whirled to look aft at the Memorial'naya Doska Bogolyubov building, which was coming in line with the rudder.

With newfound confidence, the conning officer keyed his mic. "Helm, stop the thruster . . . Ease your rudder to right ten degrees."

The helmsman repeated the order, then said, "Bridge, Helm, maneuvering thruster is stopped, and my rudder is right ten degrees."

"Bridge, Helm, Navigation concurs," Sokolov chimed in.

Konstantin crossed his arms in satisfaction.

Now they're working as a team. We'll see how these men respond when we must face a truly difficult situation.

"Helm, zero your rudder," Blok ordered at the exact moment when Konstantin would have given the command himself.

"Bridge, Helm, my rudder is amidships," the helmsman reported.

"Very well."

Konstantin felt his junior officer's eyes on him as the *Belgorod* cruised silently on course, out of the narrow mouth of Severodvinsk's harbor. Instead of giving the young officer the affirmation he was hoping for, the submarine captain kept his eyes fixed on the lapis waters of Dvina Bay dead ahead.

You did well, Blok, but not worthy of a pat on the back.

Despite its massive area of ninety thousand square kilometers, the White Sea was too shallow for the *Belgorod* to safely navigate submerged. To reach their assigned dive coordinates off the coast of the Kola Peninsula would require a seven-hundred-kilometer surface transit to the Barents Sea. For the duration of this long and wearisome journey, they would be observed and tracked by American satellites.

But this is okay, because it is all part of the game, Konstantin told himself, inhaling the ocean air.

Driving a nuclear submarine on the surface in nice weather was one of life's truly rare and precious experiences. Perfectly quiet. Perfectly smooth. No noxious exhaust gases. No squawking and complaining sailors . . .

Just me, my ship, and the sea.

Ordinarily, after making the turn northeast, Konstantin would return belowdecks to his stateroom to deal with the minutiae of command, but not today. Today, he would leave such matters to his first officer and linger on the bridge. He wanted to savor the moment and commit it to memory. Because if his plan succeeded, this would be the last time he gazed upon the shores of his beloved homeland.

3

Lieutenant Kathleen Ryan tugged at the sleeve of her jacket and leaned in beside Intelligence Specialist Second Class Pettigrew to study the image on the computer screen, jealous that the Alabama native sat comfortably in his Guacamoles, while she was in service dress blues. But then IS2 Pettigrew—Bubba, as he was known to the team, a nod to his slow southern drawl that barely masked a dizzying intellect—didn't have to brief the deputy chief of naval operations, Admiral Sarah Young, on the rising threats from Russian naval forces in the Black Sea that morning.

"What am I looking at, Bubba?" she asked, squinting at the image of a submarine on rails that would slide it into the sea from a dry dock at the Severodvinsk seaport on the Dvina Bay in the White Sea.

"Well, ma'am," her top IS said, drawling the words out and running a hand through his red hair, "that there's the K-329, a new Russki submarine based on the Oscar II platform. The official designation is Project 09852, but its name is the *Belgorod*."

She smiled patiently. She hadn't heard the term "Russki" used anywhere but in old movies.

"Yes, I'm familiar, Bubba," she said. "I recognize the boat, but I'm guessing you're showing this particular image to me for a reason?"

"Oh, yes, ma'am," Pettigrew said and traced a box around the bow of the Russian sub, clicking with the mouse to fill the screen with the selected image. "You probably remember that in all the other images we had, she was inside the covered dry dock, so we couldn't see nothing of the front of the sub. Here we got a shot of the bow before she went down the rails for launch."

Katie Ryan squinted again. "It looks different than the other Oscar IIs, but I can't put my finger on why," she admitted in frustration. Her expertise was more Russian strategy and changing geopolitics. What she knew about Russian submarines fell more into those categories, and despite the engineering courses required of all Naval Academy midshipmen, she couldn't be further from an expert on subs.

"Well," Pettigrew drawled, "she's bigger, for one—longer than other Oscar IIs, and rumored to have more displacement than even the Typhoons—but we hadn't seen the bow until now. See these here . . ." Pettigrew pointed to the bow.

"Torpedo tubes?" she asked.

Bubba nodded and clicked the mouse, opening another window in the upper right corner of the screen—an older, archive image he'd prepared in advance, Katie realized.

"This here is a standard Oscar II, and these are the torpedo tubes. See the difference?"

"Well," she said, "the standard Oscar has six and the *Belgorod* appears to only have two."

"Yes, ma'am," Bubba said, "but they're huge. I'd guess six or seven feet across."

"What does it mean?" she asked, straightening up, but still staring at the image. She knew very well that the *Belgorod* was something special to the Russian Navy. Intelligence from inside Russia suggested she was a special purpose submarine, rather than a fast-attack boat. Images of the docking station aft of the sail suggested she could serve as a mother ship for minisubs, or even autonomous undersea drones. The Pentagon was worried the sub would be used to deliver submersible drones, which could disrupt communication cables in the Atlantic, or deliver Russian Special Forces, in the same way Navy SEALs deployed minisubs out of dry deck shelters carried on the back of certain U.S. submarines.

"No idea, ma'am," Pettigrew said. "I sure ain't no engineer. But"—he leaned over and smiled—"I'm guessing that them doors is to deliver a weapon we probably should educate ourselves on real quick."

Katie nodded.

"Great work, Pettigrew," she said and clapped the sailor on the shoulder as she rose. "I'll brief this up the chain. Maybe we can get some better images on the next satellite pass that will clear things up. Although I'm assuming the bow will be hard to see now that she's in the water. We can maybe get more pictures of the docking station aft of the sail . . ."

"Don't think so, LT," Pettigrew said.

"Why not?"

Pettigrew leaned back in his chair. "She put to sea early this morning, boss," the intelligence specialist said. He clicked the mouse again, bringing up a satellite image of the submarine escorted by tugs in the Dvina Bay. The next image showed the *Belgorod* departing Severodvinsk's harbor, the tugs already behind her.

"Where is she now?" Katie asked. "Are they moving her to Polyarnyy?"

"Don't know," Pettigrew said with a shrug, "but the team is digging deeper into it on all channels."

She pursed her lips.

"Thanks, Bubba," she said, then glanced at her watch. "I gotta go, but I'll circle back later, okay?"

"You got it, LT," the sailor said and bent back over his keyboard.

She hustled down the hallway toward the skipper's office, her mind searching for a direction on the information the IS2 had shared, but not finding one. She stopped at the raised desk outside Captain Ferguson's office, the yeoman chief petty officer looking at his watch with all the subtlety of a bobcat in a coffee shop, as Pettigrew liked to say.

"I'll see if he's ready for you, Lieutenant Ryan," he said and picked up the phone. "She's here, sir . . . Yes, sir," he said into the phone. "Will do, sir." The chief gave her a crooked smile that she wondered might be pleasure at what could be coming for the young and rising star. She glanced at her own watch again—not a minute to spare. Might as well be the next day for her boss, Captain Russ Ferguson, for whom punctuality was on par with godliness— at the command level there was only early or late. "Go right in, Lieutenant."

But the skipper let her off the hook with a simple, sarcastic "Thanks for making time for me, Lieutenant Ryan" as he gestured to a chair beside where he sat at a modest-sized conference table, where he liked to conduct business.

She took her seat.

"Sorry to be late, sir," she said, noting the second hand sweeping across the twelve—making her technically right on time. "One of my people was sharing some new information on a Russian submarine we've been investigating."

"I assumed you were working," the skipper said. "Is this the *Belgorod*?"

"It is, sir," she said, surprised, but also realizing she shouldn't be. Ferguson had an amazing gift of not only eidetic memory and intelligence, but also the ability to read people in a way that bordered on mind reading. "My best IS was sharing new images of the boat, sir." She went on to describe what Pettigrew had shown her.

"Huh," Ferguson said, leaning back in his leather chair and making a little steeple with his fingers. "Work with our connections at NSA. Let's see if we can get some more images to share with the engineers over at the Undersea Research Lab, okay?"

"Sure, but it might be a while, sir," she said. "We'll have to find her."

"Find her?" Ferguson growled, now sitting up straight, his arms on the table's glass topper, under which dozens of command coins lay on display. "She's at Severodvinsk, right?"

"She was, sir," she said. "She put out to sea early this morning. Just after midnight our time, I believe."

"Well, shit," Ferguson said and slapped a hand on the tabletop. "Someone dropped the ball somewhere. We've got pretty good intel inside Russia. I can't remember the last time a Russian ship or sub put to sea on a scheduled deployment that we didn't know ahead of time. What the hell happened?"

"Not sure, sir," she said. "We'll try and find out."

"Well, if they somehow kept this one secret, that's a big damn deal, Ryan," Ferguson said. "For us to not know about it means Russian leaders are keeping secrets from each other. That means something important is happening with this submarine. We need to figure out what this boat is all about."

"I'll broaden the scope and task the rest of my team to get up to speed, sir."

Ferguson pulled at his chin, deep in thought.

"We'll need some outside help, too, Ryan," he said and looked over at her. "I'm gonna arrange for you to meet Juggernaut. Her boat is getting ready for deployment, but she'll make time for you, I'm sure."

"Juggernaut?" Katie asked, intrigued.

"It's a nickname," Ferguson said. "The perfect one, I might add. She's barely five feet tall, but tough as nails. She finished a shore tour at the undersea lab and was a genius of some sort. Smartest damn submariner I ever met, and that's saying something, because they're all smart as hell. She's the weapons officer on board the *Blackfish* now."

"The *Blackfish*, sir?" Katie asked, confused. In her job, she knew the fleet pretty well, but the only Blackfish she could think of was a movie about killer whales and a character from *Game of Thrones*.

"The USS *Washington*," he said. "SSN 787. The crew call her the *Blackfish*."

"Why?"

"Well," he said, still smiling, "why don't you ask them? I'll arrange for a visit to the *Washington* for you to spend some time with Juggernaut to get her opinion on those torpedo doors. If anyone can generate a reasonable theory, it'll be her. With deployment right around the corner it would be a big ask to bring her up here, so you'll head down to meet her. You okay with that?"

"Yes, sir. Of course. Who should I take with me?"

"No one," the skipper said. "Submariners are notoriously closed-lipped and they don't like crowds. Just you. Have your team send any imagery to me on the high side and I'll make sure it makes it to the *Washington*."

"Aye, sir," she said.

"Great," he said, rising. "Let's go meet with Admiral Young."

Her eyes widened.

"Do you want to go over what I'm going to brief her on?"

"Well, I assume you'll address the increasingly hostile activity in the Black Sea and the harassment of the fleet in the northern

Atlantic. I would hope you'll touch on the covert operations we detected in Finland, and also the false flag operations they continue to wage in the Baltics . . ."

"Yes, sir," she said, aware she was interrupting her boss. "I meant, I thought you might want to go over the specifics, sir. To make sure—I don't know—to make sure that . . ."

"Ryan, we made you a senior analyst for a reason. You promoted to O-4 below zone for a reason. If I wanted a briefing from an analyst who I needed to supervise or mentor, I would have tasked one of the JOs," he said, referring to the junior officers in the shop. "No, actually I would *not* have done that, because I'm too damn busy. Are you not feeling up to the task, Ryan?"

Katie took a deep breath and clenched her jaw.

"No, sir. I'm all good. Just want to represent our command the way you want me to."

His look softened.

"Just be yourself, Ryan. Limit the jargon and the technical details. She doesn't care about collection methods, only the facts. So give her the facts and tell her the why, but also the what—as in, what you think it means and why it matters. It's what you're best at, frankly, like your superpower. Okay?"

"Okay, sir," she said and followed him from the office and down the hall to where Admiral Young and her senior staffers would be waiting in the conference room reserved for such meetings. She felt a simultaneous grip of fear and a swell of pride. Ferguson sending her to the front of the room without review meant he trusted her—which meant a lot.

It also meant she was on her own.

If Dad could see me now . . .

4

K onstantin stared at the shattered glass screen of his mobile phone—damage that he'd elected not to repair. He'd dropped it at the hospital *that* day, and now it was a metaphor for his life. The main fissure in the glass cut transversely across Calina's neck, an ungodly reminder that his life was meant to be punishment.

He stared at this image often, the last and final picture he'd taken of his wife.

The worried look in her eyes, the waning curl of her lips . . .

In that moment, she'd known. Somehow, she'd known it would happen.

"You should have said something to me," he said to her image, tears pressing. "I could have intervened. I could have taken you to a different hospital."

A knock on the door snapped him from the macabre moment.

"Come," he said, collecting himself.

The door opened.

"Captain, I was instructed by Captain Lieutenant Blok to bring you the rig for dive checklist for your review and signature," said the messenger.

"Very well, bring it to me."

The young sailor, whose nervous face Konstantin did not recognize, entered his stateroom and handed him a clipboard with a multipage document. The captain's gaze dropped to the seaman's name tag, and he committed the name to memory as he accepted the clipboard. The messenger quickly backpedaled to the passageway outside and moved to shut the door.

"Leave it open," Konstantin said, scanning the top page. "This won't take long."

Prior to diving the submarine, a verification check was performed to validate the status and proper position of all hatches and valves associated with hull penetrations that could result in flooding when transitioning from surfaced to submerged operations. This practice, which the Soviet Navy had borrowed from the Americans, was a two-party verification—with two qualified watch standers performing the checklist separately and independently. The "independent" element was essential, with the second checker functioning as a backup to the first. During his early days as an officer in training, Konstantin had performed the rig for dive checklist many times as both first and second checker. On multiple occasions, he'd found mistakes. Sometimes a stuck valve feels like a shut valve on its seat. Sometimes people confuse clockwise and counterclockwise directions. And sometimes people are in a hurry and simply miss things.

"The ocean is an unforgiving master," Konstantin said as he flipped to the second page, scanning for two sets of initials beside every line item. "Seaman Danovich, do you know what the water pressure is at a depth of five hundred meters?"

Danovich hesitated a moment before saying, "No, Captain. I do not."

"Every ten meters of depth is one bar of pressure. This submarine's diving limit is five hundred meters, which equates to fifty bars, or fifty atmospheres of pressure. Do you understand?" The young seaman nodded, but Konstantin could see that he didn't really comprehend the significance. "If there is a leak when we are deep, it is not like on the surface. You can't stick your finger in the hole to plug it. The pressure is so great, it will cut your arm off like a laser. A hole as small as one centimeter will produce a stream of seawater so powerful that the water will atomize, flooding the air and your lungs instantly, drowning you where you stand."

Danovich swallowed hard, not liking this new knowledge. "That is terrible."

The sub captain tapped the checklist with his index finger. "Yes, which is why this checklist is so important. As part of your qualifications, someday you will do this important job. I need you to understand why it matters."

"Yes, Captain . . . I will learn and do it well."

Konstantin finished his review, signed the completed checklist at the bottom, annotating the date and time of his signature, and handed the clipboard back to the messenger.

"Return this document to the conning officer."

"Yes, sir, Captain," Danovich said and, leaving, closed the door.

A few minutes later, his telephone rang.

"*Da*," he said, pressing the handset to his ear.

"Captain, this is the conning officer," Blok said. "The ship is at the dive coordinates inside operating area KD-11. All preparations for submerged operations are complete. The ship is ready to dive."

"Very well," Konstantin said and returned the handset to its cradle.

With a grunt, he slid his heavy chair back from his desk, stood, and straightened his uniform. An old, familiar anticipation washed over him. The first dive on every underway was an exciting and nerve-racking event. A submarine on the surface was like a gladiator without his shield and sword—still a warrior, but stripped of his power. Bobbing on the surface, the *Belgorod* was slow, perceptible, and vulnerable, but beneath the waves, it was a silent, invisible killer. He couldn't wait to be underwater. However, if something was going to go wrong—and by wrong he meant terribly wrong—it would likely happen on the first submergence after leaving port.

The first dive of every underway was the risky one.

Northern Fleet Joint Strategic Command had not announced this underway. Only after the Western submarine watchers posted news online about K-329's surprise voyage would the propaganda machine kick in. Russia's public explanation for their underway would be that the *Belgorod* was conducting the final phase of sea trials. In reality, sea trials were already complete. Still, work on the hull and the large-diameter torpedo tubes had been conducted in the Sevmash Shipyard before this underway. The threat of a mistake during that work that could lead to flooding was very real, so he needed everyone vigilant during this first dive.

"Captain on the conn," the helmsman announced as Konstantin strode into the submarine's control room. All conversation stopped. Everyone standing stood a little taller, and everyone sitting sat a little straighter as the captain entered.

"Conning officer report," he said in his command voice as he took a position behind the trio of watch standers at the submarine control station, or SCS, where the helmsman, planesman, and diving officer were seated.

The conning officer handed off periscope duties to a junior officer and took position alongside Konstantin's right shoulder. "Captain, the ship is rigged for dive, on course three-five-five at twelve knots. We have one distant sonar contact, designated C-1, range twenty-two thousand meters. Based on propulsion signature,

C-1 is classified as a merchant vessel and not a tactical concern. Sounding is two hundred thirty-five meters beneath the keel and matches charted depth. Request permission to dive the ship."

Konstantin glanced at the sonar repeater display located to the right of the SCS and evaluated the lone sonar trace. The bright trace showed a steady bearing over time, a condition known as zero bearing rate—when the course and speed of both the submarine and the contact created a geometry in which the contact angle did not change. In maritime parlance, the two vessels were on a collision course. But this merchant was far away and by the time the intersection happened, the *Belgorod* would be cruising one hundred meters below the surface, making collision impossible. *Nyet*, Konstantin was not worried about this merchant vessel with its noisy twin screws and massive broadband sonar signature. The threat he was concerned about was the submerged variety—an American hunter-killer submarine silently cruising the depths with a quiet propulsor and no detectable broadband signature. This was not an irrational fear—there was always a submarine lurking out there, prepared for the hunt. With satellite surveillance, in the modern world no vessel got underway undetected and the American hunter-killers were always on the prowl. The last decades had seen a considerable asymmetry develop between the adversaries, with the American Virginia-class submarines tipping the scales in their favor. The *Belgorod*, however, would restore the balance.

It's time, he thought with a fatalistic, closed-lip smile, *to deploy this machine of war as the designers intended.*

"Conning officer, submerge the ship to a depth of fifty meters and conduct leak checks," Konstantin ordered, folding his arms across his chest.

Captain Lieutenant Blok repeated back the order, then parroted the command to the diving officer.

The diving officer keyed the microphone in his hand. "Dive,

dive," he said on the ship-wide comms circuit and sounded two blasts of the Klaxon:

AAHHOOGAA.

AAHHOOGAA.

"Dive, dive," he repeated a second time. After that, he holstered the microphone handset and operated a series of toggle switches to vent air from the fore and aft ballast tanks. "Venting all ballast tanks," he announced to the control room.

"Confirm venting forward . . . Confirm venting aft," the periscope operator reported while swiveling one hundred eighty degrees on the scope so as to visually verify the air escaping.

"Planes, make your depth fifty meters," the diving officer said. "Ease into your down bubble."

The planesman repeated the order and pressed his control yoke forward to adjust the angle of the submarine's stern and bow planes, which were linked in a coordination mode where the angles were optimized by the ship's computer. On the *Belgorod*, either control station could operate the planes or the rudder, but by convention the helmsman sat in the inboard chair and the planesman the outboard. The diving officer sat behind them and had a small control panel that he operated between them. Due to its massive size, the venting of the *Belgorod*'s ballast tanks did not happen instantaneously. Nearly a minute passed before the goliath sub tilted forward and began to descend. The diving officer called out depth changes in five-meter increments as they descended toward the target depth. Upon reaching fifty meters, the planesman eased the submarine back to zero bubble to level from the descent, while the helmsman maintained the ordered heading of three hundred fifty-five degrees.

Once on depth, the diving officer made a ship-wide announcement for all watch standers to conduct leak checks. While the control room waited for the reports to come in, Konstantin walked over to the primary sonar repeater and studied the screen. The single bright trace of the merchant contact C-1 remained the only visible vessel on the waterfall display. He knew that the American submarines used a similar display, with *time* on the y-axis and *relative bearing* on the x-axis. The noise of the sea—a combination of biologics, wind, and wave action—looked like falling snow on the screen. Somewhere in that white noise hid an American fast-attack submarine, already submerged and waiting to observe the *Belgorod*'s dive. After Konstantin submerged, the Americans would fall in trail behind him and silently track his ship from the acoustic blind spot that submariners referred to as their baffles. But Konstantin had a surprise up his sleeve for the Americans, something the Russian Navy had never tried before.

"Conning officer, dive checks are complete in all stations. No leaks detected," the diving officer said.

Blok acknowledged the report and parroted the information to Konstantin.

"Very well," he said, but was racked with a sudden stab of pain in his middle abdomen that buckled him at the waist.

"Captain, are you okay?" Blok said, reaching for the captain's arm, but stopping before making contact.

The pain would pass in a moment, it always did . . . He just needed to grit his teeth and bear it until that happened. Konstantin cleared his throat and forced himself to stand up straight.

"I'm fine," he said, putting on a stoic face. "Indigestion, that's all."

Aware of many pairs of eyes on him, he stood tall—like a captain should—until the pain ebbed. Once he'd regained his bearing and a clear head, the sub captain walked over to the closest comms box to perform the most important evolution of the day. With a deep, cleansing breath, he selected "all stations" using a selector knob and picked up the microphone handset.

"Officers and crew of the *Belgorod*, this is your captain. Today marks a historic event in the Russian Navy. This ship—our ship—is a one-of-a-kind creation. Best in class. The biggest, quietest, and most tactically important submarine in the fleet. We are a special missions boat. Never forget that. This submarine is designed to conduct operations in denied areas, where we will monitor, frustrate, and challenge our oldest and most capable adversary, and *that* is exactly what we are going to do. The Americans know we exist, but they do not know what we are capable of. On this deployment, we are going to show them just how capable we are . . ."

He pulled a folded page from his left breast pocket and opened it.

"I have received our orders and they are as follows. First, we will head north to conduct a brief training evolution with one of our most capable hunter-killer Akula-class submarines—K-335, the *Gepard*. We will simulate being an American submarine with a sound augmentation device so K-335 can test their new towed array sonar system and hunting skills. After this, we will head west. Using our stealth, we will execute our special charter and conduct a deep submersible mission, code-named Operation Guillotine, against the Americans' new, top secret deep-ocean submarine detection network. Once we have rendered the enemy blind and deaf to our presence, we will reposition off the Eastern Seaboard of the United States and deploy our Status-6 multipurpose UUV. Russia is the only nation in the world to possess this advanced technology, and the *Belgorod* is the only submarine in the fleet that is carrying it. After launch, it will travel autonomously all the way into Norfolk Harbor in Virginia. There, it will bottom and wait undetected until the day we need it to wipe the American Atlantic fleet off the map."

He paused to allow cheers and boasts from the crew, smiling at his men in the control room.

"That's right, intrepid sons of Russia. Today you make your captain proud. Your families proud. The Kremlin proud. Today, we begin an adventure that will change the balance of power in the world forever."

With a stoic smile, Konstantin returned the microphone to its cradle and walked over to look at the current sound velocity profile, or SVP, trace. Using thermographic bathymetry, the machine created a graphic representation of the speed of sound as a function of depth, temperature, and salinity. Unlike the Atlantic Ocean, with an average depth of thirty-six hundred meters, the Barents Sea was shallow, with an average depth of only two hundred thirty meters, making it not much deeper than the *Belgorod* was long. While they were stuck in the Barents, their speed and depth were significantly constrained.

As a special-activities platform capable of deploying deep-diving submersibles, K-329 had a large operating window. Normally, Konstantin would select his depth to maximize the probability of operating in a "shadow zone," an area where sound waves bent in advantageous ways, making detection of the *Belgorod* by an adversary more difficult.

But not today.

Today, I want to be found.

"Conning officer, make your depth one hundred twenty-five meters, increase speed to fifteen knots, and proceed north," he said.

Captain Lieutenant Blok echoed the order, then said, "Anything else, Captain?"

"*Da*, secure the diving and surface-maneuvering watch parties, and transition to submerged watch sections. Then send the engineer to my stateroom. I need to talk to him."

"Yes, Captain. Straight away, sir."

Konstantin gave the helmsman's shoulder a squeeze and headed back to his stateroom to prepare for the next phase of his plan.

5

R ussian president Nikita Yermilov felt a youthful vigor he'd not enjoyed for many years—perhaps not since he was a young KGB officer in the service of the mighty Soviet empire. The thought brought a smile to his face, a smile that broadened when his phone rang.

It wasn't the desk phone.

It was the *other* one.

He fished the compact sat phone from the inside pocket of his suit coat, grateful that the call had come before the meeting with the delegation from Belarus.

"*Da,*" he said, taking the call.

"It is in motion. The *Belgorod* is underway," said a gruff male voice on the other end.

Yermilov knew this already, of course. He had *ordered* the *Belgorod* to put to sea. That wasn't the detail he needed.

"What about the rest?"

"I received confirmation that everything is in place. We have the right people on board, Nikita. This is a great day," the old man

on the line said, his throat rattling from nearly a century of cigarettes.

There were few men alive whom Yermilov would tolerate addressing him as "Nikita"—in fact, so few that hearing his given
name spoken out loud sounded odd. His one-time mentor had
earned such a privilege, however.

"It is, indeed," Yermilov agreed. He had ordered the *Belgorod* to
sea through a very small and compartmentalized chain of command. The order would stoke outrage from both his military and
intelligence leadership, but to hell with them. He was the president
of Russia, and his word was final. This mission signified a new beginning. "We shall rise like a phoenix—"

"Flowery metaphors are beneath you, Nikita," the old man said
with a chuckle, cutting him off. "When it comes to words, less is
more."

Yermilov felt his face flush red and hot, but before he could
rebuke the man, the old general spoke up and returned Yermilov's
dignity as easily as he'd stolen it away.

"I will keep you apprised of all details, President Yermilov."

"See that you do."

The line went dead as the phone on his desk chirped.

"*Da*," he said, changing handsets.

"I apologize, Mr. President, but Colonel General Andreyev is
here demanding an audience," said Kierra, his tough but always
calm executive assistant. "He says it is quite urgent . . ."

"It is an emergency," he heard Andreyev, the head of NDMC,
the National Defense Management Center, say in the background.

Yermilov had expected this, in fact was surprised it took so
long, but apparently the colonel general wanted to meet face-to-
face. A bold move.

"Thank you, Kierra. Send him in, but he has only a few minutes
before I must meet with Lukashenko's generals."

"Yes, sir."

The door opened and an overweight, red-faced man strode in, his officer's cap crushed beneath his arm. Without looking over, Yermilov sensed his personal security agent, Boris, step forward to stand behind him, mirroring the aggressive posturing of the new arrival.

"What is so urgent, Oleg?" Yermilov asked, privately taking delight in how upset the general appeared. Andreyev was a powerful man who answered only to the chief of the General Staff. And that leader answered to only one man, and that man was Yermilov.

"Did you know? Of course you did!" Andreyev said, spitting as he talked. "How can I be expected to manage our combined forces when assets are mobilized without my knowledge or authorization?"

"Calm down, Oleg," Yermilov said, crossing his legs at the knee. "Take a seat for a moment, and I am sure we can figure out whatever it is that has you so troubled. Would you like a cup of tea?"

The general looked from Yermilov to the bodyguard Boris and back again, reading the room and reining in his emotions. With seemingly great effort, Andreyev lowered his considerable girth into one of the two high-back chairs facing Yermilov and his opulent desk. He placed his cap in his lap and let out a long breath.

"The *Belgorod* sailed this morning from Severodvinsk," Andreyev said with a slow, even tone. "It was my understanding that she would be undergoing continued retrofitting and then be moved to the submarine base at Polyarnyy, but that does not appear to be the case."

"And only your excellent management allowed her to complete the retrofit so far ahead of schedule, Oleg. You are to be commended for the way you are running the center."

The general clenched his jaw. "Thank you, Mr. President, but that is hardly the point. How is it that one of my submarines puts to sea and I know nothing about it? I am the director—"

"One of *your* submarines?" the Russian president said, cutting him off, his voice the black ice he'd perfected in his time at the KGB, before it became the less capable and less feared SVR that it was today. He suddenly almost desperately wanted a smoke. Most Russians still smoked, but Yermilov had worked so hard to quit, to be healthier.

"I simply meant—"

"I know what you meant," Yermilov said, staring the man in the eyes. "The *Belgorod* is owned by Russia—by the Russian people. And she is commanded by the duly elected supreme commander in chief of the Russian military, Oleg. That is still me, I believe?"

He gave the man a cold smile and leaned back in his chair. God, how he needed a smoke. Such theatrics were so much more visceral inside a cloud of blue cigarette smoke.

"*Da*, Mr. President. I serve at your pleasure, but to do my job effectively—"

"You must, first and foremost, respect the chain of command, Colonel General Andreyev. It was my intent to brief you personally on this highly compartmentalized operation later today, but since you have seen fit to come all the way over here from Znamenka 19, I will give you a short primer now."

He rose and paced around his desk, standing over the man with the desired effect, as Andreyev leaned back, away from him.

"The *Belgorod* is the jewel of the Northern Fleet, Oleg. In addition to its special mission modifications, the engineers have made it supremely quiet and stealthy—quieter perhaps than the American Block III Virginia-class submarines. Your diligence in overseeing this work is commendable."

"Thank you, sir."

"But the Americans have become belligerent and are challenging our efforts in both Syria and Eastern Europe. They view what they have seen in Ukraine as weakness—as our decline. They are wrong, and, to maintain the balance of power, we must change this perception."

"Which is why we are conducting Operation Hurricane with our flagship and aircraft carrier, the *Admiral Kuznetsov*, taking center stage. This is what you told me, Mr. President, to coordinate and conduct our largest naval exercise in a decade. Which I have done."

"Operation Hurricane is important. It will remind the Americans and the British of our naval might and our ability to project power. But it will also serve another goal, which is to keep them distracted and their attention diverted from my true objective."

"You're talking about K-329's underway?"

"*Da.* In consultation with Defense Minister Volkolov, I have ordered a bold test of K-329's capabilities. First, the *Belgorod* will slip past the American submarines who patrol our shores with unbridled hubris. Then it will drill with our Northern Fleet, and we will catalog potential weaknesses should a future conflict with the Americans occur, something I feel is inevitable. To change that inevitability, we must give the Americans pause. We must remind them that our submarine force is something to be feared. Which is why at the conclusion of the exercise, the *Belgorod* will conduct a covert operation in the North Atlantic—one that I will brief you on at the appropriate time."

He stood now behind the flag officer, who squirmed in his seat. They both knew the brutality of the Soviet Union had not disappeared, but simply moved to the shadows.

Andreyev nodded, letting out a long sigh through his nose. "I regret, Mr. President, that you did not feel you could confide in me about the exercise and subsequent operation. I have found my working relationship with Minister Volkolov to be quite effective over this year. We were classmates years ago, close comrades. If I have done something to lose your confidence, sir, I regret it immensely."

It was difficult to put a measure on how very much Yermilov enjoyed seeing the pain in the man's face. The truth was, Andreyev was an excellent director and his performance had been far from disappointing. Perhaps it was simply the old KGB man still stirring inside Yermilov who enjoyed the power of these moments. In any case, for the master plan to work, there was simply no room for Andreyev at the intimate table that he and the old man had set. And time would tell whether there would be room for him in the New Russia that was coming.

"You have no need to feel regret, Oleg. You are an excellent officer and director and I am pleased with how you run your command. But for this plan to be maximally effective, those who are read into the nature of our operation must, by necessity, be quite small. I was quite sincere when I told you I intended to brief you on the exercise later today. That is a sign of my respect for you, as it will make you one of only a few people in all of Russia who will know what we will do after."

"I see," Andreyev said, taking the gift of implied respect and clinging to it.

"I will have the full brief for you in the SCIF at Znamenka 19 later today. It will be the three of us—Sergey, you, and myself."

"Thank you, Mr. President. I am honored by your trust. And I apologize if—"

Yermilov waved a hand, shooing the apology away. "Don't be ridiculous, Oleg. Your irritation is understandable and your apology unnecessary. Now, I have a delegation from Belarus arriving, so you must go."

Andreyev stood and straightened his uniform coat. "Yes, sir. I look forward to our meeting this afternoon, Mr. President." With that, the colonel general snapped around on a heel and strode for the door, closing it behind him.

Yermilov smiled and gave a nod to Boris, who moved again into the shadows of the room.

Perhaps Andreyev would be read into the final part of the plan, perhaps not. Time would tell. When the *Belgorod* completed its special operation, he would have a weapon in place to ensure victory for Russia, should American belligerence persist.

But for the plan to work, the circle had to remain small . . .

Because the Americans have spies everywhere.

In his excitement, the thought of meeting with Belarusian military bureaucrats seemed not only unbearable, but also beneath him. He forced himself to run over the agenda in his head. The rest of the world had it wrong. Russia was not getting weaker; it was getting *stronger.* His will was absolute. It was only a question of time. Once again the Russian Federation would be the mightiest empire in the world, and he alone would be the man calling the shots.

6

Katie watched the fully kitted-up and heavily armed master-at-arms at the small brick building as he studied her DoD Common Access Card (CAC) like he thought there might be some secret code buried inside. Then he scanned it with his handheld scanner and nodded when the device chimed and turned green.

"Where to, ma'am?" the guard asked.

"What? I mean, I'm headed to Pier 14 . . ."

"Yes, ma'am, and you've arrived. Where are you headed, and who is meeting you?"

"I'm headed to the USS *Washington*. The XO is supposed to meet me."

"Very well, ma'am," he said, smiling now as if she had just given the correct coded response. "The *Washington* is on your right, at the end. The topside watch will meet you at the brow and check you in."

"Thank you, Chief," she said, noting the rank insignia in the center of the sailor's body armor.

He raised the gate and she headed down the wide concrete pier, shifting the small leather attaché case she carried on her shoulder. A large gray oiler stood on the south side of the pier, dwarfed by the aircraft carrier beyond—the *Eisenhower*, she deduced, thanks to the large 69 painted on the side of the carrier's island. The north side of the pier—her right, the MA had said, a subtle insult actually, instead of using the term "starboard," or even just "north"— seemed filled mostly with construction equipment and two barges, but then she made out the sail of a submarine, sitting surprisingly low in the water. She hadn't recognized it at first, as the sail was wrapped with what looked essentially like construction scaffolding.

She arrived at a metal brow leading up to the submarine, just aft of the sail. Another heavily armed sailor, this one considerably younger and smaller, clutched his assault rifle in a low carry, eyeing her as she approached.

Officer khakis sure don't seem to carry much weight on Pier 14.

"Help you, ma'am?" the young man asked, his finger tight outside the trigger guard of his rifle.

"Yes, I'm Lieutenant Ryan," she said. "I'm supposed to meet Lieutenant Commander Knepper."

"ID, ma'am?" She handed him her CAC, which he studied before saying, "Electronic devices in the box, ma'am. That includes phones and Apple Watches."

"I'm from ONI. I have an SCI level—"

"Not here, ma'am," the sailor said and opened a black Pelican case at his feet. "They tell me that's what the 'C' stands for."

She blushed at the reminder from the junior sailor that any clearance was "compartmentalized" and her TS/SCI clearance meant almost nothing in this "compartment." She dropped her cell phone into the Pelican, which was full to the brim with a few dozen other phones and watches.

"If it's a black iPhone, I'd tip it up in the corner to make it easier to find if you're not staying long," the sailor said.

"Thank you very much, Petty Officer . . ." She squinted to read his name tag in the bright sun bouncing off the mouth of the James River, where it emptied into the Chesapeake Bay just to her north. ". . . Roth."

"My pleasure, ma'am. Welcome to the *Blackfish*."

She smiled and glanced past him to the submarine beside the concrete pier. A green tent of sorts covered what she assumed to be the hatch leading below into the sub, and no one was making their way to her just yet.

"Why do they call it that—the *Blackfish*, I mean? Why not the *Washington?*"

"Oh, just a nickname, ma'am," the young man said with a knowing look. "Do you know what the blackfish is?"

"It's a killer whale, right?"

The man nodded.

"The Native Americans called them blackfish. The orca is the apex predator of the sea. It has no enemies that can best it and it fears no one. It can move about the ocean unchallenged and strike when it pleases."

"I see," she said.

"Just like us, ma'am. This boat is the apex predator of the U.S. Navy."

"Very cool," she said, thinking about the metaphor.

"Lieutenant Ryan?" a voice called.

Katie looked up to see a man dressed in green digital cammies— the Navy working uniform—with a tan ball cap over Oakley sunglasses, striding across the brow toward her. He had a boyish face that seemed much younger than the subdued, gold oak leaf of a lieutenant commander suggested he must be.

"Commander Knepper?"

"Call me Dennis," the officer said, extending his hand as he leapt easily from the brow to the concrete pier.

"I'm Katie," she said, shaking the strong hand.

"Afternoon, XO," the young sailor standing topside watch said.

"Roth," Knepper said in greeting, then with a deadpan expression added, "Five bucks."

"No, sir, I think you're confused. I won that bet. You owe *me* five bucks."

"No, I clearly remember my foot—and it was my right foot—crossing the finish line a split second before yours," the XO said.

"PRT?" Katie asked, referring to the Navy's annual physical readiness test.

"Yes, ma'am. We both maxed push-ups and planks, so it came down to the run. It was close, but I got him by a stride. The COB was there and he can confirm."

"Hmmm," she said, with a sly grin of her own. "How old are you, Roth?"

"Twenty-one, ma'am," the sailor said.

"Ah, well, therein lies the rub. See, Commander Knepper is older than you, quite a bit actually, so even if you did beat him by a stride, the PRT has graduated age standards, which means by tying, the XO technically wins."

"I like her," Knepper said and looked back and forth between Roth and Ryan. "I'm going to have to get you an honorary *Blackfish* cap."

Roth threw up his hands in theatrical exasperation. "How's that fair? I lose because he's old and needs a handicap. I call BS."

The three of them laughed and Knepper turned to her. "Katie, if your electronics are all squared away, I can escort you aboard."

"Great, thanks."

"Sir, if you give her a tour, be sure to keep an eye on the peanut butter," Roth called after them as they crossed the aluminum walkway.

"Will do, shipmate."

"Peanut butter?" Katie asked with a quizzical look as he gave her a steadying hand to help her off the brow and onto the deck.

"Yeah, on the last underway we had this big hullabaloo because the crew was convinced some of the riders were stealing peanut butter, which is, like, sacrilege. Anyway, it caused this whole conspiracy thing, and now it's a meme." He shook his head. "That's the thing about submarine life. We have a lot of memes."

"Well, I promise to keep my hands off the peanut butter." She noticed the black and green patch Velcroed to his left shoulder, a caricature of what she assumed was supposed to be an orca. At the top the morale patch read "USS *Washington* SSN 787," and at the bottom *Fear the Blackfish* was written in cursive. "How long have you been on the *Washington?*"

Despite his youthful face, he held all the confidence she would expect of someone who had risen to XO status in the submarine force.

"Been here four months," he said. "I was the nav on the *New Hampshire* before my shore tour."

"So, back-to-back Virginia-class tours. Nice," she said. "What about your JO tour?"

"I was on the *Jimmy Carter*," he said, and then with a crooked grin, added, "But we don't talk about *Bruno*."

It took her a second to get the joke in reference to the Navy's most secret submarine—a Seawolf-class sub that had been modified for special projects. "I bet *that* was cool."

"Oh, yeah. Stressful, but definitely cool. So . . . Is there anything you'd like to know about our boat before I introduce you to the WEPS? On the unclass side, of course. We call the WEPS 'Juggernaut,' by the way."

"I have to admit, I'm not well-versed on your community, XO," she said.

"You're not meant to be. The submarine force—and more recently the SSN community in particular—are truly the tip of the spear for America's maritime defense and global projection of power, Lieutenant Ryan. As such, we take OPSEC very, very seriously in our community."

"I gathered," she said, gesturing back at the armed sailor at the pier.

Knepper smiled knowingly.

"To be effective, we not only need the enemies of our country to be in the dark about our capabilities, but there is a tactical and strategic value in having them 'not knowing what they don't know,' if that makes sense."

"It does," she agreed. "But as a senior analyst within ONI, I'd like to think I'm more an asset than a threat," she couldn't resist adding.

"And we view you that way," he said with a nod. "That's why Juggernaut is going to share her unfiltered opinions with you. The letter of access signed by the director of ONI gives you access to questions about weapons systems and in particular her expertise on Russian weapons systems we believe are in development. But I hope you understand that we will not go beyond the strict limits of the letter of access."

"Okay," she said.

"It's not personal," he said. "I'm sure anything you need to know will be shared with you at levels above my pay grade."

She smiled now.

"I have a follow-up briefing with staff at SUBLANT later this afternoon."

"Well, there you go," he said.

"On your left," a voice said behind her, and she sidestepped to make way for a group of fast-walking sailors heading for the hatch.

"Bustling place," she said, only now realizing how many crew members were busy moving topside and back and forth across the brow.

"Yep, we're getting underway tomorrow. Not an ideal time for a visit, but when the higher-ups say jump, I say how high."

"Well, I appreciate that. Thank you."

"We won't be able to go aft, but I can show you the control room and point out a few things of interest that are unique to submariners before your sit-down with Juggernaut. The best part of my job is getting to show off the best damn boat and crew in the Navy. We have a few minutes to kill while the WEPS finishes up what she's working on."

The real and palpable pride the officer felt in his boat was infectious, and she felt her curiosity about what made this submarine so damn special kick into high gear, along with lots of new questions about the submarine force in general. The excited curiosity was an occupational hazard, she imagined. She had a few close friends from her Academy class who had gone into the Nuclear Navy, and they were the one group of friends she almost never kept in touch with. Maybe this was why.

"Come on," Knepper said and led her to a tented structure set over the top of an open hatch on the deck. "This way, and watch your head, but also your shins."

Knepper maneuvered smoothly down a step and onto the ladder, then disappeared down the hatch. Katie followed him, far less smoothly, but at least not banging her head, though she did tag a shin on the thick edge of the hatch ring. The ladder was far narrower than she expected. She'd spent her midshipman's tours in the surface fleet as well as with intelligence commands. For certain the ladder wells aboard the aircraft carrier USS *Harry S. Truman* had been easily three times the width, probably more.

She dropped to the polished, industrial-looking floor beside the ladder and followed Knepper around a tight corner into a passageway. Again, she was struck by how incredibly narrow the passageway was.

"Excuse me, XO," a sailor with a matching *Blackfish* patch on his shoulder said, and Knepper pressed himself full into the wall, which she mimicked, allowing the sailor to pass.

"Economy of space aboard our boats," Knepper said. "Follow me forward to the control room."

Katie followed him to a stairwell, which was so steep and angled it really didn't qualify as stairs.

"Down ladder," Knepper said from the top, then descended facing forward, a feat, she noted, that required leaning back and the careful placement of each heel on the steel treads. She followed him down the "ladder," which was much steeper and narrower than those aboard the *Truman*. "We're in the forward compartment, middle level now, in case you were wondering. This way to control."

The control room was smaller than she expected and she didn't see the iconic gleaming, polished periscopes anywhere that she was accustomed to seeing in the movies. Both port and starboard bulkheads were filled with computer terminals, each station fitted with an upper and lower flat-screen monitor, all of which were black presently. A waist-tall horizontal workstation beside her had a piece of finished wood covering whatever equipment lay beneath. Ahead of her, a central workstation—positioned like an island in the front forward zone of the control room—was equipped with two monitors. The height allowed either seated or standing work, sort of like a standing desk. The starboard screen showed a view of the harbor. The port screen had some other interface pulled up with data boxes. On the forward port side, she spied what she assumed was the submarine's primary control station. A pair of bucket seats, which looked like they could have been pulled from the cockpit of a fighter plane, sat in front of a wall of monitors. Instead of the yoke-style controls she'd envisioned, each station had a control stick—again like what she'd expect to see in an F/A-18 rather than a submarine.

"This is where the magic happens," Knepper said, his face beaming with pride.

"It's so small," Katie said, feeling a touch claustrophobic.

"Like I said—economy of space. Katie, meet our COB—that's our chief of the boat. COB, this is Lieutenant Ryan from ONI."

"Pleasure to meet you, Lieutenant," the large, powerful-looking man with the twin starred anchors of a master chief said, then accepted the hand she offered and shook it.

"Appreciate your hospitality, Master Chief," she said.

"Any questions, ma'am?" the COB asked.

"Well, one," she said, looking around, confused. She was totally caught up now in the world she'd entered. "Not to sound like a total ground pounder here, but where's the periscope? I thought it was, like, the central feature in the middle of the room."

"We still have periscopes, ma'am, this is a submarine, after all," the COB said with a wry smile. "But the Virginia class is the first generation of U.S. nuclear submarines to use the non-penetrating-type photonics mast. On all previous class boats, the periscope extends all the way from the sail through the pressure hull into a well. But on the *Blackfish*, all our masts are located inside the sail, with the data transferred via fiber optics." The master chief slipped onto the narrow stool of the right-hand station in front of her. He opened a small compartment and to her shock pulled out what looked like an Xbox controller—in fact it even had the Xbox logo right in the middle of it.

"You're going to love this," the XO said, his face a proud dad introducing his daughter at a dance recital.

The screen in front of the COB came to life and instantly filled with a video image looking out across the Newport News Channel at the end of the James River.

"Wait—that's the periscope, on that TV screen?"

"That's where we receive the images from the photonics mast," Knepper said.

"And you control it with an Xbox controller? Okay, you guys are totally just screwing with me."

The COB and Knepper laughed together.

"The legend is that the first generation of photonics masts came with a proprietary joystick interface that failed during its first mission at sea. The crew of that boat, which shall remain nameless, did what all good submariners do."

"And what's that, COB?"

"They jury-rigged a solution. One of the FTs donated his personal Xbox controller and they hardwired it into the system, which not only worked, but worked better."

"At a fraction of the cost," Knepper added.

"Exactly," the COB said. "So once it was reported up the chain, they did a retro on the periscope system to use the Xbox controller, which is, one, very familiar to the average sailor, and two, something you can buy everywhere."

She laughed now as well, caught up in it all.

"You guys believe that story?"

"I do," Knepper said, and his voice became somewhat more serious. "Because it tells the story of exactly the very rare kind of sailor we have in our community. There are dozens of stories, many of which I've witnessed, of sailors innovating on the fly just like that. And in submarine warfare, that kind of innovation completes missions and saves lives. Unlike an aircraft carrier, we can't just fly in missing parts or replacements. When we're on station, there is a risk of even coming to PD—"

"PD?" she echoed.

"Periscope depth," the COB explained. "It's where subs go to die."

"Right. When we're deep, there is nothing in the ocean that can find us or kill us. Like our namesake, we're an apex predator, but even orcas are vulnerable at the surface. Deep is where we're safe, but also where we execute our mission. Coming to PD for comms takes us off task. At PD, we're slow and less maneuverable. It's the only time when we're truly vulnerable. And coming off station to fix shit means the mission is over. So, yeah, I believe the story. It captures the heart and soul of the submariner."

Katie was impressed, not only with the story and what it said about the men and women of the submarine force, but also with the reverence with which Knepper told it. This was a man very passionate about what he did.

A device that looked like a cell phone clipped to Knepper's blouse rang.

"We call these MOMCOMs," he said, pulling it free. "We use these instead of the Motorola brick radios you've probably seen."

She nodded as he took the call.

"Copy that, WEPS," he said, then looked up at Katie. "Would love to show you more, but Juggernaut is ready for you. Follow me."

He squeezed past her and maneuvered through the doorway into a narrow corridor.

"We're in the command passageway. That's the skipper's cabin," he said with a tilt of his head toward the open door. She glanced in, shocked by the incredibly small space. She'd seen junior officer staterooms twice that size or more on the carrier, and this was the stateroom for the captain of the ship. "And this is my stateroom," he said, gesturing to the open door beside it. The cabin was about the same size, but had a second bunk above the first.

"You share a stateroom, XO?"

He shrugged. "It's a submarine. We share everything. But no, not routinely. The XO stateroom has a second bunk because that's where we accommodate high-ranking riders."

"Riders?"

"VIPs and such who are riding along for one reason or another," he said. "I get to be the host. Right now I'll be lending you my stateroom for you and Juggernaut to chat."

Katie frowned, not sure if that was a great idea.

"Sir, all due respect, but what I have to discuss might better be shared in a SCIF."

Knepper laughed. "This is a fast-attack submarine—a four-billion-dollar mobile SCIF with torpedoes and Tomahawk missiles. Does that work for you?"

"I suppose it does," she said.

He gestured for her to enter the stateroom. "Juggernaut will be along in a moment. Make yourself comfortable, or at least submarine comfortable."

"Thanks, XO," she said and set her leather case on the small desk. "Why do you call the weapons officer Juggernaut? Is that a sub thing, like, slang?"

He smiled and shook his head.

"No, that's a Juggernaut thing," he said. "When you meet her you'll figure it out. If not, ask me after. And Ryan?"

"Yeah?"

"Juggernaut is brilliant and insightful. She's arguably the smartest person I've ever met. But, well"—he looked at the ceiling—"she's not one for pointless courtesy and tells it how it is. She an awesome person, but in the heat of stuff she may not be as diplomatic as you're used to over at ONI. Don't let her hurt your feelings."

Now she laughed. She'd made it through plebe summer, graduated at the top of her class at the Academy, graduated Dam Neck, deployed on an aircraft carrier, and now proven herself at a command with zero tolerance for mistakes. She had thick skin by now.

"I'll be fine," she said.

"I'm sure," he said. "Just sayin'." Then he turned to look down the passageway. "She's in here, WEPS," he said. Then turned back to Katie and said, "I'll leave you to it."

And the XO was gone down the passageway.

7

I knew it was you," a woman's voice said.

Katie looked up, then readjusted her gaze down by a foot to meet the eyes of the submarine officer standing in the doorway to the XO's stateroom. The woman's hair was pulled back in a stub of a low ponytail and her thin but powerful-looking arms were folded on her chest.

"*You're* Juggernaut?" she asked, staring at the familiar face that seemed to have changed not at all from when it had first hovered inches below her own on Farragut Field. Back then, the woman had been a midshipman at the Academy, yelling at Katie during her plebe summer. Well, at least the face wasn't snarling at her this time—not entirely.

"I am," Lieutenant Commander Jackie Guevara said, and then raised an eyebrow and shot her a knowing look. "And you—you're the President's daughter . . ."

Katie's face flushed and she clenched her jaw to control her irritation.

"Actually, I'm Lieutenant Commander Select Ryan, a senior analyst from ONI here on orders from—"

"Relax, Ryan. I'm just fucking with you," Juggernaut said with a genuine laugh, her smile relaxing Katie, as she stepped into the stateroom and took a seat on the XO's rack, since there was only one chair in the space. "Honestly, Ryan, you were always so easy to spool up back then. During your plebe summer, I worried it might keep you from making it. Glad it didn't."

"Well, thanks, I guess. I never thought of myself as particularly sensitive, but you had a gift for finding a way to get under my skin. And tossing the 'First Kid' thing around really pissed me off."

"I remember," Juggernaut said. "The truth is, I admired the hell out of you—the way you worked so hard to keep your dad out of the narrative. Most people didn't even know."

"Until you told them," Katie said, feeling a tick of anger return.

"Ha," the weapons officer said. Then she leaned in, a conspiratorial look on her face. "I never actually told anyone, Ryan. In fact, only a few of the uppers knew and we kept it to ourselves. Like I said, lots of plebes might have used that to their advantage. I thought it was cool how hard you worked not to get favor. You wound up screwing yourself at times, you tried so hard."

Katie softened again and shook her head. Whenever she ran into officers who had been first class midshipmen during her first year at the Academy, they were never the assholes she remembered, almost without exception. They just all graduated and moved on to the fleet before she could ever know them as colleagues, she supposed. By the time she became a first class, she understood the importance of the upper- and lower-class relationship, but it never changed her perception of those officers who'd been above her until they reconnected.

"Well, you certainly did well for yourself it seems," Katie said. "They talk about you like you're a legend over here. My boss knew you by name as someone who could help us—or at least by your nickname."

"Who's that . . . Captain Ferguson?"

"Yes."

"Smart dude."

"I agree."

"Okay, well, I love our reunion, Ryan—like no bullshit, it's cool to see you—but I've got a lot to do. We're getting underway in the coming days and my department needs to square up. So, what's up over at ONI that they send their superstar down here to get her very clean khakis dirty and stinky on a working submarine?"

Katie shook her head. She never knew the "real" Jackie, but this was exactly what she would have guessed her to be like.

She pulled a folder out of her bag with the usual classified markings.

"This stuff is TS/SCI level . . ."

"Yeah, yeah," Juggernaut said and shut the stateroom door. "Everything in my universe is TS/SCI. What've you got?"

Katie opened the folder and spread four high-resolution pictures out on the desk.

"Well, looks like an Oscar II that's been stretched," the WEPS said, leaning in for a closer look. "That's the *Belgorod*, right? But what's up with those giant shutter doors?"

"Well, that's the million-dollar question that got me over to your stinky submarine," Katie said. "What made you say it was the *Belgorod*?"

"Lot of rumors swirling around about that boat, but the Russians have been keeping it under wraps—at least, until now."

"What kind of rumors?"

"It's supposedly their version of the *Carter*—a special missions boat with docking for UUVs and some super deep-diving sub code-named the *Losharik*, or something like that," Juggernaut said, using the acronym for unmanned undersea vehicles. "Traditionally, when you say UUVs, everyone thinks minisubs, just without the people, but there's all kinds of R&D going on right now with unusual designs and capabilities. Anyway, when I saw those giant shutter doors on the bow, it instantly made me think the *Belgorod*."

"I don't understand."

"Well, because they're not *normal*-sized torpedo tubes," she said, then gave a sheepish smile. "Sorry, sometimes I forget not everyone in the world cares about submarines and geeking out about stuff like this. Okay, quick tutorial. Your typical Russian submarine has five-hundred-thirty-three-millimeter-diameter torpedo tubes designed to carry and launch the Type 53, or Fizik-1, heavyweight torpedo. Those are being retired and replaced by the Fizik-2, but the diameter is still the same. Some boats also have six-hundred-fifty-millimeter-diameter tubes, which fire the Type 65 torpedo, designed to target carriers, and so it packs a bigger punch. The six-hundred-fifty-millimeter tubes can also launch missiles horizontally, just like we have a Tomahawk variant we can launch out of our torpedo tubes. Vertical launch is preferred, obviously, but all subs have the capability to launch missiles via torpedo tubes. But those shutter doors are huge. They must be at least two meters, which makes them three to four times the size of the Russian standard."

"To what end?"

"To accommodate a new weapons system, obviously. The *Belgorod* is their special project boat, after all."

"What kind of weapons system?"

Juggernaut laughed. "Ryan, if someone told you I can look at the doors and tell you what Russians are planning to shoot out of them, then I'm sorry to disappoint, because I'm not your girl." She scratched at her chin. "But the modifications they would have to do to accommodate something of this diameter isn't trivial. There would be significant structural changes needed to accommodate not only the mass, but also the logistics of loading and handling something that big."

"Why not just develop the new weapon so that it can be shot through the standard tubes?" Katie asked.

"Well, that's exactly my point, Ryan," Juggernaut said, leaning in for a closer look again, her interest apparently growing. "To make such a radical change there would have to be a reason. The weapon we're talking about must have capabilities that you can't cram into a six-hundred-fifty-millimeter platform. It isn't hard to imagine them launching some new armed UUV . . . or maybe a horizonal-launched hypersonic or ICBM out of these tubes. But that's what we're doing here, just using our imagination."

Dread settled in the pit of Katie's stomach. "Hypersonics have been a hot topic of late. Maybe they have a new carrier killer that's submarine launched?"

"That's where you'd be better off talking to an ONI science nerd than a fleet WEPS like me, Ryan. My job here is to be the subject-matter expert on the *Blackfish*'s weapons systems, not speculate about Russian prototypes. Speculating is supposed to be your intel superpower, right?" She leaned in close to Katie. "When I did my shore tour with three-thirty-three . . ."

"Three-thirty-three?"

"Yeah—you know, the Weapons and Payloads Division over at ONR. I was working at the Undersea Weapons Program. Anyway, we were looking into all sorts of crazy shit, and you can bet that the Russians are doing the same. Hypersonic weapons, supercavitating torpedoes, autonomous hunter-killer UUVs with learning AI—you name it."

"So . . . Best guess?"

She shrugged.

"Can't give you one just looking at the doors. It could be swim-out, stealth-torpedo bays, it could be for launching long-range autonomous UUVs, it could be for friggin' sharks with laser beams on their heads. No way for me to know." She pursed her lips. "Can't you spooks do your James Bond shit and get a closer look?"

Katie hesitated a moment, but then said, "Not right now."

"Why?"

"Because the *Belgorod* put to sea."

"Typical," Juggernaut said and leaned back. "Well, that probably means they've put to sea to test it. If there's not one up in the Barents already, you'd best recommend to your boss we get a boat up there ASAFP."

"Yeah," Katie said, nodding at the understatement.

Juggernaut looked at the ceiling, then raised a finger.

"I know someone who might be able to help you do a deep dive on this," she said. "Pete Miller is a friggin' genius on all things UUV. He was project lead on one of the crazy things I got to work on at 333. He also works closely with DARPA and—here's the best part—he's the subject-matter expert on emerging weapons technology out of both Russia and China. He's got some friggin' crystal ball in his head that converts pictures like yours into guesses about new tech that prove right a bunch of the time." She folded her arms across her chest. "I'd show these to Pete, if I were you."

"Where is he?"

"Splits his time, but is at the UWP lab at ONR more than half. You can tell him I said to hit him up. If anyone can give you a good guess, it would be Pete. Former submariner himself, did a stint at MIT, did some spooky shit at DARPA while on active duty. Retired as an O-6, but couldn't find his way to the Florida golf courses, so he works on next-gen undersea-warfare technology as a contractor and consultant. If anyone can help you figure it out, it's Pete."

Katie slipped the photos back into the folder and the folder back into the leather case.

"Thanks a ton for having a look," she said.

"Thanks for showing me. I love this stuff, actually." She rose and headed for the door, then stopped and turned around, fishing in the breast pocket of her cammie blouse, the black embroidered dolphins on her chest. She pulled out a card and handed it to Katie. "Do me a favor, Ryan," she said.

"Anything," Katie said, taking the card.

"If you learn more about the *Belgorod,* and especially anything about emerging weapon platforms the Russians may have, can you let me know on the high side?" she asked, referring to the secure and encrypted SIPRNeT communications email for classified information. "We're gonna be out there at the pointy tip. So, if the Russians have something new that tips the balance in their favor, I'd sure like to know . . ."

Katie slipped the card into her pocket. "Will do, Juggernaut."

"I'll grab the XO to escort you off the boat," the WEPS said. "It was great to see you, Ryan. Let's stay in touch."

Katie returned the other woman's parting smile, but beneath the pleasantries, she could not miss the undertone of concern in the weapons officer's voice.

8

President Ryan had learned long ago that he needed to watch the faces of the people gathered around the large conference table every bit as much as he needed to hear the words of the PDB, or President's Daily Brief. Maybe it was the former CIA analyst in him, but raw data was best evaluated against the collective milieu of the talented minds who comprised his leadership team. The expressions he noted now, while discussing the second-to-last line item inside his blue leather folder, told him that this development was the thing that had his advisers most concerned.

"So, do we think that the GRU asset is burned?" The question came from Ryan's new national security advisor, a brilliant thinker, but a man whose ideas skewed more academic than tactical.

The security advisor's role was big picture, in Ryan's mind, and details were best left to his DNI, Mary Pat Foley, and the teams she had assembled beneath her at the CIA, NSA, and NCTC. Today, only Mary Pat, the NSA, and his national defense advisor—former Marine general Nate Hammond—were present, which was not uncommon for an afternoon brief like this.

"No," Mary Pat answered, but she tapped her pen on her folder, suggesting she was unconvinced. "The CIA does not believe our asset is burned. In fact, we're still getting signals intelligence from her."

"But nothing about why they're mobilizing half the Northern Fleet?" Hammond asked. "Are we sure this is an exercise? Because we haven't seen a mobilization like this in over a decade."

"No, nothing affirming or disaffirming the Kremlin's public statements," Mary Pat conceded.

"Still," Ryan said, "we knew about Operation . . . What did they call it?" he asked, turning to Mary Pat. He knew it meant "hurricane," but the Russian word escaped him. Heck, most Russian words escaped him these days. Everyone, himself included, was reengaging their knowledge and concern about the Russian military after decades focused on terrorism and the Middle East. With their aggression in the Baltics and Black Sea, and now this, it was clear that Russia had been taking advantage of that lack of focus.

"Operation Uragan, Mr. President," Mary Pat said.

"Right—Uragan. Operation Hurricane. They mobilized more assets than we expected, but it's not a surprise . . . Correct?"

"That's correct, sir," Mary Pat said.

"It's definitely not a surprise, Mr. President," Hammond said. "But when considered in combination with the joint ground force exercises we're seeing in Eastern Europe with Belarusian troops, I think we need to keep a close eye on this."

"I agree," the national security advisor said.

"Me too, Mr. President," Mary Pat agreed.

"What do you recommend?" he asked, holding her eyes.

"We don't want to *over*react, sir. Now that their lone aircraft carrier is seaworthy and finally out of the shipyard, maybe Yermilov simply wants to remind us we're not the only ones with a carrier strike group. That said, a reaction of some sort is appropriate—to remind *them* that we're paying attention." She turned to Marine—there was no such thing as a *former* Marine in Ryan's mind. "Nate?"

"Well, the *Ford* strike group has just deployed. They're conducting a few days of flight ops off the Virginia coast before steaming east. I would argue we reposition them to keep an eye on what's going on and be a show of force in the northern Atlantic. We should coordinate with the Brits, as it looks as though this exercise will be pushing up against their backyard," Hammond said.

Ryan jotted a note to phone the British PM. "Go on."

"In addition to the usual satellite oversight to keep tabs on things, it's worth noting that we have SSN 787—the USS *Washington*—one of our best Virginia-class subs and a special-missions-qualified boat, getting underway tomorrow. We could get her to snoop around ahead of the rest of the strike group and see what she can learn."

Ryan nodded at Hammond, then turned to his DNI. "Mary Pat?"

"It's a start, Mr. President. I'll coordinate with the CIA and our European partners to see what else we can glean. And the NSA can do a deep dive on signals for us."

"Very well," Ryan said.

"The last item on the PDB is just an FYI for now, sir," Mary Pat said.

Ryan scanned over the short paragraph at the bottom of page seven and felt a tremendous wave of déjà vu. For a moment, he was a junior analyst reading a report and studying pictures of another secret Russian submarine getting underway without notice. He committed this new sub's name and hull number to memory.

The more things change . . .

"My first question is, how did we not know K-329 was about to go underway? We've always had fair warning of Russian naval advance. And the Russians don't do anything

." Ryan said.

flashed back to a heated conversation he'd once

ator skipper of the USS *Nimitz*, and his *Red Octo-*

w stronger.

He shook it off.

"It's true," Hammond said. "Thanks to Director Foley's assets, I can't remember the last time there was any significant Russian naval movement that we didn't know about, and that applies to ground force activity, too. What do your spooks with crystal balls think about this?"

He watched Mary Pat take a moment before delivering a practiced response to the question.

"The *Belgorod* has been in dry dock for a lengthy retrofit, the details of which have been rather scant. They've kept the submarine and her mission under pretty tight wraps—highly compartmentalized even from their own people at Znamenka. Our working theory is that this is a short sea trial to test some new hardware or structural retrofit and that K-329 returns to port in short order."

"Are you saying the underway is unrelated to the exercise?" Ryan asked.

Mary Pat shrugged. "We can't be sure, Mr. President, but as I said, it's our working theory. SUBLANT has the *Indiana* in theater looking for her as we speak. It is very strange how compartmentalized the *Belgorod*'s underway seems to be, though. Our assets in the Kremlin knew even less about it than our man in Znamenka, so that makes this event an outlier—at least from an intelligence-collection standpoint."

"What do you make of this written description of the sub in the PDB?" Ryan said, glancing back at the page. "Who prepared this?"

"ONI, sir," Mary Pat said.

"It sounds concerning . . . Unanswered questions about the

retrofit, a change in K-329's torpedo tube configuration? Are the Russians deploying some new weapon we need to be worried about?"

"Perhaps, sir," she said. "We're not there yet. ONI is working with the subject-matter experts from SUBLANT, and folks at the Undersea Weapons Program at ONR have been tasked to dig into the questions posed in the PDB . . ."

"I need to know more. There's nothing substantive here," Ryan said, lifting the page in the air in frustration.

"Yes, sir. I think ONI doesn't want to jump the gun, sir. As I said, we're more in the FYI stage, Mr. President."

He held Mary Pat's eyes, reading behind the look. If there was one person in the world he trusted, it was his DNI and friend. And if anyone understood the Russian mindset, it was her—and not just because she'd faced them up close and personal as a CIA operative in Moscow during the Cold War. She was also the granddaughter of a Russian colonel who had escaped the revolution and she spoke Russian like a native. Mary Pat had a very unique and personal perspective into the Russian mindset.

"Okay, well, I'd like an update on this—ONI's thoughts on the *Belgorod* as well as what's up with the naval exercise that's underway. We knew it was coming, but it sounds like a bigger operation than we anticipated."

"Yes, sir, Mr. President."

"Anything else?" he asked, glancing up at the row of clocks above the flat-screen monitors on the opposite wall. He had his next meeting up in the Oval in just ten minutes.

It's gonna be that kind of day . . .

When the others had left, Mary Pat gave his arm a tug. He turned to his friend.

"Great work, Mary Pat," he said.

"Thanks, I guess." She wasn't the kind to need an ego rub, he reminded himself. "I wanted to let you know that the Bravo Zulu for the good work so far goes to a rising star over at ONI who flagged the *Belgorod* for a closer look."

"Oh?" he said, raising an eyebrow.

"Yeah," she said. "A recent lieutenant commander select by the name of Ryan."

A proud smile curled his lips.

"Like father, like daughter. The intel brief from ONI that prompted the entry on the PDB had Katie's name on the byline. It was written brilliantly, by the way. An undertone of urgency to raise red flags, but plenty of restraint and zero hyperbole to prevent careening us into false conclusions. Ironic that another intel analyst named Ryan is shaking a stick about a Russian submarine. Destiny, I guess . . . Thought you'd want to know, Jack."

She started to walk away, but he stopped her. "Mary Pat . . ."

She turned to face him and he glanced around to make sure they were alone before saying, "I have a strange feeling about this one. It's not just the déjà vu . . ."

"I agree."

"Can the CIA or our task force assets figure out where the disconnect exists inside Russian command and control? I'm worried about what seems like a fracture in the normal lines of communication between Russian military and the Kremlin here. Something strange is going on."

"Of course."

He saw something in her look.

"Mary Pat, if this turns out to be real, I think we should keep all our field *options* open. What do you think?" he said, dropping a not-so-subtle hint about the right asset for the job.

"I agree completely, Jack," she said, and on that note they parted company.

If Katie's instincts about K-329 were right, they needed

information, and they needed it now. But they also needed a team ready to react.

Mary Pat would know right where to go for that . . .

He sighed, tucked the blue folder under his arm, and headed for the Oval Office, where the signing ceremony awaited him.

My other enemy . . . bureaucracy.

9

J ohn Clark—actually traveling on this trip *as* John Clark for a
pleasant change—pulled the starboard engine throttle to neutral, spun the wheel, and bumped up the port engine throttle
just a touch. The Bertram 61C responded perfectly, angling toward
the end of the dock. A mischievous grin curled Clark's lips as the
dock attendant sprinted forward to meet him. The kid surely expected Clark to cut power and throw a bowline for a nice slow
docking by hand, but Clark had no intention of doing any such
thing.

The deckhand's eyes went wide as Clark kept coming under
power. The kid scrambled to figure out how this lunatic was going
to stop the Bertram from smashing into the dock and damaging it,
the expensive boat, or both. At the last second, the former bosun's
mate turned SEAL turned spook expertly worked the throttles
and wheel to stop the boat perfectly parallel and dead center
against the pier, the gunwale just inches from the edge. He smiled
down from the cockpit at the young man, who, line in hand, stared
up at him with reverence and awe.

"Do you speak English?" Clark called down.

"Yes," the deckhand said.

"Good."

"Do you need petrol, sir?" the young man asked as he worked quickly to tie off the bow and stern cleats of the Bertram while Clark dropped two bumpers over the side.

"No thanks, I'm heading back out." Clark jumped to the dock and slapped a ten-euro note into the attendant's hand. "I'll top off when I return."

"But the sun is setting. It will be dark soon," the deckhand said with real concern in his voice.

"There's still an hour of twilight. Besides, I've got lots of practice driving in the dark."

The kid glanced at the cash in his hand and smiled. "Yes, sir. Thank you, sir."

Clark looked up the long pier to where a man, almost certainly *his* man, walked from the wide, dirt parking lot along Spinčićeva Road. The CIA officer was carrying a small cooler, a backpack, and a fishing pole. A *freshwater* fishing pole, Clark noted, shaking his head.

Instead of walking to meet the guy, Clark waited beside the Bertram.

"So great to see you, John!" the man Clark had never met said, once he was in range.

"You too, Tommy," Clark said with a fake smile.

The truth was, Clark was irritated. He was forty-eight hours from heading home to his wife and a week off with the grandkids. Before doing that, however, he needed time to decompress and purge the stress and emotions from a harrowing mission inside Ukraine. He'd learned that a day or two to get centered before crashing through the front door made him a much, much better husband. Back when he was a young man named John Kelly, Clark had never needed "time off" in the classic sense. But decades in this business had made him wiser and more self-aware. Men like him needed time to reflect and contemplate. The only place he did that well was alone on the water. He'd thought chartering a boat and exploring the Dalmatian Coast was the perfect solution.

Apparently, he'd been wrong.

The message he'd received via a secure satellite link on his computer had suggested this meeting was urgent, but "D.C. urgent" rarely met Clark's operational definition of the term. Whatever was going on, this dude had scrambled for a face-to-face. And in fairness, Mary Pat Foley had signed off on the meet.

So . . . urgent may well mean urgent.

After shaking hands, Clark boarded the boat. He then turned to receive the guy's gear. The spook handed Clark his backpack, which, as expected, was heavier than it looked. Next, he passed his fishing pole, then walked to the stern and stepped onto the boat by way of the transom.

"How's the fishing?" the man asked, walking forward to join Clark.

"Been quiet out there," Clark said, the irony of the challenge response not lost on him.

"Well, I'll be your good luck charm," the man said, completing the ritual and confirming he was the CIA officer that Mary Pat had sent to meet him.

"I doubt that very much," he grumbled, this no longer part of the rote exchange, as he signaled to the deckhand to cast off the bow and stern lines.

Clark set the fishing pole on a long bench seat and then tossed the heavy backpack onto the couch in the salon before ascending the ladder to the flybridge. The man followed, dropping into the oversized captain's chair beside Clark, who stood at the controls. With the lines cast off, Clark gave a two-fingered salute to the deckhand, then tapped both throttles out of idle. The younger CIA man opened his mouth to speak, but Clark cut him off.

"Not until we're out," was all he said.

The spy sighed and clenched his jaw at being managed, but didn't argue.

Clark spun the boat around expertly and headed out to sea. Once clear of the pier and the no wake area, he opened up the throttles on the twin Cat C32s. The Bertram accelerated smoothly, and the bow dropped slowly as she auto-trimmed. He enjoyed the silence, the smell of salt, and the sea breeze as he maneuvered them south and east, away from the shipping channel and into the deep waters of the Jadransko More between the mainland and Brac Island to the south. Once he'd traveled a good two miles offshore, he eased the throttles back to idle. The Bertram rocked in the gentle waves, then windsocked into a stable heading of northwest. Clark scanned around them, saw no other boats anywhere nearby, before shutting the engines down.

"Come on," he grumbled and beckoned the CIA man to follow him down the ladder.

Clark walked through the open slider into the spacious salon, picking up the man's backpack as he passed the sofa and then dropping it onto the dining table before sliding around the breakfast bar into the galley. He bent over and pulled two Nova Runda beers, a local favorite, from the fridge without asking the CIA man if he wanted one.

If he doesn't, then it's two for me.

He sighed, trying to shake off the funk, and slid one of the bottles to the younger man already seated at the table.

"Thanks," the spy said, raising it in a salute of sorts before taking a sip. "Wow, that's really good. I bet you're a microbrew guy . . ."

"What do you want?" Clark said, slipping into a white leather seat. "I'm on leave, as you may be aware," he added, taking a long pull on his own beer. "Headed home in a day and a half to my grandkids."

"Yes, and I'm sorry about that. Actually, I'm supposed to tell you that the DNI is sorry to interrupt your time off." The man shook his head. "This was my first personal directive from her. Seems you have friends in high places, Mr. Clark."

That brought the first real smile to Clark's face, but he didn't know this guy and had zero obligation to share anything about his relationships up the chain.

"What is it I can do for the CIA, Tommy?"

The man opened his backpack and pulled out a small tablet. He tapped in a password and then slid the tablet across to Clark, who glanced at the pictures that were fanned out in tiles.

"Looks like a submarine," Clark said, then took another long swallow of cold beer. "If you're hoping for more than that, you may have been given some bad intel. Submarines aren't my area of expertise."

"Right, sorry," the CIA man said, pulling the tablet back and zooming it in with two fingers. "The submarine is the *Belgorod*, a heavily modified version of the Oscar II, which I, also, know little about. What has the analysts spooled up is a few things." He slid the tablet to Clark again, this time showing what he guessed were torpedo tube doors. "Those torpedo doors were what got someone's attention. This is a big modification, which the eggheads think is designed to accommodate a new—and I guess we read that as scary—weapon. There are other people working on that."

"Well, that's good, 'cause I got nothing to offer so far," Clark said.

"Again, just background. The other modification to the sub is a docking station midship that the engineers think is part of a system to deliver special minisubs—like our SEAL team delivery vehicles, probably—but also some sort of underwater drones or something . . ." He raised a hand when Clark started to speak. ". . . another thing I know nothing about and suspect you are the same. The thing that has everyone in a tizzy is not just the strange modifications, but that this submarine has put to sea from the yard where she was undergoing the retrofit—headed out to the White Sea from Severodvinsk. A Russian boat putting to sea without us knowing is very, very unusual . . ."

"Some scary new submarine puts to sea without us knowing, and it has everyone spooled up. Got it. But where do I fit into this?"

The man shot him a look, and Clark felt a little bad about giving him a hard time.

"The unprecedented degree of compartmentalization is what has the DNI concerned."

Clark leaned in, intrigued now.

"What are you talking about?"

"The Russian military complex," the man said. "We have an asset inside Znamenka 19. Think Russian version of the Pentagon—"

"I know what Znamenka 19 is," Clark said, "but go on."

"Right, so this asset claims that the head of the NDMC, a General Andreyev, was furious that he didn't know what was going on. Imagine the chairman of the Joint Chiefs not being in the loop when we deploy a new, high-tech submarine."

"Hold on," Clark said, realizing he was already all in, his interest beyond piqued. "Why do you say deployed? Why do we think she's on deployment and not just doing some testing or even just moving to a permanent duty station?"

"That's a good question. We're not sure, but everyone is playing the worst-case-scenario game here. The CNO is concerned this sub is a special missions platform that not only has the ability to conduct secret missions off our shores, but also can carry nukes. Add to that the deep compartmentalization inside Russia and the sub going to sea without any forewarning, I mean—dude—you see how it looks?"

"Yeah," Clark said, his mind now spinning furiously between doomsday scenarios and a deep sense of déjà vu. Talk about Cold War–era chess moves that feel like a bad dream. "But I still don't see how the DNI thinks I can contribute?"

The CIA man smiled and pulled the tablet back, tapped again, and then slid it back.

"You know this dude, right?"

Clark stared at the image and felt himself stiffen. "Where did you get that?"

"It's all good, bro. I'm read in."

"The circle of people who know about this asset is supposed to be small," Clark grumbled.

"And the circle is *still* small. I work with a special task force on emerging Russian threats and I'm the only guy on the team who knows about VICAR. I was briefed in the SCIF at ODNI by his handler."

"Is that so. What's the handler's name?" Clark said, deciding that a little test seemed appropriate.

"Well, the handler's NOC is Adam Yao. I'm not at liberty to say more."

"What do I call you, by the way?" Clark asked, softening a bit. "Tommy?"

"You can call me James."

"Okay, James," Clark said. "Dovzhenko—code name VICAR— is a deep SVR asset who has taken decades to develop. What are you saying? The DNI wants to risk burning VICAR for this? She wants me to make contact?"

"Yes," James said, closing the tablet to a dark screen. "Yao will make the initial contact with VICAR, but DNI Foley wants you to take the lead. We'll set up the meet, provide you whatever support assets you need, and back you up. For the sake of expediency, I have a small team of seasoned field officers and ground branch operators at my disposal. The goal is to learn what's happening within the Kremlin that has things fractured and compartmental-ized in a way that we've not seen before. The hope is VICAR can provide insight for us on this matter."

For the sake of expediency, eh? Translation: my guys are too busy to pull.

He laughed softly.

"Something funny?"

"Nah," he said. "Where is best to schedule a meet? I assume you've coordinated with Yao already?"

"Yao is in the loop, but we were told to wait to pull the trigger until you were in and to get your thoughts. My guess is that VICAR may run the play for a meet, based on his own risk assessment and where he can make it happen without it raising flags."

"Makes sense," Clark said. "I trust Yao to get it set up. I can get my team here pretty quickly—"

"ODNI thinks we need to move fast, so there's no time for that. Like I said, we have a team here, so we'll support you on the meet, which needs to happen ASAFP."

Clark frowned. He didn't like working with strangers. Still, if it was just a meet for a data dump, that should be okay.

"It's too bad we don't have someone in the GRU who might have more insight on the military side of the house," Clark said. "Does the CIA have any assets on that side we can use to vet whatever we learn from VICAR?"

James shrugged, but said nothing.

"Okay, well, any additional materials you need to share can go to my high side. In the meantime, I should drop you back at Lucica Zenta."

"I can make calls from right here," James said, "if you want to get some fishing in?"

"No," Clark said. "Make your calls, but we need to head in. Looks like my vacation is over."

He also needed to get in touch with Mary Pat and mobilize *his* team to Europe. If the meeting uncovered something actionable, then he'd need to be able to react quickly. And "actionable" wasn't something he intended to manage with strangers.

Foley wasn't using him for this meet unless she thought there would be follow-up work—something black and off the books . . .

10

Hey, Supe, I think I got something," Sonar Technician Second Class Xavier Harris announced, craning his head to look back over his shoulder at the sonar supervisor on watch, Chief Schonauer.

Schonauer slipped into the chair at the workstation beside Harris. "Broadband or narrowband?"

"Narrowband—a 151-hertz signal, bearing zero-two-one," Harris said.

Unlike previous classes of U.S. submarines, the Virginia class had done away with the separate sonar shack. On the *Indiana*, the sonar operators stood watch in the control room alongside the fire control technicians, quartermaster, pilot, and copilot, and the officer watches. Together, this multidisciplinary team formed the section tracking party, a watch team specifically organized to find and track adversary submarines. Harris hadn't served on an LA- or Ohio-class boat, so this was all he knew. The chief often talked with nostalgia about his previous tours and loved telling anecdotes about the antics that went on in "the shack."

There were days Harris wished sonar was separate from the conn, but having everyone in the same room certainly had advantages. As an ST2, he was a junior watch stander, but on the *Indiana*, that didn't mean his observations and insights weren't valued. Being valued was probably his favorite thing about his job . . . That and getting to go on liberty in foreign ports. He was still a few months from pinning on his dolphins, and once he had his "fish," the respect his shipmates had for him would level up considerably. In the submarine community, competency was the only currency that mattered. Earning his warfare pin meant everything.

"Signal-to-noise ratio is good," Chief Schonauer said, mirroring Harris's display on his terminal and slipping on a pair of headphones. "Anything to correlate on that bearing?"

"No," Harris said, barely able to contain his excitement that he might be the one to find their mission target—a new Russian submarine called the *Belgorod* that nobody had ever tracked before.

Schonauer announced the new contact.

"Conn, Sonar—new narrowband sonar contact designated Sierra Seven, bearing zero-two-one. Possible submerged contact in the vicinity of where intelligence indicated our target of interest could be," Schonauer announced while looking at the OOD, the officer of the deck.

"Schonar, Conn, aye," acknowledged Lieutenant Commander Yu, the OOD, riffing off the sonar supe's last name while impersonating Sean Connery's iconic accent.

No matter how many times the OOD did this schtick, Harris couldn't help but laugh. Yu was the navigator on the boat, and he was funny as hell. If there was one thing that made life bearable on deployment, it was a sense of humor. Well, that and pizza night. The cooks on 789 could make a mean pizza when they tried.

The OOD and the contact manager, an experienced female

junior officer named Lieutenant Crystal, who everyone called Crystal Light, stepped over to caucus with Schonauer.

"Where's the ACINT, dude?" Crystal said, looking toward the port rear corner of control where the acoustic intelligence rider usually camped out.

"I think he went to the head, ma'am," Schonauer said.

"Of course he did," the OOD said, "because that's the perfect place to be when we get a new submerged contact."

"Do you want me to go find him, sir?" the control room messenger asked, taking initiative.

"Check crew's mess first," the OOD said. "He's been gone awhile. Five bucks says he's playing cribbage."

The messenger shot a finger pistol at the OOD and said, "My thoughts exactly."

"I can search the acoustic database, sir . . . if you'd like," Harris said. As far as he was concerned, they didn't need outside ACINT.

Anything that dude can do, I can do, Harris thought with more than a little irritation. *Just another rider taking up a bed so more of the crew has to hot rack.*

"Hop to it," the OOD said and then walked back to the command workstation in the middle of the conn.

Lieutenant Crystal, whose job was succinctly defined by her title of contact manager, stayed. Schonauer leaned in, too, and they became a three-body investigative huddle as Harris opened the ASD, or acoustic signature database, that ONI maintained. The ASD was made for submarines on deployment by other submarines on deployment.

"What's that?" the junior officer of the watch, a brand-new and unqualified ensign fresh on the boat, asked after walking over.

"Well, sir, you know how every human being possesses a unique set of fingerprints?" Schonauer said as Harris entered "151 Hz" into the query window.

"Yeah," the ensign said.

"Well, every submarine has a unique *acoustic* fingerprint. If one of our sister boats has encountered this 151-hertz signal before in the Barents Sea, it will be logged in the ASD. The intel guys at ONI sift all the data, correlate it, and try to identify the exact model and hull number of the submarine with that frequency vulnerability," the sonar supe said. "ST2 Harris is looking to see if we can ID the Russian boat we're tracking as Sierra Seven."

"Cool," the JOOW said.

The computer thought for a second, then populated a list of hits at 151 hertz.

"Must be a popular frequency," Crystal said.

"You're going to want to refine your search, Harris," Schonauer said.

"I found the rider," someone announced with bravado, and Harris turned to see the messenger strolling onto the conn with a red-faced ACINT specialist in tow. "He was in crew's mess playing cribbage with Fitzpatrick."

Good-natured public ribbing was another central tenet of submarine life.

"Sorry," the intelligence specialist said, looking at his hands. "Just needed a brain break."

Harris resisted the urge to roll his eyes. *Yeah, because you were working so hard in the corner.*

"Hop on over there and take a look at what ST2 Harris found," the OOD said, leaving it at that. "I'm gonna give you guys a couple more minutes, then I'm turning."

Harris had logged enough hours on watch to understand the unspoken meaning in the OOD's statement. Everything in undersea operations could be distilled down to geometry. Driving a submarine was, basically, math. Since they'd acquired Sierra Seven on narrowband, the OOD had maintained a constant course and speed. That was great for sonar techs like Harris, because in this current geometry, the *Indiana*'s TB-29C towed array had a strong lock on the signal. The problem, however, was that with only a single leg of bearings from the emitter, the *Indiana* had an incomplete tactical picture. The target could be close, or it could be far away. It could be driving toward them or driving away. It could be going slow; it could be going fast. To determine the range, course, and speed of the target, the officer of the deck needed to change the geometry and that meant turning. But with every course change came the possibility of losing the signal and not being able to reacquire it.

Nothing in their undersea game of cat and mouse happened without risk.

"Pull up a new query window," the ACINT rider said, joining the ever-expanding huddle at Harris's workstation. "This time, go ahead and put the decimal in—151.7 hertz."

"Yeah, but it's walking all over the place, 151.6 to 151.9," Harris said, pointing at the trace on the upper monitor.

"I know, but the trend line is around 151.7. If you don't put the decimal in, the database will give you all 151-hertz emitters. Also, add a location tag, Barents Sea. That will narrow the list."

Harris did as the man said and pressed enter. This time only two results popped up: K-335 and K-391.

"K-391 is decommissioned," the ACINT guy said. "Click on K-335."

Harris clicked the listing and a new window opened with data.

NAME: K-335 *Gepard*

TYPE: Akula III–class submarine

PENNANT #: 895

STATUS: Active

FLEET: North / Arctic

PORT OF RECORD: Polyarnyy

PROPULSION: Single 7-bladed propeller

SOUND OFFENDERS: 151.7 Hz on port aft quadrant

"Bingo," the ACINT dude said.

Harris deflated a bit at the news he hadn't found K-329. "I was hoping it was the *Belgorod*."

"No, this is a good thing. The *Belgorod* is in the final phase of sea trials. It probably has orders to conduct exercises with the *Gepard*. If we follow them, chances are good they could unwittingly lead us to the boat we've been tasked to find."

"Agreed," Chief Schonauer said. "Great work, Harris. Looks like you hooked your first shark."

Harris felt his cheeks flush with pride at his chief's shout-out and the possibility that his find could lead them straight to the *Belgorod*.

"*Akula* is the Russian word for 'shark,'" the ACINT rider said. "In case you didn't know that."

Harris shot the guy a look. Of course he knew that, but he was too excited to get defensive.

I found my first Akula . . . how friggin' cool is that?

"Officer of the deck," Crystal said, turning toward the command station, where the OOD was standing. "We have a hit in the ADS on the narrowband contact. High confidence that Sierra Seven is the *Gepard*, hull number K-335—an Akula-class submarine homeported in Polyarnyy."

"Good work, team," the OOD said, addressing the group. "Time to turn and call the captain. Let's see if we can get a good fire control solution on this guy and fall in trail."

11

Q uartermaster, how much longer can we maintain our current course and speed before we exit our operating area?" Konstantin asked.

The man turned to his chart, took a measurement with calipers, and said, "Approximately one hour, Captain."

In the Army, quartermasters oversaw rations, supplies, housing, and the logistics pertaining to those things. But in the Navy, the quartermaster was a member of the navigation department, and his job was to plot the ship's position and course on the navigation charts. On the surface, geolocating was easy and automatic. Because of GPS, the days of determining a ship's position by shooting lines of bearing to landmarks and dead reckoning were over. However, for submarines operating at depth, GPS was not available. While submerged, quartermasters still needed to use the dead-reckoning technique of determining where you *are* based on where you've *been*. To help mitigate the uncertainty, modern submarines used inertial navigation systems that measured three-axis accelerations to estimate the effects of set and drift. Regular soundings from the sub's Fathometer were compared to bathymetric data on the navigation charts to help validate the sub's estimated position. A good quartermaster was always vigilant, anticipating undersea hazards and not afraid to make course and speed recommendations to the conning officer. The *Belgorod*'s quartermaster, Starshina First Class Fyodorov, was such a man.

"Very well, quartermaster," Konstantin said. "Conning officer, maintain this course and speed for thirty minutes, then turn east. We will secure the acoustic augmentation device on the next leg. In the meantime, I'm going to tour the ship."

"*Da*, Captain. Shall I inform the department heads?" the conning officer asked.

Konstantin smiled at the question and the fact that the conning officer had the wherewithal to ask it. "That will not be necessary. I am just a captain touring my ship."

As soon as he stepped out of the conn, the news of his "tour" would travel fast. Like spreading wildfire, the control room messenger would telephone all watch station leads and division chiefs to tell them that the captain was conducting a surprise inspection. This was to be expected, and a positive reaction in Konstantin's mind. A crew should stick together and have each other's backs. A healthy crew cared about their collective success and performance.

So far, he'd been satisfied with this crew's aptitude and attitude. They'd taken the *Belgorod* through sea trials without incident. But did this crew have the mettle to execute the mission he would ask of them?

I hope so. It would be a shame for them to all die for nothing.

The *Belgorod* was a big submarine . . . a very big submarine. With five levels and dozens of compartments, his tour would take every bit of an hour. He would start forward and work his way back into the engine room. The purpose of this tour was not to look for contraband, or to check equipment logs, or to mete out discipline for substandard cleanliness or improper stowage for sea. No, this tour was not for them; it was for *him*. Inside this engineering marvel made of steel and wires, a captain had to trust his senses. Odors, sounds, and vibrations told him things that the dials and gauges did not. Over the years, he'd come to view a submarine as a hybrid creature—part man, part machine—and neither part could complete the mission without the other. Just as a physician must put his hands on the patient to make a proper diagnosis, the same was true of a sub captain. Konstantin could not take the pulse of his men and his ship from his stateroom.

And so . . . he toured.

I must know the health of the beast before I order it into battle.

At the thirty-minute mark of his tour, he felt the ship heel to starboard as the conning officer turned east per his instructions. A few minutes later, the report was given to him in person by a breathless messenger that the ship was on course zero-nine-zero at twelve knots. He acknowledged the report and told the messenger to have the ship's engineer meet him in the propulsion bay in half an hour. By the time the sub captain arrived in the propulsion bay, the engineer—whom Konstantin had kept waiting—was dripping with sweat. The temperature in the vicinity of the propulsion turbines and main reduction gears was a sweltering forty-eight degrees Celcius; it was a place where no one liked to loiter.

"Captain, you wanted to see me?" the engineer said while blotting his forehead with a wadded-up grease towel.

Konstantin checked over his shoulder to make sure they were alone, with no messenger or watch stander hovering nearby eavesdropping. This location, in addition to being the hottest on the ship, was also the loudest and the perfect place for a confidential conversation.

"Is it done?"

The engineer nodded. "I switched documents in the safe while he was on the toilet. He doesn't know that I have the combination."

"And the seal on the original was intact?"

"*Da.*"

"Well done."

"What do you want me to do with it?"

"Incinerate it," Konstantin said and clapped a hand on his department head's shoulder. He'd mentored Tarasov for the past eleven years and thought of the man like a son. Like Konstantin, Tarasov had suffered great personal tragedy in his life and through their mutual pain they had bonded. Tarasov was a true believer and only one of a handful of crew members read into the plan. Fate had done its best to derail their operation when the ship's weapons officer had fallen ill with pneumonia and required hospitalization. The replacement, Captain Lieutenant Morozov, was not a member of Konstantin's inner circle and was the one man on board with the know-how and potentially the will to undermine their mission.

"I have my doubts . . ."

"Don't tell me you're getting cold feet," Konstantin said with a smile meant to reassure.

"Not about the mission, never. I'm talking about Morozov. He's clever and observant. He could be a problem for us."

"I know, which is why I want you to keep a very close eye on him. Report directly to me any behavior you think is concerning."

"Yes, Captain."

"All right, time for us to go silent. Captain Lieutenant Tarasov, secure the noise augmentation device."

"Secure the noise augmentation device, aye, sir," the engineer said with a crooked smile and walked over to turn off the precision frequency emitter bolted directly to a steel mounting bracket. Unlike every other bracket that had sound-dampening rubber spacers, this bracket was welded directly to the pressure hull to create a perfect path for sound to travel from the inside of the submarine to the ocean. After powering down the sound emitter, the engineer turned and said, "Noise augmentation device secured, sir."

"Very well," Konstantin said and turned to make the trek back to the control room, where he would give the order to reverse course and head west. He'd not taken two steps, when he stopped. "Engineer, have your mechanics remove the noise augmentation device from the mounting bracket and stow it . . . I would hate for it to accidentally turn on at an inopportune time."

Tarasov gave a slight bow of deference. "A very wise precaution, Captain. I will see it done."

12

ST2 Harris cursed under his breath as he scanned for the 151.7-hertz signal.

"What's the problem, Harris?" Lieutenant Crystal asked.

Harris pointed to the bright green narrowband trace on the waterfall display that abruptly ended, drifting down on the screen. "Lost the narrowband signal on Master One. The trace was strong one second, then gone the next."

"Maybe they turned," she said.

"Mmm, I don't think so. We held contact through their last turn and there's no bearing drift at all. It just stopped."

"Then they probably changed up their equipment line. Maybe that 151.7 hertz was from, say, number one lube oil pump and they shifted to number two," she said. "Why don't you ask the ACINT guy what he thinks, while I inform the OOD."

Harris nodded and waved both the ACINT rider and Chief Schonauer over to his station. "Just lost contact on Master One. The narrowband signal stopped."

"That's typical in my experience," the acoustic specialist said. "Quite frankly, I was surprised how long we held the signal, and

through aspect changes, no less. Even when he turned east and his port quarter was away from us, we maintained contact."

"The signal-to-noise ratio degraded after the turn," Schonauer said.

The ACINT guy pursed his lips. "Yeah, but not as much as I would have expected. According to the logs, we're the only boat to maintain contact off K-335's starboard beam."

"Captain in control," the copilot announced from his inboard chair at the SCP.

Harris glanced over his shoulder to check the commanding officer's expression and demeanor, which didn't look upset. *Thank God,* Harris thought, and quietly exhaled with relief as he turned back to his display.

"We lost him, huh?" the *Indiana's* CO, Commander Bresnahan, said as he walked over to join the growing huddle of people around Harris's console.

"Yes, sir, but we're going to get him back," Harris said, surprised by the bravado in his voice.

"I like that attitude, ST2," the captain said. "Have we managed to get any additional frequencies or broadband signature on Master One?"

"Not really, sir. Other than the 151.7 hertz, it's not putting out much noise," Lieutenant Crystal said, answering first.

The CO scratched his forehead and leaned in for a look at the display. "Dead quiet out there now."

"Yes, sir," Harris said.

Nobody said anything for a long, uncomfortable moment.

"Remember, folks," the captain said, talking louder so everyone in control could hear him. "Intelligence thinks there are *two* Russian submarines out here and they are playing cat and mouse with each other in a hunter-killer exercise. They're looking, and I mean *really* looking for each other, and we've put ourselves right in the middle of their game. I'm glad we found Master One, but we're not out here to track Akulas. Our tasking is to find and monitor the *Belgorod*. We have no data on this monster and the folks with stars on their shoulders back home are very interested in what it can do. I know she's quiet, but our job is to find her and build an acoustic profile for the fleet to leverage. What we do today could save lives in a future conflict if things were to heat up with the Russians and, God forbid, we were to find ourselves in a shooting war."

"Yes, sir," the officer of the deck said, responding for the entire watch team. "We'll find her, sir."

"Good, because I'm in the mood to tango, but at the moment I don't have a dance partner."

13

K atie loved everything about her Jeep Grand Cherokee—the styling, the comfy leather seats, the four-wheel drive—everything except for the color. She'd picked white because that day on the dealer's lot it had looked so striking and beautiful. Her dad had told her to buy a darker color, but she'd not listened. Listening had never been one of her strengths. As usual, her dad had been right, and now every time she passed a car wash, she could practically hear it whispering to her:

Hey, you, in the dirty Jeep. Yeah, I'm talking to you, Ryan. For twenty bucks, I'll get you looking good as new. C'mon, pull over and get wet.

Her phone chimed, alerting her to an incoming text message.

"Siri, read me my newest message," she said.

"Would you like me to read your newest text message?" Siri asked with an Irish accent.

She rolled her eyes. "Yes, please."

Unlike most people, Katie was nice to Siri.

"Pete Miller says you're not going to find any parking on the street,

but the office has a garage you can use. Access is on the west side via Randolph Street," Irish Siri dictated. *"Would you like to reply?"*

She thanked Pete for the heads-up and Siri sent her text back "hands free."

Katie had changed Siri's default voice to an Irish accent one day to amuse herself, but she'd ended up keeping it because the Irish Siri just seemed cooler than the American one. This current incarnation of Siri was a simple AI and not nearly as capable as a lot of others, but it was proof positive that AI was everywhere now. It wasn't clear to her—in a way that made her think of their older brother, Jack Junior—just what her brother Kyle did, but the Task Force 59 team in Bahrain worked with what she could only imagine was an immensely powerful AI, crunching and managing terabytes of data. Like submariners, she supposed, Kyle was very tight-lipped about his role in whatever TF59 was doing in the Middle East, but she knew that artificial intelligence was going to be a sea change in how wars were waged over the next decade. The speed and asymmetric impact of that sea change was what had her concerned. Would America lead the vanguard as it had always done? Or would it cede advantage to China, which was plowing forward without any regard for the unintended consequences of rolling out unproven AI systems too quickly?

Save that worry for another day, she told herself. *You've got enough on your plate.*

Her GPS navigation app delivered her safely to Randolph Street and she parked in the garage, as her contact had advised her to do. She got badged at security, checked her iPhone into a locker, and waited for Pete. He arrived in the lobby a few minutes later and greeted her with a handshake and a smile.

"Hi, I'm Pete," he said with a firm but not too firm grip, smiling at her with a handsome and weathered face that said it had seen the world.

"Katie," she said, flashing him her pearly whites.

His business casual attire, laid-back manner, plain eyeglasses, and comfy Rockport shoes told her everything she needed to know about him. Pete was here because of the work, not to build his résumé or pad his ego.

We're going to get along like two peas in a pod, she decided.

"Have you ever been here before?" he asked, holding the security door open for her like a gentleman.

"Nope," she said.

"In that case, welcome to the Office of Naval Research."

"You must be busy, with the pace of technology accelerating daily."

He smiled, and gestured with a hand toward the elevator bank down the hall.

"Well, certainly busier than when ONR was founded in 1946," he said. "Our work is primarily funded with grants, so we get to contract research scientists, engineers, and academics in several spheres: basic research, intellectual property development, applied science applications, and prototyping."

"Do you do all the research here?"

"No," he said. "This building is basically a giant project-management facility. We contract and collaborate with universities, NGOs, the national laboratories, and defense contractors, but the vast majority of our work is overseen by the Naval Research Laboratory."

"Sounds like a lot to manage."

"It is, but that's the nature of the beast. Turns out, the world's smartest people don't all work at the same place." He pressed the button for the elevator.

"Ain't that the truth," she said. "Juggernaut said you're the guru of the Undersea Weapons Program."

"Guru, huh? I guess I've been promoted. I'm going to have to

add that to my business card," he said with a charming smile as
they stepped into an elevator. "I work in the Weapons and Payloads
Division, or Code 333, and I have the coolest job in the ONR."

"Why is that?"

He fixed her with a crooked grin. "Because I get to blow stuff
up, Lieutenant, *duh.*"

"You sound like my brother."

"Which one?" When she hesitated to answer, he said, "Yeah, I
did my homework. Sorry, I'm thorough. That's the nature of
nuclear-engineer-trained retired submarine officers like me."

"In that case, the answer is both brothers," she said. "And I can't
fault you for being thorough, that's why I'm here. Juggernaut said
if anybody could help me, it would be you."

"Jackie Guevara is a force of nature, that one. Her nickname
suits her perfectly. She's on the *Washington* these days, right?"

Katie nodded. "She's the WEPS."

"Of course she is."

The elevator chimed and they exited on the seventh floor.

She followed him through a warren of offices and cubes. "When
Juggernaut worked here, what type of project was she working
on? . . . That is, if you can tell me."

"I ran your clearance before you arrived. Looks like somebody
somewhere high up on the food chain gave you a big fat rubber
stamp of approval to look at anything your heart desires, and that
includes the highly compartmentalized stuff."

She shrugged. "What we're investigating is important," she said,
wondering if it had been her dad and hoping not. Unless it was her
dad just being President—God, it was so exhausting.

"Roger that," he said. "My group is focused on next-generation
torpedo and UUV propulsion technology, maneuverability, and
stealth. But 333 is also tasked with increasing kill and counter-
kill probabilities, engagement tactics, warhead lethality, sensor

performance, and autonomy," he said as he gestured for her to enter a vacant breakout room with a round table and four chairs. "Juggernaut was working on counter-kill applications for the Mk 48 ADCAP torpedo. She had some real outside-the-box, cutting-edge ideas while she was here."

"That's cool," she said and took a seat.

He sat down opposite her, fixed her with an easy smile, and said, "So, what would you like to talk about?"

"Do you have a laptop computer we can use? I have a photo on my encrypted file vault at ONI that I want to get your opinion on."

"Sure do, I'll be right back," he said and popped to his feet. At the threshold, he stopped and turned back to her. "I've forgotten my manners. Can I get you something to drink—we have coffee, soda, water?"

"No, thank you, I'm good," she said.

While he was gone, she stared out the room's lone window, which faced the facade of the building across the street. *I wonder what they do over there*, she mused. A weird, *Twilight Zone* thought flashed before her mind's eye of her mirror image staring back at this building pondering the same question. She squinted to see if she could see—

"I'm back," Pete said, snapping her out of her rumination as he dropped into the chair beside her.

He opened the laptop, logged in, and slid it in front of her.

"Thanks." She clicked into the secure web interface, logged into the encrypted cloud server, and opened the file folder she'd prepared for this meeting. Using the touch pad, she selected and opened the picture of the *Belgorod* that had been taken inside the covered dry dock at the Sevmash Shipyard in Severodvinsk. "Do you know this submarine?"

"Of course, that's the *Belgorod*—K-329," he said.

She pointed at the bow of the sub. "These six large openings here—they look too large to be torpedo tubes. What do you think they are? Could they be horizontal ICBM launchers?"

"No," he said. "Those are large-diameter torpedo tubes. Two meters, to be precise. We're pretty sure they're designed to launch Status-6 UUVs."

"Status-6 . . . What's that?"

"That's the Russian code name for one of the Kremlin's new strategic WMDs designed to terrorize the civilian world. They call it Status-6; we call it Poseidon."

She swallowed, not sure whether she should be relieved or not. "So it's not some kind of new super torpedo, is that what you're saying?"

"Oh, it's definitely some kind of a new super torpedo."

"But I thought you said it was a UUV?"

"A 'torpedo' is what we called UUVs before people made up the term UUV," the former submariner said. "If you think about it, the only real difference between a torpedo and a UUV is that the former has a warhead slapped on the front."

"Oh," she said, deflating. "Do we need to be worried about this?"

"Most definitely," he said, scooting his chair back and turning it so he could look at her. "The Poseidon is a nuclear-powered, nuclear-payload-carrying vehicle. It's fast, stealthy, and designed to travel long distances autonomously."

"When you say long distances, how far are we talking?"

He fixed her with a tight smile. "It's nuclear-powered, Katie. Just like our submarines. That means it has a virtually unlimited range."

"Are you saying they could launch this weapon off the coast of Russia and it could patrol the entire Atlantic Ocean looking for a target?"

He nodded. "Or it could cross the Atlantic and target a city on the Eastern Seaboard."

"What kind of yield are we talking about here? When you say nuclear payload, I assume you mean a tactical nuke."

"This thing is huge, Katie. It's six feet in diameter and we estimate sixty-five to eighty feet long. That's bigger than our Trident ICBMs, which means it's easily capable of carrying a warhead in the two- to ten-megaton range."

"Dear God . . . If they sent one of these things into the Hudson River, they could take out New York City."

"That's right. But I have other concerns about this weapon."

"What can possibly be worse than a ten-megaton stealth nuclear-tipped torpedo?" she said, crossing her arms.

"A ten-megaton nuke with a salted warhead."

"I don't know what that is."

"No problem, I'm going to walk you through Nuclear Weapons 101. Your typical nuke is a fission bomb. When it detonates, it creates a massive exothermic reaction—which is the fireball and shock wave combo they like to show in the movies—but it also releases a ton of radiation. And there are different types of radiation, at that. The bad ones are: gamma, which are like X-rays; alpha particles, which are basically helium atoms; and neutrons. If you're not underground or in a shielded location when the bomb goes off, you'll get bombarded with a lethal dose of radiation and die within days. But after that initial blast, the radiation levels drop pretty quickly. Sure, there are nasty radioactive fission products that linger, but the worst offenders decay away within a couple of months. A salted bomb, however, is an entirely different animal—a weapon designed with a single, malevolent purpose."

Gooseflesh stood up on her neck at the timbre of his voice. "And what is that purpose?"

"To render the target uninhabitable for a generation."

"I still don't understand."

"The way it works is, they put a jacket of cobalt 59 around the warhead so when it detonates the metal is transmuted into highly radioactive cobalt 60, the atoms of which get distributed for miles and miles around the blast sight. The half-life of cobalt 60 is five and a quarter years. Even after one half-life, a person who was unlucky enough to wander into the contamination zone would get a lethal dose of gamma radiation within an hour. It would take twenty half-lives, or a full century, before the radiation in the area reached livable levels, and even then those levels would be thirty times greater than typical background radiation levels. Do you see where I'm going with this?"

She shifted uncomfortably in her seat. "A cobalt bomb is basically the mother of all WMDs. Not only does it destroy like a nuclear bomb, but it renders the target area uninhabitable in the aftermath."

"Exactly. That's why they call it a doomsday weapon, and the only people insane enough to actually build and threaten to use them are the Russians."

She blew air through her teeth. "Do you think the Status-6 torpedoes have salted warheads?"

"I don't know. The question is academic at this point."

"Why do you say that?"

"Because the Status-6 UUV is still in development. As far as dreaming up terrible weapons, the Russians win the gold medal every time, but when it comes to actually executing on those ideas, they have a pretty spotty track record. From what I understand, they're still working on proof-of-concept testing with a prototype. And as you can see from your picture, the delivery platform is in dry dock. We're several years out from Status-6 entering service, provided it works at all."

She clicked on a new photo, this one a satellite image of K-329 leaving harbor. "Unfortunately, Pete, I'm concerned that the Russians are much further along than you think. This picture was taken yesterday. That's the *Belgorod* departing Severodvinsk. We tracked it by satellite into the Barents Sea, but lost visual contact after it submerged."

Pete took off his glasses and rubbed his eyes. "Do you know if they loaded Status-6 torpedoes before they got underway?"

"No," she said. "But if they did, it would have happened while K-329 was in the Sevmash covered dry dock and out of view from our prying eyes in the sky."

"These weapons will be immensely heavy and, due to their size, impossible to load pierside. I suspect they are loaded tail-first into the tubes externally. And if that's the case, because the shutter doors are below the waterline, loading the weapons in dry dock would be their standard operating procedure."

She zoomed in on the image of the surfaced *Belgorod* to evaluate where the waterline fell on the hull. Then she clicked back to the previous image of the sub from the front and saw that he was right. "The tubes are definitely below the waterline."

They sat for a moment in silence, both lost in thought.

Eventually, Pete spoke. "What can I do to help?"

"Send me everything you have on the Poseidon program and generate some spec sheets and diagrams for me that I can use in a presentation. I want to know your estimate of what the torpedo's predicted and worst-case capabilities would be. I'm going to need to brief, well, probably everyone about this threat."

"No problem, I'll get on it straight away. I'll email your high side a link to an encrypted file share."

"Great," she said and scooted her chair back from the table. "I probably should get going."

"Let me walk you out," he said, closing the laptop screen and pressing to his feet. "I just have one request going forward."

"What's that?"

"Promise me you'll keep me in the loop on this one. If this

weapon is legitimately operational, you're going to need my help to devise the techniques and technology necessary to detect and destroy it."

She took a page from her dad's playbook and clapped a hand on his shoulder. "Pete, not only can I promise you that . . . I'm willing to guarantee it."

14

I n the old days, Clark would have casually concealed himself behind an open newspaper as he surveilled the lobby for his mark. Today, reading a newspaper in a lobby—open or not—would make him the most conspicuous man around. Instead, he sat on a low, modern, gold-leafed love seat beside the concierge desk, sipping a drink and scrolling with a thumb through the news feed on his phone. From this spot he had sight lines on the entrance, the elevator bank, and the opulent staircase leading up to the second level. Most important, his back was against the wall, so he didn't have to worry about his six.

The hotel design reminded him of a stack of donuts, and the lobby was the donut hole. Look up and a towering open foyer extended multiple stories, with hotel rooms on each level that looked down—balcony-style—from around the perimeter. The spook in him appreciated the visibility, but the operator in him hated the vulnerability. Anywhere above him could be a sniper ready to end him with a headshot or Russian operatives listening in with modern, augmented listening devices.

Clark stretched his back and rolled his head, eyes half closed, as he scanned the east side of the lobby and floors with a line on his partially covered position in the corner—just a tired businessman, waiting for a meeting or a call.

Clear.

The few people on the floors peering down from above were moving—heading to elevators or to their rooms. The one exception was the red-haired woman in a blue knee-length dress at the door to her room on the third floor across from him, her suitcase wedged into her door to keep it open, giving the appearance she was waiting on someone.

She was his wingman.

Inside the room, out of sight, a ground branch operator was waiting with a long gun—just in case. Clark would have preferred Adara to be the one in that doorway and have the comfort of knowing Ding Chavez, the former Army operator turned CIA operative turned team member and friend, was his backup, but the short-fuse nature of the meet precluded mobilizing The Campus.

Adapt and overcome, he reminded himself.

Nothing in the lobby tickled his sixth sense as he processed the activity of dozens of people simultaneously. The hotel was classic Berlin. The old, regal mid-century exterior reflected prewar opulence, while the uber-modern interior and slick, well-dressed employees gave off a trendsetter vibe. The Westin, like Germany, was sprinting toward the future it believed it deserved, yet no matter how hard it tried, it seemed incapable of escaping the shadow of the past.

Then, in his peripheral vision, Clark spied someone entering the lobby from the street.

He waited a three count before letting his gaze flick to the new arrival, who walked toward reception, expensive shoes clicking on the polished floor. The man was middle-aged, but fit and athletic, making him appear ten years younger than Clark knew him to be.

This was his mark—Erik Dovzhenko, a deeply embedded Russian double agent, code-named VICAR.

Clark watched with little interest as VICAR went through the motions of checking in.

"*Kann ich ihnen helfen?*" the man at the desk asked. "*Einchecken?*"

"I'm sorry, my German is terrible," VICAR said in perfect English with just a hint of New England. "*Weiss du wie sach mann das auf English?*" he asked in poorly accented German.

"Of course, sir," the man at the desk said. "Are you checking in?"

"Yes, thank you," VICAR said, his voice crisp and easily audible from where Clark sat. "Robert Manning."

"May I please see your passport and the credit card you reserved the room with?" the check-in attendant said.

Checking in as Robert Manning meant Dovzhenko believed he was in the clear. Had he checked in as David Marsh, it would mean he had concerns and Clark's team would clear the man's six and make contact later. Had he checked in as William Hunt, then Clark would know to abort.

"Bobby?" he called out from his seat to the man at the desk. "Bobby Manning, is that you?"

Had Clark called him Robert, it would signal he had concerns they were being watched.

He didn't—not yet.

"Carl Bates?" VICAR said, smiling broadly as Clark rose and approached him. "What are you doing here? My goodness, what a small world."

"I'm here on business. Wait— Are you here for the bank summit?"

"I am," VICAR said as they shook hands. "I came in early to spend some time in the city. I love Berlin."

"Same," Clark said, and the challenge-and-response protocol was complete. "What are your plans? Is your wife with you? Do you want to grab a drink?"

"I'm solo on this one, and absolutely," VICAR said.

"Great." From the corner of his eye, Clark watched the female CIA officer that James had "loaned" to him slide her suitcase back into the room, close the door, and head to the elevators.

Dovzhenko turned to the reception agent and handed him twenty euros. "Can you see that my luggage is taken to my room for me? I'm gonna grab a drink with my friend here."

"Of course, sir," the desk agent said and came around to take the SVR agent's roller bag.

"Come on, I know just the place," Clark said, gesturing toward the door where the red-haired CIA agent in the blue dress had just pushed through to clear the street outside. In a few minutes, the man still in her room would leave the hotel and clear their six and then function as trailing security.

James ran the show from his own room with three ground branch officers ready to jump in as a QRF, a quick response force, if things went to hell. The micro earpiece deep in Clark's left ear suggested nothing had James spooked as of yet.

Minutes later, Clark and Dovzhenko were seated in club chairs inside Bar Rouge—a dimly lit pub on Französische Strasse known for its leather-appointed furniture, heavy curtains, chandeliers, and red wallpaper. The bar seemed almost a caricature of where Russian and American spies would have met when Berlin was a divided city at the very heart of the Cold War. Over Dovzhenko's shoulder Clark saw the redhead CIA agent, who had introduced herself that morning as Ginnie, seated at the bar, sipping a martini and talking up the bartender. Clark imagined that Dovzhenko almost certainly knew she was there with Clark. For him to stay alive this long as a double agent inside the SVR, the man would have to possess impeccable tradecraft. It didn't matter—Ginnie, her partner, Tom, out on the street, and the QRF back at the hotel were there as much for Dovzhenko's safety as his at this point.

Unless this was a trap and Dovzhenko had turned.

Always a possibility . . .

"So," the spy code-named VICAR said, crossing his legs at the knee and taking a sip of his bourbon, "what is so important that Yao would risk such a meeting?"

Clark took a sip of his own drink.

"First let me say I understand the risk you've taken, my friend," he said. "We would never have pushed for it were it not important at the highest levels."

Dovzhenko nodded.

"There's a lot of activity in both Moscow and the Arctic these days. We were hoping you might give us an"—he smiled—"insider's perspective."

"What is it you're referring to?" VICAR said, but his face suggested he had an idea.

"A rumor of a schism between the Russian military and the Kremlin," Clark said, hedging a bet.

Dovzhenko laughed at this and took another sip of bourbon.

"It is Russia, my friend," he said, watching Clark carefully. "There is always division within the military and the Kremlin. This is true now more than ever. You will have to be more specific."

"Okay, let me be more specific," Clark said, scanning the room and leaning in closer. "A few days ago a new special missions submarine, K-329, put to sea—possibly with some sort of new weapons technology aboard. That's of great interest to my bosses, as you can imagine. But what is far more concerning is that Colonel General Oleg Andreyev, head of the NDMC, was left in the dark about its highly compartmentalized mission. It caused quite a stir . . . Or so we hear."

Dovzhenko looked uncomfortable now, maybe even afraid.
"This is new information to me," the Russian said.

"We can ensure your safety, Erik," Clark said, sensing he needed
to reassure him, "even get you and your family out—"

"Oh, please," Dovzhenko said, waving a hand. "We both know
that is untrue. I work with Yao not because I am a traitor to my
country, Mr. Bates, but because I love my country. I do not care for
what has become of Mother Russia—politicians have become more
like mob bosses, working closely with Vory to line their own pockets. There's much concern for personal power and profit, but little
for the Russian people. I assure you that, if I am burned, you will
not be able to get me out. When the time comes, I have my own
plans. So please, do not insult me by treating me like some fright-
ened bureaucrat or scientist hoping to defect."

Clark felt admiration for the man across from him. This face-
to-face meet had put the spy in a very compromising situation. It
had taken serious balls to come to Berlin and answer his questions.

"Fair enough. But just know that I will personally help you
should you need it—should the time come." He held the man's eyes
and something passed between them—something that said they
were both men of action who respected both the cause and the
risk. When Dovzhenko nodded, Clark said, "Should we try again?
You look like you have something to share."

"Nothing of substance, I'm afraid. I'm SVR, not GRU or military, so the operations and movements of the Northern Fleet are
not in my wheelhouse, as you Americans would say. But I can
confirm that everything you have said is true—about Andreyev
being kept in the dark." Now he, too, leaned in closer. "My concern
is something much larger, Mr. Bates. There are rumors—things
talked about in hushed tones over drinks, by men like you and
me—about a growing power structure that now has influence in
the Kremlin . . . Influence at the highest level."

"What, like some sort of secret cabal?" Clark asked, dubious.

Dovzhenko's expression darkened. "I believe there is a faction with designs on a post-Yermilov Russia."

"Who are the members of this faction?" Clark asked, the Russian spy's words giving him a chill.

"I do not yet know . . . Old men, I believe. Old guard, you might say. Those who wish to see Russia returned to the empire it once was. Russians who miss the old ways of power and control. My concern," he said and now leaned in so close that they were only inches apart, Clark able to smell the bourbon and cigarettes on the man's breath, "is that if this cabal exists and does, indeed, have tentacles into the military through the office of Yermilov, and if K-329 has been dispatched on a secret mission carrying Poseidon torpedoes . . ." He leaned back and took a slug of his drink. "Well, this would be very bad indeed, yes?"

A hint of his Russian accent had slipped in.

Clark watched the man and digested his words. They sounded like the mad ramblings of a conspiracy theorist. But VICAR was a well-vetted, reliable asset who had provided mission-saving intel in the past. If there was even a grain of truth to his suspicion . . .

"Can you try to identify the principals of the cabal?"

Dovzhenko shrugged. "Perhaps. But looking behind this particular curtain could be very, very dangerous. I may have to execute my own exfiltration plan at the end."

Clark understood, and that meant losing the most valuable asset they had inside the Russian intelligence community. But if Dovzhenko was right about this . . .

"I understand, but this information could be vital to both our countries. If a coup happens and our government is not prepared. If a nuclear submarine has been given orders by someone outside the Russian presidential chain of command . . . Let's just say wars have started because of less. Knowledge and understanding are the antidote to escalation."

"True," Dovzhenko said.

"I will meet you in Poland in two days," he said. "I will try to find out more—not for you, Mr. Bates, but for us all. Power-hungry men playing games with doomsday submarines is dangerous. One wrong move could destroy the whole planet. I have children, Mr. Bates. This is not the future I want."

Clark's mind went to his wife, waiting even now for a promised week together watching the grandkids at home.

"Where in Poland?"

"InterContinental hotel, Warsaw. We will meet the same way." VICAR smiled. "You can even bring your lovely lady friend in the blue dress and your friend standing there outside at the corner."

Clark smiled at this one. "Out of curiosity, what does the SVR think you're doing in Berlin today?"

"Recruiting a new American mole inside the U.S. intelligence community," he said with a smile and a wink. "A disgruntled American CIA man who works as Carl Bates."

They both laughed and then clinked their glasses together.

"Two days, then," Clark said.

The Russian mole rose and turned for the door.

Clark caught the eye of the redhead at the bar and gave her a nod.

Feeling worse than he did before the meeting, Clark took a swig of his bourbon and wondered, *What the hell are the crazy Russians up to now?*

15

Katie glanced through the partially opened door into the conference room while the United States Marine security guard used a hand scanner to check her CAC microchip. It beeped and turned green, just as her face turned red. Captain Ferguson, whom she'd briefed after talking to Pete Miller, had taken the news quite seriously and run her concerns up the flagpole. Apparently, the news had gotten a lot of high-level attention because they'd been summoned to the White House Situation Room within the hour.

Contrary to popular belief, the Situation Room was not, in fact, a single room. In its current incarnation, the WHSR was a six-thousand-square-foot communications and command and control center—a SCIF inside the West Wing with a watch center, briefing rooms, and the famed videoconference room that most people imagined when they thought of the Situation Room. Despite being a daughter of the President, this was Katie's first time in the WHSR in a professional capacity, and her nerves were starting to get the better of her.

"How many people am I briefing to, Skipper?" she asked as she took in the room packed with not just flag-rank military officers, but also a half dozen civilians in suits. She felt her pulse quicken as her face flushed. "I thought you said it was for the DNI and the national security advisor."

Ferguson smiled beside her as the Marine scanned his CAC.

"A few more than we thought initially. The President and the DNI both felt we needed the key members of the National Security Council as well, and, of course, they bring their aides . . . You get it, the room fills quickly."

"Wait, so the SecDef is going to be here, too?"

"Yeah, presumably. Also, the secretary of state and someone from the Joint Chiefs—the chairman, I imagine. The vice president couldn't make it, I heard."

"But the President . . ."

"Oh, he'll definitely be here."

"Why didn't you tell me, sir?" she asked, unconsciously smoothing the front of her uniform.

"Oh, did I forget to mention that?" Ferguson said unconvincingly. "Look, just relax, Ryan. Remember you're the expert on this stuff, okay?"

"Actually, Captain Miller is the expert. He's the guy who should be briefing this, not me."

Ferguson gave her a stern look. "He's a subject-matter expert. You're the analyst in charge of the *Belgorod* threat."

"Since when?" she said, screwing up her face.

He checked his watch. "Since I made you the case manager two hours ago."

"Thanks a lot, sir."

"Look, Ryan, no one in the room knows more about this threat than you at this moment. These guys only deal with big picture, they're not going to get into the weeds and try to test you on technical minutiae. So just share what you know and answer their questions succinctly and directly."

"Okay," she said, a wave of nausea hitting her.

They entered the conference room and were largely ignored, as some of the most important people in the country in regards to national security policy had divvied themselves up into little subgroups, talking animatedly among themselves. The seat at the head of the table was empty at the moment. She connected her tablet at the podium and then, hands shaking, followed Ferguson to their seats at the table.

"Sit down, Ryan," Ferguson said with a paternal smile. "And good Lord, take a breath. You look like you're about to pass out. It's gonna be fine, kid."

She tried to look over her notes, but found it impossible to concentrate, instead catching snippets of conversation from the powerful men and women around her. Then, suddenly, everyone stood up and she reflexively did the same, turning toward the door to see President Ryan and DNI Mary Pat Foley enter the room.

"Please, please—take your seats," the President said with a humble smile that just made his presence even more larger-than-life. Perhaps it was the setting or the people in the room or the topic at hand, but the man taking a seat at the head of the mahogany table was the President of the United States. She could barely even imagine him as the "daddy" she'd had dinner with just a few nights ago.

"Thanks to those of you that hung around after the PDB earlier and those of you who came in for this. Everyone is busy, I know, so we'll get right to it. Captain Ferguson, you have emerging details to share? Something, I hope, that will expand on the written brief we've all read, I assume?" he added, which Katie took to mean *Don't waste our time here.*

"Thank you, Mr. President. In the interest of time, I am going to turn the floor over to the lead intelligence officer and case manager on this threat, Lieutenant Commander Select Ryan—if you please?" Ferguson said, gesturing to the podium. She stood, suddenly wishing she had something in her hands to keep them from shaking—note cards or something, though she'd probably drop them on the floor and then collapse in on herself like a dying star . . .

She took the podium, tapped the tablet, which brought it to life, and the screen behind her filled with the amazingly crisp, clear satellite image of the *Belgorod* that had kicked this odyssey off in the first place.

"I'll try not to repeat information you already know, but will be happy to answer questions at the end, of course," she said, hating herself for saying "of course," of course. "As we all know, the heavily modified Block II Oscar submarine *Belgorod* put to sea yesterday, something that caught us by surprise in light of our robust intelligence network within Russia. There are two things that make this event more concerning. The first is the unusually large torpedo tube shutter doors we discovered just before she launched from Severodvinsk. The written report includes speculation about these doors, but I have more information to share now after meeting with retired Navy captain Pete Miller, who is a program manager at the Undersea Weapons Program at the Naval Research Lab. Based on the large diameter, his team believes that these doors could be designed to accommodate a new multipurpose UUV being developed by Rubin Central Design Bureau. Code-named Status-6, aka the Poseidon, the Status-6 represents an evolution of torpedo technology—"

"Hold on, are you saying the Poseidon is *real*?" a four-star admiral she recognized as Lawrence Kent from the Joint Chiefs said. "The last brief we had on that program indicated Status-6 was more propaganda than reality—Russian bluster and fearmongering—but you're saying it's operational? What the hell, Mary Pat?"

"Let's hear the whole brief, Larry," the President said before the briefing could devolve into a free-for-all. The admiral folded his arms across his chest and for some reason glared at *her.* "Lieutenant Ryan, please continue."

"Yes, Admiral Kent, many *supposed* leaks about new weapons systems and technological breakthroughs have proven to be controlled propaganda campaigns from the GRU, but the Weapons and Payloads Division that Miller heads up stays on top of the science. They tell me that the large-diameter torpedo doors necessary to accommodate the Status-6 align with what we see in these photos. As I was saying, the Poseidon UUV represents an evolution in torpedo design. They are estimated to be two meters in diameter and use a nuclear-powered propulsion system, which gives the platform theoretically unlimited range and the ability to travel at very high speeds."

"How high?" Kent asked.

"Upward of eighty knots." That piece of information caused grumbles and gasps around the room. "Also, there are concerns the Russians have incorporated AI technology into the weapon, giving it the ability to navigate autonomously and employ sophisticated counter-detection and evasion strategies, which makes it hard to defend. The other problem—"

"The other problem is the payload," an Army general she didn't recognize said, interrupting. "We were told that they were developing this damn thing as a doomsday weapon to carry high-yield nuclear warheads that can create radioactive tsunamis."

She looked at the President, who nodded at her and smiled.

"You're right, General," she said and tapped her screen to bring up the schematic Miller had shared of the terrifying torpedo. She went on to summarize what the retired submarine officer had shared about the doomsday variant with a cobalt 60 salted warhead. "Our further concern is that the *Belgorod* is a special missions boat. We do know—and this is information confirmed through sources at the CIA—that the sub was designed to carry and deploy advanced submersible technology capable, we think, of tapping into and disrupting our undersea sensor and communications systems, which are also largely linked by undersea fiber optics."

"So, it's both a saboteur and a first-strike platform," the SecDef said solemnly. "Wonderful."

The President was still staring at her, so Katie continued, tapping the tablet again. The screen filled with images of Russian president Yermilov, the Russian defense minister, and Colonel General Andreyev, who headed the National Defense Management Center.

"General Andreyev, on the right, met with President Yermilov briefly right after the *Belgorod* sailed. We learned, through other intelligence assets within the Russian military, that Andreyev was upset because he was not informed of the sailing of the *Belgorod* . . ." Admiral Kent leaned in to say something, but the President cut him off with a simple raised finger. "We have hints of divisions and compartmentalization of information as it relates to the *Belgorod* at a level unprecedented for the Russian military and the Kremlin. This is concerning as well—"

"Obviously," the SecDef said.

"Yes, sir," she said, her face flushing.

She tapped the tablet.

"This is the captain of the *Belgorod*, Captain First Rank Konstantin Gorov. He has been a star in the Russian Navy and was selected to command the *Belgorod*, we believe, by President Yermilov himself. His bio reads as one would expect," and she quickly summarized the man's stellar military career, including two previous submarine commands and numerous awards. "What's a little more interesting is something the Defense Intelligence Agency provided."

Tap.

An older picture, clearly from before high definition was even a thing, appeared.

"This is Dimitri Gorov, Captain Gorov's father—"

This time it was the President who interrupted. "Wait, you're telling us that the *Belgorod* is skippered by the son of the lead engineer on the *Red October?*"

"Yes, Mr. President," Katie said, and she wondered for a heartbeat how he knew the elder Gorov was the lead designer of the *Red October.*

That wasn't in the written brief . . .

"What's the *Red October?*" one of the staffers, a blond woman in a power suit, her hair back in a bun, asked.

"*Red October* was a Typhoon-class Russian submarine reported to be equipped with propulsion technology that was rumored to be revolutionary—at least in its day. The *Red October* was lost in the Atlantic Ocean during exercises, but under very mysterious circumstances. There are tons of rumors around her disappearance, but I'll stick to what we know with certainty. Most of the crew was rescued after a significant accident involving the submarine's reactor leaked radiation into the boat. The submarine's captain, a man named Marko Ramius, went down with the ship, scuttling the vessel to keep it out of American hands, along with the XO and a few others. One rumor that is worth mentioning is that Captain Ramius may have been trying to defect, though I found no evidence of that in CIA records—at least those available to me." She couldn't help glancing at DNI Foley, trying to read her expression, but the woman's face was a mask. "In any case, I mention this interesting legend only because I did discover that there was, around the same time, a sanctioned CIA operation to extract Captain Gorov's father, Dimitri, with a promise from the scientist that he would exchange detailed plans for the *Red October* in exchange for a new life in the West with his family."

"Wait," said President Ryan, who in that moment looked more like her dad, a strange expression on his face, "Dimitri Gorov defected?"

Katie wasn't sure what to make of the stunned look on her dad's face, a look he rarely wore. She wondered, with his CIA pedigree, if her dad might have insight into the mystery of the missing Typhoon-class submarine, but she quickly dismissed it as coincidental.

"No, sir, Mr. President," she said. "It turns out that Dimitri Gorov died before he could be extracted."

"Was it an assassination by the KGB?" President Ryan pushed. "Was the operation compromised?"

"I don't know, sir," she said. "The official report is an accidental death—a drowning. Apparently, he fell through the ice on the river in Leningrad around the time of the meeting with the agent in charge. The body was reportedly never recovered, but that's the official story—gleaned, it would seem, from sources inside Russia, so make of that what you will. Honestly, there's not much in the case file on this. It could be he died accidentally or maybe committed suicide. A KGB assassination seems unlikely to me, however. It seems implausible that the son, Konstantin, would have risen to his rank and station in the Russian Navy had the KGB known about his father's planned treason. Sins of the father were not readily forgiven in the Soviet Union."

President Ryan's face suggested his mind was churning related to something she'd said. He traded glances with DNI Foley and seemed to have a silent meeting of the minds that Katie couldn't interpret. She stole her own glance at Ferguson, who shrugged, clearly as confused as she was. After an awkward silence, her boss gestured for her to press on.

"In conclusion, the *Belgorod* putting to sea took us by surprise and the two-meter-diameter torpedo tube shutter doors indicate the Status-6 program may very well be more than theoretical. In fact, this underway could signal that Status-6 is—best-case scenario—ready for deep-ocean testing. Worst-case scenario, it could be fully operational—"

"Lieutenant Ryan, did the Russians load *nuclear*-tipped Status-6 torpedoes on the *Belgorod*, yes or no?" Admiral Kent asked, getting straight to the point.

She measured her response, acutely aware that saying the wrong thing could have significant tactical and strategic implications. "It seems unlikely given the nascent nature of the program and the current defense condition, Admiral," she said. "But honestly, sir, we just don't know."

"The IC is working on this as we speak. We have assets already in place seeking clarity on the payload question," Mary Pat said to Katie's relief and surprise. "We're also looking into the compartmentalization, infighting, and confusion among the Kremlin power brokers. We hope to have clarity on both matters very soon."

"Is there some sort of shake-up happening in the Kremlin? Is Yermilov cleaning house again?" the SecDef asked, his voice tense with worry.

"Again, we'll have more soon," was all DNI Foley said.

"Based on your findings, Lieutenant Ryan, do you have any recommendations?" President Ryan asked, taking the floor and signaling it was time to wrap up.

"Recommendations, sir?" Katie asked, caught off guard.

"Yes," Ryan said gently. "What is the Office of Naval Intelligence recommending in light of this potential new threat? Where is the *Belgorod* now?"

"We don't know, sir. The USS *Indiana* is in the Barents and tasked with finding the *Belgorod*. The *Indiana*'s last report indicated they had intermittent contact with a Russian submarine, but based on the preliminary assessment, it appears to have been an Akula, not the *Belgorod*."

"What other activity from the Russian Northern Fleet are we seeing?"

Her brain raced to unpack all the ship names and data she'd crammed before the brief just in case she was asked this very question. "Satellite imagery indicates increased activity at Severomorsk—they are loading stores and conducting power plant start-ups on the battle cruiser and Northern Fleet flagship *Pyotr Velikiy*, as well as the frigate *Admiral Flota Kasatonov*. Also, K-560, the Yasen-class SSGN *Severodvinsk*, got underway this morning from Olenya Bay. There is a Russian Northern Fleet Artic exercise previously announced for this week to showcase their carrier the *Admiral Kuznetsov*, which is already at sea, so I suppose this is not surprising, but it is something we need to watch for any changes. The *Gerald R. Ford* strike group is conducting training exercises in the Atlantic off the Virginia coast as we speak. We could reposition them north as a show of force, balancing the Russian activity, and use that as cover for further interrogation of K-329 if its true mission is to head south. The USS *Washington* was scheduled to go underway tomorrow to participate in the strike group exercises, but it could be retasked to work in tandem with the *Indiana* to find the *Belgorod*. But for all we know, the *Belgorod* may very well still be in the Barents, waiting to participate in the upcoming Artic war games. Regardless, the situation needs to be closely monitored and the carrier strike group should be notified of the threat."

"I agree," DNI Foley said, looking satisfied.

The President, for his part, wore an unmistakable expression that she recognized from her lacrosse-playing days at the Academy whenever she scored a goal . . . *Dad pride.*

She resisted the urge to beam, but she felt herself blush, regardless.

"The Pentagon is eyeing these developments closely and I agree with your assessment. Nice work, Lieutenant," Admiral Kent said, the hard edge to his voice easing.

"I'd like to head up the coordination between ONI and the strike group . . . if possible," she said, looking at Captain Ferguson, assuming it would be him making the decision. "That is to say, sir, I think I can be most effective if I were to be aboard the *Ford*."

"You want to deploy?" Ferguson asked.

She nodded.

"I'd like to take my best IS with me and set up with the N2 team on board. I can keep my fingers on the pulse of what they're learning, while coordinating information from ONI."

"Sounds like a reasonable plan," DNI Foley said. But she glanced at the President, who looked less enthusiastic.

After a long beat he said, "I tend to leave decisions like that to those of you in uniform. But keep us in the loop of all findings."

This was a very Jack Ryan position to take. Translation: *Fine, I'll give you enough rope to hang yourself, so long as you don't keep me in the dark.*

The President rose, and everyone else did in unison, which she assumed meant the meeting was over. Before he turned to the exit, he gave a parting glance to Katie. She saw a hint of both anxiety and affection in his eyes, and she put herself—maybe for the first time—in his shoes. For a fleeting instant, she felt the same weight he must, trying to be a father to a daughter who'd just declared her intent to charge headfirst into harm's way and a father to a nation that knew nothing of the dangerous Russian leviathan potentially carrying a doomsday weapon. She smiled at him and then he was gone, whisked away by his chief of staff, Arnold van Damm, and the cadre of White House power brokers who kept the machinery of the United States government running.

As the others filed out, her boss intercepted her at the podium.

"Nice work, Ryan," Ferguson said and gave her a genuine, proud smile. "You struck a perfect balance between managing the urgency of the situation and triggering World War Three."

"Thank you, sir," she said, having not really thought of it in those terms, but realizing he wasn't joking.

"Did you mean it when you said you wanted to embark on the *Ford*, or was that just bravado in the moment?"

"I meant it," she said. "Can you help make that happen?"

"Of course," he said. "Pack your seabag and we'll get you out there tomorrow."

"Nice work, Katie," said a woman behind her.

She turned to see Mary Pat Foley, who had lingered as the rest of the uniforms and suits shuffled out.

"Thank you, ma'am." Then, realizing the opportunity would likely never present itself again, she decided to press. "Madam Director, is there a way I could find out more about Dimitri Gorov and his failed defection in the winter of '84?"

There was a flash of something that told her Foley knew more than she was letting on, but it was gone from her face as fast as it had appeared.

"I was in Russia House in the day," the DNI said. "But I wasn't involved in an operation to snag Gorov. I can dig in, if you like, and share what I learn. I'll find out if the agent running the op is still around. If so, you can meet with him before you head out."

"Thank you, ma'am," she said. "I just don't want to miss anything important. Best to have a full picture."

With a smile and a pat on Katie's shoulder, the DNI excused herself and left the briefing room.

"I assume you'll be taking IS2 Pettigrew with you?" Ferguson said, returning to the conversation they were having.

"If possible, sir. Bubba is my right-hand man and stays on top of this stuff like nobody else."

Ferguson nodded. "I'll coordinate with Captain Mackenzie, the skipper of the *Ford*, and get you out there and embedded with their intel shop by late tomorrow. I have a meeting at the puzzle palace next, but you head back to the shop, get things squared away, and let Pettigrew know the plan. After, I want you to head home, get packed, and, for God's sake, get some sleep, Ryan. You've got a long few days ahead of you."

"Yes, sir," she said and followed him out of the Situation Room, the most famous and secure briefing SCIF in the world, wondering to herself . . .

What the hell did I just get myself into?

16

Instead of going home to pack and sleep like she'd been ordered to do, Katie did the opposite and scrambled to exploit every second of remaining time she had in D.C. before embarking on the *Ford*. Mary Pat had kept her word and surprised Katie by providing her with the information she'd promised and done so in less than two hours from when they'd parted company in the Situation Room.

Katie eased her Jeep Cherokee to a rolling stop in front of the modest two-story residence on Jackson Street in the heart of Arlington. From the driver's seat, she squinted to read the house number beside the front door and checked it against the address on her GPS app.

"Yep, this is the place," she murmured, spinning the steering wheel and pulling into the narrow driveway.

While her visit wasn't technically unannounced, she'd not given retired CIA officer Matthew Reilly much advance notice of her visit. Twenty-two minutes, to be precise. Name-dropping Mary Pat Foley had insured the man couldn't refuse her request, but it also didn't start things off on the note Katie would have preferred. Transactional interactions had never been her MO. She liked to take her time with people and form a connection before she even thought about making an ask, but the last thirty-six hours had forced her to repeatedly violate her natural protocol and it was starting to make her feel, well, uncomfortable. Sweeping in and pumping this guy for information on Dimitri and Konstantin Gorov, only to disappear never to be seen again, felt so sterile and callous. Consequently, she'd stopped at a florist on the way here and picked up a potted orchid to give the guy.

Why arrive with a plant? Why an orchid? Who knows . . .

It had been a gut impulse.

Now looking at the two-stem, yellow-petaled orchid on the passenger seat, she felt stupid, and she questioned the whole ludicrous idea.

"Hi, I'm Katie. If you tell me everything you know about a couple of Russian dudes, I'll give you this flower," she said, playacting the absurdity of the situation.

I guess I'm transactional after all.

She exhaled, left the orchid on the passenger seat, and climbed out of her Cherokee. She made it halfway up the driveway, cursed to herself, and ran back to grab the stupid orchid. Tucking the little pot under her arm, she retraced her steps and made her way up and onto the adorable little covered front porch and rang the doorbell. Thankfully, the chime was not accompanied by barking and frenzied scraping of claws on the inside of the front door. She didn't have the time or energy for big friggin' dogs today.

On hearing the sound of the dead bolt shifting, she put a pleasant smile on her face.

The front door, which was painted an interesting shade of green, opened and she was greeted by a sixty-something, pleasant-looking man with thinning sandy-blond hair. His azure-blue eyes—framed by trendy tortoiseshell spectacles—stared out at her with something that looked like a cross between expectation and weariness.

"Hi, I'm Katie Ryan," she said.

And I brought you this orchid, added the voice in her head.

"Come on in, Ms. Ryan," he said, taking a step back to give her room to enter.

"Thanks."

On entering the foyer, she immediately noted the smell. That was the thing about homes. Everybody's smelled different and unique, like an olfactory fingerprint. Matthew Reilly's house had a pleasant odor that her brain identified as lemons and soap.

Or lemon soap?

"Is that for me?" he asked, his gaze settling on the orchid.

No, it's my pet orchid. We're besties. We go everywhere together, the snarky voice said in her head immediately.

"It is," she said and presented him with the five-inch glazed ceramic planter and yellow orchid.

"Thank you," he said, accepting the plant and turning his back on her. "We can put it with the others . . . I assume Mary Pat told you."

"Told me what?" she said, chasing after him after an awkward beat.

"That I collect orchids."

"Um, no, actually she didn't . . . I just, I don't know, stopped by a florist on a whim," she said, sounding more tongue-tied than normal.

"Mmm-hmm," he said, apparently not buying it.

He led her into a tiny, but nicely appointed, glass-enclosed four-season porch at the rear of the house that was filled with all kinds of cool plants, half of which happened to be orchids. He shifted two similar-sized pots with orchids—a white- and a purple-flowered pair—to make room for the one she'd given him.

"Thank you for the orchid," he said with a polite smile and gestured to a wicker love seat with pastel-colored cushions. "Can I get you something to drink, Ms. Ryan . . . water, iced tea, soda?"

"No, thank you," she said.

He sniffed, then lowered himself into a matching wicker chair, catty-corner from the love seat. "How may I be of assistance?"

She crossed her legs and placed her folded hands on top of her knee. "I was hoping to talk to you about a defection case you managed when you were a case officer in Leningrad during the eighties. I know it was a long time ago, but any details you might remember would be very helpful to, um . . . to a case I'm working on presently."

"Did you know that orchid flowers have bilateral symmetry?" he said.

"I . . . did not," she said, the non sequitur catching her by surprise.

"Do you know what else has bilateral symmetry in nature?"

She thought for a moment. "Faces."

"That's right. Other flowers have radial symmetry, but not the orchid," he said with an approving smile. "When you look at an orchid, subconsciously the mind has the sense that it's looking back. I think that's why I like them. Every plant feels unique, like an individual, if you will. Did Mary Pat really not tell you about my collection? Please be honest."

Unblinking, she met his stare. "No. It was pure coincidence. The truth is, I felt guilty barging my way into your home on short notice to badger you for information. Coming empty-handed felt wrong, so when I passed a flower shop on the drive here, I decided to stop."

He nodded, seemingly satisfied. "Let's call it good karma, in that case."

"Great, I could definitely use some of that," she said and gave him a tired smile.

"You're here to talk to me about Dimitri and Konstantin Gorov, aren't you?"

"Yes."

"Just a moment." He stood, exited the sunroom, and returned a moment later with a well-worn and bulging accordion-style folder that was held closed by a pair of rubber bands. To her surprise, he handed it to her. "Here, it's yours."

"What is it?" she asked, lowering the hefty folder to rest it on her lap.

"That is everything I know and collected on both father and son for the past forty years," he said as he lowered himself back into his chair. "This is open-source information—nothing classified or out of place. I knew in my gut that, someday, this information would have a role to play. Apparently, that day is today. Honestly, it feels good to be rid of it."

Katie hard-swallowed. "You've been tracking Konstantin Gorov for forty years?"

"Yes."

"Why?"

"Call it curiosity. Call it guilt. Call it compulsion . . . Maybe all three. Whatever the reason, the simple fact is that I needed to know what happened to the boy."

She resisted the urge to open the folder and start digging into the files. There would be time for that later; while she was here, she needed to leverage the opportunity to dialogue with him. "From what I understand, the father, Dimitri, was an asset you were running who wanted to defect, but he died mysteriously on the night of his extraction. Is that accurate?"

"No," Reilly said. "Not exactly. Dimitri wasn't an asset. He never provided any actual intelligence."

"I don't understand."

"He was the lead project engineer for the Typhoon SSGN

program at Rubin Central Design Bureau for Marine Engineering. Rubin is the Soviet—or Russian now, I suppose, though the difference seems semantic these days—anyway, the Russian analogue to General Dynamics Electric Boat. Dimitri was smart and calculating. He also understood risk, which is why he wouldn't agree to be a managed asset. We negotiated a simple deal. The plans for the *Red October* in exchange for a new life in the West."

"And what happened?" she asked, leaning in.

"Marko Ramius happened," he said. "I can see from the blank look on your face you don't know what I'm talking about, do you?"

"No."

"I just assumed with you being his daughter and the by-name request from the DNI and all . . ." He blew air through pursed lips. "Fuck it, if you don't find out from me, you're going to find out one way or another. You're a Ryan and if you're anything like your father you won't leave any stone unturned."

She smiled at the comment. "Yep, that's how we roll in my family."

"Marko Ramius was the Russian submarine captain of the *Red October*, the first and only Typhoon SSGN with an advanced magnetic-ionic silent drive. He defected in December 1984, and when he did, he hand-delivered the *Red October* to the United States Navy. It was the single greatest intelligence coup and transfer of military intellectual property during the Cold War."

I can't believe he never told me, she thought, feeling a flash of something best described as a cross between anger and incredulity. But instead of saying this, she said, "I can't believe the Navy managed to keep this compartmentalized for all this time. Hiding a Typhoon-class submarine is no small feat."

"Indeed," he said. "But remember, back then nobody had iPhones, or TikTok, or quadcopter drones with 4K streaming video cameras on them. It was a different time."

"That's true," she said, her mind racing as fresh deductions began popping inside her head like kernels in a popcorn machine. "Thanks to Captain Ramius, you didn't need the plans from Gorov anymore."

"That's right."

"The head shed in Langley canceled the defection?"

"Right again."

"And I bet you had to deliver the bad news to Gorov, didn't you?"

He tapped his temple with his index finger and pointed it at her. "Winner winner, chicken dinner. The lady wins a prize."

In that moment, she became aware of the weight of the accordion folder on her lap. "That must have been rough for you."

"It was the most difficult thing I ever had to do as a case officer. We're supposed to be the good guys, the guys who keep their word. The betrayal I saw in Dimitri's eyes that night . . . It's haunted me ever since."

"If you don't mind me asking, what actually happened to Dimitri Gorov?"

His lips pressed into a thin, hard line for a moment before he said, "That's the worst part about the whole damn thing. Maybe suicide, maybe the KGB . . . I tried for years to find out, but it was literally as if after our conversation, Dimitri vanished off the face of the earth."

"So all of this," she said gently, tapping the accordion folder, "is information on the son, Konstantin?"

"Call it the product of a guilty conscience."

"How? I can't imagine the Company gave you resources for this."

"It did not."

"Are you saying you paid sources out of your own pocket to keep tabs on him?"

He nodded.

"My God, that must have cost you a fortune."

"Why do you think I'm divorced?" he said with a sad, self-deprecating laugh.

"I'm sorry."

"Don't be. It was self-inflicted."

I bet the orchid collection was his wife's, she thought. *He probably talks to them like they're his kids.*

She tucked an errant strand of hair behind her left ear. "I'm going to venture a guess that you are already aware that Konstantin Gorov is the captain of the Russian special missions submarine *Belgorod* K-329?"

"Yes," he said.

"The Navy has both tactical and strategic concerns about this submarine. The Russians . . . Well, all I can tell you is we have some concerns about what Gorov might be up to."

"Concerns?" the former operative said.

"I wish I could share more with you but, well, you get it. Obviously, I'm going to review this file you gave me, but I'd like to get your unfiltered impressions of Gorov while I'm here. It could be immensely helpful."

Reilly exhaled with the weariness of a person who'd just been asked to climb ten flights of stairs after having just climbed fifty, but he answered her anyway.

"Konstantin Gorov is the consummate, successful Russian warrior. What I mean by that is that he is stoic and unyielding in the face of adversity. His life has been difficult. Can you imagine being raised by a single mother in the Soviet Union, orphaned at sixteen, and finding the courage and motivation to rise to a captain first rank in the Russian Nuclear Navy?"

"I can't imagine that, actually," she said. "So, if you could only use a single word to describe him, what would it be?"

"Tenacious," he said without a second's hesitation.

"If you could pick only one of the following, would you say Gorov is a rule follower or a trailblazer?"

He narrowed his eyes at her. "Is that your way of asking me if Gorov is another Ramius?"

"Maybe . . ."

Damn, this guy hasn't lost a step.

The corners of his lips curled in wry amusement. "The *Belgorod* has put to sea and nobody can find her. Is that it?"

"I'm really not at liberty to say."

"Mm-hmm, well, in that case there is something else you should know."

"And what's that?"

"His wife died during childbirth ten months ago. He married quite late and she was the bright spot in his life."

"And the child?"

"Stillborn."

"Oh, dear God," she said and felt a heaviness in her gut. "That's terrible."

"Gorov is no stranger to adversity and loss, but I can't imagine he's in a good place," Reilly said. "Even stoic Russians need time to grieve. The command should have put him on a leave of absence."

"This might be a strange question, but do you think there's any chance that Gorov would be considering defecting with the *Belgorod* like Ramius did forty years ago?"

The old spook surveyed his orchid collection for a long moment before turning to meet her eyes. There was pain in the man's eyes—guilt maybe. "From what I know about the man, not a snowball's chance in hell."

17

GLAVPIVTORG RESTAURANT AND BAR
BOLSHAYA LUBYANKA STREET, HOUSE #5
MOSCOW, RUSSIA
1931 LOCAL TIME

Colonel General Nikolai Ilyin arrived first at Glavpivtorg. Most people didn't realize that the bar's name was an acronym fashioned in the Soviet tradition, with GlavPivTorg meaning "main beer cooperative." Most people didn't know that the restaurant's owner was former KGB. And most people hadn't seen the multiple reincarnations of the establishment over the decades like Nikolai had seen.

The thought made him smile.

Reincarnation of the establishment . . . This is the Russian way.

Reincarnation was the purpose of the clandestine meeting he'd arranged tonight—a meeting brazenly happening in the heart of Moscow.

This is also the Russian way.

He took a final drag from his Prima, stomped out the butt on the sidewalk, and grabbed the door handle. Once upon a time, this building had been the foreign ministry office, located across the street from the old KGB headquarters. When the foreign ministry office was relocated, Glavpivtorg had opened in its place. As a young KGB officer, he and his comrades had come here to drink, to commiserate, and to talk politics. Back then, the interior had been unapologetically plain. But like everything else in Moscow, Glavpivtorg had changed with the times and now could best be described as "proletariat chic," a swanky attempt to capture the nostalgia of days past, but with comfortable seating, a proper menu, and none of that Soviet-era grime.

The purveyor of the establishment had become a trusted comrade of Nikolai's over the years. With a phone call and the implicit promise of a favor, the owner would close early, kick out all the restaurant's patrons and staff, and turn the upstairs dining balcony into a virtual SCIF with all the beer, *vobla*, and *pelmeni* his VIP guests could consume. A half dozen of Russia's most audacious operations had been planned in Glavpivtorg.

The thought made Nikolai smile.

Who would think that Glavpivtorg, not the Kremlin, was the true seat of power in Moscow?

"General," his old friend said, walking up to embrace him with a bear hug.

"Anatoly," Ilyin said, hugging the restaurant owner and giving him an affectionate triple back slap. "How are you, my friend?"

"Honestly, I'm tired. I turned seventy last week. I think I'm ready to retire."

"*Da*," Ilyin said, "but retirement is a risk for men like us. Stop working and in two weeks you'll be dead."

Anatoly responded with a sandpaper chortle. "You think I don't know this? Like I said, I'm tired. I need a very *long* rest."

Both men laughed at the earnest black comedy of the quip. But then, like a sniper's bullet, the payload hit home and a powerful tsunami of emotions washed over Ilyin. Regret for the past, hope for the future, uncertainty about his plan, and the weight of his mortality turned his mind into a salty, cloudy soup of indecision. He shuddered.

What am I doing? Do I have the right to wield this power? Who am I to change the fate of man?

"You look like you saw a ghost, my friend. Is the Grim Reaper here for me already?" Anatoly said, still smiling.

"*Nyet.* He works for me, remember?" Nikolai said, forcing a smile onto his face. "I promise to give you a fifteen-minute warning before I dispatch him for you."

The barman laughed and gestured to the staircase leading up to the empty balcony. "Your table is waiting, General. When the others arrive, I'll send them up."

"Thank you, Anatoly. You're a good man."

"*Nyet,* I'm just an old communist parading as a poor capitalist."

"Don't worry, I know you had to close early. I'll make tonight worth your while."

"Concern about such things never crossed my mind. Are you famished? What would you like me to bring you?"

Ilyin began unfastening the buttons on his dress jacket in subconscious preparation for the gut-expanding feast he was about to consume. "The usual."

"The usual it is."

He ascended the staircase to the balcony, but took care with each step, as his left knee had developed a nasty habit of alternating between locking up and giving out on him these days. Thankfully, he made it to the top without incident and took a seat at a dining table positioned along the back wall. The wall was decorated as an antique bookshelf with leather-bound tomes that stretched corner to corner. A brass banker's lamp with the iconic green glass shade provided the lion's share of illumination in the otherwise dimly lit space. He snacked on a bowl of mixed nuts while he waited for the others, three men of equal station as himself in the upper echelon of power and influence in the Russian military and intelligence apparatus.

They arrived within short order and feasted together as they had done many times over the years—laughing and making jokes at one another's expense. Forty-five minutes later, bellies full of salted Caspian fish and lamb dumplings and their minds well lubricated by pints of Baltika #9, Russia's longest-serving power brokers got down to the business of plotting their coup.

"We all agree that President Yermilov is a cancer that must be removed," three-star Admiral Boldyrev, commander in chief of the Russian Naval Fleet, said, and slammed his fist down on the table.

"He lied to us. This is not the Russia he promised. He's turned a once mighty and noble government into a kleptocracy to serve his whims. Our people are as poor and weak as the worst days of the Soviet era," Admiral Rodionov, second-in-command at the GRU, said.

"I don't care about the people," General Aralovich, head of the FSB, quipped. "What matters is Russia's standing on the global stage. Yermilov is only about serving his ego and his legacy. If he keeps up this way, there will not be a Russian Federation left when his grip on power finally wanes."

When Ilyin didn't pile on the presidential-insult bandwagon, Boldyrev addressed him. "Nikolai, do you have nothing to say on the matter?"

Ilyin cleared his throat, inhaled deeply, and said, "Remember two months ago, Ivan, when you and I had drinks with Captain First Rank Gorov in St. Petersburg?"

"*Da*, I remember."

"Do you remember what he said when I asked him why he would volunteer for such a mission?"

"Isn't it obvious? Gorov is a dead man walking," Boldyrev said, then took a slug of beer from his pint glass.

"I could say the same for all of us. That's not the reason. Do you *really* not remember what he said?"

Boldyrev waved his hand dismissively. "Too much vodka that night."

"What he said drilled into my mind . . . It's all I can think about since."

"What did he say?" Aralovich asked.

Ilyin paused and swept his gaze across his comrades for effect. "He said, 'I volunteer because there is beautiful stability in parity.' Gorov understood that it is time for the world to have two superpowers once again. Today's Russia is weak. Yermilov confuses the capacity for thuggery with power. There was a purity and strength in the politburo. When we make decisions as a group, like we are doing tonight, we separate the ego from the equation . . . It is time for a new Cold War, comrades. Time to return to the status quo. I want our people to be proud to be Russian again. To rise, to compete, to push himself, a man must have a worthy adversary. This propaganda state we live in today has only one objective, and that is to exalt Yermilov and make excuses for his poor leadership and terrible decisions. America is his scapegoat, and he denigrates them at every turn. They won't admit it, but the people know this. We need to give the Russian people an adversary that they fear, but also respect."

"But we also need to weaken America. They have grown too powerful," Aralovich said.

"Agreed. Which is the genius of this plan. By detonating a single Poseidon in Norfolk, the heart of the American Atlantic fleet will be destroyed. Norfolk will be contaminated and useless for decades. Think of the losses: Second Fleet command and control, Naval Special Warfare, DEVGRU, naval aviation, UWDC Det

Norfolk, and on and on. The loss of talent, leadership, infrastructure, and assets will set them back two decades."

"What happens if the Americans retaliate in kind? We need to consider the possibility they launch a nuclear counterstrike," Rodionov said.

"*Da*, but *we* will intervene before that can happen," Ilyin said. "We will control the narrative, blame Yermilov on the attack, and initiate the coup. We swiftly remove him from power—not only remove him, but execute him, publicly, as an enemy of the people. We will give the Americans their pound of flesh. And we sacrifice the *Belgorod*. We let the Americans destroy it, and if they can't find it, we sink it ourselves. Instead of escalating, we, the Russian military, stands down. We make concessions. And we do this until the time for standing down and making concessions is over and Russia rises again. As they rebuild, we will build . . . And the dance will resume."

"Stability in parity," Boldyrev said.

Ilyin nodded back.

"To Captain First Rank Gorov," the three-star admiral said, raising his glass.

"To Captain First Rank Gorov," Nikolai echoed, clinking glasses with his comrades-in-arms. "The man and the martyr who will restore Mother Russia."

PART II

There is beautiful stability in parity.

—Captain First Rank Konstantin Gorov

18

S T2 Harris yawned as he listened to a broadband recording of the K-335 *Gepard* . . . but *not* the data the *Indiana* had collected while shadowing the Akula. The recording he was listening to was archive data compliments of the ACINT submerged-threat-training database. From the moment he'd picked up that 151.7-hertz signal, something felt off about the *Gepard*. Since Harris couldn't quit the feeling, he decided to camp out at the vacant workstation in the back port corner of control that was typically reserved for the ACINT.

"Dude, Harris, this ain't your watch section. Why aren't you in the rack, brother?" ST2 McCullough said to him in a quiet voice, leaning over from where he sat in front of the narrowband stack.

"Can't sleep," Harris lied.

The truth was he was tired as hell, but what he was doing was more important than sleeping, or watching a movie, or working out. He'd missed something important about K-335—they all had—and damn it if he wasn't going to figure out what it was.

"Getting in some extra training?" McCullough asked, not letting it go.

"Yeah, something like that," he said.

His fellow sonarman held out a fist to Harris. "Hashtag Extra-Mile."

Harris bumped knuckles with his shipmate, then replayed the recording for the umpteenth time. In his peripheral vision, a body appeared beside him. Harris slipped the left headphone cup off his ear and looked up to see the ACINT guy standing there holding what looked like a folding camp stool in his hand. Harris raised an eyebrow at the dude whose name he couldn't remember. Chief Schonauer and everyone else in the division were so enamored with the shore command sonar expert, but Harris couldn't see why.

"Hey," the dude said with an expectant look.

"I know what you're going to say," Harris grumbled, and started to get up. "I'm in your seat, I know."

"Actually, I was going to say that I think you and I got off on the wrong foot. I'm Torvik. Jason Torvik."

Harris, who'd not expected this, said, "Oh . . . I'm Xavier Harris."

Torvik unfolded the little stool and took a seat beside him. "Look, I get it. You've got all these riders on board for your deployment, taking up racks, breathing your oxygen, eating your food, and drinking your bug juice. It sucks, but you know, I used to be a sonar tech just like you. I did four deployments before I went ACINT. I have dolphins, and I've eaten more than my fair share of death pillows. Heck, I probably go to sea more than you guys . . . 'Cause they send me from boat to boat to boat."

"Oh," Harris said. "I didn't realize that. I thought you were a civilian."

"Yeah, well, your skipper's policy is as long as it says 'Indiana' on it, I can wear it underway," Torvik said, gesturing to his maroon

IU sweatshirt and embroidered track pants. "I never liked poopy suits."

"Me either," Harris said with a new and sudden respect for the guy.

"I've seen you up here a couple times in your off-watch time. What are you working on?"

Harris felt a little uncomfortable telling Torvik the truth, worried that maybe the guy would be offended or something, but he decided to be honest anyway. "I've been comparing the recording we have of the *Gepard* to the one in the ACINT database."

"Do you mind me asking why?"

Here it comes, Harris thought. *The CYA routine.*

"Well, not because I'm questioning your classification or anything, but something just feels off to me."

"Dude, you don't have to worry about that," Torvik said. "I leave my ego on the pier, bro. You literally can't offend me. Acoustics before self, that's my motto."

"Ah, that's good to know."

"So, let me have it. Both barrels. What's really on your mind, Professor X?" Torvik said, riffing off Harris's first name and the famous X-Men character.

Harris felt energized at where this was going, and the fog of sleep boiled off instantly. "Okay, so when we first acquired the *Gepard* on narrowband, of course I thought it was the *Belgorod* because that's who we were looking for. But then we found the match in the database on the 151-hertz freq, and it was a match for K-335—which is in the Northern Fleet and confirmed by satellite imagery not to be in port. So, case closed, because it was a perfect fit."

"Yep, agreed," Torvik said.

"But it's not a perfect fit . . . That's the problem."

"Go on," Torvik said, his gaze shifting to Harris's terminal and his tone indicating his mind was already working the problem.

"Okay, so this gram is showing an archive broadband collection on the *Gepard* from three years ago . . ." He clicked to minimize the pane and reveal another broadband file he had cued up. "And this is broadband that *we* recorded on the *Gepard* . . . To my ear, they don't sound like the same boat. The ACINT data is so much cleaner. I think it must have been recorded at a much closer range than what we got. To be honest, our recording's not great. It took me hours to isolate the best segment, and I still gotta jack the volume up because the signal-to-noise ratio is shit."

"Do you mind if I take a listen?" Torvik said.

"Really? Cool," Harris said and handed his headphones to Torvik. "I'm going to play the cleaner version from the archive data first so you can get your baseline. Then I'll play our recording."

"Ready," Torvik said and closed his eyes.

Harris played the thirty-second segment.

When the clip ended, Torvik said, "Again, please."

Harris played it again.

"Okay, now the other."

Harris switched panes and played the *Indiana*'s recording for Torvik, whose eyes were still closed.

"Once more, please . . ."

Harris replayed the second clip and waited. Once the recording had finished, Torvik opened his eyes and removed the headphones. "I have my own opinion, but I'd like to hear yours first, if you don't mind."

"Sure, simply put, they don't sound like the same boat," Harris said. "In fact, I think I hear two screws. Akulas only have one. I know it sounds crazy, but that's where I'm at."

Torvik nodded. "I agree."

"You do?"

"Yes. Does that surprise you?"

"Well, I kinda thought you'd fight me on it so you wouldn't have to change your finding and risk looking stupid in front of the captain."

Torvik smiled. "Like I said, I check my ego at the pier."

"I guess you weren't bullshitting about that."

"Are you familiar with something called hydrodynamic acoustic effects?"

"Yeah," Harris said. "It's the sound generated from water moving over a vessel's hull and control surfaces."

"That's right, and every submarine has a unique hydrodynamic acoustic fingerprint. Even two boats in the same class will vary. In the case of the Virginia class, the difference between, say, one Block III boat and another are so insignificant you wouldn't be able to tell them apart. But that's not what's going on here. In this case, we should be listening to two different recordings of the same hull number, which means they should sound identical. They do not. It's not the same boat. In fact, to my ear it's not even the same class of boat."

Harris couldn't help but grin. His hunch had been right. "Now what do we do?"

"We're going to import this broadband recording into the narrowband analyzer, which will let the computer deconstruct the symphony of frequencies into their constituent parts."

"I get it," Harris said, loving the metaphor. "The broadband recording is like all the instruments in the orchestra playing at the same time, but we're going to separate each one into a solo."

"Exactly," Torvik said. "We're going to do that for both the archive *Gepard* and our *Gepard*, and compare them. If our ears are telling us the truth, they're not going to match."

"And we're going to reject the nice and shiny convenient 151.7-hertz signal, right?"

"Absolutely. If you're right, and I think you are, then we can positively conclude that that signal was broadcast on purpose to deceive us."

"And what do we do if I'm right, and the boat we were following was the *Belgorod* and not the *Gepard*?"

"We call it in to the big bosses and we look like badasses instead of dumbasses."

"Then let's do it," Harris said and held out his fist to Torvik. "Kick ass . . ."

"Battle Bass," Torvik said, using his adopted crew's slogan, and bumped knuckles with Harris, one sonar tech to another.

19

President Ryan dropped the leather folder containing the forty-year-old classified intelligence brief on Dimitri Gorov on the Resolute desk and let out a long sigh.

"Do you agree with Reilly's findings, Mary Pat?" he asked, looking up and reading the face of his most trusted adviser—especially when it came to . . . *such things.*

"I do," she said. "I know Matt Reilly personally and he was a fine case officer and a man of integrity. It's why I authorized him to talk to Katie. But don't worry, he is a man who knows how to keep secrets. He knows to stay in his swim lane. The true fate of the *Red October* and Captain Ramius are still sealed."

Her eyes sparkled a moment, but other than that her face betrayed nothing.

"Do you think I should have shared more about the *Red October* at this morning's brief?" he asked.

"That's your call, Jack. Honestly, I'm not sure it changes the calculus here. Nor do I think keeping such a highly classified operation deeply buried has a negative impact on Katie's investigation.

If I believed otherwise, I would have said so, but that's not the case."

He nodded and tapped the intel brief written by his daughter.

"I don't like coincidences."

"Nor do I."

"So, why didn't we get Gorov and his family out, back then?" Ryan asked. "It sounds like the wheels were already in motion and then he was just cut loose, after taking the risk of making contact."

Mary Pat watched him closely, as she often did, as he spoke. Ryan knew she had an almost supernatural ability to read him, but then again, he considered himself an open book, written in black and white.

"I assume the director at the time conducted a cost-benefit analysis. With the *Red October* already in our possession and Captain Ramius safely in CONUS, the risk simply outweighed the reward—especially in the wake of what must surely have been going on in the Kremlin at that time."

He nodded absently, but then turned and looked her in the eyes. "Do you think Gorov was killed by the KGB?"

"No. Like Katie said, the Russians are not the type to exonerate sons for the sins of the father. Konstantin Gorov would not be commanding the *Belgorod* as the son of a traitor."

"So, an accidental drowning?" he asked, but she knew what he was really asking.

"Perhaps." They both knew that the timing suggested the Russian scientist may well have committed suicide. "In the shadows, events are never black and white, Jack. We work in shades of gray."

"I know that, Mary Pat," he said and heard the irritation in his voice. "But our decisions, and the criteria we use to make them, must always be based on right or wrong."

"Yes, sir, Mr. President," she said, placating him, because this was a conversation they'd had many times over the years.

"In any case, that was decades ago. But it does give insight into the history behind the man in command of the *Belgorod*. In the case of the *Red October*, I risked everything because of Ramius's character. I wonder if Gorov is cut from the same cloth?"

Mary Pat pressed her lips into a tight line, but didn't comment.

He shoved the thought aside. "Anything from your investigation into the chaos in Russia?"

"Not yet. But my operative has made contact with the necessary asset."

Ryan knew full well who her "operative" was likely to be. And why. If anyone could get to the bottom of this . . . "If we understood what was going on inside the Kremlin, it would help provide context to this *Belgorod* situation. Unpublished underways, stealth deployments, trying to penetrate enemy waters undetected—that's what submarines do. Ours and theirs."

"Yes."

"But something about this situation feels different to me. More desperate and belligerent," he said and turned to the window and the garden beyond. "Echoes of December '84 . . ."

Again, Mary Pat didn't say anything, letting him work the problem out loud.

"We need to know if there are nuclear-tipped torpedoes aboard that submarine," he said finally. "If there are, it means the *Belgorod* is operational and on patrol. Is this platform a nuclear deterrent like our boomers, or is it meant to be something else?"

"The Russians have their own boomers. They have two BNs on patrol right now."

"And that's the problem," he said, scrubbing his face with his hands. "The *Belgorod* is something different. Like Katie said, it's a special missions boat. It's not intended to lie in wait in the shadows until called upon. K-329 is intended to be at the pointy tip of the spear, penetrate our defenses, and conduct operations to destabilize our advantage."

"Yes."

"This may be a first-strike weapon," he said, pacing, "and it just deployed."

"Yes, Jack."

He paused behind the desk, grabbed the chairback in his fingers, and squeezed. His mind filled with unexpected thoughts and memories—all his family had been through when they were young and all the patience and grace his wife had given him and his calling over the years. He thought of Jack Junior, who right now was in harm's way, and how Katie would be aboard the pointy tip of the spear in a confrontation that could easily escalate out of control. Wars started when adversaries crossed swords like this. And, once again, his family was in the middle of it. He sighed.

It's not the same. They're not kids anymore. They chose this life—a life of service.

"Anything else?" Mary Pat said, shaking him from the rumination.

"Actually, yes. There is one more thing," Ryan said. "I feel like we need an outside perspective—someone who can help me get inside the heads of both the *Belgorod* captain and what Yermilov is cooking up."

She cocked a quizzical eyebrow at him. "An outside perspective?"

He nodded.

"How far outside?"

He could already picture the man's weatherworn face twisting in irritation upon being summoned. But this man would answer the call, because that was how he was forged.

"He goes by Mark Ramsey these days. Rumor is, he bought a ranch in Montana."

Mary Pat's lips curled up at the corners as she connected the dots. "I'm sure *Mark* will be delighted to see you, Jack."

"I don't know about delighted . . . But he certainly can't say no. I outrank him this time around."

The man once known as Soviet Navy Submarine Captain First Rank Marko Ramius was still not one who enjoyed being *summoned*, but this was the way it had to be. As President of the United States, every trip he took—even trips inside CONUS—prompted speculation and signaled something. He wasn't some junior CIA analyst who could fly out and have a drink on the man's ranch. This was how it had to be. "Get him here as soon as possible."

"You got it, Jack," Mary Pat said and walked out of the Oval.

Ryan looked at the clock.

Two minutes to collect himself before his next meeting.

Time . . . I never seem to have enough.

20

Every once in a while, Lieutenant Commander Dennis Knepper would feel overcome by the strange sensation that he needed to pinch himself, because no way was this his life. He had to be dreaming. Walking onto the conn of the *Blackfish* today—America's most deadly and stealthy fast-attack submarine—qualified as one of those times. Was he really cruising six hundred feet below the surface of the Atlantic Ocean? Was he really the second-in-command of a four-billion-dollar nuclear-powered warship at age thirty-three? Were one hundred and twenty-eight souls really depending on him to maintain order, discipline, safety, and quality of life for the next one hundred and seventy-eight consecutive days on deployment?

Yes, yes, and yes.

With a little smile, he went ahead and pinched his cheek anyway.

"XO, if you need a cup of coffee, all you have to do is ask," the control room messenger, Culinary Specialist Third Class Sullivan, said with a big ol' Cheshire cat smile spread across his face. "It's just like Starbucks. I can get you whatever you want. Black and bitter? Blond and sweet? A mocha . . . You name it, sir. Sully's got your back."

"Black and bitter? Blond and sweet?" one of the JOs said. "You a barista or a fucking pimp, Sullivan?"

"All right, all right, fellas," Knepper said, chuckling. "Let's dial it back. The OOD has sensitive ears, and she doesn't appreciate crass innuendo and language."

"That's right," Juggernaut said. "I don't tolerate any bullshit on my watch. Especially fucking cursing."

This tongue-in-cheek pronouncement got a laugh from everyone in control.

And all is right in the world.

One of the greatest things about being a submariner was the banter. STEM sarcasm, jokes that somehow served as both compliments and insults, and ironic observations about submarine life in general and life on the *Blackfish* specifically, made every day underway hilarious and interesting. But the humor didn't mean the crew didn't take their jobs seriously—in fact, nothing could be further from the truth. Every man and woman on board would give their life for each other. Nowhere was this better represented in the Navy than in the submarine community, where every single crew member was cross-trained in firefighting and damage control and a Culinary Specialist served as control room messenger. Underwater, there was no cavalry to rescue them in the event of an accident. If the proverbial excrement hit the rotating apparatus, the crew had to save itself. Earning one's dolphins, aka "fish," was more than a badge of honor. To wear a submarine warfare pin was a pledge that one was willing and able to risk their life for their shipmates. Competency was independent from rank and gender. And on the *Blackfish*, they took it one step further. There were no gold officer dolphins or silver enlisted dolphins—every pair of dolphins earned on this ship, regardless of rank, were painted black.

On the USS *Washington,* a crew member didn't earn dolphins . . . they earned their Blackfish.

Knepper walked over to stand next to Juggernaut. "How's it going?"

"Living the dream," she said. "I was just about to head to PD to catch the top-of-the-hour broadcast. Are you planning to hang out while I do?" she asked, referring to an ascent up to periscope depth.

"Have I told you lately that I'm jealous? If there's one rub about being XO, it's that I don't get to take the boat to PD anymore. I miss those days."

"If you want the conn, sir, all you have to do is ask. I'm happy to have you as my U/I," she said with a wry smile, using the acronym for unqualified under instruction watch standers.

"I'd hate to embarrass you in front of your watch section with my perfect execution," he quipped back.

"'Embarrassment' is not in my vocabulary," she said. Then he announced, "All stations, Conn, make preparations to go to periscope depth. Pilot, make your depth one-five-five feet."

Immediately upon this pronouncement, the mood in the control room shifted. Like a soldier ordered to attention, all chatter stopped. The opportunity for banter was over; it was time to go to work. The senior watch standers at each station responded their acknowledgment in practiced, rapid-fire fashion.

"Make my depth one-five-five feet, Pilot, aye."

"Sonar, aye."

"Fire Control, aye,"

"Quartermaster, aye."

"Conn, Radio, aye," came the final acknowledgment over the control room speaker from the radio room.

Knepper watched the pilot enter the new depth of one hundred fifty-five feet into the interface on the ship's control station, and the *Blackfish* tilted up as the computer determined the optimal amount of bow and stern planes angle to change depth. For a submarine, going to periscope depth was an evolution that put the boat in a compromised position. For a Virginia-class sub operating deep, the risk of collision with another vessel or being counter-detected was practically zero. Going to PD, however, meant traveling to the surface and breaking the waterline with the periscope—or in their case, the photonics mast. The entire evolution was conducted at a slow speed so as not to leave a visible white wake, or "feather," from the mast cutting through the water that could be detected by ships, aircraft, or satellites. The slow speed also made the *Blackfish* less reactive and dramatically reduced its capacity for evasive maneuvering. To prepare for the evolution, the *Blackfish* typically made a stop at one hundred fifty-five feet to clear baffles, reassess the surface contact situation, and decide upon a final course and speed for the trip.

Once on depth, the boat leveled out and the pilot reported, "Officer of the deck, the ship is at one hundred and fifty-five feet."

"Very well, pilot. Contact manager, report all contacts," she said, stepping over to look at the contact management plot.

"Officer of the deck, we hold four sonar contacts—Sierra One, the USS *Ford* CVN-78, bearing zero-nine-one, range eight-two-hundred yards, on parallel course of zero-two-five at fifteen knots. Sierra Two, USS *Mason* DDG 87, bearing zero-seven-one, range eleven thousand yards, on course zero-two-five at fifteen knots. Sierra Three, USS *Gettysburg* CG-64, bearing zero-eight-two, range five-four-hundred yards, also on course of zero-two-five at fifteen knots. And Sierra Four, merchant vessel bearing two-nine-two, range nineteen thousand yards, on course zero-seven-three, making eighteen knots," Lieutenant Junior Grade Rucker reported, giving her the complete contact picture of the carrier strike group that they were escorting, as well as a lone, and distant, contact heading east.

"Very well," she said. "Pilot, come right, to new course one-four-five."

"Come right to new course one-four-five, aye."

Knepper watched as the pilot entered the new speed request into the digital engine order telegraph, which transmitted the new speed demand to the propulsion plant operator in maneuvering, which was located in the engine room. Next, he entered the new course into the SCS and the ship's computer calculated the optimal rudder to execute the turn without cavitating or sinking out of the depth band as the submarine slowed. The sub heeled slightly to starboard, leaning into the turn like an aircraft would.

Knepper watched the broadband sonar screen—the trace lines for contacts Sierra One through Four changing as the boat turned. Once they steadied on the new course, the two fire control technicians would firm up their solutions on all four contacts having two legs of data to work with. Driving a submarine and managing contacts by sonar was, at its core, a geometry problem. But the maneuver was not just to help the contact manager and FTs hone their solutions. By turning sixty degrees to starboard, the OOD was on a new vector where the *Blackfish*'s hull-mounted wide aperture array sonar panels could now peer into the sub's "blind spot." If a contact was hiding in the baffles, then a new broadband trace would appear on the display in the range of relative bearings that had previously been blocked by their own ship.

As the *Blackfish* steadied on to the new heading, Knepper saw nothing new or of concern.

"Officer of the deck, ship is on course one-four-five making turns for five knots," the pilot reported.

"Very well, pilot. Sonar, Conn, report new contacts."

"Conn, Sonar, sonar holds no new contacts," the sonar supervisor said.

Juggernaut turned to look at Knepper and said, "XO, I plan to go to PD on course zero-two-five."

As a fully qualified watch stander and experienced OOD, she didn't need to get his permission, but the comment was meant to be a professional courtesy. Her boss was on the conn, and she'd shown him respect by offering him an opportunity to provide input or guidance on her decision.

"Agreed," he said simply.

She could have decided to come to PD on the current course of one-four-five. Tactically, there was nothing wrong with that, but the carrier strike group was steaming north at twelve knots, and so every minute they wasted going the wrong direction was multiple minutes it would take them to catch up. By going back to the Ford's course of zero-two-five, they would still fall behind, but at least be doing it slower.

"Contact manager, do you have what you need?" she asked Rucker, referencing time on the new leg to dial in their contact solutions.

"We're good to go, ma'am," he said.

"Very well. Pilot, come left to course zero-two-five. Raising number two scope. Up," Juggernaut said and used the Xbox controller on the OOD workstation to raise the port photonics mast.

The moment the photonics mast exited the housing on the top of the sail, the right-hand monitor on the OOD workstation came to life with a dark blue underwater view of the Atlantic. Bubbles and flotsam zipped by the lens as they turned. As soon as the heading indicator on the display read 025, the pilot reported as such.

"Very well. Pilot, make your depth six-three feet," Juggernaut said, staring at the scope display with the Xbox controller in her hands.

The pilot acknowledged the order and called out depth in increments as they ascended, his voice the only one in the otherwise silent control room: "Passing one hundred feet . . . nine zero . . . eight zero . . . seven five . . . seven zero . . . six five . . . On depth at six-three feet."

The moment the periscope camera broke the surface, Juggernaut completed a twenty-four-second-duration, three-hundred-sixty-degree sweep in a clockwise direction, scanning just over the white crests of the three-foot wave action.

"No close contacts," she announced in a loud, clear voice, and the conn took a collective breath of relief.

While the risk was small, a submarine *could* collide with a surface vessel that was at sea anchor or dead in the water while coming to PD. A surface ship that wasn't moving and running its engines had no broadband signature or narrowband frequencies for the *Blackfish* to detect. Not until the scope broke the surface and the OOD completed the safety sweep could everyone truly relax.

"Conn, Sonar, holds no close contacts," the sonar supe announced, backing her up using the ship's ears to complement the visual survey.

Knepper glanced at the clock, which read two minutes before the hour. Juggernaut had executed a perfect PD trip, getting the sub up safely and in time to receive the satellite broadcast of the *Blackfish*'s dedicated traffic as efficiently as possible. If they missed it, they'd have to try again and go back to PD in an hour.

"Radio, Conn, do we have any outgoing traffic?" Juggernaut asked over the open mic.

"Conn, Radio, that's a negative," the report came back on the 27MC.

"Radio, Conn, aye," she said as she trained the scope to look at the USS *Ford*, which, thanks to its massive size and giant freeboard, was visible even at the current range of nine thousand yards.

"Visual observation on Sierra One, bearing mark." She used the "pickle" button on the joystick to send a bearing to fire control. Then she zoomed in to the maximum magnification.

"Looks like they're conducting flight ops," Knepper said, watching a black cross that he knew to be an F/A-18 arc into the sky from the carrier.

"They've been at it for over an hour. We can hear the catapult strokes," the sonar supe said.

"Really?" he said, cocking an eyebrow.

"Yeah, do you want to take a listen, XO?" the supe said, holding out a pair of headphones from the console beside him.

"Sure," he said and began to mosey that way, only to be interrupted by the radioman.

"Conn, Radio," the radioman said on the control room speaker. "Is the XO on the conn?"

"He sure is," Juggernaut answered.

"Request he come to radio? We've got a new alert he's gonna wanna read, ASAP."

"Roger that, I'm on my way," he said.

Listening to flight ops on sonar would have to wait.

Apparently, something big had happened, and from the gravity of the radioman's voice, it sounded important.

21

VRC-40 DET 2 GRUMMAN C-2A
CARRIER ONBOARD DELIVERY (COD) PLATFORM
2,200 FEET ABOVE SEA LEVEL OVER THE ATLANTIC OCEAN
   EN ROUTE TO THE USS *FORD*
1438 LOCAL TIME

Katie looked at her watch, sighed, and pressed her head back into the insanely uncomfortable airplane seat inside the C-2A Greyhound turboprop. She'd been flattered by CIA officer Reilly's comparison of her to her father, the person she most admired in the world. She tried hard to embody his good qualities, but unfortunately she'd inherited one thing from her dad she could definitely do without. Like him, she was afraid of flying.

Unlike her dad, Katie had no legitimate reason to be afraid. What she knew of the story of her dad's fear—of the crash in a helicopter that had nearly killed him as a young Marine—she knew mostly from open-source information about the American President. Her dad had never talked about it, nor had he added much detail when asked about it. So his fear made sense. But hers?

It's probably his fault. Because it's the only thing I ever saw him nervous about as a kid. Fighting terrorists—no problem. Turbulence—oh shit, clutch the armrest, we're going to die.

When it was time to fill out her "dream sheet" at the Academy for the community in which she hoped to serve, she'd not even listed aviation—had, in fact, laughed out loud when she saw it on the list. So many of her classmates were at the Academy with the sole purpose of earning aviator wings. Not her.

She looked at her watch again to find, no surprise, less than two minutes had passed. That she'd been in the air for over three and a half hours sure as hell didn't help—that was a long time to think about how this antique plane was going to basically crash-land on a boat and be stopped by some metal wire. Add in that she was in arguably the most uncomfortable aircraft known to man, and she had achieved a level of misery not experienced since her plebe summer—worse by far, in fact.

"First arrested landing?"

She looked over at the man across the aisle, one of only two others on board, the other being Bubba, who was all the way in front of her—at the rear of the plane from her aft-facing seat—after saying he wanted to be as close to the door as possible. The man had yelled to be heard over the noisy airplane and wore the green flight suit of a naval aviator, had a Top Gun patch on his shoulder, and a real fighter pilot helmet in his lap. She'd taken off the "brain bucket," as the crew member who handed it to her called the helmet and goggles, shortly after takeoff.

"Yeah," she said. "Not you, obviously."

He smiled.

"True," he said. "But I don't like it when someone *else* determines whether we bolter or not." He shot her a grin from under a cheesy, eighties-style mustache. "And I have the not-being-able-to-see-out thing, too. Add to that we're sitting facing backwards . . ."

"I get it," she said, trying to be polite. She closed her eyes again, but then they popped back open and she turned to the pilot, noting the silver oak leaves of a commander on his shoulder. He'd been around a bit. "I mean, this is totally safe, right?" she asked nervously, which only made her seem more manic. "They land these things on the carriers all the time, right? I mean, like, what are the odds of something bad happening?"

"Very, very low," the pilot said with a knowing smile. "And this plane is super stable, has a nice straight wing, and a very slow approach speed."

"Right," she said, convincing herself now. "It's gotta be even safer than landing a fighter jet on board, right?"

"Right," he said with a reassuring nod. "You hardly ever hear about something bad happening."

She let out a sigh and closed her eyes again.

"I did hear about this one time," the pilot said, a bemused edge in his voice, and she snapped her eyes back open and turned to him. "A Greyhound was bringing a bunch of VIPs from the beach in kind of sketchy weather, you know?"

"Okaaay . . ." she said, staring at him.

"Anyway, they caught the boat as a swell brought her up—this was the *Nimitz*—and, you know, just bad luck, right? Anyway, the port main gear collapsed and the plane skewed off left . . ."

"When you say 'off' . . . "

"Afraid so," the pilot said. "Tossed right over the port side of the ship," he said, a twinkle in his eye like he was somehow enjoying telling this horrible story.

"Did anyone die?" she asked, unable to resist.

The pilot leaned in.

"It was almost a miracle," he said. "The left wheel had departed entirely, and the left main strut caught the wire before she slipped over the side. So there she is, this giant C-2 Greyhound, pointing nose-first at the ocean in rough seas, hanging by the number three wire, which has the left main strut and the tailhook, which is still engaged on the number two wire. It was insane. They were able to get chains on her—I mean, the flight deck crew are amazing on a carrier—and so they get her chained to the boat and evacuate all the VIPs and crew. Only a few bumps and scrapes." He sighed but was still smiling, like he'd told a story about a time rain ruined a picnic. "Crazy. You gotta know those two pilots shit their flight suits, right? I mean, they're hanging over the side, staring at white-caps just feet away."

She stared at him, mouth open, unable to speak.

"Anyway," he said as he turned and grabbed his helmet, slipping it on his head. "That's the only real story about a Greyhound I know."

"Great," she said, looking at her watch, and then, a new dread rising inside her, slipped her own "brain bucket" onto her head.

A minute later, the almost-teenage-looking kid at the rear ramp of the cargo plane began waving his arms back and forth, the signal they'd briefed her to mean that they would be on the ship in less than fifteen seconds.

Katie gripped the armrests after tightening her four-point harness, then leaned back and pressed her head into the top of the seat as they'd told her to.

It's 2024, Katie. I could have done all of this from my office in D.C. with a secure Zoom link . . .

She jerked back into the seat a moment later, despite having readied herself, as the sounds of the engines spooling up made her think maybe they'd missed the approach just seconds before the plane was jerked to a stop—from over a hundred miles an hour to zero in under two seconds.

Then the engines whined back down. For some reason it felt like they actually went backward for a second, and then she felt them veer to the right, presumably safely aboard the USS *Gerald R. Ford*.

"See?" the pilot said, turning to her and flipping down the clear portion of his visor. "Piece of cake."

She gave him an appropriate stink eye and noted the gold aviator wings embroidered on the brightly colored rectangular patch on his left chest as he turned in his seat. Beneath the wings was his name—or at least his call sign nickname.

Mr. Pibb

She shook her head and then her eyes were blinded for a moment by the sudden onslaught of light as the ramp at the rear of the plane lowered.

She rose, grabbed her backpack and duffel, and followed the funnyman pilot out the back of the plane, patting Bubba on the shoulder, who looked like he might be a bit motion sick and gave her a grim smile back, then fell in behind her, his own gear over his shoulder. They weaved around some heavy equipment as she found herself right beside the island towering above her, and a moment later they were through a hatch that was dogged behind them, and she pulled off her helmet and goggles.

"I'll take those, ma'am," the thin flight crewman said, and she handed them over, Bubba doing the same. "Thanks for flying with the Rawhides, ma'am."

She wanted to point out that she'd had no choice, but decided to be nice, despite the queasiness still ebbing inside her gut.

"Thanks for the ride," she said.

"Nice to be the only game in town," the young man joked.

The aviator she'd followed into the conning tower—aka "the island"—disappeared around a corner, leaving her and Bubba with a female petty officer wearing blue overalls. The blue patch on her left chest had a surface warfare pin embroidered over her name, Caspar, with IS2 COMBAT beneath it. The left side of the patch was a compass rose.

"Lieutenant Ryan?" the petty officer said.

"Yes."

"Ma'am, I'm IS2 Caspar from the N2 shop. If you'd like, we can drop your gear in your stateroom and then"—she glanced at her watch—"the XO would like to meet you. IS2 Pettigrew, I can take you right to the intel shop if you want, after I drop off the lieutenant, and introduce you around."

"Great," Bubba said, then turned to Katie. "Worst airplane ride of my life, ma'am. Thanks so much for bringing me along." His voice was a thick mix of good ol' boy charm and sarcasm.

"My pleasure, Bubba," she said, just grateful they'd survived. Then to Casper, she asked, "Will the CO be there, too?"

"The meeting is in the CO's reception quarters, ma'am, but Captain Mackenzie may or may not join us. Depends on his schedule."

"Understood," she said.

Caspar handed her a key card, not unlike a hotel room key card, and then she followed the woman, about her own age, down the passageway and then down a metal ladder well, descending two levels, with Bubba in tow. This all felt far more familiar than being aboard the claustrophobic sub, and brought back nostalgia from her fleet tour, underway on the *Roosevelt*.

"First time on a carrier, ma'am?" the intelligence specialist asked.

"No, but the first time arriving by COD. I did a tour with the *Roosevelt*."

"Gotcha," Caspar said. "The *Ford* is a whole new boat, so your tour on the *Roosevelt* may help you a little, but not much in terms of finding your way around. The system of giving you directions by level and frame number still works, so I'll give you some important ones to write down when we drop your bags—the intel shop, CIC, wardroom, gym, stuff like that. We have you sharing a stateroom with Lieutenant Commander Kumari, who leads the N2 shop.

Officer quarters mostly have their own heads, so no wandering around in shower shoes to find a women's shower anymore."

Despite trying to pay attention to the route, Katie was already turned around. After rounding an L-shaped corner, Caspar stopped.

"This is you, ma'am," Caspar said, standing outside a closed door. "Write down the number and then the level and frame number underneath."

"Okay," she said as Caspar rapped on the door.

"Will you be okay to find the shop if I give you the level and frame, ma'am? Or do you want me to wait for you and escort you down?"

Katie was about to answer when the door opened.

"Good afternoon, Commander," Caspar said to the officer in the doorway, a fit, serious-looking woman in Guacamoles, instead of the blue jumpsuit IS2 Caspar wore. The name tape read KUMARI.

"Afternoon, IS2," the woman said and smiled—not just with her mouth but with big brown eyes that held warmth despite the initial taken-aback look on her face. "Thought I'd meet Lieutenant Ryan ahead of the XO and skipper. If you want to take Petty Officer Pettigrew to the shop, I'll take the lieutenant to the skipper's reception quarters."

"Thank you, Commander."

"No problem, Caspar," Kumari said. "We'll meet up with you there when we can, but you get Pettigrew all set up with access and workstation, okay?"

"Will do, ma'am," Caspar said, then gestured with her head for Bubba to follow her, and the two disappeared down the passageway.

"You coming in, Ryan?"

She nodded and entered the surprisingly spacious stateroom,

two matching desks flanking multi-compartment metal cabinets and then bunks with blue privacy curtains at either end of the room. A single stainless steel sink sat beside a metal door, presumably the head.

"Sorry to break up your solo accommodations," Katie said, dropping her bags beside the clearly empty desk and cabinet.

Kumari smiled.

"No problem. We have an odd number of female officers and I got lucky, but to be honest, I prefer a little company."

"Well, then, happy to help," Katie said, looking around. "This is way better than what I remember from my tour on the *Roosevelt*. I can't believe we have our own head and shower."

"Yeah, we share it with the stateroom next door, but I went to sea on the *Vinson* and this is like the Four Seasons after a JO tour on that boat. Wait until you see the gym."

"She's different topside, too," Katie said. "I know about the EMALS catapult system and the advanced arresting gear, of course, but it's more than that . . ."

Kumari smiled at her.

"XO loves to give the brag tour, so you'll learn more than you need, probably, but we're proud of this ship. Up top looks different for a couple reasons, but one of them is that the entire island superstructure is set way back aft compared to other carriers, which improves the flow of aircraft off the arresting gear as well as onto the cats," she said, using the carrier slang for catapults Katie was already familiar with. "It greatly improves the efficiency of flight ops."

"Maybe that's it," Katie said.

"The deck is also much more open, because both weapons and fuel come up from down below. No more stacking weapons all over the deck and no more pulling fuel lines across the busy flight line."

"Yeah," Katie said. "I think that's the real difference. I remember the flight deck being such a jumble of stuff, and it seemed, by comparison, almost barren up there."

Kumari nodded.

"It's a dramatic difference and one of the reasons why, as XO loves to say, we're now the biggest and baddest warship on the seas. Make a quick head call—you must need one after such a long shitty ride in the COD—and then I'll take you down to the XO for your brief, get you badge access, and then get you to the shop."

"Thanks, Commander," she said.

"It's Jaya," Kumari said. "Or just Jay. I'm really dying to hear just what it is that ONI sent you out here to do. XO is read in, I'm sure, but down in N2 we're still waiting for someone to tell us what's up. All we know is there's a large Russian naval exercise spinning up and for some reason we're headed north instead of east, as planned."

Katie gestured with her head toward the door to the head. "I'll get you, and the XO, up to speed," she said, "but first, um, I do need to use the bathroom."

22

Clark and Dovzhenko, the Russian double agent known as VICAR, crossed the hotel lobby, chatting loudly—just two American friends working abroad. Clark resisted the urge to sweep the lobby. To do so would make *him* look suspicious, should anyone be watching. He let James and the rest of the CIA clandestine services team do their jobs, trusting they would clear his six for him. So far, the CIA team had proven quite capable, but they weren't *his* team—bonded together through shared triumphs and defeats, victories and blood. But if VICAR came through tonight and delivered the intel they needed, maybe he wouldn't have to put Ding, Leanna, and the others in harm's way and he could go home to make good on his promise to spend time with the family.

They weaved through the blue and white furniture of the well-appointed lobby, chatting like old friends, and went to the hostess stand at Platter, a restaurant known for modern Polish cuisine. The young male host—who wore his hair up in a man bun—escorted them to a quiet table in the back, along a wall of glass looking out onto the street.

"You're clear," said James's voice in Clark's micro earbud transceiver, having received a clean report from the two CIA observers positioned in the lobby.

Despite his plastered-on smile, Dovzhenko seemed nervous, stoking Clark's ill ease.

"Is there a problem?" the Russian asked in flawless English.

"No," Clark said. "We're clear."

Dovzhenko's eyes seemed different than in Berlin. Tired—no, *haggard*. And Clark thought he noted a fleeting glimpse of fear, an emotion he imagined both uncommon and unfamiliar to a man such as VICAR.

"You have the same CIA team as in Berlin keeping watch?"

Clark nodded. "What about on your side?"

Dovzhenko shook his head and gave him a tight smile. "*Nyet*," he said in Russian, surprising Clark. "I am here alone this time. Alone and unsanctioned, Mr. Bates. And you should know, this will be the last time we will meet."

Clark felt his pulse quicken at the statement.

Shit, he better not be compromised.

"I heard," James said in his ear, sensing the danger the message implied. "I'm mobilizing our backups. One in the bar at the restaurant, one additional in the lobby, and one on the street."

Clark studied Dovzhenko. Clearly, something had gone wrong since Berlin.

"What happened, Erik? Can we help you—help your family?"

"No," the Russian mole said. "My family is safe. I will be with them soon, but we must disappear. I can't risk coming to America—and I don't want to, frankly."

"Are you blown at SVR?"

Dovzhenko gave a soft chuckle. "No."

"Okay, so what happened?"

The Russian stared out the window a minute, then looked back at Clark. "It is as I feared, Mr. Bates . . ."

"Call me John," he said, trading his name for trust.

"It is as I feared, John. There is something happening. Something big. Chess pieces are moving. The power brokers want change."

"Who?"

"Old men with a vision to restore Russia to what it once was."

This was not the update Clark had imagined. He'd been certain VICAR would tell him of a coup that had been put down, of young Russian visionaries now being tortured in a gulag or the victim of an "accidental" fall from a high window. But to hear his fears confirmed . . .

"I understand how stressful this must be for you. I know how much you have risked, but Erik, I need names. Who are the men plotting the coup?"

"I will tell you what I know and then I must go."

"I understand," Clark said, and he did. He would do anything to keep his family safe under similar circumstances.

"This is not confirmed, but I suspect Colonel General Nikolai Ilyin may be in charge. He was observed at Glavpivtorg in Moscow with Admiral Rodionov—"

"Wait, Rodionov—the head of the GRU?"

"Yes, yes. The same. Also, Admiral Boldyrev, who commands the Russian fleet, was seen at this meeting, along with General Aralovich, who leads the FSB. Nothing happens in Russia that these men don't know about."

Clark rubbed his chin. "What is their endgame? Do they want to overthrow Yermilov, or control him?"

"I don't know. But you must understand the Russian mindset, John, especially for the old guard. For these men, the Cold War era represented the height of the Soviet empire. Do you understand?"

"Yes," Clark said.

"I don't think you do, my friend, because your country was the victor. In losing the Cold War, these men lost their identity. They lost their pride. They lost their purpose. That is something that fancy houses, rich bank accounts, and even putting on a general's uniform cannot replace. During the Cold War, Russia was a superpower. Russia was strong. Russia was feared. There are many inside Russia who wish to return to the glory days. Do you understand what I am saying? For Russia to rise, America must fall."

A chill ran down Clark's spine.

"What are you implying, Erik? If I didn't know better, it sounds like you're suggesting these men are plotting to move against the United States with or without Yermilov's blessing?"

The Russian spy let out a long, shaky sigh. "I am not sure, John. But that is my concern."

Clark scrubbed his face with his hands.

But how does the Belgorod *fit into this puzzle?*

Mary Pat had forwarded additional details about Russia's new, potential doomsday weapon, details that a part of him wished he didn't know.

"Erik, there are rumors of a new kind of Russian torpedo— nuclear-powered with a nuclear payload designed to travel very long distances and evade our early-warning and detection systems. Code name Status-6. Do you know of the weapon I speak?"

"Ah, the Poseidon. Yes, I've heard of this."

"Is it operational?"

"I don't know."

Clark tamped down his irritation and tried his damnedest to keep his voice even. "Erik, it's imperative that I know if this weapon is deployed on the *Belgorod.*"

"I understand," Dovzhenko said. "But I simply do not know.

There is an engineer named Popov who works in the weapons division at Sevmash Shipyard at Severodvinsk who might—"

Dovzhenko stopped midsentence, turned his head left, and looked out the floor-to-ceiling window to scan the street outside. Clark glanced to his right, his back to the corner wall, but saw nothing that raised alarms.

"Is everything okay? Did you see something?" Clark asked.

"No," VICAR said. "Nothing. I'm just tired."

Dovzhenko turned to him, his eyes dark and his expression grim. But just as the Russian opened his mouth to continue, a shadow caught Clark's eye.

"Get down!" Clark shouted.

As the floor-to-ceiling picture window exploded, Clark was already in motion, diving under the table for cover against the raining glass shrapnel. He felt glass shards cut through the shirtsleeve of his right forearm as he reached for the compact Wilson Combat EDC X9 in the holster at the small of his back. He glanced to where Dovzhenko was huddled on the floor, stunned, the man's face scratch art of bleeding lacerations. He, too, was reaching under his coat for a weapon, when the first pair of booted feet appeared on the sidewalk a yard away.

"No!" Clark barked, but it was too late.

Two muffled pops of suppressed gunfire reverberated in time with Dovzhenko's head jerking left and then right as bullets tore first through the center of his face and then split his forehead. A second pair of boots joined the first and Clark reacted immediately before his own death shots punched through the tabletop.

He fired two sets of two rounds each in rapid succession into the right knees of both pairs of legs, the bones shattered and the bundle of nerves, arteries, and veins shredding from his nine-millimeter bullets. Twin screams rang out as both shooters—killers he could now see clad in black from head to toe—collapsed to the ground.

He delivered a single nine-millimeter kill shot to each assassin's head to take them out of the game.

With VICAR beyond saving, Clark rolled left and leapt to his feet, scanning through the shattered window for fresh targets. Seeing none, he bolted across the restaurant just as the stunned diners and waitstaff panicked in unison and stampeded the exits.

"Viking One, sitrep?" James said in Clark's ear.

"The asset is dead," Clark hollered, the mic of the tiny device in his ear picking up his voice and cutting through the din. "Two shooters also down on the sidewalk outside the restaurant. I'm moving toward the lobby."

"We have three tangos headed toward you from the lobby, One," came a voice from the CIA team, he wasn't sure which, since the man didn't use his own number call sign.

Clark shifted left, away from the wide entrance to the restaurant, colliding with a waiter who stood open-mouthed beside the tray of food he had dropped. The man simply fell to the ground without a sound, then curled up into a ball as Clark jumped over him while scanning over his pistol.

Two shooters surged forward, each scanning left and right over compact machine pistols. These men were dressed in slacks and sport shirts, each with a leather satchel over their shoulders from which the weapons had no doubt been drawn. Clark stayed low, his pistol sight lined up on the temple of the closest man as the shooter turned his way. The man's eyes widened in realization as he finally spied Clark, but too late.

Clark squeezed the trigger.

The bullet tore through the man's head as the Russian squeezed his own weapon, a spray of gunfire blasting through the glass hood over the salad buffet and then licking a trail of destruction up the wall beside the double doors to the kitchen. Clark was already on a knee, dropping his sight onto the chest of the smaller man behind the first, who turned toward him and dropped into his own tactical crouch just as Clark fired.

The man pitched forward as Clark accelerated toward the wall beside the entrance, firing a round into the top of the man's head, just to be sure.

A woman, short and compact, dressed in workout clothes with a gym bag over her shoulder, whirled to face him. The assault rifle she carried identified her as a hit squad shooter and Clark dropped her with a head shot.

"Coming to you," a voice in his ear said.

"Negative—hold position!" Clark said.

Right now he was the only target. There was a good chance none of his teammates had been made. Best to not change that and leave them in reserve for now.

"Cover my six as I exit," he said, exchanging his pistol's partially spent magazine for a fresh fifteen rounds, and slipping the mag with three rounds into his pocket. "And pick me up."

You never know, he thought.

"Check," James said. "Name your egress."

"Śliska Street," he said, scanning for threats as he visualized the mental map he'd memorized for the op.

"The truck will come from the west, turn the corner from Sosnowa Street. Viking team, we'll use contingency Charlie for exfil," James said, his voice calm in Clark's ear.

Clark peered around the corner and into the lobby. Not the chaos he expected, but probably because everyone had already fled. Man Bun crouched behind the narrow hostess stand and looked at Clark with terrified eyes.

Clark gestured for the guy to stay put and checked over his shoulder, to where VICAR lay unmoving in a growing pool of blood and gore. The attackers had been professionals, but didn't move like Spetsnaz.

Must be Wagner Group.

But not the lowlife hired guns that the black ops mercenary out-fit sometimes employed. Probably a mix of former military or GRU. If they were thorough, they'd have both a primary and a flanking team to cut off escape in case the street team botched the hit.

They'll have the lobby covered as a backup for the shooters who came through the window . . .

"Viking, change of plans. I'm not going through the lobby," he said. "Variable, whoever you have on the street should slowly and without raising suspicion reposition to the corner at the alley be-tween us and the building south. Egressing through the staff en-trance to the alley."

"Variable, check. Five and Six, acknowledge."

He could hear the huffing in James's voice as he was on the move, but still coordinating.

"Five," said a gruff voice in acknowledgment.

"Six," said another, the driver, Clark thought.

He spun a hundred and eighty degrees and crossed behind the destroyed salad buffet. Leading with his shoulder, Clark burst through the double doors into the next room. Pistol up and swivel-ing, he cleared his left corner quickly, then swept his pistol over the tight, narrow kitchen. Saucepans swayed from hooks on the lip of a ventilated hood that ran above the long row of gas burners and the grill. The movement distracted him momentarily as he scanned for threats, but he found no targets. In the movies, he would have breached to find a terrified kitchen staff, screaming and cowering at the sight of his gun. In real life, people tended to run *away* from danger, and in the wake of the gunfire, the kitchen was completely empty. He moved swiftly, grabbed a white, high-collared chef's coat from the rack full of them in the corner, and slipped it on over his jacket, buttoning it up to mid-chest, but kept his pistol in hand.

He headed for the staff entrance, through which workers came and went and food deliveries were made. He took a slow breath, held his pistol to his chest in his right hand, and pressed the beater bar to open the heavy door with his left. He peered out through the crack, saw nothing, and egressed into the dark alley. After clearing left and right, he slipped his weapon into its holster in the small of his back. Having confirmed he was alone, he ditched the bright white chef's coat and walked at a brisk pace toward the corner, where his team was to pick him up.

His Spidey sense tingling, Clark glanced over his shoulder just in time to see a figure with close-cropped hair turning into the alley behind him. With menace in his eyes, the man opened his jacket, hollering something over his shoulder as he did, and pulled a machine pistol from under his left armpit. With no time to draw his pistol, Clark dove left behind a dumpster as a barrage of bullets impacted the huge, blue metal garbage receptacle. Sparks flew as bullets pummeled the steel container, the ricocheting rounds echoing loudly. He pressed against the wall and pulled his pistol.

The barrage stopped, and Clark deduced the assaulter was swapping mags. Two shots rang out, fired from a different weapon on a different vector, followed by a thud. Clark rose from a knee to a combat crouch behind the blue dumpster just as a voice came into his ear.

"Shooter down, Viking One. You're clear."

Clark turned in time to see the CIA man who called himself Tom give a short wave of his left hand, still scanning over the pistol in his right. But before Clark could take a step, the top of Tom's head exploded and he pitched forward onto the ground.

"Sniper!" James said in his ear. "Who has eyes?"

"Looks like he fired from the roof of the northwest building across the street. He just fired at Three. Do you have eyes on?" Five said.

"Three is down—KIA," Clark said, shifting back behind the dumpster. "Viking, do not give away anyone else. They don't know who you are unless you engage. Variable, exfil, exfil, exfil."

"We're not leaving you, One," James said.

Clark clenched his jaw in annoyance. "I'm not proposing I sacrifice myself, Variable. Exfil the team. Once I'm clear, I'll give you a new pickup point."

"Roger that, Actual. Sniper elevation is only four stories, so his line into your alley is limited."

Clark gave a tight grin. James, or whatever his real name was, knew his stuff. This was valuable information. Had the sniper been on a taller building, Clark would have very few options to exfil.

Maybe James is a former operator.

"Copy, Variable. See you soon," Clark said.

He snuck his head around the corner of the dumpster, pulling it back instantly and reconstructing what he saw in his mind's eye. No sight line on the building James described from his pos, but the shooter on the roof might also be coordinating and directing other Wagner shooters toward Clark.

He popped up, aiming over the dumpster, and sighted on a man kneeling beside the dead shooter, who'd pinned him down originally. The man screamed, threw up his arms, and ran.

Civilian.

With his six clear, Clark spun on a heel and sprinted west. He made it to the corner in a dozen strides, full tilt, his pistol in a low ready. He came to the corner just as someone rounded it, and they collided into each other.

"*Przepraszam,*" he muttered in apology, but then noticed the FB VIS nine-millimeter pistol in the man's hand.

He wrapped his left arm tightly around the operative, pinning the man's gun hand to his side. As the shooter struggled to get free,

Clark dropped to a knee, angled his own pistol upward as he jammed the muzzle into the middle of the assaulter's back. He squeezed the trigger twice. The rounds shattered the man's spine and the rounds drilled into the thoracic cavity. With the spinal cord severed, the body went instantly limp. The smell of piss and excrement filled the air as the man's bowels let go.

Clark shoved the body off him and into the street.

"Oh, shit!" a voice cried over the whine of an oncoming scooter.

The driver swerved to avoid the dying man and wiped out directly in front of Clark. A bag bungeed to the back of the Vespa dumped books and papers all over the gutter and sidewalk as the kid scurried away from the body in horror, looking every bit like a panicked crab on the beach. Clark slipped his gun into the waistband of his slacks, righted the fallen Vespa, and climbed on. A heartbeat later, he was screaming west on Sienna on the stolen scooter. He came to the six-lane main road, gave a quick glance left and right, then shot across all six lanes, weaving the Vespa like he was on a motocross track as horns blared all around him.

"Viking team is clear," said James into Clark's ear. "We're heading west on Listopadu."

Clark vectored the Vespa south, nearly wiping out as he maneuvered off the road into a small parking lot in front of a bodega-style food mart. He stepped off the Vespa before coming to a full stop, and ditched it against a light pole. Then he wiped the blood from both of his hands on the inside of his sports coat, buttoned it closed to conceal the gore on his shirt, and stepped into the store. A little bell at the top of the door announced his entry. He moved toward the back, looking left and right as if looking for something, then scanned the last shelf of items, glancing over the shelf at the door, ready to jump back into battle if someone he deemed a threat entered.

"*Czy moge pomóc ci cos znalezc?*" a female voice asked.

He turned to the short woman, an apron tied about her generous waist, smiling at him beneath gray hair pulled back tightly in a bun, asking if she could help him find something.

"*Znalazłem to,*" he said, grabbing a box from the second shelf without looking and then holding it up, smiling.

I found it.

The woman laughed, then told him he was a good husband in Polish.

He looked at the box in his hand.

Tampony—Polish for tampons.

He smiled and headed to the register.

"I have your tracker, Viking One," James said into his ear. "Confirm you're inside a store called Żabaka on Sienna."

"Hell if I know," he grumbled, his eyes scanning desperately for threats. "I'm in a grocery mart, and yes, it's on Sienna."

"Two mikes," James said.

"Perfect," he mumbled. "Just enough time to pay for my tampons."

There was a pause.

"Say again, Viking One?"

"Just meet me at the south entrance," Clark said, pulling out crumpled bills of Polish currency—the zloty—and handing them to the younger girl at the register. She smiled, dropping the box into a plastic bag and handing him his change.

He watched through the glass door until the white Jeep Avenger pulled up. He ducked out of the store, jumped into the back seat, and chopped a hand forward for the driver to go. James looked over his shoulder at him from the front passenger seat as the SUV pulled away, back onto Sienna, where it turned north at the first corner.

"You intact?" James asked.

Clark rolled his neck and did a mental check for pain other than

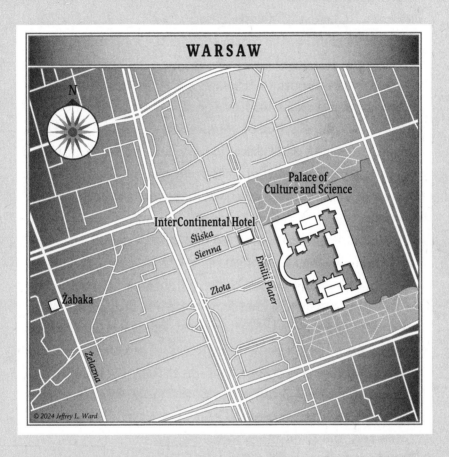

his arm, which still burned like hell from the dozens of small cuts. He opened and closed both fists.

"Five by . . ."

"Copy," James said. "We lost Tom."

"I know," Clark said. "I'm really sorry."

"Not your fault," the CIA man said. "In the meantime, we need to find somewhere to lay low."

"Head to the airport," Clark said. He pulled his weapon from the holster, and the CIA woman named Ginnie immediately read his mind and pulled a box of ammunition from a gray backpack hanging on the back of the driver's seat. Clark ejected the magazine from the X9 and topped it off with fresh nine-millimeter rounds, and then fished the nearly expended magazine from his coat to do the same.

"What . . . Why?" asked the CIA officer at the wheel, the sniper that he thought they called Spencer. "We need to retrieve our man first. We need to get his body home."

Clark gave a tight smile to the man driving.

"I understand that, but we're compromised on foreign soil. We'll arrange retrieval of the body through State. I promise, and it'll be done with the dignity he deserves."

"We'll take care of Tommy," James said to the driver, squeezing his shoulder, and then turned and held Clark's eyes. "What's next?"

"You and your team are exfilling," he said.

"And what about you?" James asked. "We're in this together."

Clark shook his head. "Not anymore. The stakes have evolved. My team is inbound, and we'll take it from here."

"Now, hold on . . ." James began.

He got it. If he'd lost a man and then was told to stand down, it would have sat wrong with him, too. But the situation called for a different level of compartmentalization and operational experience level.

"Listen, you guys are pros—you did everything I asked of you— but this thing is going deep dark now. That's where me and my team operate."

James nodded, but clearly didn't like it. "You're going into Russia, aren't you?"

Clark held his eyes and said nothing.

"Okay, okay, I get it. But there has to be some way we can help?"

"Get me to the airport and then get your man and your team home," Clark said.

"I think we've earned a seat at the table, John," James said solemnly.

"Probably," Clark said. "But this table is invitation-only and I don't control the guest list. And believe me, what happens next you don't want to know anything about."

James sighed, then fixed Clark with a tight smile.

"You move pretty good for an old man," Ginnie said beside him.

Clark gave a snort and looked at the CIA operative.

She handed him a medical kit from her gray backpack. "For your arm."

"Thanks," he said, opening the kit in his lap, then rolling up his sleeve to reveal dozens of cuts, some with bits of glass still in them, which he picked out and dropped on the all-weather floor mat.

They drove in silence, Clark planning the next steps in his head. He needed to get to Severodvinsk and find the Sevmash worker named Popov. That was the next play if they were to uncover what was going on with the Status-6 torpedoes. After that, they would do whatever needed to be done to stop whatever coup the "old men" in Moscow were planning. In the meantime, he needed to share with the DNI what he'd learned and of VICAR's fate. The loss of their top-placed mole in Moscow was a terrible blow to the IC.

He blew air through pursed lips.

In a few hours, he and the Campus team would be diving

headfirst down a very deep, very dark bunny hole and prepping for one of the most dangerous denied missions imaginable.

They were going to infiltrate the Russian Northern Fleet's most secure shipyard and naval base.

Which meant cuddling the grandbabies would have to wait a bit.

Fuckin' Russians. This is the worst vacation ever.

23

Russian president Yermilov tapped his finger on the armrest's drink holder in the rear of his Aurus Senat limousine, trying to quell the anger he felt. He had indulged the old man, had embraced the retired defense minister's vision and accepted his help to restore Russia to the world power it could be—*should* be— but he was still the president, after all. This late-night summons was simply too much. He had great respect for his mentor, but he could simply not let such a blatant abuse go unanswered. In the end, Ilyin would remain his close ally and confidant, but first he must remind the old-timer who ruled Russia.

He glanced at Boris, his personal, hand-selected bodyguard, who had been with Yermilov for years now. This was a dangerous time in Russia, and one could not be too careful. Friends, enemies, confidants, traitors—titles were changed in the blink of an eye in Russia. This was the downside of capitalism, but also its strength. Yermilov paid Boris ten times what rank-and-file soldiers made and used funds from his personal treasure chest. He also took care of the man's family. Boris was loyal only to him, and answered, there-fore, only to Yermilov.

I am very well familiar with the story of Julius Caesar.

The monster of a man stared straight ahead, a wall of muscle. But Yermilov knew better. Behind the man's brute strength was a competent, educated warrior. He had plucked Boris from Spetsnaz because he'd wanted more than a guard dog. He'd wanted a tacti-cian at his side.

"You alone will come inside with me, Boris. The rest will re-main outside."

"As you wish, Mr. President," Boris said. "I will post them to the perimeter."

"I only trust you," he said, not sure why he'd vocalized the sen-timent.

Maybe because it was true.

Boris met Yermilov's gaze and nodded as if to say, *A prudent philosophy.*

The lead vehicle in the presidential convoy slowed and made the left turn, arriving at a towering wrought-iron gate set in a ten-foot brick wall surrounding the estate. The private home of "retired" Colonel General Nikolai Ilyin was opulent—no doubt funded by dubious revenue streams. The irony that the man talked often about returning Mother Russia to greatness, after having person-ally amassed great wealth after the fall of communism, was not lost on Yermilov.

Would Ilyin cede his wealth and privilege in the coming days?

Yermilov certainly wasn't prepared to.

They weaved down the long gravel drive, the two-story home of brick and Spanish tile coming into view. The first vehicle came to a stop at the front of the house, Yermilov's vehicle standing off by more than thirty meters, and the third vehicle in the convoy turn-ing to block the drive behind them an additional thirty meters back.

"We will hold here for a moment, Mr. President," Boris said.

He let out a long, frustrated sigh. He didn't relish this meeting, but it simply had to be done.

And most certainly could not be done at the Kremlin.

Boris raised a finger to his ear, touching the earpiece there, then looked at him. "All secure, sir."

With that, Yermilov followed Boris out of the limo.

The two minutes passed slowly as Yermilov ran over in his head how he would reprimand his former boss, rein him in, but without breaking the man's spirit. He knew how much he needed Ilyin. The legendary soldier and spymaster had weaved a complex web of connections and debts. Those connections, and the small but powerful committee dedicated to restoring the homeland, were completely necessary in order for Yermilov to remain in power. The committee formed by Nikolai Ilyin were all loyal to the old man. It was unclear to Yermilov exactly what "restoring the homeland" meant to Ilyin, but certainly a return to communism was both unrealistic and impractical. More control, more propaganda, more military might: these were certainly the things Ilyin and the others had in mind.

More influence over me . . .

The plan to deploy the *Belgorod* to disable the American mid-Atlantic sonus net and then secretly deliver a Poseidon nuclear-tipped torpedo into Norfolk Harbor had been Ilyin's brainchild. Truth be told, Yermilov was annoyed *he* hadn't thought of it. Russia had hundreds of missiles in silos ready to launch at a moment's notice, but those missiles had limitations. Launching them was an observable event by the American spy satellites. They took time to fly to their target and they could be shot down by antiballistic missile defensive systems. But to have a nuclear warhead sitting undetected and unknown in the heart of the American fleet, ready to detonate at a moment's notice . . . This was true power. It could not be shot down. It could not be defended against. He relished the idea of having it in position. It would change the balance of power when bargaining with Washington.

And Ilyin had assured him an accidental detonation was impossible.

The plan was brilliant.

If it worked, why not repeat it and have K-329 use its stealth to deliver a Poseidon to every major American port city: New York, Boston, Groton, Charleston, Jacksonville, Miami?

Just the thought made him grin like a mad scientist.

His propaganda machine had already leaked information about the Poseidon torpedoes, exaggerating slightly the speed, range, and stealth. The Western news media had latched on to the release and ran dozens of stories about nuclear tsunamis and Russia's new doomsday weapon. He loved it—the frenzy of fear and doubt.

The Americans had no one to blame but themselves. They'd taken their eye off the prize in the quest for superpower dominance, distracted by hunting down goatherds in Afghanistan—a mistake he supposed the former Soviet Union had made as well. The irony was not lost on him, that a pointless war in the Middle East that had cost the Soviet Union the treasure and national resolve needed to retain *her* place in the world order had now allowed America to weaken her own resolve for conflict and allow her military to degrade.

The door opened.

"All is secure, sir," Boris said.

"Very well," he replied.

First, I will remind Colonel General Ilyin who it is who leads Russia. Then we can get to the business at hand.

He passed through large double wooden doors leading into the house, annoyed when neither of the large men in dark suits flanking the door came to attention as he passed. But then again, this was a highly secret meeting.

Ilyin has probably ordered his men to pretend I was never here.

A stern woman waited just inside, thin, older, her graying hair pulled back tight from her pale face.

"This way, please, Mr. President," she said. Unlike the brutes outside, she offered a deferential bow of her head. "He is waiting for you in his study."

She led him through the cavernous, regal foyer, with furnishings and memorabilia of an age long past. Next they passed a wonderful dining room of stone and marble, a table with seating for twenty calling back to a time of castles and kings. She stopped outside a heavy decorative wood door, which stood unguarded.

"If it pleases the president, the general would like to see you alone," she said.

Boris stepped forward, a hand raised to protest, but Yermilov stilled him with a look.

"He is *alone*, Mr. President," she said and opened the door.

Boris stepped in front of him, cleared the room quickly, then stepped back out and gestured with a hand that all was well. The protection officer then positioned himself beside the door, hands crossed in front of him.

Yermilov nodded at Boris and entered the room, the heavy door closing behind him with a resounding thud. The general was seated in an oversized high-back leather chair behind a more modest wood desk, his elbows leaning on the green felt inlay. It occurred suddenly to Yermilov that this desk looked like the desk Lenin used in so many of his portraits and photographs. Hell, knowing Ilyin, it was possible that this was the actual desk once belonging to Lenin. He shook away the urge to comment. To acknowledge the desk would be to elevate the man, and this was something he refused to do.

Not today.

"It is good to see you, Nikita. Please, sit," Ilyin said.

The informality bristled the Russian president.

"I prefer to stand, Nikolai," he said, eschewing honorifics as the old man had done. "We have an urgent matter to discuss, you and I. Something that was brought to my attention on the drive here, no less."

"Of course, Mr. President," Ilyin allowed, but his eyes conveyed less respect than the title deserved. "What has you upset?"

Yermilov paced, but forced himself to pace slowly, with authority and power, as if contemplating how best to deal with this uncomfortable situation. He stopped and turned to the man still seated at what he was now sure must be Lenin's original desk.

"I demand to know what you know about the killing of an SVR agent in Warsaw this very evening," he said, holding a steady gaze on the man.

Rather than cower or even give him a deferential look, Ilyin laughed.

"Is that what has you worked up? Please, Nikita, sit down. If we are to spend the next decade together, raising Russia from the ashes of its former self under the inferno of this failed capitalist experiment, we must be able to speak of difficult things. Sit and drink with me. Let us drink vodka and talk as men—like the Russian leaders we both are."

Ilyin had already rolled his chair back, pulling open a drawer from which he retrieved a bottle of Russian Standard and two glasses. The bottle immediately fogged with condensation, suggesting a chilled compartment or a box of ice inside the drawer.

The wind dashed from his sails, Yermilov took a seat, aware of the optics of him sitting in *front* of the desk at which the general sat. But then, it was just the two of them. Still, the point needed to be made. He accepted the proffered glass of chilled vodka from his host, but did not take a sip, holding it in his lap instead.

"From your response, I can only assume you know exactly what I am talking about, Nikolai."

"*Da*," Ilyin said, taking a generous gulp of the liquor and then refilling his glass. "The SVR agent's name is Erik Dovzhenko. He was making inquiries—dangerous inquiries—through a colleague at the GRU. Silencing him was necessary to protect our operation—to protect *you*, Nikita."

"Be that as it may . . ." he said, allowing irritation to creep back into his voice. He took a swallow of the cold, smooth vodka. Not to match pace with Ilyin, but to *not* drink would be a show of weakness. "It is not the point. Need I remind you, Nikolai, that I am no longer your pupil, nor even your colleague."

"You seem upset?"

He slammed the glass down on the desk. "I am the president of Russia! I am in charge, not only of Russia, but of the military, the SVR, and the GRU. And I am in charge of you. Is that clear?"

Ilyin once again fixed him with that irritating, condescending smile. Before answering, he topped off Yermilov's glass, replaced the cap on the bottle, and returned it to his desk drawer, the gesture not lost on Yermilov.

"Tell me, Mr. President," Ilyin said, rising, drink in hand. He walked to a large window that looked out over the garden behind the house, a view all the way to the lake. "Were you aware that Erik Dovzhenko was an American mole? Surely you knew he was a double agent working for the CIA?"

"What?" Yermilov said, dumbfounded. "That is impossible. I would have been immediately notified and would have ordered his execution myself."

"One would think," Ilyin said softly, not turning back from where he stared out at the lake. "And yet, there it is, eh?" He drank down the second glass of vodka, then turned slowly to face Yermilov. The smile was gone from his face. "Dovzhenko was a double agent, Nikita. He had been for some time, it seems. After meeting with an American agent in Berlin two days ago, he began asking questions about K-329 and its mission. He also inquired after Rodionov and Boldyrev and we believe passed their names to the Americans as being tied to the operation. They may also know of Aralovich, we are unsure. In any case, I had no choice but to take action. I instructed Rodionov to mobilize assets from the Wagner Group to kill Dovzhenko before more damage could be done."

"You should have kept me—"

"Don't be a child, Nikita," Ilyin snapped, cutting him off. "You must put this mission ahead of your own ego if we are to succeed. It is what I taught you to do, or have you forgotten all that you learned . . . Mr. President?"

Ilyin returned to his seat, dropped his glass into the drawer of his desk, and stared at Yermilov in the long awkward silence.

"There is no going back now, Nikita. You have but one hope to retain power—to be the president of the *new* Russia that is coming—and that is for us to succeed and to succeed in secret. We have plugged the hole, but we do not know what was told in the few minutes that your traitor met with his American handler. We must, therefore, proceed with caution."

Yermilov rose, ignoring the glass on the desk, and paced away, his mind reeling. How had he not known all of this? The answer was clear. Ilyin—it was so obvious. Ilyin, Rodionov, Aralovich, and Boldyrev—and God only knew who else was in the circle he now realized he was on the outside of—were controlling the flow of information from their respective organizations to him in the Kremlin. This was not a group of loyalists, protecting him with a degree of deniability should things go wrong or come to light. No, this was a group of old men who saw him standing in the way of progress. What Ilyin called New Russia was, in fact, *old* Russia.

He looked at his vodka glass sitting on the desk. Lenin's desk . . .

These men truly wished to turn back the clock to the days of the Soviet Union. By controlling information available to him, they had control over him. Like a frog in a pot of slowly boiling water, he had ceded power to a cabal of old men and he hadn't even noticed.

He felt sick.

The *Belgorod* mission.

What if it fails? What if the Americans monitor the launch and recover the Poseidon weapon?

They would pin it on me. Shout for my resignation. Certainly, that is their contingency plan.

"You are right to worry, Nikita," Ilyin said, and Yermilov turned back to find him reclined in his chair, hands pressed together and his chin on his fingertips, eyes young and clear in his old and weathered face. Yermilov felt faint. "There will be a coup, Nikita. This will be a bloodless coup, because the transfer of real power occurs behind the scenes, you see? You retain your position—and your wealth. And we will work with you, rather than for you, to bring America to her knees so that Russia can rise again. You see? It is the only way."

"You betrayed me," he hissed.

"Bah," Ilyin said, waving a hand. "Again, don't be a child. It is better this way. Far better than the other type of coup, *da*? Now, finish your vodka like a man."

Yermilov returned to his seat.

I'm safe. I'm in control, he silently told himself.

Boldyrev might have operational control over K-329, but presidential authorization was required to launch a nuclear-armed Poseidon. He could withhold this. As president, he alone had control over the codes needed to arm and launch all nuclear weapons. Without the codes, K-329 was more show of force than weapon. It was nothing but bravado without the codes.

Ilyin thinks he's backed me into a corner, but he's wrong.

He picked up his vodka, drained the glass, and stared at the traitor seated behind Lenin's desk. "It seems we need each other more than ever. And will for a long time."

"Do not feel betrayed, Nikita," Ilyin said, his voice fatherly and his face softening. "We both serve, not ourselves, but Mother Russia. The time for a new Cold War is now. Together we will stand against American hegemony and once again become a superpower. And when that time comes, we will share a meal and laugh about today."

You will pay for your arrogance, old man.

Yermilov rose, stretched his hand across the desk, and said, "For Mother Russia."

Ilyin took it, the squeeze so much stronger and more powerful than Yermilov expected from the aged man.

"For Mother Russia."

"Keep me informed," he said, holding the general's eyes. "I don't like surprises."

"I will do better in this regard, Mr. President."

"It is all I ask."

He released Ilyin's hand and headed for the door, where Boris would be waiting. A sudden flash in his mind's eye—of Caesar, stabbed by every member of his own senate.

Ilyin could easily murder me here and now if he so chooses.

Yermilov's hand shook as he reached for the doorknob. Did death await him on the other side?

If he wanted me murdered, I would already be dead. But I won't make this mistake again.

Ever.

He opened the door and stepped out of Ilyin's office, where Boris dutifully waited . . . alone. Without a backward glance, President Yermilov—billionaire, dictator, and supreme commander in chief of the Russian military—marched toward his limousine, his head held high.

24

With all the subtlety of being launched from a catapult, a siren's wail popped Avgust Vladimirovich out of his captain's chair and onto his feet. There were over two dozen alarms on the control console of the *Finitor*. He didn't have all of them memorized, but *this* one he knew at a glance.

OVER TENSION ALARM: PRIMARY WINCH flashed red on the alarm panel.

"Move," he barked in Russian and shoved the young sailor at the helm out of the way so he could take control of the ship's wheel and throttle.

He yanked the twin throttle levers back to neutral, then pulled them down to reverse thrust. The *Finitor* shuddered as the twin screws cavitated, battling to slow the vessel. He glanced at the nav screen, which displayed speed over ground, and watched the number drop.

He'd been fast, but would he be lucky enough that the cable wouldn't snap and cut somebody in half, or worse, send a five-hundred-million-ruble high-resolution scanning sonar probe to the bottom of the Atlantic? He couldn't afford another black mark on his record. Black marks were the reason he was the captain of this rust bucket instead of one of the vaunted Admiral Grigorovich-class frigates where he should be.

His eyes shifted to the black-and-white video monitor streaming live footage from a camera on the fantail, where two crewmen were fighting with the cable reel. They couldn't hear him, but he shouted anyway. "Get away from that thing, you idiots! Do you want to die?"

"Here, Captain," the young helmsman said, handing Avgust a handset microphone. "I tuned it to broadcast ship-wide."

At least this one has a brain, the captain thought as he snatched the handset and ordered the two operators by name to get clear of the cable drum. At first the men froze, but hearing their names and the captain's angry voice on the loudspeakers seemed to do the trick and they evacuated the winch room. He glanced back at the navigation display and saw that speed over ground had dropped to 0.7 knots. The *Finitor* was still shaking, but less violently as it settled into a productive backing harmonic.

A heartbeat later, the siren stopped wailing.

"Captain, the over tension alarm is clear," the helmsman—who was the only other person on the bridge—reported.

"I'm not deaf, Yuri," he said with a growl, but inside he was glad the young man was making an effort. He eased off the throttles as the speed over ground reached 0.2 knots in the reverse direction. "Why haven't they radioed to tell us what happened?"

"Do you want me to run aft and find out what the problem is?" Yuri asked.

"*Da*," he said, earning an enthusiastic smile from the kid. "But, Yuri . . ."

Yuri stopped at the threshold of the port bridge door. "Yes, Captain?"

"Don't go anywhere near that winch."

"Understood, Captain," Yuri said with a smile.

Craving a cigarette, Avgust worked the throttles and wheel, fighting the wind, waves, and ocean current to maintain station and keep the ship's speed over ground as close to zero as possible. This was not the first time he'd had to take the wheel from a junior watch stander to safeguard the *Finitor* and its crew from an accident. It was trusting incompetent underlings who'd made bad decisions on his watch that had derailed his naval career in the first place.

I'll never make that mistake again.

Just as his anger was reaching the boiling point at being kept in the dark, the bridge radio squawked at him.

"Captain, this is Kozlov," the ship's civilian operations officer said.

He hated having a mixed crew. Civilians were lazy, entitled, and always complaining. But that was part of the subterfuge of this mission, and there was nothing he could do about it.

"Did we lose the sonar head?" he said, getting straight to the only question that mattered.

"*Nyet*. It is intact, but the winch is jammed."

Avgust cursed. "How much cable is spooled out?"

"Eighteen hundred meters, Captain."

"Listen very carefully to me," he said. "I want you to install a cable clamp on the cable just above the stern spool eye. Rig a come-along to the cable clamp and take all the pressure off the winch. If the cable is going to snap, I want it to snap below the cable clamp, where it can't hurt anyone. Do you understand?"

"I understand," Kozlov said.

"No work on the winch or the cable drum is permitted until the cable is secured as I described. Repeat this back to me."

"No work on the winch or cable drum until the cable is secured with a clamp and a come-along," Kozlov said.

"Good. Now, work fast, the sea state is picking up and maintaining station is going to be difficult. And send Yuri back to the bridge."

"*Da*, Captain."

"And tell him to fetch my cigarettes from my stateroom on the way."

"*Da*, Captain."

Avgust took his hand off the throttles just long enough to wipe the sweat from his brow with his sleeve.

Fate, it seemed, had smiled on him this morning. No one had died and he'd not lost the one piece of equipment that would cost him his ship and what remained of his reputation. If this secret mission was successful, there was a chance he could turn things around. Maybe he'd even be offered command of the *Admiral Grigorovich* itself. He exhaled and permitted himself a tight-lipped victory smile as he imagined himself back in uniform standing on the bridge of an actual warship.

Now, where are my damn cigarettes?

25

Katie glanced at her watch. She wanted to make sure she had plenty of time to make it to the next, and perhaps one of the most important, meetings of her deployment aboard the *Ford*. Her *almost* eidetic memory had allowed her to orient to the *Ford* pretty quickly, but outside of the wardroom, gym, and her stateroom—all of which she still had to reference deck and frame numbers for—she had no idea where anything was. Fortunately, Jaya Kumari was going to accompany her to meet Bentley Kiplinger, the rear admiral commanding Carrier Strike Group 12, and Captain Martin Vasquez, the commander of the embarked air wing, or CAG.

"Does the strike group commander usually meet with lowly O-3s assigned to augment the N2 shop?" she'd asked Captain James "Spacecamp" Huddleston, the DCAG, or deputy commander, of the air wing, which included all aircraft squadrons embarked aboard the *Ford*. The DCAG had been with Captain Otis "Opey" Mackenzie, the skipper of the *Ford* and a former EA-18G Growler naval flight officer, or NFO. The two were, despite their rank and commands, laid-back, like most aviators she'd known, and seemed to be good friends from before their current commands.

"Oh, hell no," Huddleston had said, laughing and exchanging a knowing look with Mackenzie, who had summoned her to the XO's wardroom, where, with *Ford*'s XO, Sarah "Baby" Williams, the three aviators had been having dinner and, apparently, speculating about Katie and her agenda.

"Admiral Kiplinger said he wanted to meet the JO who had single-handedly changed Group 12's orders and mission," Mackenzie had said. "I think the CAG was egging him on. CAG's not a fan, Ryan."

"Not a fan of what?" she'd asked, confused.

"Anything," the aviators had said in unison, and laughed.

Now Katie let out a long, nervous sigh and glanced at her watch yet again. There was still time to get more work done before the meeting, which would take place in the skipper's reception quarters, where she'd met Captain Williams, the XO and an F/A-18 pilot, when she'd arrived. The XO had been affable and also immensely proud of the ship she helped lead, the first in a new class of ultra-capable, next-generation aircraft carriers. Williams had given her a rundown of the many improvements the *Ford* brought to the fleet, and then had heard Katie pitch on what brought her aboard—though she seemed already fully briefed on both the activities of the Russian Northern Fleet and the mysterious, modified Oscar II–class submarine that had kicked the whole thing off.

"Lieutenant Ryan?"

She looked up from the desk, set up for her in a latrine-sized pocket office across the shop from Jaya Kumari's.

"Hey, Caspar," she said to the IS2. "What's up?"

"Couple of quick things, ma'am," the intelligence specialist said. "I know you have a meeting with the admiral and the CAG later, so the boss said to make sure you're read in on anything new or different."

"Okaaay," she said, drawing the word out.

"Well, first Bubba—that is, IS2 Pettigrew—"

"Bubba works," Katie said.

"Okay, so Bubba wanted you to know that there's nothing new on the sub hunt, but we also don't have any new comms from the undersea assets. That's typical, ma'am," Caspar said. "The *Washington* will only be in comms when she comes up to PD, though they have a way to data dump anything important without coming up, so usually no news means, well, no news."

"Okay," Katie said. She would probably not be sharing any "no news" with the admiral or the O-6 commanding the air wing. "I mean, yeah, of course," she said, rising from her rather cramped desk in her very cramped office. She bumped her hip on the corner of the desk trying to maneuver over to the door.

"Sorry we don't have a better space for you, Lieutenant," Caspar said.

"All good, IS2," she said with a genuine smile. "I like being with you guys where the real work gets done, anyway."

She followed Caspar to the office across from hers and rapped on the door as Jaya Kumari looked up, pushing her glasses up onto the top of her head.

"Hi, Katie," Kumari said with a nod and a smile to the petty officer beside her. "What's up?"

"IS2 wanted to give us a brief together on some development— I don't know what yet."

"Yeah, I'm sorry," Caspar said. "I'm not sure where Lieutenant Ryan fits in the chain here, ma'am." She gave an apologetic look to Katie.

"I'm just here to help," Katie said. "Just think of me—and IS2

Pettigrew—as a resource up and down your chain. I'll share with you guys, but I really am here to help, not get in the way."

"Thank you, ma'am," Caspar said and seemed to mean it.

"Ryan is part of the team now, IS2, so go to her with anything and then either of you can brief me as you see fit. I trust her."

"Yes, ma'am," the shop's LPO said.

"So, what's up?" Kumari asked.

"Ma'am, we got a routine flag on the multi-brief," Caspar began. Like her shop at ONI, Katie assumed one of Caspar's collaterals in the *Ford*'s N2 shop was to scan the daily, looking for anything relevant to their tasking or intelligence streams they were prosecuting. "There's a ship called the *Finitor* that was spotted during routine coastal surveillance—satellite, in this case. It's a Cyprus-flagged vessel, but popped because in reality it is a Russian surveillance ship. The *Finitor* operates under a fabricated cover of being a research vessel with a multinational oceanographic organization, but we've pierced that original content."

"Okay," Kumari said and glanced at her watch. "Might need you to get to the point, Caspar. Sounds like a nothing burger so far."

"Right," Caspar said, "Sorry. The point is, it's been a while since the *Finitor* has been outside the Med and the Black Sea—she was off the Florida Keys in 2019 during a naval aviation exercise—and so, popping up off the East Coast seemed unusual. But the satellite found it loitering around 35-60."

"Well, that's a development," Kumari said.

"Wait," Katie said, trying to catch up. "What's 35-60?"

"It's shorthand for a more specific lat-long, Lieutenant," Caspar said.

"It's the location of the mid-Atlantic data node for the DASH network," Kumari said.

"And the *Finitor* is right over top of it, ma'am," Caspar said.

"I'm not familiar with the DASH network," Katie said.

"It started as a DARPA project, stands for Distributed Agile Submarine Hunting," Caspar explained. "Think of it as a successor program to SOSUS."

"Ah, because SOSUS is ineffective now?"

"Yeah, I don't know a ton about it, only that as Russian submarines got quieter and started achieving parity with our own in terms of acoustic stealth, they had no trouble cruising past the SOSUS nodes undetected. I think when the *Severodvinsk* popped up off the coast of Norfolk and said hello, having penetrated our coastline waters entirely undetected, it raised some eyebrows. DARPA was tasked to fast-track a solution and DASH was their answer."

"Is it a passive hydrophone network like SOSUS, or does DASH also use active sonar?"

"Like I said, I don't know much about it. Everything I'm telling you is what I looked up today," Caspar said. "The only other thing I know is that after proof of concept, the Naval Information Warfare Center took ownership. The *Finitor*'s presence has got NIWC Atlantic's antennae up, obviously."

"So," Katie said, pacing the two steps back and forth available to her in the small space, "if a foreign adversary wanted to penetrate the East Coast sensor net, like say with a stealthy, special mission submarine, disrupting this data node would be a logical first step."

Caspar nodded her agreement.

"Thanks for being all over this," Katie said. "This is a really big deal, Caspar."

"I'd love to tell you I put the pieces together, ma'am, but it was Bubba who flagged this one as important. Also, it seems, from the satellite imagery—and we're still doing a reconstruct, so this is preliminary—that the *Finitor* was hung up on something at the site."

"Hung up?" Kumari asked.

"Yes, ma'am," Caspar said. "She was trailing something off a cable winch, and it appears—again this is speculation based on imagery—she got snagged on something."

"Well, that's a red flag. We need to figure out what the hell they're up to," Katie said.

Kumari rose. "Ideally, but that's not our call, Lieutenant. We're scheduled to meet with the admiral right now, so are you comfortable briefing on this as well?"

"Sure," Katie said. "I mean, I'm not a fleet sailor, but I've done intel with a strike group before. With the *Belgorod* slipping past the *Indiana* and now the *Finitor* probing a critical early-detection sonar node, I would imagine the strike group commander would like to know if the two are connected."

"I would imagine so," Kumari agreed. "Thanks, Caspar. Let me know if anything new comes up about that ship or anything else. You guys will get busy with a data dump and keep an eye on that Russian Northern Fleet exercise."

"Yes, ma'am," Caspar said and then turned to go.

Katie looked at Lieutenant Commander Kumari. "This feels like a big deal to you, too, right?"

Kumari shrugged. "We're what I call 'mission myopic' out here sometimes, so it just depends. And understand, we're mission-first by design, and we're not always fully read in and up-to-date down in the N2 dungeon."

"The N2 dungeon?"

"That's what our LCPO calls it. Most of his time has been doing analysis with NSW, so he's adjusting."

Kumari rapidly ascended a ladder well, and despite the multiple triathlons Katie had run over the past few years, she pushed to keep up as she said, "Well, 'N2 dungeon' and 'mission myopic' are both now in my repertoire."

Minutes later, Kumari rapped on the wood door labeled:

USS GERALD R. FORD
COMMANDING OFFICER

"Come." It was the skipper, Captain Mackenzie's, voice.

Kumari gave Katie a look, opened the door, and ushered her in. She maneuvered past the large desk and then around the glass case housing the enormous, detailed model of the aircraft carrier.

Kumari first greeted the skipper of the *Ford*, who sat at the middle of the mahogany table and wore an aviator's flight suit and a pair of gold wings. Then she addressed the other ranking members. "Admiral Kiplinger, Captain Vasquez, this is Lieutenant Katie Ryan, our rider from ONI."

Katie's gaze ticked from the CO to the head of the table, where the flag officer, Rear Admiral Kiplinger, sat. At the other end of the table sat an officer in a flight suit, arms crossed at his chest. She assumed he must be the CAG, Captain Vasquez, and the DCAG, Captain Huddleston, was the man sitting beside him.

"Honored to meet you, Admiral," Katie said, addressing Kiplinger first, before turning to the other end of the table. "Captain Vasquez."

Vasquez, who commanded the air wing, looked up, but she couldn't help but notice the scowl forming on his face.

"Have a seat, Lieutenant Ryan, and please sit down as well, Commander Kumari," the admiral said. He gave a polite smile and gestured with a hand, and Katie took a seat, trying to read the mood behind the steel-blue eyes set in a weathered face beneath close-cropped gray hair. "We have your intelligence brief from

ONI, Ryan," he said. "But when I have the opportunity to meet the officer behind the report, I always take it."

The unspoken implication was clear—he was vetting her, not the intel.

"Of course, sir," she said.

"Like I said, Lieutenant, we have the brief, but why don't you summarize for us, and then you can give us any relevant updates."

"Yeah, pitch us your theory, Ryan," Captain Vasquez said at the other end of the table.

Katie took a beat, swallowing down her irritation.

"Well, sir, first off I'm not operating off a theory, with all due respect—"

"All due respect usually implies none—in my experience," the CAG grumbled.

"I assure you that's not the case here, sir," she said. "It's not a theory that a brand-new, highly modified Oscar II submarine, the *Belgorod* K-329, set to sea without our normal advance notice—"

"Advance notice?" the admiral interrupted, far more politely than the CAG, whose eyes she felt boring a hole into the side of her head.

"Uh, yes, sir. Without giving away the store here, the intelligence community, including the DIA, manages assets inside Russia—in the Kremlin, SVR, GRU, and the military. My point being that a lack of notice to us implied significant subcompartmentalization within Russia, something confirmed by our own agents and operatives through a reliable source. Specifically, even the head of the National Defense Management Center, Colonel General Andreyev, was caught completely unaware when the *Belgorod* sailed."

"That sure sounds like a big effin' deal, don't you think, Marty?" the admiral said, raising an eyebrow at the CAG, who shrugged.

"Maybe—if it's real."

"Go on, Ryan," Admiral Kiplinger said. "Don't mind the CAG—he's in a mood."

Captain Vasquez's face flushed, and Katie had a feeling that any hope of winning the man over just went down the shitter.

She went on to summarize everything from the beginning—from Bubba making her aware of the bow of the *Belgorod* and her unexpected putting to sea, to her disappearing, the confusion inside Russia, her conversation with Miller about the Status-6, nuclear-tipped, nuclear-powered UUVs. She reiterated that intelligence assets inside Russia had confirmed what they knew and were working to get more information. She gave an update on the *Indiana*'s missed unfruitful search for the *Belgorod*, and then she briefed them on Konstantin Gorov, his dad, and the surprise connection to the legend around the *Red October* and her conversation with CIA case officer Reilly.

"We've all heard the legends of the *Red October*," the CAG said with a snort. "She sunk in the Atlantic and we had to rescue her crew. Doesn't say much about the Russians' submarine engineering ability, does it?"

"That was a long time ago, Marty," the admiral said. "And I've heard some other versions of that story over the years."

"Yeah, me too," the CAG grunted. "Including one that involved UFOs."

"Well, these Status-6 torpedoes are pretty damn worrisome," Captain Mackenzie said.

"We know about the Status-6," Admiral Kiplinger said. "The Russians call them Poseidon torpedoes. They put together a whole propaganda video with CGI showing one blow up off the coast of New York and destroying Manhattan with a nuclear tsunami. My favorite, of course, was the animated video of a Poseidon evaporating an aircraft carrier at sea along with her entire escort. But I was under the impression this was all bluster because the project was still in early development. Do we have reason to believe they're operational and on board this submarine, Ryan?"

"We're working on that, sir. ONI is coordinating with all the assets under ODNI to answer that very question. I hope to know more soon."

"Well, shit," Mackenzie said, a strain now in his voice. "If there's a rogue submarine out there and it's carrying a doomsday torpedo, that could start a nuclear war. I'd say that's a big damn deal."

"Well, me too," the CAG agreed. "If . . ." He turned to Katie and she held his stare. "How's your dad doing, Ryan?"

The words were a gut punch and she felt herself flush.

"Kumari, can you give us the room a minute, please?" Admiral Kiplinger said, holding up a hand to Vasquez.

"Of course, sir," the intelligence department head said, shooting Katie a short but quizzical look. Then she rose, strode quickly across the ornate room and its memorabilia to the late President Ford, and left, closing the door behind her.

Katie felt her anger grow and turned to the CAG, a voice screaming for her to stop and wait, and said, "My dad is fine, sir. How are your parents?"

"Dead," the CAG said and snorted. "But when Daddy's little girl shows up to 'give us a hand' during a deployment, it makes me go, 'Huh?' And when friends in the intel community whisper that the girl's daddy was the CIA man who got it wrong about a Russian submarine called the *Red October*, it makes me wonder if the Ryan family has some score to settle. Helluva reason to reposition an entire strike group and put them in slapping distance of the Russian Northern Fleet."

"I'm guessing you didn't vote for him, sir?" she swiped, earning a giggle from the XO.

"No," the CAG said, leaning in with fire in his eyes. "I did not, because I don't think spooks should be President."

"That's enough, Marty," Admiral Kiplinger snapped. He turned to her. "Ryan, I admire that you keep your—let's call it an uncomfortable relationship—with the White House a secret as best you can, but you must have known the leadership here would know about it."

"Of course, sir," she said. "I just didn't think it would matter. I thought my graduating with honors from the Academy, top of my class at intel school, in FITREPs, and below-the-zone promotion might speak for itself." She immediately regretted it, her dad's sage words from a decade ago coming to her:

If you ever find yourself giving someone your résumé, you've lost the argument already . . .

"Yeah, 'cause those accolades couldn't be related to your uncomfortable relationship."

She snapped her head and raised a finger at the CAG, but Kiplinger took care of business for her, probably saving her career from her temper—the other thing she got from her dad.

"Damn it to hell, Marty, I said that's enough!" the admiral snapped.

The CAG folded his arms and leaned back, looking smug.

Katie did a short round of four-count tactical breathing and felt her pulse slow.

"I appreciate your being aboard with us, Ryan," the admiral said after an uncomfortable beat. "Anything else to add?"

She almost chickened out, giving in to her anger, but the right thing was always the right thing.

"One last thing, sir," she said. She gave him a quick overview of the *Finitor* and why there was reason to be concerned.

"Suspicious, I agree," the CAG said, perhaps his version of an apology.

"Might be useful to take a look aboard that ship, sir," she said.

Kiplinger laughed. "That's above my pay grade, Ryan. I can't authorize an intervention on a commercial vessel operating in international waters, especially one we know is a Russian false flag. But I agree it's a worry, especially with everything else going on . . . And I do hate coincidences." He tapped his pen on a blank notepad in front of him. "Well, I guess that's about it. Marty, Spacecamp, thanks for coming. I'll catch up shortly. And Opey," he said, using the CO's call sign, "can I borrow your office for a minute?"

"Of course, sir," Mackenzie said. The three aviators rose and left, but through a door behind the desk instead of the main entrance she'd come through.

Katie felt her pulse quicken again. She'd overstepped with a command-level officer and she had a feeling she was about to pay the price.

She felt her pulse slow, though, when Kiplinger smiled and leaned in on his elbows.

"Don't worry about Captain Vasquez, Ryan," he said. "He can be a dick, but he's all bark. We flew together back in the day, and he was a prick then, too."

A relieved smile spread on her face. "Yes, sir."

"This is real good work, Ryan," he went on. "Maybe the *Belgorod* putting to sea and the *Finitor* probing our coastal surveillance are connected, maybe not. But . . . If that sub is carrying doomsday nuclear torpedoes in its inventory, then it's sure as hell worth postponing our Med run and sticking a little closer to home. Also, if that Northern Fleet exercise 'drifts' south, then we might have a problem. Like I said, I hate coincidences."

"Me too, sir," she said.

"Do me a favor, Ryan," he said. "Route your briefs and recommendations to ONI and ODNI through me. I'll give my comments and endorsement, in case the opinion of a salty fleet sailor carries any weight."

"That would be great, Admiral. Thank you, sir. If the higher-ups do green-light a collection op on the *Finitor*, can we execute it from the *Ford* if needed?"

"No," the admiral replied. "That would be less than ideal. I imagine a hit out of Virginia Beach with the JSOC. Tier One SEALs would be preferred. And anyway, I doubt it'll get the green light—hitting a Russian ship in international waters is a helluva provocation, Marty's right about that. But who knows?"

"I was still planning to recommend it."

"I had a feeling you would," he said.

"Do you still want me to route it through you, sir?" she asked, giving him an opt-out, since he clearly wasn't a fan of the plan.

"I thought we agreed on that already, Ryan."

"You'll have it within the hour, sir."

"All right, then," the admiral said and signaled the meeting was over by standing and proffering her his hand. "Keep me in a close loop on all of this business, Ryan."

"Yes, sir," she said and headed for the door.

The admiral went to the other door, and just before the main door closed she heard him call the CO and CAG back in to "talk this through," ending with "And, Marty, if you're gonna be an asshole, I'll forget to invite you next time."

She smiled. There were definitely worse things in the world than having the admiral in charge of the carrier strike group in your corner.

26

This was how Ryan preferred it, frankly—just the two of them, sorting out the best course of action. He looked at Mary Pat, who was tapping a pencil on the side of the table, her mind deep in concentration as they looked over the latest intelligence brief. It wasn't that he didn't value his entire team—in fact, nothing could be further from the truth. President Jack Ryan had assembled some of the most brilliant geopolitical and military minds of a generation, and did so with a mandate that this was an administration that served the people. Any "rice bowl," self-serving attitudes, any decisions made to advance careers or shift blame, would be dealt with quickly and harshly. And he had done just that more than once, early in his presidency. Nearly a half dozen senior-level members of his administration and cabinet had been given walking orders when their motivations didn't align with his vision for the nation. Most were good people and all were brilliant.

They simply didn't put the country first.

Alone, with Mary Pat, he felt free to be himself—free to voice his questions, opinions, and doubts that would be difficult for him in a formal brief or larger group.

"Here it is," Mary Pat said finally in response to his question. "So, the last time the *Finitor* was this close was . . . about fourteen weeks ago. Same basic pattern in and loitering over the same coordinates."

"Are we positive the *Finitor* is a Russian spy ship?" he asked, loosening his tie. He wished he could take it off. Hell, sometimes he wished he could doff the whole President business and head down to an office at Langley, where he could do the people's work all day every day. So much of his job these days felt ceremonial and constantly pressured by politics. There was a purity to analyzing intelligence data, drawing a conclusion, and recommending—and even executing—a response.

"Oh, one hundred percent, Jack," she said, looking up. "The *Finitor* is in our confirmed database. We routinely harass her with signal jamming, that kind of thing. The concern is the location, and that it's a repeat location, especially in light of the developments with the *Belgorod*."

"The DASH node," he said, nodding.

"Yes," she said.

Of course, he saw the implications. The *Finitor*, flagged in Cyprus, was loitering over a critical DASH sonar network hub. Were the Russians mapping . . . or were they sabotaging? It mattered.

"If the Russians disrupt the mid-Atlantic DASH hub, it wouldn't take down the entire system, correct?" he said.

"That's true, Jack. That was one of the design criteria for DASH—it's supposed to be a *distributed* and *agile* sensor network, where the loss of a single TRAP, transmitter, or hydrophone array does not compromise the entire network."

"But this is a node, which I assume means it aggregates the data from multiple collectors in the area?"

"That's correct."

"Taking out this node would create a blind spot—or a deaf spot, to be technically precise—that the Russians could sneak a submerged asset through."

She pressed her lips into a tight line, then said, "In theory, I would think so. But we could try to plug that hole with ASW assets."

He sighed and his thoughts went to the *Belgorod* and Katie.

Katie, who'd authored the brief he'd just read, was making a case that the *Belgorod* putting to sea and the *Finitor* interrogating the DASH data node may not be independent events. Could the Russians have deployed the *Finitor* to damage the data hub so that the *Belgorod* could slip through America's newest state-of-the-art submarine detection network undetected?

"If the *Belgorod* is carrying the Status-6, they have quite a stand-off capability. If it really is nuclear-powered with an unlimited range, they could launch it a thousand miles out."

"That's true," she said.

"My worry is that they could time the disruption to align with an inbound weapon that's already been launched. This brief says the weapon travels up to seventy knots . . . Of course, anything traveling at that speed is going to be putting out a ton of noise. We'd probably hear it coming well before it got to any gap in the DASH network."

"They said it *can* travel up to seventy knots," Mary Pat said. "It doesn't *have* to. What if it's traveling at ten knots? Maybe it is virtually silent at low speeds. The truth is, we just don't know enough about this weapon, because its development was highly compartmentalized and our assets in the Kremlin, SVR, and GRU simply don't have any information to share. We are working on it, but right now we're still in the dark."

He tapped a finger on a supposed photograph of a Status-6 weapon half covered by a tarp that was taken in a Russian shipyard. "Well," he said. "We need to get aboard the *Finitor* and see what the hell they're up to. We have NSW assets available and on standby for operations like this, right?"

"Yes, but, Jack, for all we know, the *Belgorod* is going to surface in the Barents and return to Sevmash at any minute. Boarding a Russian ship in international waters is a pretty hefty escalation, especially as we're steaming a strike group toward the Russian fleet conducting an exercise in international waters."

"If we do a flyby on the *Finitor*, do we learn what we need to know?" he said.

"No. Best case she just sails away."

"Leaving more questions than answers."

"I suppose."

Ryan smiled now, pulling the picture of the *Finitor* toward him.

"I know that smile," Mary Pat said.

"You said the *Finitor* is flagged from Cyprus?"

"Yes?"

His smile broadened. "Then why would we believe we're hitting a Russian military vessel? As far as we know, it's from Cyprus."

She leaned back, narrowed her eyes at him, but the hint of a smile started to form on her face. "Well, we do know."

"But nobody can *prove* what we know and what we don't know. To incriminate us, the Russians would have to admit what they're really doing and publicly shatter the *Finitor*'s official cover. They're not going to do that."

"What about the media?" she said. "When they get word of this, the story will break."

"We're looking for drugs, not spies. The drugs pouring into this country are an absolute scourge, Mary Pat," he said theatrically. "Americans are suffering from drug abuse and addiction at all-time highs. This vessel has been inside our national waters on numerous occasions. I bet the DEA is highly suspicious that this might be a drug-smuggling operation."

"I bet they even have a report circulating to that effect," Mary Pat added, the epiphany complete and her smile large and genuine now.

"That would be a nice touch with the press—after. This is clearly a drug-running ship, Mary Pat. Order our JSOC SEALs out of Virginia Beach to conduct an operation to seize and search the drug-running vessel *Finitor* operating off our coast, and have the Coast Guard intercept and take custody of it—but only after the raid. We can't risk spooking them. I want to catch the *Finitor* in the act."

"And once we 'discover' that the crew is manned by Russians?"

"We'll release the ship and crew, while demanding an official apology from Moscow, of course."

"Okay, just give me the word."

"Do it, Mary Pat."

She rose. "Yes, Jack."

While she packed up the files and her laptop, he checked his watch.

"Has our acoustic specialist arrived on the *Ford* yet?" he asked.

"Should be landing as we speak. Just out of curiosity, how did *that* conversation go?"

"He's excited to help," Ryan said.

"Really? What about the trap landing? Was he excited about that, too?"

"That part required a little more coaxing, but we eventually *landed* on the same page," he said with a chuckle.

Mary Pat rolled her eyes.

"Sorry, I couldn't help myself," he said.

"For a man who hates flying, I would have expected a little empathy from you," she said.

He shrugged. "Let's just consider it friendly payback for what he put me through on the *Dallas* all those years ago."

27

K atie blinked, the harsh light from her computer screen starting to bother her eyes, despite the filter placed over it. With little new intelligence to sift through, she had spent the last few hours scouring intelligence reports on Captain Gorov. She'd learned nothing new, and found even less about the man's father, the engineer who had died after his defection plan was pulled out from under him. Other than routine background information about the man, his education, his family, and, of course, the work he did on the *Red October*, there was very little data available. Again, she'd learned nothing new. The *Red October*—now, that was something different. TS/SCI files on the Russian submarine abounded, the threat it posed, and the now-deceased captain, Marko Ramius, who had gone down with the ship, quite literally, after a nuclear disaster aboard, saving his crew before scuttling the sub to keep it out of the hands of the Americans. What was curious, however, was the incredible, detailed technical specifications about the *Red October* contained in the CIA and ONI files. Everything from engineering to operations specifications, all in rich detail. Of course, Miller had told her that the skipper of the *Red October* had defected, so that made sense—if you knew the truth. After her visit to the USS *Washington*, she couldn't imagine being under the ocean in one of those damn things. Sailors volunteering for submarine force duty were special—or strange.

A knock made her start, and she looked up to see IS2 Caspar at the doorway to her tiny office space.

"Sorry, ma'am," the intelligence specialist said. "I didn't mean to startle you."

"Not at all," she said sheepishly. "What's up, Caspar?"

"Just wanted to let you know your guest has arrived, ma'am," Caspar said.

"Wait, wait," Katie said confused. "Who are you talking about? What guest?"

Now Caspar looked confused. "Ummm . . . There's a civilian who just arrived by COD to join the team. The request was routed from ONI, so I thought . . ."

Katie sat back and looked at the intelligence specialist, confused.

"I don't know anything about it."

A civilian? Who the hell could that be? And why had Ferguson not given her a heads-up?

"Okay, well, here he is," Caspar said and stepped aside to allow a thin, middle-aged African American man dressed in khaki pants, a button-down shirt, and a sports coat step in from the hallway.

The new arrival gave her a smile—a courteous smile—but his eyes suggested he was less than happy to be aboard. He let go of the handle of a small roller bag and extended a hand to her.

"I'm Dr. Ronald Jones," he said.

Bubba, who was working at the desk beside her, popped to his feet and beat her to the handshake. "Dr. Jones—like *Raiders of the Lost Ark*. I love it."

The man gave a polite, perhaps placating smile. "Yes, well, *that* Dr. Jones was a fictional archaeologist with a whip, whereas I have a PhD with an emphasis on mathematical acoustic algorithms and I carry a laptop."

"So . . . You're smart," Bubba said.

"Well, educated, I suppose."

"Welcome, Dr. Jones," Katie said and greeted him with a handshake of her own. "But, um, why are you here?"

"A great question," Jones said. "Short answer is I'm here because your father threatened me with involuntary recall to active duty if I refused, and so, this seemed the path of least resistance."

She flushed and looked at her hands.

"Wait, who's your father, Lieutenant Ryan?" Caspar's eyes went wide. "Oh my God, are you kidding me? Ryan as in—"

"Doesn't matter," Katie said, more abruptly than she intended. "We're not here to talk about my paternity. All banter aside, Dr. Jones, how much do you know about the situation here?"

Jones smiled and shrugged off his sports coat, as if signaling he was ready to get to work. "From what I understand, you're on the hunt for a Russian submarine, and that just so happens to be an area where I have considerable expertise and experience."

"So . . ." Katie said, eyeing him. "You're a former submarine officer, I'm guessing?"

"Submarines, yes. But not an officer. I was a sonarman in a previous life. In fact, my name might have cropped up in stories your dad's told you over the years."

"My dad doesn't tell many stories," she said, cutting a look at IS2 Caspar and praying Jones would stop bringing her dad up. "But I'd love to hear some of yours, Dr. Jones, and learn what you can do to help us find a particularly troublesome, missing Russian submarine."

"Then you're in luck because finding missing Russian submarines is my speciality," he said. "Oh, and since we'll be working closely together, you can drop the 'Doctor.' My friends call me Jonesy."

"All right, Jonesy," Katie said. "IS2 Caspar will show you where to stow your gear, and then we can meet the *Ford's* intelligence officer, Lieutenant Commander Kumari."

"Stowing my gear is not the priority. Finding this Russian sub is. How about we leave my bag and go meet the intel boss so we can get to work?"

"Great," she said and decided she liked this guy. "But first we should probably find a SCIF and bring you up to speed."

"Jones is cleared TS/SCI," Caspar said, reading her mind.

"And already fully read in," Jonesy added.

"Okay, well, there's been at least one new development while you were en route." She leaned in and whispered, "A SEAL team is spinning up to hit a Russian spy ship that's interrogating the mid-Atlantic DASH node. We're about to poke the bear."

"Of course we are," Jonesy said and shook his head. "Because that's what you Ryans do best."

28

C lark hauled in his end of the fishing net, working in tandem with the Russian fishing boat captain, who he'd come to like and respect during the dangerous infil on the White Sea. Clark's gloved hands were freezing from the cold water, but the heavy roll-neck wool sweater he wore was at least keeping his core temperature toasty.

At least until I jump in the water.

After a half dozen hand-over-hand tugs, the job was done, and he nodded to the burly, bearded Russian. They'd not caught any fish, but they hadn't been trying to, either. Ivan's job had been to get Clark and his team this far into the White Sea. The next phase of the infiltration would be more dangerous. He walked forward and stood beside the wooden mast, which could add sail power to the family-owned fishing boat for those times when the engine needed repairs or the cost of fuel was simply out of reach. The money the Russian fisherman and his wife would make for risking his life on this particular voyage would keep them in boat fuel for quite some time.

Clark steadied a shoulder against the mast and pulled out an
infrared night-vision monocle and began a slow and steady, three-
hundred-and-sixty-degree scan, searching the horizon for lights
and patrol craft. Fortunately, the only other vessel he saw was the
Sadovsk, a much larger fishing boat that crept along just north of
them. Satisfied they could make the transfer, he slipped the monocle back into the baggy canvas pants he wore and pulled out a
small flashlight. He waited until the *Sadovsk* was nearly abeam
before signaling—three short followed by two long flashes. The
sound of the *Sadovsk*'s engines going to neutral and then shutting
down served as his acknowledgment. The squeal of the winches
and the splash of nets being let out from the pickup vessel's twin
outriggers that followed meant that it was time to go.

He hustled belowdecks, where the other three members of his
team waited—Ding, Midas Jankowski, and Adara Sherman. On
the outside they were dressed like Russian fishermen, but underneath they wore wetsuits and held fins and dive masks at the ready.
Adara, who had her hair back in a tight stub of a ponytail, gave him
a solemn nod, but none of them looked particularly excited for the
part that came next.

"How cold's the water?" Ding asked.

"Freezing," Clark said, tugging the zipper up to the neck on the
wetsuit beneath his sweater. "We'll only be in the drink for a few
minutes, but without dry suits there's still risk of hypothermia, so
stay together and swim directly to the *Sadovsk*. They have a net
out on the port side. It's a short climb up, but easy to get tangled
and harder when your muscles are cold and sluggish. Stay beside
your swim buddy and keep an eye on them."

The guidance was a good general reminder, but more for Adara
than Ding and Midas. Adara was as tough as nails, but this evolution was a bit outside of her wheelhouse. Midas, a former Special
Forces colonel, wouldn't be bothered by the cold. Hell, the man

wasn't bothered by anything. As for Ding, well, if given the choice, he'd trade this arctic evolution for a jungle op any day of the week.

"Cold water is the reason I didn't become a Navy SEAL," she grumbled, the comment tongue-in-cheek.

"Well, now's your chance," Clark said, thinking back on his grueling time in the teams—the best and worst years of his life.

"We need to get moving," Ding said. "The *Sadovsk* can only loiter alongside for a few minutes without raising suspicion if anyone is watching."

"If anyone is watching," Midas said, pulling the mask onto his face, "we're fucked already."

They stayed low as they came topside, Clark leading them aft, over the transom, and into the dark, frigid water. As his wetsuit filled with icy water, the cold instantly took his breath away. The few people who knew he'd once been a SEAL sometimes asked him if all that training made him immune to the cold. As his teeth chattered, he reminded himself that the opposite was his truth. BUD/S and all his later time in the teams had made him despise the cold.

He finned quickly while checking periodically to make sure his assigned swim buddy, Adara, was still with him. She kept pace, side by side, showing no overt effects of fatigue or cold. The woman was a badass, Trident or not. By the time they reached the net, Clark's hands were trembling and his fingers had gone numb. Despite the cold sapping his strength and dexterity, he was still able to haul himself up the net and roll over the gunwale onto the deck of the fishing trawler. He landed in a deep crouch as Adara dropped in beside him, breathing heavily. A moment later Midas slipped nearly silently over the rail, landing in a kneeling position, a pistol already up in his hand.

"Holy shit it's cold," Ding said, teeth chattering, arriving last onto the deck.

A Russian man with thick, powerful arms stepped out of shadows.

"Come, come," he said in heavily accented English. "We go below. Quickly."

Legs trembling and cramping from the cold, Clark followed the fisherman into the boat's main cabin. The warmth from the twin space heaters hit him and he let out a sigh of relief.

"Take off water clothes. Here, please to take off," their escort said, handing each of them a large, but rough, towel.

They stripped off their clothes and then their wetsuits, each wearing black formfitting Under Armour pants and T-shirts underneath. A middle-aged Russian at the helm, cigarette dangling from his lips, looked them over head to toe—then shrugged, apparently not impressed by America's top superspies.

"Come, come," the first Russian said and ushered them to the stairs leading belowdecks.

On reaching the bottom of the steps, a familiar, booming Russian voice as warm as the space heaters that had greeted Clark. "John!"

Dima Aslanov, their host, wrapped Clark in a back-arching bear hug that lifted Clark's feet literally off the floor. Clark grunted as the Russian fisherman with the body of a bear set him down and stepped back to arm's-length reach to get a look at him.

"It's good to see you, too," Clark said, wiggling his arms to get the blood flowing.

"You look good, John," Dima said. "How are you, my friend?"

"Cold. I'm too old for this shit," Clark said, toweling the cold salt water out of his hair. "Swimming in the Arctic and climbing a fishing net with frozen fingers is a young man's game."

Dima replied with a big, barking laugh, and turned his attention to Clark's teammates. "This man is Peter Pan, yes? Never does he age, yet still he complains."

"He complains *a lot* these days," Ding said with a sly grin.

"That's because you guys give me a lot to complain about," Clark said, dishing it back. He gestured to their Russian host. "These days, Dima is a fisherman, but once he was a great warrior. And he is a very old friend of mine."

"And friend to anyone who would do for my family what you did, John," Dima said with a deferential nod.

Clark introduced his teammates by first names only as they dried off and accepted the stacks of clothes provided by Dima's wife, Merda, who'd been waiting in the adjacent compartment.

"When do we dock in Arkhangelsk?" Clark asked.

"A few more hours of fishing and then we head in," Dima said. "We will arrive while it is still dark, and the docks will be mostly empty. I have arranged for your stay at a house we use for seasonal workers."

"Good. What about transportation?"

"Yes, a truck as you requested, older model, but reliable."

"And the rest?"

"I have procured the weapons you requested, but I am very curious to know why you need GRU uniforms," Dima said. "They were not easy to obtain, especially on short notice, but I have done it."

"Thank you, but as far as the reason why . . . It's best you don't know," Clark said.

Dima laughed. "'Best not to know' is the Russian motto."

They changed into the dry clothes as Merda prepared and handed each of them a mug of hot tea and a glass of cold vodka.

"You will rest in the crew racks up forward," Dima said, gripping the handrail of the ladder leading up to the pilothouse. "Get some sleep while you can. Whatever you are planning, my friend, I am imagining you will need it. I will wake you thirty minutes before docking."

And with that Dima was gone, and Merda disappeared into what Clark imagined was either an office or galley.

"Not sure about getting any sleep," Midas said, holding Clark's eyes. "Seems a little risky."

"This isn't the first time I've put my life in Dima's hands. I can promise you we're safe, but do whatever makes you comfortable," Clark said.

Midas sniffed, unconvinced, it seemed.

Clark, for his part, definitely planned to hit the rack. Sleep was a weapon, and his tired body could use every minute of shut-eye he could get. But first, one more thing to do.

He picked up the shot of Russian vodka, lifted it to his lips, and said, "*Nu, poehali!*"

29

Special Operations senior chief Max Harden stared out the cockpit window of the sleek CCM Mk1 fast boat as it zipped across the Atlantic at forty-five knots.

"Want me to slow it down?" the SWCC (special warfare combat crewman) pilot at the helm asked him with a sideways glance.

Harden checked the Suunto watch on his left wrist, then looked at the moving map display beside the helm. He noted the position of the target, their position, and the magenta line predicting their course and time to the checkpoint, and the green triangle that was Ghost Two—the fast boat running parallel and carrying the other half of their twelve-man assault force.

"Nah," he said. "This new boat is quiet as hell. No chance they hear us until we're inside a half mile—maybe not even then."

The SWCC senior chief gave Harden a nod. "Roger that. I'll keep the pedal to the metal."

"Do you like this better than the Mark V?" he asked, referring to the recently retired previous-generation multi-mission platform.

"Better engines, better handling, better stealth . . . But I'm still gonna need spine surgery before I retire," the SWCC said, running a gloved hand through his long, sandy-blond hair, which made him look more like a surfer than a badass operator.

"I hear ya," Harden said, using his legs to augment his shock-absorbing seat as the double-walled aluminum V-hull carved a path through the surface chop. Tonight's infil wasn't too bad, but in rough seas, going fast in a fast boat was murder on the body.

"She is whisper-ass quiet, though, huh?" Sandy said.

That was for sure. A water jet propulsion design ran the boat so quietly that the water on the hull was louder than the engine.

Harden knew "Sandy" from way back when the boat driver was with Grey Squadron, the SWCC team supporting the secretive Tier One SEAL team from Joint Special Operations Command. Harden had rotated to Group Ten for a three-year stint, but Sandy was still driving when Harden got back to the unit last year. The Tier One could be like that—people either stuck around or eventually found a way back. There was an officer in the med shop Harden knew—a former enlisted SEAL 18 Delta and sniper who'd gone to PA school and earned a commission—but instead of moving on to do other things, he'd transferred back and been at the Tier One for all but two of the last eighteen years.

Harden looked at the ETT—estimated time to target—display, which read ten minutes. In this case, the "target" was not the *Finitor*, but a waypoint a mile from the Russian spy vessel where Harden and his team would be dropped to start their swim to the actual target.

"Ten minutes out," Harden announced in his boom mic, updating his five fellow SEALs in the boat.

"Perfect," Navy SEAL Chief Petty Officer Reed Johnson—the 18 Delta combat medic on the stick—said as he checked over his swim gear and weapons. "I'm finally dry and almost warm, so for sure let's get back in the water."

"Dude, how the hell did you get through BUD/S and then Green Team? You complain like a Long Island grandma," Billy Harper said with his thick Brooklyn accent.

Billy, who was also a chief, was one of the best breachers Harden had ever worked with. The Tier One was a command where a guy could pin on anchors and celebrate making chief one minute, and the next be told to empty the garbage. At JSOC, chiefs were still low men on the proverbial ladder.

"Complaining is my way of embracing the suck," Reed said and flipped "Billy the Kid," as he was nicknamed, the middle finger.

Reed was right, but that was the job.

The only easy day was yesterday.

"Twelve Tier One operators to take down a little research vessel with only sixteen heat sigs on it? Kinda overkill, if you ask me," said Owen "Del" Delacorte.

"That's the idea, Del," said Marty Rich, their team sniper. "We're trying to give them pause so they throw up their hands, bro. Not an ideal situation—these are Russian sailors in real life. Kind of a big deal if we show up and cap a bunch of Russians in international waters. Get it?"

"I get it," Del said with a shrug. "Just sayin'."

Harden, who'd been listening to the exchange, had already given the matter quite a bit of thought himself. A capture/kill mission against a bunch of terrorists was straightforward—you shoot who you need to shoot and black bag the rest. But the rules of engagement for this op were very different. He and his team had to board and secure the *Finitor* without bloodshed. Yes, they could return fire in self-defense, but killing even a single Russian sailor would create an international incident.

This is how wars get started, he thought as he swept the Copenhagen snuff from his lower lip and tossed it over the side. He removed his ball cap, stowed it in his kit, and pulled his wetsuit hood over his head, getting ready to go. Next, he began a reflexive check of his gear, hands moving with minds of their own across pistol, magazines, and his assault rifle, grenades, blowout kit, radio . . .

Personal inventory checks complete, he looked at the ETT and signaled Sandy with a flat hand moving up and down. The SWCC pilot pulled the twin throttles back, and the boat's twin 1250-horsepower engines fell quiet to barely a whisper.

After a few minutes at a quiet, low-speed cruise, they reached the waypoint and Sandy pulled the throttles to idle. Masks and fins in place, the six SEALs lined up on the gunwale.

"Olympia, Neptune One—we're Michelob," Harden reported softly into his mic.

"Roger, Neptune One—we show you Michelob," the operational coordinator back at their TOC, or tactical operations center, said. For tonight's op the SEALs were using the call sign Neptune and the TOC was designated Olympia.

After a pause, Dwight Merrell—the Navy SEAL known as "Annie"—chimed in: "Two is Michelob."

Harden had heard three different versions of the story that had led to Dwight being called Annie back in the day at SEAL Team 5—each more hysterical than the last. Annie, who was also a senior chief, led the other stick of SEALs who were riding on Ghost Two.

"Roger, Two," came the reply from Olympia. "Show you Michelob North."

Harden knew the command had satellite coverage monitoring them in real time, so the confirmation from the TOC team—who were working aboard the Sentinel-class Coast Guard cutter the *Lawrence O. Lawson*—meant they still had the all-important eyes in the sky. The *Lawson*, which was cruising to the near south, was serving as the head shed for the op, the comms relay station, and medevac platform. It also happened to house another six-man

team of SEALs in standby as a QRF, should things go bad. But in Harden's experience, the JMAU emergency surgical teams spent most of their time operating on bad guys, not SEALs.

Harden gave a thumbs-up and six SEALs rolled backward off the boat in unison. Cold salt water flooded his suit, chilling him instantly. It took time for his body heat to warm the water—from freezing to just cold enough to be bearable—and provide a thin layer of insulation that stopped the ocean from sapping all his heat. He kicked off their swim, finning powerfully toward the northeast, his right hand stretched out in front of him and his left bent at the elbow so he could monitor the moving map display on his left wrist. He left his night-vision goggles up, focusing only on the track, knowing that the men around him had his back. They moved almost silently through the ocean waves, predators on a stealthy approach to their unsuspecting prey.

It took less than ten minutes to cover the distance.

At a hundred yards out, Harden tipped his face out of the water to confirm that the *Finitor* was still at sea anchor and the readiness condition had not changed. The ship was definitely not underway and he couldn't perceive any activity. He raised a closed fist and stopped finning, just as Annie's voice came into his ear.

"Neptune Two is Budweiser."

"One is Budweiser," Harden replied.

"Olympia shows One and Two are Budweiser," Olympia came back. "Stand by."

He visualized his teammates from the Gold Squadron, who were manning the TOC, taking last looks at satellite and SIGINT feeds. He'd been there—stuck in a TOC on the radio supporting his brothers in the field—and he hated it.

The most helpless feeling in the world, Annie had called it, and Harden agreed.

He fished a scope out of his kit, selected "day," since the well-lit ship had plenty of lights on, and scanned the superstructure and deck as best he could from his low angle in the water. He concentrated the bulk of his scan on the rails of the one-hundred-seventy-five-foot target ship, but saw no standing or roving sentries. The only movement he observed was inside the well-lit bridge.

"Neptune Two, One, I hold no standing sentries or roving patrols from my pos."

"Roger, One," Annie said in his earpiece. "I hold two dudes at the stern having a smoke, but little else."

"Neptune, Olympia, we show tangos as follows: Five thermals in the bridge, plus one that appears to be outside on the rail just forward of the ladder well on the starboard side. Two thermals on the fantail near the winch. Four tangos appear sitting around a table just forward of midships—estimate this to be belowdecks in the crew lounge. We then show five static thermals in the aft, supine, so likely asleep in the crew quarters. Show one thermal in solo cabin, supine—guessing this is the captain in his stateroom. Only live video imagery is of the two figures at the stern, who do not appear to be armed, at least not openly."

"Neptune One, roger," Harden said.

"Two," Annie said, acknowledging the report using his call sign, as was their practice.

Harden finned gently, keeping his head just above the water to minimize the chance of being spotted by a lookout with binocs.

"Two, One," he said softly into his boom mic, pressing his push to talk on the shoulder of his kit. "We'll board amidships aft of the pilothouse and clear aft to the fantail. You mirror us, but stay low until we clear the tango on the catwalk aft of the bridge."

"Two, copy."

With any luck, the tango on the catwalk would wander back inside before it mattered. Anything forward of amidships would be a terrible spot to breach with so many thermals in the bridge, as

the pilothouse on the *Finitor* was located seventy-five percent forward in this design. Aft was crammed with superstructure and
heavy equipment and there were no aft sight lines from the bridge.

*If the asshole on the catwalk would just go away, it would make life
so much simpler.*

Harden signaled with a hand over his head and, with him at the
tip of the arrowhead formation, SEALs finned to the target. Minutes later, they bobbed in the swells alongside of the *Finitor*, finning
gently to avoid being slammed into the hull.

"One is Corona," he whispered and switched from PTT to VOX
on his radio.

"Check," Olympia said simply.

Moments later, Annie's voice called, "Corona," announcing that
the other six SEALs were in position on the opposite side of the
ship, ready to board.

"Roger, Two. The tango on the catwalk is now back inside,
which makes six tangos on the bridge. Two tangos are still manning
the stern, smoking and talking by the cable drum. The rest of the
tactical picture is unchanged."

"One, roger. Two, we'll infil together," Harden said.

"Two."

An instant later, Olympia gave them the green light. "Neptune,
you are go."

Harden nodded to Billy the Kid, who finned to the side of the
ship. The SEAL waited for a swell to lift him to the apex, reached
high, and locked an electromagnetic handle onto the metal hull.
The swell fell away, and for a moment Billy hung by one arm, then
he attached another electromagnetic handle. Harden watched as
his fellow SEAL scurried up the side of the ship like Spider-Man,
using the lockable handholds and special pads on his knees to "grip"
the outward-sloping hull. At the top, Billy secured his harness to
one of the locked handles and hung while he secured five other

handles with ropes that dropped back into the sea for his team-mates.

Harden and the four other SEALs removed their fins, which they secured to their calves in case they needed them later. The operator clipped a battery-powered, gear-driven ascender onto a rope, and fixed it with carabiners to the harnesses they wore under their kits. With a flick of the directional switch, and a squeeze on the ascender handle to control the rate of ascent, the motorized ascenders whisked them up the side of the ship, their booted feet walking quietly up the hull. Upon reaching the top, Harden peered onto the deck through the large two-foot-diameter porthole in the gunwale. He stuck his head through the hole cautiously, looked aft, then forward, then pulled his head back.

Having seen nothing of concern, he said, "One is clear."

"Two," acknowledged Annie, who Harden imagined was hanging on the other side.

Harden took a long, slow breath. This was the most dangerous part of any shipboard infil—coming over the rail. His attention, but more important, his hands, were fully engaged on getting over and onto the deck, making him unarmed and vulnerable during the transition.

He glanced at his teammates, getting a thumbs-up from each.

"Neptune, go," he said, giving both squads the green light to breach the deck.

Gripping the top of the gunwale, he heaved himself up, rolled over the rail, and dropped into a kneeling crouch. His custom assault rifle was in his hands, up, and scanning a heartbeat later. He could barely hear the other SEALs dropping in near unison behind him as he cleared aft along the rail. Seeing nothing, he continued to scan his sector, knowing his fellow operators had his back.

"Two is Coors," Annie reported, signifying his team had breached successfully on the opposite side of the boat.

"One is Coors," Harden said.

"One and Two, I show you both Coors," the TOC reported, knowing that neither squad could see the other because of the superstructure—aka "island"—between them.

Harden gestured with three fingers, pointing to Marty, Reed, and Special Operator Second-class Scott Todd, the junior SEAL on the stick. Then he chopped a hand forward toward the end of the island, where a switchback metal staircase rose from the deck level to give external access to the levels above. At the end of the chop, he closed his fist to complete the nonverbal order.

You three, position at the stairwell—hold and cover.

Then he chopped a hand aft and led Billy and Del toward the stern, where the two tangos by the cable drum were smoking.

Harden scanned over his rifle as he advanced, quick-stepping in a combat crouch. He was confident that Olympia had eyes clearing his path, but he was also experienced enough not to take anything for granted. Nothing was ever as it seemed in special operations. For example, the supine thermals Olympia had reported below-decks as sleeping in a bunk room could turn out to be tangos lying on the deck, ready in ambush. Satellites were great, but they didn't give a three-dimensional picture—even with advanced software that tried to account for the top-down view.

They passed what Harden guessed was the control shack for either the large deck crane or the winch and cable drum at the stern. Maybe this was where you controlled both. He held a fist up at the rear corner of the shack, took a knee, and peered around the edge.

Clear.

Back up—hand chop forward—and he passed his team under the orange lifeboat hanging from cables that held it taut to the launching device. He arrived at a short staircase, cleared left toward centerline, then silently ascended the eight steps to the raised stern deck. He moved swiftly around a large capstan and then to the edge of the raised superstructure supporting the massive cable drum.

He peered around it and spied the two men leaning casually over the stern rail looking out into the water, laughing, each with a cigarette in hand.

"One in position," he said, his voice barely a whisper, but augmented in the earpieces of his teammates.

"Two in position. Your count, bro."

Harden nodded. "Three . . . two . . . one . . ."

On the zero count, he rose and surged forward, feeling his teammates spread out beside him, and watching as Annie moved around the corner from the opposite side of the men at the railing. The tango closest to him dropped his cigarette at the sight of Annie and the other two armed SEALs moving in on him with green laser designators hovering on his chest. The tango facing Harden just froze, mouth open, eyes wide.

"Quietly, sit against the rail," Harden growled in Russian, and both men complied, not making a sound. "Hands above your head."

Again, the men complied, their hands shooting up while a wayward cigarette caught by the breeze tumbled overboard. Harden kept his weapon pointed squarely at the center of his target's face. Scott and Billy surged around him, and in seconds both seated Russians were bound to the railing with zip ties.

Harden looked over at Hernando "Hondo" Rodriguez, a SEAL breacher from Annie's stick.

"Security here," he said.

"Aye, boss," Rodriguez said and disappeared into the machinery bay, which was forward of the stern deck and cable drum. Inside the garage-like structure, he'd be shielded from view from the outside and above, but could keep an eye on the bound crewmen.

"Olympia, any movement?" Harden whispered.

"No change," Olympia replied.

Had there been movement below, he would split the two sticks and clear the bridge and belowdecks simultaneously. But since the Russians were making it easy, he'd err on the side of caution.

"Take the bridge together, then we move below," he said to Annie.

Annie moved back to the starboard rail, while Harden led his two SEALs forward along the port side. "Neptune Six," he called, releasing Marty as they moved. "Find your hide." A double click told him the team sniper had heard him and would find a perch from which to provide overwatch support for the remainder of the op.

In no time, Harden was back where he started, kneeling beside Del and Scott where he'd left them at the stairwell in cover.

"One, set."

"Two."

"Neptune Six is now Zeus," Marty announced, changing call signs and indicating he'd found a satisfactory spot from which to plink bad guys if needed—probably the crow's nest above the aft stack, as he'd suggested in the brief.

"Roger, Zeus," Harden replied, then gave the green light to both squads to secure the bridge. "Go, Two."

Harden and his four fellow SEALs moved like a fluid single-cell organism, each clearing their own sectors as they silently ascended the switchback metal stairs, the only sound his own breath in his augmented ears.

"No change—six tangos on the bridge," Olympia said with perfect timing as he approached the top landing of the stairwell. "As you breach, four tangos forward of the entry doors, one beside the port door, and one, center aft, appears to be seated."

He double-clicked his push to talk with his left hand, stepping up now onto the catwalk and dropping low so as not to be seen through the single round window at the top of the wooden door.

He then rose and pressed against the door outboard of the window. Two of his teammates—Billy and Scott—were crouched on a knee, low beneath the window, weapons leveled at the door. Reed and Del had stopped at positions on the ascent, Del at the switchback and Reed just below the catwalk on the second level, covering their six o'clock.

Twelve SEALs still seemed overkill for taking the bridge, but bringing overwhelming force made it less likely they would encounter resistance.

"Two, set," came Annie's call.

Harden reached slowly for the door handle as he whispered his count. "Three . . . two . . . one . . ."

On the zero beat, he pulled the door open, stepping back as he did to give a lane to his teammates behind him. Billy entered first, clearing right and immediately kicking the legs out from under the man by the door. Scott cleared left, Del surged forward, and Harden followed last, clearing center right as he hollered, "Hands up," in Russian.

Everyone on the bridge complied, hands shooting into the air, except for a man across from Harden, standing in the front starboard corner. Despite being dressed the part, this Russian was no sailor. He moved like an operator as he dropped to a knee and pulled a pistol in a single, fluid motion. Harden had a solution on the man, his red dot on the man's forehead, finger inside the trigger guard, as the Russian brought his pistol up.

Shit, he's going to shoot.

Driven by both instinct and experience, Harden shifted left as the Russian's pistol roared, the bullet tearing through the thick, angled glass of the bridge window behind him. No choice in the matter, he shifted his targeting dot to the shooter's right chest and fired.

The man screamed as the bullet tore through his upper torso

below the collarbone and a palm's width from the shoulder. Harden heard the clatter of the man's pistol as it fell to the deck. Annie was on the shooter instantly, forcing the Russian to the ground with a booted foot in the center of his back between the shoulder blades.

"Secure these assholes," Harden growled, acutely aware of the implications of having just shot a Russian national—even if the shooter was a member of the GRU or SVR operating under a NOC. "Damn it. Neptune Five to the bridge," he said, summoning his combat medic. "Got a tango down, need medical assist."

"Five. On my way," came the reply.

Harden's teammates worked in a flurry around him, and in seconds the bridge crew were secured with zip ties. He scanned their faces, looking for one that looked like it could belong to the ship's captain. Not finding anyone with command presence, he said, "Where's your captain?"

No one answered.

"I said, where is your captain?" he repeated, this time dragging his laser target designators across their chests for effect.

"Captain in stateroom," one of the Russians said in heavily accented English.

Harden knelt beside the Russian he'd shot, who had a crimson stain growing on his shirt. "What the hell, bro? Why take a shot when you had no chance?"

The man glowered at him, but his face was pale—maybe from shock, or maybe from fear, or maybe from both.

"Boss, we need to clear the crew spaces belowdecks ASAP," Annie said. "Someone might have heard the gunshots."

"Yep," Harden said. "And we need to secure the captain."

"Two from my stick can get the captain and bring him back here," Annie said. "The rest of us will clear belowdecks with you."

"Scott, you stay here and watch these yahoos," Harden said and did the math. With Rodriguez watching the guys aft and Marty in overwatch and the three they'd just assigned to secure the captain and the bridge, that left seven. He looked at Annie. "That leaves three and four, you comfortable with that?"

"How about we have Rodriguez make sure those two assholes on the stern are double secure and we use two teams of four," Annie suggested. "Those two at the stern were just sailors, but we had a shooter in the mix here. Maybe they've got some hitters belowdecks, too."

Harden agreed. The guy he'd shot was a pro, it seemed, so there were likely more. And if they'd lost the element of surprise . . .

"You're right, let's do that." He radioed Rodriguez the plan, then requested a sitrep from Olympia.

"Neptune, Olympia. No changes. Repeat, all the same. Crew lounge with four tangos, three seated at a table or workstation and the fourth standing at the rear of the room to your left as you breach. Bunk room still shows five supine tangos. No indication they've been alerted to your presence."

"Roger, copy all."

Minutes later, they'd formed up in two teams of four, Harden leading one team to hit the crew lounge, while Annie took his team to the bunk spaces aft. They moved swiftly and quietly, lethal instruments of violence of action, down the port ladder well. On reaching the bottom, Harden turned left, toward the bow. They shifted into diamond formation, Harden in the lead with two SEALs hugging the walls of the passageway and the fourth man covering their six.

They paused at a white-painted metal hatch, which instead of being dogged shut, hung open a few inches. Harden drifted left to the hinge side and crouched low below the round, ten-inch porthole in the middle. Rodriguez fell in behind him and gave his shoulder a squeeze to indicate he was set. Billy and his wingman set up on the opposite side of the passage and gave a curt nod to Harden, his weapon angled down at the deck at a forty-five.

Harden gave him a nod back, then indicated with hand signals to toss a flash-bang.

Billy pulled one from his kit.

"Two, call your breach," he whispered.

He didn't want the sound of the flash-bang to alert the sleeping men and make Annie's assault more dangerous.

"Stand by," Annie said and after a short hold reported, "Two, going . . . Now."

On that cue, Billy, who was gripping the flash-bang with his left hand, pressed the door open wide enough with his rifle and tossed the nonlethal grenade into the crew quarters.

Harden squeezed his eyes shut to protect his vision.

A dull *whump* followed—soft and painless in his protected ears, but deafening and disorienting for anyone in the space on the other side of the hatch. The smell of sulfur filled Harden's nostrils as he shoved the hatch open and breached in the lead. He moved in swiftly in a low combat crouch, using his laser target designator to intimidate and deter as much as he was to mark targets in the smoky room. More green lasers joined the fray, cutting swaths in the haze, as his teammates poured into the space. He cleared his left corner, then spun right to drop his laser designator on a figure he deemed as the highest threat—a Russian crouched by the coffee station with his hand on the butt of a gun in a holster on his belt.

"No," Harden shouted, his voice booming, as his laser settled on the man's forehead and his finger put tension on the trigger.

The Russian glowered at him, but moved his hand very slowly away from his weapon and then raised his hands in the air.

Harden held his position while the other three SEALs dragged three men from chairs, shoving them face-first onto the floor and pressing knees between their shoulder blades in preparation for cuffing. The armed Russian stared back at him, seemingly unintimidated by the glow of the target designator dancing on the center of his face. A second later, Billy pulled the man's pistol from its holster, forced the Russian to the ground, and flex-cuffed his hands like the others.

"What in the hell is this?" Rodriguez said, winking at Harden. "I thought this was supposed to be a drug-running vessel. But I don't see any drugs, just sophisticated electronics, boss."

"Looks Russian," Billy said, feigning shock and barely containing his own grin.

"One, Two, bunk room secure," Annie reported in Harden's ear.

"Check. Securing crew quarters now," he said.

"One, Seven, ship's captain has been secured and taken to the bridge," Scott reported.

"Roger that."

"One, looks like we have a problem. This crew is Russian," Annie said, playing along.

"Yeah, same here," Harden said, getting it all out there for the recording that would be made in the TOC of their comms. "This ain't no drug-running operation. Looks like we stumbled onto some sort of very sophisticated spy vessel—a Russian spy ship, from the look of things."

"I agree," Annie said.

"Olympia, this is Neptune One. Target vessel has been secured. We have one wounded tango who engaged us first and we returned fire—require CASEVAC. Be advised this appears to be a Russian spy vessel rather than a drug-running operation. Please advise."

He held the stare of the Russian still staring at him, now from the floor, where Billy stood over him with a boot in the center of his back.

"You will pay dearly for what you have done," the man said in clear, accented English. "We are a research vessel operating in international waters."

Harden smiled at the man.

"Well, we were told this was a drug-running ship. The DEA must have given us bad intel. But I am curious why you're flying a Cyprus flag. You are clearly not from Cyprus, as your crew speaks Russian. So, why is a Cyprus-flagged ship operating with Russian Navy aboard? That's a flagrant violation of international law."

"And so is espionage, ain't it, Senior Chief?" Rodriguez asked, having a little fun now that the danger was past.

"Yes, it is," Harden said.

"Neptune One, Olympia."

"Go for Neptune, Olympia," he said.

"Neptune, contain the crew without harm. CASEVAC for the wounded en route and will be on scene in minutes. Coast Guard vessel *Lawrence O. Lawson* will be on station in forty minutes. Conduct inventory of the *Finitor* to ensure no drugs are on board. Then release the ship to Coast Guard custody until we sort this out with the Pentagon."

"Copy all. Billy, get these guys secured in the crew mess after you search them. The Coast Guard will be here shortly. In the meantime, we're supposed to have a look around," he said and gave the glaring Russian a wink. "We'll start with their computers, then I say we take a look at what's connected to the submerged end of that cable hanging off the stern."

30

Katie made a quick scan to take the temperature of the assembled officers around the table, all of whom outranked her. The admiral, who sat at the head, wore an inscrutable neutral expression, one that flag officers all seemed to have mastered; she couldn't help but wonder if there was some secret mandatory school taught by Robert De Niro that O-7 selects were required to attend. He was flanked by the CAG on the left, whose face seemed stuck in a permanent scowl, and the much more likable and laid-back DCAG, Captain "Spacecamp" Huddleston, on the right. Down the line from Huddleston sat the *Ford*'s XO and CO. The former looked concerned, leaning in with elbows on the table, while the latter sipped casually at his coffee. Last but not least, Kumari, who sat beside Katie, looked a bit bedraggled as she ran the computer, putting slides of information recovered by the JSOC SEALs up on the big flat-screen TV for all to see.

"The op confirmed that the *Finitor* is a Russian spy boat," Kumari said. "The SEALs have inventoried state-of-the-art spy gear aboard, and we have positive identification of half the Russian Navy crew on board and at least one Russian GRU officer."

"I can't believe they shot him," the CAG grumbled. "I mean, what the hell? Hitting a Russian ship in international waters was provocative enough, but the damn SEALs had to go and shoot a Russian GRU officer as well? Are they trying to start World War Three?"

Don't do it, the voice of caution said in Katie's head. *Just let him ventilate.*

But when no one came to the SEALs' defense, her big mouth seemed to open without authorization from her brain.

"I'm sure they did their best to avoid casualties, sir, but the GRU officer fired," Katie said. "They managed to take the ship with only the single casualty, and no blue side wounded. I'd consider that a success."

"A success? Let's see if you still feel that way after the Russians respond in kind," the CAG said, glowering at her.

With great effort she didn't take the bait, and turned back to Kumari, who continued.

"Our cyber team is hacking into the recovered hard drives, but it's taking time. What we do know is that whatever piece of equipment they were towing was lost. When the maintenance team from the *Lawrence O. Lawson* got the cable drum working, they didn't find anything on the other end of the line . . ."

"But we confirmed they were directly over the DASH data hub and feeds?" the admiral asked.

"Yes, sir," Kumari said.

"So they were planning to sabotage our deepwater sonar network?" Spacecamp asked.

Kumari turned back to Katie.

"That is our working theory, sir," Katie said. "NSW has an EOD and salvage team en route to try and recover the device. It's possible the *Finitor* is a bottom-mapping platform, but they could also have been using a submersible with the capability to do more. We have to assume worst-case scenario for now, is our thinking."

"I agree," the admiral said.

"Well, good Lord," the CAG said. "Disrupting our sonar surveillance systems and comms could be prelude to a first strike. We need to know where that Russian submarine is."

"We need to know if she's carrying those Status-6 nuclear torpedoes," the XO added. "From what you briefed, Lieutenant Ryan, one of those things could be used to take out the entire strike group."

"Yes, sir," she said.

"Admiral, I recommend we spread the strike group out significantly in case that's what's on the Russians' minds," Captain Mackenzie, the *Ford* CO, said, his face tense with the rising gravity of the situation. She knew he'd flown hundreds of combat sorties in the war on terror as weapons systems officer in the Growlers. The man was no stranger to the gravity of war.

"We will," the admiral said. "We're also waiting to see what the White House and Pentagon think about raising the defense readiness condition. We need to stand firm and project confidence. Satellite imagery has the Russian carrier and battle group repositioning south. I assume in reaction to our hit on the *Finitor*. I've recommended repositioning the strike group north, right up against the Russian fleet."

"Why?" the CAG asked. "Sir, we have tensions quite high already. This hit on their ship will demand a response from the Russians. If they are steaming south, it means they're looking to pick a fight. Do we really need our jets challenged by Russian MiG-29K fighters on every sortie? And what if they have their new fifth-gen fighters aboard?"

"The Checkmate fighter is still a prototype and only two Felons are operational, and those are not carrier-capable," Kumari said.

The CAG turned on her, red-faced. "Yeah, well, you intel weenies said the *Belgorod* was in development and the Status-6 was just a propaganda tool, so screw your reassurances. We're inviting a mishap that could drive us into a shooting war in a blink."

"I get it, Marty," the admiral said. "But if these nuclear torpedoes are aboard the *Belgorod* and are meant to be used against Strike Group 12, then having our carrier in close proximity to theirs is the best way to give them pause. I imagine the Russian admirals are less inclined to fire a nuke torpedo if their own fleet is in the blast area and at risk of the fallout."

"Makes sense," Mackenzie said.

"Where is the *Belgorod*, Lieutenant Ryan?" the admiral asked. "And how close are we to finding it?"

Katie took a moment to choose her words. "Sir, we're waiting to hear from the *Indiana* as well as the *Washington*. Both are hunting the *Belgorod*, but we have no comms until they come up to share data. They could be tracking her, for all we know, but submarines on mission only transmit when it's absolutely necessary, otherwise they compromise their stealth."

"These are two of the best crews in the submarine force," the admiral said. "If the *Belgorod* can be found, I'm confident they'll find her."

"But what if they don't?" Sarah Williams, the *Ford*'s XO, asked, her arms crossed over her green flight suit.

Everyone turned to look at her, and the question hung in the air.

"In that case, we have to pray that the worst-case scenario we're all concerned about is simply that," Admiral Kiplinger said at last, "and the Russians are just flexing their muscles a bit and nothing more."

The XO nodded.

What else could be said? Modern submarines operating in the world's oceans did so with absolute impunity, because that was what they were designed to do. Subs like the *Belgorod* were not meant to be found, and that's why it was such a terrifying adversary.

"All right," the admiral said, his tone suggesting they were done. "We meet back here in twelve hours, or sooner if new information warrants." He rose. "In the meantime, we should expect the Russians to begin harassing our flight operations and buzzing our damn ships as soon as they're in range. Brief your people to keep cool heads and not do anything stupid. Naval Special Warfare has already poked the bear. Let's be careful we don't do the same."

Everyone stood, Katie included, and the senior officers shuffled out the door of the SCIF.

"I need you to reach out to your contacts at ODNI and wherever else," Kumari said. "I'll work with Dr. Jones on plans for how our surface assets can contribute to the hunt for the *Belgorod*."

"I'll get with Captain Ferguson and our connections at ODNI right away," Katie said.

"Good," Kumari said, then sighed and held Katie's eyes. "We're running out of time. And I'm gonna be honest—this whole thing scares the hell out of me."

Katie clenched her jaw.

Me too.

31

The phone on SecState Scott Adler's desk chirped and he pressed the intercom button, a smile turning up at the corners of his mouth.

"Yes, Elizabeth?"

"Mr. Secretary, Russian ambassador Darmatov is here, sir."

"Thank you, Elizabeth," he said, grinning ear to ear. He took a sip of his Earl Grey tea. "Please send him in."

He knew he shouldn't be enjoying this as much as he was. Hell, the stakes of the game they were playing were actually quite high. The Russian Northern Fleet was already repositioning south, closing aggressively on the *Ford* strike group. Not to be intimidated, the *Ford* was responding in kind, pushing north to intercept the Russian fleet. The response had been predictable, with aggressive harassment by Russian aircraft of U.S. patrols. There had already been one near miss this morning as a Russian fighter buzzed a Seahawk helicopter crew. Tensions were danger-high in the North Atlantic. His objective for this meeting was not to stoke the fire, but to gain the upper hand in a way that perhaps gave everyone pause.

They needed the Russians to take a slow breath and back off. Wars too often started by mistakes on the front lines.

The door opened and the tall, flabby, bald-headed man who served as the Russian ambassador to the United States entered, his face set with well-rehearsed indignation. Adler knew better than to underestimate the man on appearances. He'd been handpicked by President Yermilov himself, and Adler had seen firsthand the cunning and aggressive brand of diplomacy Sergey Darmatov was capable of. The looming conversation might not be actual combat, but it was a very high-stakes chess match, the outcome of which could easily open the door to war.

He stood and extended his hand across his desk. "Sergey, it is a pleasure as always. How can I be of assistance? Your office said it was most urgent, but I must confess, I am very busy this morning."

The Russian ambassador ignored his outstretched hand and took a seat in one of the two antique Elizabethan-style chairs in front of the desk, smoothing his slacks as he did.

"I think we must both make time in our busy schedules for this conversation, Mr. Secretary. You know that a military operation against a Russian vessel in international waters is an overt act of war. Is that your government's intention, to go to war with Russia?"

A warning salvo right out of the gate . . . Darmatov isn't messing around.

Adler's smile went wooden, and he took a seat, crossing his legs at the knee and reaching for his tea.

"I'm sorry, Ambassador Darmatov," he said, switching to the more formal address, despite having shared dinner and drinks with this man on several occasions. Diplomatic sparring was an odd beast. Darmatov was usually measured and reasonable—but maybe he had different marching orders today. "I'm afraid you have me at a disadvantage. I have no idea what it is you are referring to." He set his tea down. "What happened that has you so upset?"

Darmatov shot him a dirty look, his double chin vibrating.

"You want to play games, I see. Very well. My country demands a response to the illegal military action against our research vessel conducting peaceful, oceanographic research in international waters. We consider this assault to be an act of war and demand the immediate return of our civilian sailors and the privately owned research vessel."

"Ah, now I understand," Adler said, still smiling, but his eyes hardening. He leaned forward, placing his elbows on his desk and holding the man's eyes. "I was confused, I think, because you referred to it as a Russian vessel."

"You know full well—"

"We do know full well, Sergey," he said, cutting the man off. "We know full well that a Cyprus-flagged vessel was operating off the American coast. This very ship has been documented by our Coast Guard conducting operations of a questionable nature off the mid-Atlantic states, as well as in the vicinity of Kings Bay in Georgia, Naval Air Station Key West, and even in the Gulf of Mexico. It has been placed on a watch list by our Drug Enforcement Administration as a probable drug-smuggling platform. I don't have to tell you, Sergey, that we are stepping up our battle against the drug cartels who pour deadly, illicit drugs into our country. We reserve the right to protect our citizens from this scourge, and we conducted a counter-narcotics operation on the vessel you are referring to—the *Finitor,* I believe."

"You are claiming—"

"I am *telling,* Sergey. It's all documented."

"But once you boarded the vessel you knew . . ." Darmatov started to say, but stopped, his voice having lost its hard edge.

"Indeed," Adler said, leaning back in his chair and making a little steeple with his fingers, elbows on the armrests of the high-back leather chair. "Imagine the surprise of our counter-narcotics team upon boarding to discover that the *Finitor* was not a drug-smuggling platform parading as a Cyprus-flagged vessel. That it was actually a Russian spy vessel conducting sabotage operations of American property while operating under a false flag. Imagine President Ryan's dismay upon learning the crew aboard the *Finitor* were not drug runners but, in fact, Russian Navy personnel, commanded by a Russian naval officer, and with additional crew identified as members of the Russian military's intelligence apparatus. Imagine the conversations that unfolded in the Situation Room . . . *once we knew.*"

Darmatov shifted uncomfortably in his seat. "The United States regularly conducts spying operations in the Black Sea—"

"We're not talking about our well-publicized peacekeeping patrols in the Black Sea," Adler said and slammed a hand on his desk, allowing his face to cloud with anger. "We're talking about the *Finitor.* We caught you, Mr. Ambassador, caught you in the act . . . Conducting espionage and potential sabotage operations against the United States. A Russian spy ship, operating near sensitive communications and other equipment maintained by the United States for the defense of our East Coast, must certainly be viewed as an act of war and a prelude to a first strike against our Atlantic fleet."

"What? That's ridiculous, Mr. Secretary. No sabotage was conducted."

"The *Finitor* was operating something off a winch cable, a device that was lost, but that we have every intention of recovering."

Darmatov narrowed his eyes. He hadn't considered that possibility, apparently, and didn't like it.

Instead of letting the man off the hook, Adler decided to see how far he could push before getting the reaction he was looking for.

"Why is your Northern Fleet repositioning south into the North Atlantic? Is Russia preparing for war with America?"

Darmatov swallowed and Adler saw a flash of something new in the man's eyes.

"It is dangerous to use such rhetoric, Mr. Secretary. Words matter," Darmatov said.

"And so do actions, Mr. Ambassador. Why has your fleet suspended its Arctic exercise and steamed south? How can we not view this as an act of aggression?"

"It is in response to your illegal military operation against our vessel. You should advise your President that detaining the crew of the *Finitor* can also be interpreted as an act of war. So I ask you the same question in reverse—is America preparing for war with Russia?"

"War is the last thing we want, Mr. Ambassador. We would prefer a diplomatic solution—which is why you and I are talking. To that end, a public apology and admission of guilt from the Kremlin over this incident would demonstrate your government's desire to de-escalate. We would respond to said apology by releasing your spies, Russian Navy crew, and vessel. But a failure to de-escalate will be met with a very different response." He leaned in now, eyes narrow. "Sergey, I should tell you that President Ryan does not fuck around when it comes to safeguarding the United States of America. Your fleet needs to back off."

The Russian ambassador sat red-faced, staring back at him, but said nothing.

Adler reclined in his chair, letting out a slow breath, as if trying to rein in his emotions. "President Ryan expects an official response from the Kremlin within the next six hours. The nature of that official response will factor heavily into the drafting of our own statement, which the Secretary of Defense Burgess will make later this afternoon."

"Mr. Secretary, I know nothing about the espionage operations that you are accusing Russia of conducting, but I will pass along this information to my superiors in the Kremlin."

"See that you do. With all that is going on in the Atlantic today, I'm afraid I have other pressing matters to attend to. Six hours, Mr. Ambassador. Good day."

He made a show of shifting his chair forward and opening a leather folder and examining what was inside it.

"Good day, Mr. Secretary," Darmatov said, rising and heading for the door.

Adler resisted the urge to look up.

He'd achieved the upper hand in the short meeting, but he was no longer enjoying himself. Because the truth was, the *Finitor*'s activities very well could be a prelude to war. The Russian Arctic "exercise" no longer looked like an exercise, as the bulk of the Northern Fleet was steaming south toward the *Ford*, the Russian submarine the *Belgorod* had not yet been found, and DNI Foley was reporting chaos that might represent a coup inside the Kremlin and the various Russian intelligence agencies. He'd chosen *not* to broach the last two topics . . . this time.

Adler glanced at the closed door.

What if we're at war already and we just don't recognize it?

Darmatov had played his role flawlessly, but there'd been a moment when he cracked. It had been fleeting, but Adler had seen a look.

A look of surprise.

A look of fear.

He hoped DNI Foley had covert operations in the works to gain actionable intelligence before it was too late. There were simply too many unknowns. If there was one thing he'd learned during his tenure as secretary of state, it was that fear and paranoia flourish in uncertainty. He waited a few beats, then pressed the call button on the intercom of his phone.

"Yes, Mr. Secretary?"

"Elizabeth, I need you to schedule a call with the President," he said, but then reconsidered. "Actually, I'm going to head to the White House. Get my detail together and let the chief of staff know I'm en route to brief the President on my meeting with the Russian ambassador."

"Yes, Mr. Secretary."

He closed the empty leather folder on his desk and let out a long sigh.

The shit was about to hit the fan.

32

A knock on his stateroom door caused Konstantin to look up from his desk.

"Come," he said, hoping the knock would be the messenger returning with his tea service.

It was not.

"Captain, we just received a confidential sitrep that impacts our tasking," his communications officer, Captain Lieutenant Blok, said, standing in the doorway.

Konstantin looked at the monitor mounted on the wall beside his rack, which live-streamed the view from the periscope's camera. A steel-blue roller washed over the lens momentarily, then cleared.

"Why are we still at PD? I told the conning officer to quickly get the broadcast and go deep."

"We're downloading a data package. It appears to be quite large and related to this message," Blok said and waved the brown folder in his hand for emphasis.

"Come in and shut the door."

Blok did as instructed, then handed Konstantin the decrypted message from the folder.

"Who else has read this?" he asked after he'd finished reading it.

"Only you and me, sir."

"Are you positive the radioman who downloaded the traffic and printed the message did not review this?"

"It is my policy that I am present in the radio room for all excursions to the surface. I alone handle the confidential traffic."

"Good," Konstantin said. "Find Stepanov and tell him to report to my stateroom."

"Aye, Captain," Blok said.

"And Lieutenant . . ."

"Sir?"

"Do not discuss this with the other officers."

"Never, sir," Blok said with a stoic nod and shut the door.

Konstantin reread the message, then took a long, deep breath to calm his mind and look for an opportunity in this wrinkle. According to the sitrep, the *Finitor* had been seized by the American Navy while conducting high-resolution bottom mapping of the mid-Atlantic DASH network's primary data node. This latest development did not bode well for the *Belgorod* and his plans.

When his first officer, Captain Second Rank Yuri Stepanov, arrived moments later, he handed the man the printout.

"What is this?" Stepanov said.

"Just read it."

The first officer did, and when he was finished, he looked up and met Konstantin's eyes. "This came in on the most recent broadcast, I assume?"

Konstantin nodded.

"Can we trust this information?"

"I don't see any embedded code words that would lead me to believe otherwise. Do you?"

"No, sir. It looks authentic," Stepanov said. "If the Americans truly boarded the *Finitor*, we must assume it was a military operation and the intervention was intended to prevent the *Finitor* from completing its mission."

"Northern Command is transmitting a large data package as we speak. They would not do this unless the *Finitor* was able to obtain the critical data we need to complete our tasking. The Americans certainly did their best to intercede, but it appears they intervened too late," Konstantin said.

"Sir, even if the *Finitor* completed the bottom mapping, the gambit is up. We have to assume the Americans know our plans to sabotage the node."

"Not necessarily, Yuri," Konstantin said with a smile. "All they know is that the *Finitor* was mapping the seafloor bottom."

Stepanov looked at him with open-mouthed incredulity. "Mapping the seafloor at the exact location of their mid-Atlantic data hub for their top secret, second-generation SOSUS array!"

"*Da*, but they don't know about our mission. They still think we're in the Barents Sea," Konstantin said, waving his hand dismissively.

"But, Captain, the American fleet is present in the area. If we go there, we'll be walking into a trap."

"Maybe . . . Maybe not." When Stepanov didn't respond, Konstantin said, "Covert, deep submersible operations are what this vessel was designed to do. Correct?"

"Yes, Captain, I know, but maybe it would be wise to avoid this area. I say forget the sabotage, we change course and proceed to the launch coordinates. The Status-6 is quiet. They will not find it in time."

"*Nyet*," Konstantin said. "Did you not do your reading? This new system is very advanced. It utilizes both active and passive sonar to locate and track submerged targets. The plotted track is over nine hundred kilometers. We must assume they *will* find it, because now they are looking. That is the cruel irony of our situation. Had the Americans not intercepted the *Finitor*, I would have risked the launch—after all, it is a very big ocean—but now they are on alert. The only way to avoid detection is to cripple this system before we launch."

"But, Captain, we'll be walking into a trap. They will be waiting for us at the data node."

"If I didn't know better, I might think you are afraid of the Americans."

At this comment, Stepanov cleared his throat and stood up a little straighter. "No, sir, I was just presenting you with options to consider. I will support whatever decision you make."

"I know you will, Yuri," he said, just as an acute burning pain beneath his rib cage flared.

"Captain, do you want me to fetch the ship's doctor?"

"*Nyet*," he said, doing his damnedest not to buckle over. "Go to the conn and supervise. Every second we're at periscope depth we are vulnerable. The second the download is complete, take us deep."

"Yes, Captain," Stepanov said and promptly left.

The moment his stateroom door shut, Konstantin gasped and let out a guttural moan. The flares were progressively getting worse. This one had practically taken his breath away. Hunching at the waist, he shuffled from his chair to his rack and curled up into the fetal position on his left side, which was the only position that seemed to ease the agony. He lay there, counting the minutes, until finally the pain began to ebb.

A knock shook his stateroom door inside the frame.

"Not now," he barked and felt his rack begin to tilt as the *Belgorod* nosed down.

"Captain, the dataset was downloaded successfully, the ship is going deep," Stepanov said, speaking loud enough to be heard through the door.

Konstantin didn't answer.

"If you need me, I'll be in my stateroom, Captain."

"Very well," he said, his voice more croak than speech.

Stepanov and Tarasov were the only members of the crew who knew about Konstantin's "condition." He trusted both men to keep his secret to the end, but for entirely different reasons. In the event he became physically unable to fulfill his duties as captain, as the first officer, Stepanov would assume command of the submarine. Whether Konstantin would be *ready* to delegate his authority when the time came was another matter altogether. Ultimately, he'd decided that it was better that Stepanov respect and want to please him than feel suspicious and resentful for being kept in the dark.

On the flip side, he'd told Tarasov the truth out of necessity. The ship's engineer was a co-conspirator—one of three men who knew the true nature of their operation. As far as the rest of the wardroom and crew were concerned, the Poseidon torpedo they intended to launch was the UUV variant without a nuclear warhead. Only Tarasov, Blok, and the original weapons officer were part of the inner circle who knew the deadly, world-changing agenda. But with the weapons officer replaced by Morozov at the last minute, everything had become immensely more complicated.

The original plan had been simple—the weapons officer would alter the documentation to swap a nuclear variant for a conventional variant. When the Poseidon was launched, not even Stepanov would suspect what they'd done. The crew would not discover the truth until after the nuke had detonated and it was too late to do anything about it. That, however, was no longer possible.

Morozov was a detail-oriented and by-the-book type of officer. He'd been present when the weapons were loaded and documented everything with meticulous precision. The *Belgorod* carried six Poseidon torpedoes—two equipped with nuclear warheads, two equipped with conventional ordinance, and two UUV deep-diving drone variants. Due to their massive size and weight, they were loaded directly into the *Belgorod*'s large-diameter tubes in the Sevmash Shipyard, where they would be stowed indefinitely or until such time they were ordered to be fired. Not only did Morozov personally oversee the loading of each weapon, but he had the serial numbers and tube locations memorized. In addition, he'd posted this information on a status board at the weapons launch control panel and physically marked the tubes with colored hanging tags as a visual safety reminder to all. Morozov was exactly the kind of naval officer the world deserved to have in charge of nuclear weapons.

And exactly the wrong kind of officer Konstantin needed to help him execute this act of defiance that would upend the world order. He and the engineer had a backup plan, but it required a good measure of subterfuge and would be much harder to pull off without a mutiny.

Konstantin sat up on his rack and exhaled a shaky breath.

It is time.

With the pain having subsided enough that he could talk, he pulled the telephone handset from the wall cradle and rang the conn.

"This is the conning officer," the voice said on the other end of the line.

"Conning officer, have the quartermaster calculate a new course at fifteen knots to the following location," he said and read off the latitude and longitude of the *Finitor*'s last position in the North Atlantic.

"Aye, Captain," the conning officer said.

"Tell him to plot a course that takes advantage of any and all bathymetric difficulties, which will mask our presence and minimize our chance of being detected . . . The game is on, conning officer. Rig the ship for silent running."

33

C lark sat in the passenger seat of the absurdly bright orange van, scratching at his neck. He'd never been a coat and tie guy. The stiff collar and pressed shirt he wore with his black suit and tie were driving him crazy. To make matters worse, he'd shaved for the first time in days, and with a cheap plastic razor at that, and had nicked himself in a half dozen places. He wasn't worried about being spotted in the bright orange van. In fact, he wanted to be seen—because his two teammates were dressed in Russian military uniforms with patches indicating they were with Russian Special Forces. That, combined with his suit, which screamed GRU, would intimidate anyone with the guts to approach them.

He listened via the micro earbud transceiver in his left ear as Adara—who was serving as their honey trap for the op—talked with perfect Russian. Her mark was Vasili Popov, the Russian engineer and Sevmash Shipyard Status-6 program manager whose name VICAR had given his life to share with Clark in Warsaw. Clark and his team had been forced to work quickly, but they'd managed to learn a few useful things about the man that had guided their approach.

Popov frequented the Moloko Restaurant after work, usually ordering the stroganoff and having a few drinks before retiring to his small apartment for the night. He was married, but his wife and two kids lived in St. Petersburg. Certainly, the attention of a woman as attractive as Adara would be a rare treat in a town as remote and industrial as Severodvinsk.

Clark couldn't help but shake his head as he eavesdropped on the cringeworthy conversation.

"If you're looking for stroganoff, you've come to the right place," Popov said. "The fine dining options are severely limited in Severodvinsk. We don't see women as beautiful as you here often."

"You are too kind," she said, and Clark could almost picture her flashing Popov a coy smile while she tried not to gag.

"Are you dining alone tonight? If you are, perhaps you would care to join me? I've ordered a plate of stroganoff. We could share it and order another entrée of your choosing."

"That sounds lovely, thank you."

"Here, let me get your chair for you . . ."

Clark looked over at Midas, whose eyes sparkled with amusement. "She's got him hook, line, and sinker."

"Pulling off a honey trap is way easier when you're hot," Ding said from the back, tugging at the coarse fabric of his military uniform.

"Don't think for a second she's actually enjoying herself," Midas said. "Cozying up to this douche wasn't the kind of work she signed on for when she joined The Campus."

That was only half true. Recruiting assets and collecting human intelligence *was* a dance of seduction, even when sex wasn't involved.

Clark was following Adara's conversation in Russian with Popov better than expected. Maybe it was being in Russia, maybe it was reconnecting with Dima after all these years, but his Russian-language skills had just come pouring back to him. Still, he would leave most of the talking to others. Clark's role was to be intimidating.

And that's something I'm still very good at.

"*Da*, but so boring," Adara was saying. "I am here with the inspection team from Polyarnyy, but I am just an assistant, so I do not have clearance to be on the base with them. I do not even know why they made me come along, except that the pig, Colonel Captain Vasilyev, likes to look at my ass."

Popov laughed, and she laughed with him. Clark could picture her gently putting her hand on the man's arm. She was good at this game.

"And how can you blame him?" Popov was saying.

"Do you work on the base?" she asked.

"Yes," he said. "I am an engineer. I develop the weapons that our Navy uses to destroy the enemy. What use is a submarine without a torpedo? The ship captains might get all the accolades, but they would be nothing without me."

"Oh, I agree," Adara said.

After the wine arrived, the conversational rhythm felt more organic. Adara worked Popov like the pro she was, asking nothing else about the Navy, his job, or the base, but rather keeping him talking about himself. Time passed slowly for Clark, but no doubt quickly for Adara. Soon Popov was insisting that he pay for her dinner.

"Let's see if she can close the deal," Ding said.

"Thank you for a lovely dinner. Too bad I have to go back to my hotel room by myself and drink alone," Adara said, slurring her words just a touch.

"You wish to drink alone tonight?"

"No one wishes to drink alone, Vasili."

"Then don't," Popov said. "Why don't you come to my apartment? We can continue talking and drinking there. I will buy a bottle of wine to take with us."

"I would love that," Adara said.

He listened as Popov paid the bill. A moment later, the chair legs scraped on the floor as the would-be couple scooted their chairs away from the table.

"Here we go," Clark said as Adara and Popov emerged from the restaurant, a bottle in the engineer's left hand and Adara's hand on his right arm.

As they neared the van, he caught Popov's eye and saw a flicker of worry, but then Adara said something and hugged his arm, and the engineer broke eye contact. As they reached the van, Ding slid open the door and stepped out onto the sidewalk, standing tall and threatening.

"Vasili Popov?" he said, hands on his hips.

"*Da?*" the engineer said, stuttering the word slightly and now taking a long look at Clark, who stared daggers at him. Even in the chill of the night air, he saw beads of sweat suddenly pop up on the man's forehead.

"We need to speak with you," Ding said, his Russian as polished as Adara's. "It is urgent."

"Why? I have done nothing wrong. There must be some mistake."

"There is no mistake," Adara said, letting go of his arm and taking a step away.

"What is happening? You are trying to trap me." He turned now to Clark, speaking directly to him. "If this is a test of loyalty, I assure you I am loyal. This woman may have tried to seduce me, but I would never reveal state secrets."

Clark broke his stare and turned away, as if bored.

"It is urgent and vital to national security that we speak with you," Ding said. "Get in the van and do not make a scene."

"People will notice if I go missing," Popov said, and he looked terrified now. "My work at Sevmash is important. Critical even . . ."

"We know, comrade," Adara said, her Russian now clipped and serious, nothing like the tipsy, flirtatious girl she'd been moments ago. She placed her hand on the back of his neck and pushed him toward the van. "Now, get in."

Popov climbed in the slider door, followed by Ding, then Adara. She slammed the door shut and Midas put the van in gear, pulling away from the curb. As he did, Clark turned in his seat to look at the petrified engineer.

"There are traitors in Russia today, working to damage our motherland, Comrade Popov," he said, finding the Russian words he'd practiced flowing out. "Have you been approached by anyone in the past year asking questions about the confidential nature of your work?"

The engineer opened his mouth, said nothing, then snapped it shut again. For a moment, Clark worried the man might pass out.

"You are GRU?"

"Don't be an ass," Ding said. "You know exactly who we are. You will answer our questions and never speak of this conversation again. If you do, we will know. Is that understood?"

"*Da*," Popov choked. "I understand."

"Very good," Clark said softly in Russian and turned away with a wave of his hand.

This might be easy after all.

They drove south a few blocks and parked in the dingy parking lot of the Flagman, Magazin motel. Moments later, Popov was inside the room they'd rented, seated in a faded vinyl chair at a round table, the stained yellow curtains drawn shut. Popov's left leg bounced up and down and his eyes darted repeatedly to the door, where Midas stood watch, a subcompact machine pistol in his hands. Adara took the other seat, crossing her legs at the knees, and placing a cell phone–sized device between them on the table.

"I will be recording our converation," she said simply. Again Clark was surprised to see how quickly his Russian skills had returned.

"Yes, of course," Popov said, trying to sound calm, but his voice trembling. "I have nothing to hide."

"We shall see," Ding said, glaring at the man from where he stood by the dirty wall beyond the cheap, sagging bed.

Clark held up a hand and shook his head, a superior urging patience and calm in a subordinate. Then he crossed his arms, observing.

"Has any person outside of your command approached you with questions about the Status-6 project, Vasili?" Adara began, her voice calm and direct, her hands in her lap. But it was clear Popov was having trouble keeping his eyes off the MP-443 Grach pistol on her hip, which was in clear view now that her jacket was off and lying on the bed.

"No. I only discuss this program with others on the project," he said. "And inspection teams who have come to visit."

She nodded. When he simply stared back, she gestured at him with her hand. "Who else?"

A bead of sweat trickled down the man's left cheek.

"There was another contingent from the GRU led by Admiral Rodionov that came last month to tour the facility and conduct interviews. But you already knew this, of course."

"Yes, of course. Do not waste our time," she said. "This is a follow-up visit."

"What other ranking officials from Moscow have taken an interest in your work?" Ding prompted. "Who else have you spoken to?"

"No one other than those inside the project. Um . . . As far as other ranking visiters, Admiral Boldyrev and his team flew in for an update recently. They wanted to make sure we would achieve our production and testing milestones, which we did, of course."

"What about your wife?" Adara asked, raising an eyebrow and watching the man's face flush. "What have you told her about your work?"

"Nothing," he said, his voice a tight cord. "She knows nothing. She thinks I'm a maintenance engineer. I swear it."

"Perhaps during your infidelities, you have mentioned your job to another woman. Perhaps trying to impress, yes?"

"*Nyet*," Popov said, the word a sob.

"You tried to impress me. You told me you designed weapons, did you not? Might you have elaborated—bragged, perhaps—should that help you get me into bed with you?"

"Never," Popov said, and was crying now.

Clark watched as Adara let a long, heavy pause hang in the air.

"Who, outside of your team, have you spoken with about the Poseidon project since testing ended and the torpedoes became operational?" Adara asked.

"What?" Popov said, distressed, but now also clearly confused. "You are trying to trick me."

"Why would you say such a thing as that?" Adara said, leaning in.

He looked nervously back and forth between Adara and Clark, and Clark indicated with a hand that he should answer. But he felt relief swell inside him and struggled to hide it from his face. Maybe the Status-6 was not operational. Maybe it was little more than a propaganda tool, as previously thought.

"You are GRU," Popov said, the strain almost more than he could bear. "So you must know that I was ordered not to brief Colonel General Andreyev that the torpedoes had become operational. It was your boss—Admiral Rodionov himself—who gave this order to me and my team."

Clark felt his relief wiped away in an instant, replaced by dread.

"And," Popov added, "Admiral Boldyrev ordered the dry dock cleared of all nonessential personnel when the six torpedoes were loaded on the *Belgorod*. I can assure you that absolutely no one, outside of the ship's crew and Sevmash's weapons-handling team, knows the Poseidons are aboard the *Belgorod*. I swear on my children's heads that if there has been a leak it is not from me. I swear it."

The man wept openly now. As he put his face in his hands, Adara looked up and held Clark's stare, her look mirroring, for a moment, the dread he felt.

Unexpectedly compelled, Clark strode suddenly across the room and struck Popov with a backhanded blow across the cheek, nearly knocking the man from the chair. He felt angry, but also in character owning the room.

"Stop weeping, you're an embarrassment," he growled. "Were Admiral Boldyrev's orders followed to the letter? What was the mix of conventional and nuclear warheads?"

"Six torpedoes. Two nuclear warheads, two conventional warheads, and two prototypes equipped with ISR collection packages. All safety protocols and documentation requirements were satisfied, I swear. I personally confirmed the serial numbers myself."

Clark turned away, waving a hand. "Get this piece of shit out of here."

"Please, don't kill me. I have done nothing wrong. I have a wife and children . . ."

"Yes," Adara said, her look hard on the engineer. "I know. I heard you swear on their heads. What kind of man swears on his children's heads?"

He stared at her in terror, and she pulled her weapon from her holster.

"*Nyet*," Clark said, just before the man passed out in fear.

Adara sighed in disappointment at the rehearsed intervention.

"So," she said, tipping the man's head up by the chin with the barrel of her Russian pistol. "It seems the bosses still need your expertise, perhaps, eh? But know this—should you tell anyone of this conversation, even Rodionov himself, I will kill you in your sleep. But not before I show you video of me killing your children as they sleep. Do you understand?"

Unable to speak, Popov nodded.

"Take him back," Adara said, slipping her pistol into its holster and then walking away from the shell of a man sobbing by the table.

Ding jerked the man to his feet and pulled him out the door, Midas following.

The door closed behind them and Clark watched Adara's shoulders sag.

"Oh my God, John," she said, once again herself in the literal blink of an eye. "Are we on the brink of World War Three?"

"I honestly don't know, but this is bad," he said, feeling as though he was suddenly carrying a hundred-pound rucksack on his back. "And whoever is pulling the strings—whether Yermilov or someone else—it's clear that Rodionov and Boldyrev are involved."

"At least we got the inventory out of him," Adara said, taking a seat on the edge of the bed. "Two nukes . . . But it could be worse."

"Two nuclear-armed Status-6 torpedoes is two too many in my book."

"Now what?" she asked.

"We report what we know to ODNI and the President."

"And get the hell out of Russia, right?"

"No," Clark said, stone-faced. "Not yet. Unfortunately, we may still have work to do."

34

Mikhail Morozov sat at the wardroom table, cleaning his eyeglasses with a handkerchief. He felt nervous and uncomfortable and needed something to distract himself so he wouldn't appear that way in front of the others who were gathering. The first officer had summoned the ship's entire officer complement for an unscheduled briefing—with the exception of Lieutenant Blok, who was the conning officer, and Lieutenant Shanklin, who was standing watch aft as the engineering control room supervisor.

"Does anybody know what this is about?" the mechanical division officer asked.

"We'll find out soon enough," the reactor controls officer replied in a hushed tone.

Someone bumped the back of Morozov's head from behind as bodies shuffled to claim the few seats remaining at the table. The latecomers would have to sit on the bench seat along the wall or stand along the inboard wall.

"Apologies, Captain Lieutenant," a young officer who was still in training said, but Morozov couldn't tell from the man's tone if the apology was sincere.

There was something odd about this ship. Well, not the ship per se, but rather the senior officer corps. Since the day he'd reported aboard he'd felt a palpable distrust from Captain Gorov, cold aloofness from First Officer Stepanov, and downright enmity from the ship's engineer, Captain Lieutenant Tarasov. At first, Morozov had chalked this up to the simple fact that he'd been a last-minute replacement for the ship's regular weapons officer, who'd been hospitalized with pneumonia a week before the *Belgorod*'s scheduled underway. That the leadership team would feel frustration and disappointment at this development was certainly understandable, but the frosty reception he'd received had yet to thaw.

Why don't they like me? he thought, pressing hard with his thumb as he cleaned the left lens with a circular motion. *I've done nothing but work hard and by the book since my arrival.*

In fact, he'd made a point of trying to go overboard in that respect. He'd endeavored to impress his comrades by working extra-long hours, personally supervising key evolutions prior to the underway, and being meticulous with his paperwork. Perplexingly, his efforts had seemed to have the opposite effect, and he felt more isolated and disconnected from his fellow officers than on the day of his arrival. On the day he'd been informed of the order modification, he'd told his wife that the universe had provided him with a golden opportunity. The *Belgorod* was the jewel of the Northern Fleet and Captain Gorov was the most respected commanding officer in the entire Russian submarine force. Even a temporary posting would raise his stock and possibly open the door to early selection for first officer. He remembered how her face had lit up and how she'd hugged him and told him that his hard work was finally paying off.

"Take the assignment and don't worry about us," she'd said, beaming at him. "The girls and I will be fine until you get back."

I'm a lucky man to have a wife like Nina.

The captain's arrival caused Morozov and the rest of the assembled officers to pop to their feet.

"Sit down, sit down," Gorov said, waving his hand as bodies shuffled out of the way to make room for him to get to the vacant armchair at the head of the wardroom table.

Morozov donned his spectacles, shoved his handkerchief into his left breast pocket, and lowered himself back into his chair.

"I've called this meeting because on our last excursion to periscope depth we received some disturbing news," Gorov said, his eyes scanning the faces in the room as he spoke. "Tensions with the Americans have reached a level not seen since the days of the Cold War. It appears that the American Navy has boarded and commandeered one of our research vessels operating in international waters, captured and detained the crew, and are even now rattling their sabers toward war. We received an encrypted message that I am certain will elevate our readiness condition."

Chatter erupted in the room, with most of the officers indignant at the news and mouthing blustery threats against or complaints about the trigger-happy, overly aggressive Americans. Morozov, for his part, held his tongue and focused his attention on the first officer, who didn't have quite the poker face that the captain did. Stepanov must have felt Morozov's gaze because he met the weapons officer's stare with a blank-faced, tight-lipped one of his own.

A knock at the wardroom door caused all heads to swivel en masse to look at the closed door.

"Come in," the captain barked.

The door opened and the control room messenger stood in

the doorway holding a red legal-size envelope. "Captain, Communications Officer Blok directed me to bring you this decrypted message."

"Very well, bring it to me."

The messenger hand-delivered the red envelope to the captain, who accepted it with a nod. A lump formed in Morozov's throat. Red envelopes signified top secret information or order modifications, aka ORDMODs.

This cannot be good.

"Shut the door on your way out," Gorov said as he opened the envelope and extracted a single sheet of printed paper. As he read, his expression hardened. When he finally looked up, his eyes locked with Morozov's. "Weapons officer . . ."

Morozov hard-swallowed. "Yes, sir."

"This message directs me to remove safeguards and enter authorization codes to arm the Number One Poseidon Torpedo."

He felt all the blood drain from his face and felt lightheaded, despite sitting down. "But, Captain, Number One Poseidon is a nuclear variant . . ."

"That is correct, Captain Lieutenant. I need you to go to your safe and retrieve the sealed authentication code for Number One Poseidon so that you and I and First Officer Stepanov can validate the authenticity of the code provided in this message."

"Yes, Captain," he said and scooted his chair back from the table.

He walked out of the wardroom, down the corridor, and entered his stateroom as if his body was on autopilot, a marionette controlled by an invisible puppeteer from above. He stooped in front of the weapons officer's safe, and when his fingers turned the combination dial, it was as if he were watching it happen on a movie screen. Then time seemed to skip, because the next thing he knew, he was handing the captain the sealed authentication code sleeve for Number One Poseidon. When the captain cracked the plastic, Morozov felt his heart skip a beat.

I can't believe this is happening, he thought, and his mind went to Nina and his two daughters, Lucia and Svetlana. Snapshot images played in his mind of his girls laughing and running at the local playground—

"Captain Lieutenant Morozov," the captain said, his voice like the crack of a whip.

"Sir?"

"I asked you if you concur."

Morozov blinked and the two printouts came into focus. He compared the authentication code on the message to the authentication code on the paper from the safe. The sixteen-digit alphanumeric sequences matched.

"The codes are a match," he heard himself say.

"Very well," Gorov said and handed both printouts to Stepanov. "First Officer Stepanov, accompany Captain Lieutenant Morozov to the torpedo room. Remove the mechanical safety interlocks from torpedo tube number one. Enter the authorization code into the computer for Number One Poseidon and establish a data link with the weapon's computer. Enter the target latitude and longitude and change the status from standby to armed. Do *not* flood the tube. Repeat this order back."

Stepanov repeated the order back verbatim.

"Go—do it now," Gorov commanded.

"Yes, sir," Stepanov said, then turned to Morozov. "Let's go."

Morozov had never heard the wardroom so quiet. It was as if the CO had given the order for a collective breath hold. He followed the first officer out into the central corridor and shut the wardroom door behind him. Expecting that Stepanov would say *something,* he paused.

"What are you doing?" the first officer said when he didn't follow.

"Sir, this is madness," he said, his tongue feeling thick as he tripped over the words. "Even if the Americans did seize one of our research vessels, we cannot launch such a weapon."

"It is not our place to decide such things, Captain Lieutenant. We are naval officers and our only job is to follow orders."

"But, sir—"

"Enough!" Stepanov barked, stepping so close their noses were in danger of touching. "You authenticated the message. You heard the captain's order. We will remove the safeguards and arm the weapon . . . But we are not flooding the tube. These are preparatory actions, not a firing order. Do you understand?"

"Yes, Captain," Morozov said, his voice just above a whisper.

"Hopefully, the situation with the Americans will de-escalate and we are not asked to do the unthinkable," Stepanov said, and then in a quiet voice added, "I have a family, too."

"Yes, sir."

"All right, now we go and do our duty. No matter how bitter the pill, we are men of action and we will swallow it," the first officer said and gave Morozov's shoulder a fraternal squeeze.

Feeling even more discouraged than before, the weapons officer of the *Belgorod* followed the first officer to the torpedo room. As his fingers unlocked the mechanical safeties on torpedo tube one and entered the authorization code into the computer, he imagined the radioactive tsunami that would wipe out Norfolk Naval Base and contaminate half of the Eastern Seaboard if they launched this terrifying, ungodly weapon. Then something unexpected happened. A single thought popped into his head, a thought he'd never imagined considering since the day he joined the Russian Navy.

Sabotage.

35

Ryan swallowed down his irritation as the makeup artist tucked paper towels into the collar of his shirt and began to apply powder to his face. The news of the *Finitor* incident had broken and the pundits were driving the conversation in a direction he didn't like—posing questions that echoed Kremlin talking points, while at the same time stoking fears about the Russian Northern Fleet moving into the North Atlantic. Most of the time he left the talking heads to yammer and stir the pot of controversy and conspiracy, but not today. He refused to let them control *this* narrative, and wanted the American people to hear from him directly.

Normally, counterespionage operations like the *Finitor* operation never saw the light of day. And the few times that they did, the White House messaging machine deftly made sure that a blip stayed a blip. Russia spied, America spied, China spied . . . everybody spied. And the public knew it.

But this was different.

The story had picked up a head of steam because of the Russian response of repositioning their carrier battle group south. The media zeitgeist sensed the escalation. And even though the talking heads had yet to articulate the truth, Ryan could feel that they were close. The *Finitor* incident was a precursor to something big. Just as Ryan knew it in his gut, so did the hawks, and the Russophils, and all the retired military brass who worked as network "contributors." When he moved the *Ford* into position to head off the Russian fleet, a media frenzy would ensue. He believed that ordering America's sons and daughters into harm's way was the most serious responsibility he had, and that laying out the circumstances and rationale that led to this decision should be presented by him, and him alone.

The SecDef could field questions tomorrow, but the announcement he would own and it needed to happen today.

"Five minutes, Mr. President," his press secretary, Jeanine, said from the corner of the Oval Office. She leaned around the single camera set up in front of the Resolute desk to be sure he had heard, and he gave her a tight smile.

"Thank you, Jeanine," he said, and then to the makeup assistant, he added, "I think we're good here. Thank you."

"Mr. President?" Mary Pat said off to his left, and the woman with the powder and paper towels quickly tidied up and excused herself.

Ryan turned to the private door, his stomach tightening at the sound of Mary Pat's voice. She wasn't interrupting five minutes before he addressed the American people on live television because she had good news.

"Everything all right?" he asked, but her face told him it wasn't. He turned to the press secretary and her team. "Can you give us the room a minute, Jeanine?"

Jeanine nodded and hustled her small media team out through the main door, closing it behind her.

"Tell me," Ryan said, pulling the paper towels from his collar.

"It's Yermilov," Mary Pat said. "He released a statement fifteen minutes ago. It's getting picked up by the majors as we speak."

Of course . . . Yermilov is no fool.

The White House communications team had announced that Ryan would be addressing the nation, which may have been a mistake. That miscalculation practically invited the Russian president to get his own statement out first.

"Any surprises?"

"Well, we certainly didn't get the apology and admission of guilt that Secretary Adler demanded during his meeting with Ambassador Darmatov," she said. "Not that we expected we would."

"Russians don't apologize," Ryan pointed out. "What did Yermilov say?"

"The usual drumbeat—America is once again provoking conflict by illegally attacking Russian interests. He's trying to spin the *Finitor* incident as an unprovoked attack by the U.S. Navy on a civilian research vessel operated as a joint venture between Russia and other partner nations. He went on to claim that we *kidnapped* Russian nationals on the crew and have illegally detained a vessel operating in international waters."

"We're not going to let them off the hook," Ryan said. "I want to use the curated video clips from the SEAL operation as planned. We will show the world what the *Finitor* really is—an espionage platform with sophisticated spy gear manned by Russian intelligence agents. We'll post their pictures and superimpose them against the files we have on the men. It'll be hard to argue with that."

She nodded. "Yermilov also claimed that American naval forces are moving into position to attack his Northern Fleet, which is engaged in a preplanned military exercise . . ."

"Yeah, well, they're the ones steaming their battle group south to harass us. We didn't make them move, they did that all on their own. The American people are smart, Mary Pat, and so are the citizens of the rest of the world. Most people are tired of Russian lies and bravado. Their destabilizing efforts in the Baltics and the false flag operations in South America are still top of mind for most people. I'll lay out our response as a defensive maneuver meant to preempt Russian aggression."

"What about the *Belgorod*?" she asked.

He sighed. "What about it?"

"I hope you're not planning to tell the American people that there's a super-stealthy Russian submarine carrying long-range nuclear torpedoes somewhere in the Atlantic?"

"No," he said. "Creating a panic only plays into Yermilov's hands, and besides, we still don't know if the threat is real or if it's Kremlin propaganda."

"Unfortunately, I have some more clarity on that front," she said, her face turning grave.

His stomach sank. "Tell me."

"My assets in Russia have confirmed that the Status-6 program *is* fully operational," she said, her voice conveying the gravity of the news as much as her words. "Six Status-6 torpedoes were loaded onto the *Belgorod* before it got underway, Jack. Two of them are armed with nuclear warheads."

"And the good news?" he said sarcastically through gritted teeth.

"There is no good news," she said. "And to make matters worse, our team has supporting evidence that the *Belgorod* could be a pawn in a chess match unfolding between a shadow organization and the Kremlin."

Ryan tried to imagine a worse, more dangerous situation than what Mary Pat was describing. Short of inbound Russian nukes, he couldn't think of one.

"Hold on . . . Are you saying Yermilov has lost control of his own Navy? That the *Belgorod* might be taking orders from some rogue faction?"

"It's not clear, Jack. But that's my concern and why our team is heading to Moscow."

"What?" He stared at his DNI. "That's very dangerous, Mary Pat. What is their tasking?"

"I'm leaving them kinetic . . . Like you said, there are important questions that we need answers to. We need to know who's really running the show in Moscow."

He glanced at his watch.

"Go to the Situation Room and wait for me there. I'll join you after I address the country," Ryan said. "I want the SecDef and the chairman of the Joint Chiefs there as well. If there has already been a breakdown in the Russian military chain of command, we need to start preparing for different contingencies."

"Yes, sir," Mary Pat said, turning back to the private door.

"And Mary Pat," he called. She turned. "If the *Belgorod* is actually a rogue asset not under Yermilov's control, then we're in uncharted terrority."

"I know," she said.

"I need to understand what's going on in the minds of the key players. Russians don't think like we do."

"Yes, Jack."

"Which is why I need to talk to Ramius."

"It's in the works, Jack . . . I promise I'll get him here."

36

THE BELGOROD (K-329)
HOVERING OVER TARGET DASH NODE
NORTH ATLANTIC
THURSDAY, APRIL 11
0724 LOCAL TIME

orozov paced in his stateroom—alone, fretting, and talking to himself.

"None of this makes sense. The Americans would not risk nuclear war, and nuclear war doesn't serve Yermilov."

It's just saber rattling, said the voice of reason in his head. *Nothing more.*

"*Nyet,* there's something else going on. I can feel it. This is the captain's doing. He's up to something. Something dangerous and terrible."

What proof do you have?

"Look at the man—all is not well with our intrepid captain."

Everyone knew about the personal tragedy Gorov had suffered with the loss of his wife and unborn child not even one year ago. Despite Morozov not being a crew member of the *Belgorod* at that time, tragic news spread like wildfire among the spouses of the tightly knit Northern Fleet submarine community.

"That poor, poor man," his wife, Nina, had said the night the gossip reached the Morozov home. "They say he wept for two days over her body and refused to release her to the morgue."

This detail was certainly hyperbole, but wasn't that the point of gossip and legends? Konstantin Gorov had lost the love of his life and his unborn child at the same time. Loss like that could make a man question the point of carrying on. Equally concerning as the captain's mental state was Gorov's physical condition. Morozov had seen his commanding officer turn white as a sheet and buckle over in pain on two separate occasions on this underway. Gorov already looked thinner and paler than he had three weeks ago when Morozov had joined the crew.

"It's because he's dying."

You don't know that, countered the voice in his head.

"But I do. I can feel it in my soul."

And therein lay the problem. He didn't have any proof that Gorov was not long for this world, or that the orders had been tampered with, or that the vaunted captain of the *Belgorod* had some vendetta to settle with the Americans. But in his heart of hearts, Morozov knew. For some insane reason, Gorov intended to launch a nuclear-tipped Status-6 torpedo at Norfolk Naval Station, and that order had *not* come from the Kremlin.

Impossible. The order was received by satellite transmission.

"That's what he wants us to think. Don't you see, it was theater. He assembled the entire officer corps in the wardroom on purpose. Only his two most trusted servants, Tarasov and Blok, were on watch. And Blok is the communications officer. He screens all messages and could have easily changed it. What are the odds *that* order came in while we were in the middle of the brief?"

But the authentication codes matched. This cannot be faked.

"They must have found a way . . . I don't know how, but they found a way."

Impossible.

A manic laugh erupted from his lips. "Listen to me. I'm arguing with myself like an insane person."

Maybe it is you who is unstable. Not the captain.

"Maybe so," he muttered, turning to face himself in the small mirror glued to the back of the stateroom door. A haggard complexion and bloodshot eyes stared back at him. "If only there was someone else I could talk to about this. An ally, perhaps . . ."

Unfortunately for Morozov, he didn't have a single ally on the *Belgorod*. He was an outsider and had not had time to develop trust or comradery with any of the junior officers or the senior noncommissioned officers on board. But that probably didn't matter anyway, because he suspected the senior staff were complicit. Tarasov and Blok were in on it, of this much he was certain. As far as the first officer, Stepanov, he wasn't sure. The man idolized Gorov, but he did not seem blindly loyal like Blok and Tarasov.

One man does not a mutiny make. Go to Stepanov. Make your case, the voice of reason said in the mirror. *Express your concerns, but tread carefully. Gauge his reaction and then we can decide what to do.*

"Okay," he said, reaching an accord with himself. "I will do this."

He swallowed, smoothed the collar wings of his coveralls, and reluctantly made his way to Stepanov's stateroom. When he reached the command passage, he paused outside the first officer's door, which was barely cracked open thanks to the latch mechanism resting against the leading edge of the catch plate. Through the three-millimeter gap, he heard a conversation between Stepanov and a voice he recognized as Tarasov's.

"When the time comes, he's going to be a problem. He's a rule follower—a by-the-book kind of guy. There's no way he obeys the order."

"I think you're seeing things backward, Eng. It is because of these qualities that he won't be a problem. Morozov has an exemplary service record. He follows orders blindly because that is the kind of officer he is."

"And what if he doesn't? What then? He wears the launch key around his neck. We cannot afford to let the mission hinge on one man's compliance."

"Then what do you suggest we do, Tarasov? Hmm? Take the key and confine him to quarters?"

"*Da,* that is exactly what I suggest."

Despite desperately wanting to loiter, Morozov's feet seemed to move without an order from his brain. He'd heard enough. Getting caught eavesdropping would jeopardize what could be the only moment that he had to act.

Looks like I owe you an apology, said the voice in his head. *It appears you were right.*

"I wish I wasn't," he murmured as he left the command passageway and made his way to the forward auxiliary mechanical room, where the pump stations for potable water, sanitation, and the trim and drain systems were located.

The space also served as the sub's repair shop. He'd served on an unmodified Oscar II as a junior officer, and this space was one of the few that had not been modified on the *Belgorod* from the original design. In trying to think of a place to hide his weapon-launch console key, his subconscious had brought him here. The on-watch auxiliary man greeted him with a look of surprise, as this area of the ship did not fall under the weapons officer's regular purview.

"Are you lost, sir?" the senior mechanic said with a wry grin, then jerked a thumb over his shoulder. "The torpedo room is that way."

Morozov nervously wiped the sweat from his brow with the cuff of his sleeve. "I need to get a nut and M20 washer from the hardware cabinet."

"Do you need my help finding what you need?"

"*Nyet.* I can get it."

"In that case, help yourself, Captain Lieutenant," the mechanic said with a bored shrug of his shoulders.

He walked to the afterpart of the auxiliary room, where a simple workbench was bolted to the deck. All the fasteners and tools were maintained in special cabinets with latch drawers so they could not open or spill during angles and rolling maneuvers. After checking to make sure he wasn't being watched, he quickly removed the steel launch console key from the chain around his neck. Next, he opened the drawer containing M20 stainless steel washers, hid his silver key under a mass of them, then took a single washer off the top for himself. He then fetched a stainless steel nut and turned to leave.

"Did you find what you need, sir?" the mechanic asked.

"*Da.*"

He opened his palm to show off the washer and nut as proof, then left the machinery room without another word. On the way back to his stateroom, he stopped in the officer's head and locked himself inside a stall. He sat on the toilet seat, carefully threaded the washer onto the chain around his neck, then slipped it under his T-shirt, where the key usually hung. The nut he deposited in the waste bin inside a wadded-up paper towel. After this, he went to the sink and splashed cold water on his face. Without his key, launching Number One Poseidon would be virtually impossible.

Unless the captain keeps a backup key in his safe, he thought with a creeping sense of dread. Such a thing would not be surprising on this ship.

"Think, think, think . . . There has to be another way," he murmured.

If Gorov wants to start World War Three, save a mutiny, there's nothing I can do to stop him.

Just then, a paradigm-shattering epiphany occurred to him.

But what if I don't have to? What if the Americans can do it for me?

A broad smile spread across his face as a brilliant, tactical, treasonous idea came to him—an idea that no one, not even Gorov himself, would anticipate.

Now if only the Americans are smart enough to figure it out.

37

Commander Brian "Mr. Pibb" Hanson, executive officer of VFA-31, the Tomcatters, pressed the twin throttles forward and eased his jet into a right turn as he climbed.

"Copy, Ace Zero One," he said, his voice low and calm. "We have your bandits, twenty-five left at angels two-seven."

"Roger, Thor," said the young controller managing his merge with what Hanson assumed to be a pair of Russian fighters headed toward the strike group. "That's your bandit. Flight of two fast movers making seven hundred knots, maneuvering, with number two, three miles in trail. You are cleared to engage."

Hanson glanced right where Lieutenant Ashley "Fodder" Cannon now pushed out from his wing, increasing the distance between their jets as they turned, and setting up a combat spread before he even made the suggestion. He liked the JO and enjoyed flying with her. She was one of the most intuitive pilots he'd served with and would make a great leader. He felt no need to gum up the channel with unnecessary chatter when she was on his wing.

He leveled his Hornet at thirty thousand feet and watched his center screen as the two Russian jets made a slight turn, coming nose to nose in a wide combat spread, and began a climb out of angels two-seven for thirty, he assumed. With some junior officers, he'd call out that he was taking the MiG to the east, but felt no need to make the call with Fodder, who already angled left to come nose to nose with the Russian jet slightly west. He pressed the throttles forward slightly, increasing his speed, the closure rate on the MiGs now passing more than twelve hundred miles an hour.

"All right, Ivan," he mumbled, "what's on your mind, comrade?"

A dot appeared at his twelve o'clock through the HUD, growing inside the red targeting box, which had already acquired and locked on the bandit, ensuring that a simple trigger squeeze would send the AIM-9 missile he'd selected off the outboard rail and screaming toward the Russian. A warble in his headset suggested the Russian had the same idea and had radar lock on his jet.

Now it was a game of nerves.

Nerves, discipline, and self-control. He hoped the Russian pilot had the same measure of all three that he and his wingman did.

The Russian jet filled his screen and he held his jet steady on course. Deviating now without knowing the Russian's intent could lead to a midair collision, since the crazy Russian was intent on passing danger close.

The MiG flashed past him, to his starboard side and slightly above, no more than twenty feet away. The wake turbulence buffeted his jet as Hanson pulled the stick back and advanced the throttles, wrenching the Hornet into a high-G, climbing right turn, while doing his damnedest to watch the target on his HUD.

Crazy asshole almost hit me.

His G suit inflated, squeezing his legs and waist as he grunted and bore down in an M1 maneuver, intent on keeping the blood in his brain as the Hornet grumbled and shook through the 7 G turn.

He rolled the jet inverted and let up some of the back pressure on the stick, his vision clearing.

Then a call came in his headset that caused his chest to tighten.

"I'm hit . . . I'm hit . . ." said Fodder, her voice tight but controlled. "Thor Two is hit. Thor Two is going down . . ."

The warble in his headset became a squeal.

Hanson watched the target on his HUD, still being tracked by his jet's computer, as it generated a line for the MiG's projected course. He rolled his jet on its side, pressed the twin throttles forward, and pulled the stick back into his lap, initiating another high-G turn. His F/A-18E went inverted through the turn, then he rolled and returned the wings to level. A heartbeat later, he yanked hard and entered the nearly straight vertical climb as the MiG overshot and passed him. He pushed over, the negative Gs making his face feel full and his eyes ache, then rolled inverted again and pulled the nose down. He grunted hard as his color vision faded and the G suit squeezed. The nose pulled all the way through the horizon and he lined up the targeting pipper on his HUD with the red box.

The two aligned.

His headset chirped.

Commander Hanson pulled the trigger on the stick and felt the jolt as the missile left the rail. He rolled the jet back over level and then pushed into a negative-G push over, watching the white smoke trail of his missile streak toward its target, as he searched now for the first MiG that had shot his wingman. He found it first on the HUD, then easily saw it in the distance, streaming smoke and flame just a mile or so away. As he watched, a flash of fire signaled the pilot ejecting from the damaged jet.

It all became clear. The Russian hadn't fired at Fodder—he'd collided with her.

What a dumbass. And now his wingman locked me up and I had to shoot him down. That idiot just started a shooting war.

"Thor Two is good chute," he heard his wingman's strained voice announce and he felt his shoulders sag with relief.

"Thor Two, roger. SAR en route. Hold on," came the cool voice of the controller aboard the E-2C, indicating that the *Ford* had already scrambled a search and rescue helo.

"Ace Zero One, Thor One will remain on station with Thor Two," Hanson said, letting the controller know he had no intention of leaving Fodder alone, bobbing in the middle of the freezing Atlantic Ocean.

"Roger, Thor One. Stay frosty," the controller said.

So long as I have gas, I'm staying.

He'd just shot down a Russian MiG and that pilot was in the drink as well. He wouldn't put it past the other Russian pilot to strafe Fodder in the water. He was pretty sure they were at war now, so he'd cover her six and shoot down any asshole that tried.

38

Captain "Spacecamp" Huddleston, the deputy commander of the embarked air wing, stood behind the air boss and did his best to let his people do their jobs without interference. They'd launched the four jets from VFA-37, the Ragin' Bulls, early in an effort to accelerate the recovery operations of the jets now low on fuel. That included the XO of VFA-31, who was covering his downed wingman and had to be nearly at bingo gas. Already the *Ford* was turning back into the wind as two of the three F/A-18Es from the Tomcatters called inbound. The E-2C had plenty of gas to loiter for now, but he needed to get Mr. Pibb home. He glanced out the window as the *Ford* entered her turn.

What he saw made him reach for the phone to the bridge, but it rang in his hand.

"Air," he said, "this is the DCAG."

"Spacecamp, it's Opey," his lifelong friend and the ship's CO, Captain Mackenzie, said. "Are you seeing what I'm seeing?"

"Yeah," he answered, eyes glued to the Russian warship in the near distance, which had just maneuvered into a position to squat on the *Ford*'s track as she came to a new heading into the wind to recover planes. This was a common Russian and Chinese tactic meant to harass and stymie flight operations. But today the stakes were much higher—missiles had been fired and aviators were in the water. Diverting the jets that were low on gas was not an option. "How long do we have on this course before we have to turn?"

A pause followed and Spacecamp could picture the skipper conferring with his bridge crew. The Russian frigate would slow and maneuver in a manner that forced the *Ford* to reduce speed or change course to avoid collision, robbing the *Ford* of the precious wind and constant heading they needed to conduct safe recovery operations.

"We have some wind now, so I'm gonna slow to fifteen knots, but we need to get the planes on deck ASAFP," Mackenzie said.

Huddleston caught the eye of the air boss, who nodded.

"We'll ditch the break and keep them away from Ivan," the DCAG said. They didn't need the planes doing overhead recoveries and breaking right over the enemy. "And we'll stack 'em up for fast straight-ins, but we'll need to get Mr. Pibb heading home."

"I'll give you as much time as I can, Jim," Mackenzie said, and then he was gone.

"I gotcha," the air boss said before Spacecamp could even speak. The DCAG folded his arms on his chest, wishing like hell there was something more he could do other than watch. Thank God the men and women serving on the *Ford* were some of the Navy's best and brightest.

The ballet unfolded, the sailors on the deck and the sailors in the PriFly working in perfect harmony as planes began to recover. The new, enhanced arresting gear did its part, keeping the recoveries smooth and on centerline. After each trap landing, the crew cleared the arresting gear with remarkable speed and efficiency. Then the pilot would taxi clear and the cable would rebound with mere seconds to spare before the next plane made its approach. The DCAG gave a satisfied smile as jet after jet arrested perfectly— he'd never seen so many two-wire passes back to back in his career, despite the danger close separation.

He felt his pulse slow as Spartan One—the helo providing search and rescue for the downed aviator from VFA-31— announced they had Lieutenant Cannon aboard. Unlike Mr. Pibb, the helo had plenty of fuel and didn't need the ship heading into the wind for recovery. He glanced aft and saw the short line of jets still on the straight-in waiting to land.

"Thor One is headed back, but he's still sixty miles out," the air traffic control sailor working the "stack" announced, coordinating with the real-time data coming from the airborne controller, Ace Zero One.

Spacecamp reached for the phone that would connect him to the bridge.

"Bridge," the bridge phone talker said.

"It's DCAG for the skipper," he said.

"Stand by one," the sailor answered.

The thirty-second wait for the CO felt like a day. As they got closer, the Russian frigate grew larger through the glass of the PriFly. The frigate's wake was a series of S-turns as the Russian captain snaked back and forth across their track—slow enough to make things dangerous and just fast enough to counter any course adjustments the *Ford* made. If the *Ford* turned into the wind now to recover the F/A-18E, it would get danger close to colliding with the Russian frigate. Even though the *Ford* was orders of magnitude bigger than the Russian warship, collisions at sea were deadly and unpredictable. Despite her size advantage, the carrier could become crippled or, worse, suffer catastrophic flooding from a hull breach and sink. On the other hand, if Mackenzie veered out of the wind, they might just lose the VFA-31 jet and the squadron's XO.

"These guys are such assholes," he said, glaring at the frigate.

"Like splashing one of our jets wasn't already escalation enough," the air boss agreed. "We oughtta sink that son of a bitch."

Spacecamp nodded, but that wasn't really an option . . . At least not yet, it wasn't. He glanced at his watch, then back at the electronic board. Only Mr. Pibb was left, but the Hornet was still several minutes out.

"Skipper," Mackenzie said into the phone at last. "I'm running out of ocean, and I'm running out of options. How many more?"

"One. Mr. Pibb," the DCAG said. The XO of the Tomcatters was one of the best pilots in the Navy in his opinion. A Top Gun graduate, former Top Gun instructor, and recent instructor at VFA-106, the Gladiators, the fleet replacement squadron for all of the East Coast–based Hornet squadrons. "You okay if I tell him to bring the heat?"

"Do it," Mackenzie said. "Just get him aboard before I'm forced to make a hard turn to starboard."

The skipper was gone and the DCAG replaced the phone with a snap.

"Boss, tell Thor One to bring the heat."

"You got it, boss," the man said with a grin. He reached over his sailor and picked up a mic. "Thor One, you're cleared for a shit-hot break. Bring the heat, 'cause we're gonna make a hard turn to starboard in just a minute."

"Thor One," came the low, cool voice of Mr. Pibb. "Bringing the heat. On the deck in ninety seconds."

The air boss glanced forward to where the Russian ship now loomed off the bow.

"Make it eighty, Pibb," he said.

The deck was clear now, the last planes recovered and positioned out of the way along the starboard side ahead of the island. The DCAG watched aft as the fighter jet grew larger off the stern of the ship, screaming toward them just a couple hundred feet off the deck. Just as it crossed the stern of the carrier, the jet rolled left and condensation streamed like white fire from the wingtips, then the entire wings, and finally even the fuselage itself as the pilot pulled through an insanely high-G turn, looping around the carrier in a physics-defying tight turn with the gear, slats, and flaps lowering to bleed off speed. He watched the pilot roll the jet out of the maneuver and onto a perfect approach vector a mere five hundred yards off the stern. The maneuver, known as the "shit-hot break," was once a favorite way to test the mettle of "shit-hot" fighter pilots, but had long since been relegated to only emergencies such as this—and only with approval of the air boss and the skipper of the boat.

Seconds later, landing gear barked and smoked as the Hornet hit the deck. The tailhook snagged the number two wire—a perfect "okay pass"—and the jet jerked to a stop, the engines on full afterburner. The pilot immediately returned the throttles to idle and the Hornet rolled backward as the carrier deck tilted sharply from the hard, starboard turn.

The DCAG watched as the Russian ship passed impossibly close to the port side of the carrier, and then smiled as the sailors in the PriFly pressed raised middle fingers against the glass.

Then his smile faded.

They'd survived this engagement, recovering their downed pilot, whose injuries were yet to be determined. But they were in a shooting war now. The Russian Navy might be no match for the *Ford* strike group, but that didn't mean everyone would be coming home from this one.

39

Ryan scanned the faces of his defense team as Admiral Lawrence Kent from the Joint Chiefs briefed the room on an engagement between two F/A-18E Super Hornets from the *Ford* and a pair of MiG-29K Russian fighters from the *Kuznetsov*. The grim expressions told him everything they needed to know. He'd assembled the nation's most formidable minds as his military leadership team—people he trusted, who were the best in their fields—but would their collective experience and judgment be enough to navigate this crisis and keep this situation with Russia from spiraling out of control?

Behind Kent, the center monitor showed a bird's-eye view of the North Atlantic Ocean with clusters of green triangles, each labled with the names of the ships within the USS *Gerald R. Ford* strike group. The scattered red squares were labeled with the names of the Russian Northern Fleet ships, including the fully operational *Admiral Kuznetsov*. Plenty of experts in and out of the DoD had believed that the beleaguered, accident-prone aircraft carrier—which had spent nearly a decade in and out of the shipyard—was not capable of flight operations.

The pilots of VFA-31 had just proven that assessment incorrect.

"What is the condition of the pilot of the downed Hornet?" the SecDef asked, demonstrating once again that he understood and valued the human cost of combat operations.

"She has minor injuries—a dislocated shoulder, I believe— related to the ejection, and is suffering from cold exposure. A full recovery is expected," Kent said.

"And the Russian pilot?" Ryan asked. It mattered politically, but personally as well.

The human toll.

"Well, we can't be sure, sir," Admiral Kent said. "The Russians claim that he died, but we have imagery confirming his ejection and we also have video from the guard helo showing a pilot being picked up by the *Kuznetsov*'s recovery team, and in the video he is clearly alive. The aircrew couldn't get too close because the Russian recovery team fired on them. Predictably, the Russians claim we fired first—though our helicopter crew never fired a shot. It is possible that the Russian pilot sustained injuries he later succumbed to."

"I always assume everything out of the Kremlin's press office is horseshit and then work backward from there," General Bruce Kudryk growled.

Ryan held up a hand, looking at the screen to the left, which was on a loop, showing the AIM-9 air-to-air missile impacting the MiG, the collision between the MiG and Lieutenant Cannon's jet from her gun camera's point of view, her ejection from the plane, and the ejection of the Russian pilot after the XO of VFA-31 shot him out of the sky.

Good Lord . . . What a fiasco.

Admiral Kent continued, pivoting to ship movements. As he

spoke, Ryan glanced again at the screen showing the green triangles and red squares. Even in the zoom of just the AOR, the red and green markers seemed incredibly close.

Danger close.

"All of these icons are surface combatants, which we are tracking. We do *not* know, however, the location and position of the three Northern Fleet submarines that are presently unaccounted for: the K-329 *Belgorod*, the K-335 *Gepard*, and the K-560 *Severodvinsk*. Submarines in general pose a significant risk to the carrier because of their stealth, torpedoes, and the Kalibr-class anti-ship cruise missile, which the *Severodvinsk* is known to carry. But the *Belgorod* poses a particularly grievous risk to the strike group with the nuclear-tipped Status-6. As everyone in this room is acutely aware, intelligence has confirmed the *Belgorod* is carrying two of these long-range standoff weapons. If the Russians decided to attack the strike group with a Status-6, the weapon would not have to directly hit the carrier to be effective. Our analysts estimate a detonation anywhere inside two nautical miles could be catastrophic. That said, the close proximity of the Russian fleet should give their leadership pause before using a nuclear weapon in the event tensions continue to escalate," Kent said.

"I understand," Ryan said, a little annoyed. He'd authorized the strategy, after all. "Anything else?"

There was an awkward silence, then General Kudryk cleared his throat. Ryan figured it would be Kudryk who would point out the elephant in the room.

"Mr. President, we shot down a Russian MiG in international waters—"

"After his wingman collided with an American jet operating in international waters," Kent interrupted, his face turning crimson. "They drew first blood."

"I'm not debating that point, Larry," Kudryk relented. "The

Hornet pilot reacted properly. It's my understanding that the second MiG had missile lock on the Tomcatter's XO when he engaged and splashed the Russians. He did the right thing. But, Mr. President, this is clearly an escalation and we need to define the rules of engagement for our fleet that will provide clarity for the ship captains and pilots without risking full-scale war."

"I would argue we're already at war," Ryan said grimly and allowed the words to bring the expected hush to the room. "But what I don't understand is why now? Nothing happened geopolitically to change the status quo. Our stance and policies on Russia have been consistent. We've done nothing overtly or covertly to antagonize or provoke Moscow." He looked at Mary Pat, giving her the green light to say what needed to be said.

"My worry, Mr. President, is that Yermilov may not be the one making the decisions anymore. Our intelligence indicates that there are fractured lines of command and control at the highest levels of the military and intelligence aparatus. I'm concerned the Russian president might be the president in name only. It's possible we're witnessing the early stages of a coup led by a cabal of senior-ranking officials to either remove Yermilov from power completely or to strip him of real authority and turn him into a figurehead. We need more confirming details, but if I had to speculate, I'd say Yermilov's grip on power is slipping," she said.

Ryan let himself do something he rarely did—speak off the cuff. "I don't like speculating. I don't like making tactical and strategic decisions based on assumptions. If the command and control in the Kremlin is fractured, then I have questions that need answers quickly. Who is directing the Northern Fleet? Who has control of Russia's nuclear arsenal—the bombers, the SSBNs, the ICBMs? Taken as an isolated incident, the *Belgorod* going to sea would not normally stoke my concerns. But K-329 is not a Russian SSBN going on a scheduled deterrence patrol. It is a special missions boat carrying a new class of first-strike weapon—a nuke designed to be launched submerged so we can't detect it. The Status-6 is not like an ICBM. We can't see it coming. We can't shoot it down. Our only early warning against this weapon is our DASH sonar array and we just caught a Russian spy ship interfering with that. This can't be a coincidence."

To his surprise, nobody said anything.

He sighed.

"Our posture internally must be that we are *already* at war," Ryan said. "I refuse to be caught unprepared and on my heels. I refuse to make the mistake of pretending away early-warning signs preceding a Russian first strike that could cripple our ability to respond in kind. That said, I strongly believe and always have that discretion is the better part of valor. While we prepare for the worst, there *are* steps we can take to reduce the risk of escalation to global conflict. Our posture should be defensive, rather than provocative."

Kent pursed his lips and Ryan nodded his agreement at the un-spoken concern of being tasked with the near impossible.

"I know, Larry," Ryan said. "What I'm asking is a difficult dance on a very thin tightrope. We keep the strike group in close proxim-ity to the Russian battle group, we continue surveillance and flight operations meant to protect our fleet—combat air patrols for air superiority twenty-four seven—and we do it without provoking them. We need time . . . time to get all our forces on war footing without signaling an offensive, time for our covert assets to gather additional intelligence and provide clarity on this possible coup, and time for me to pursue a diplomatic solution with President Yermilov."

"Yes, Mr. President," the SecDef said, answering for the group.

"What about the *Belgorod?*" Admiral Kent asked. "If we find it, what are the rules of engagement?"

Ryan had already given this thorny question considerable thought. "*When* we find the *Belgorod*, not *if*, Admiral, I want one of our attack submarines following in its baffles with torpedoes loaded and a firing solution ready to go. If the *Belgorod* so much as floods a tube while pointed in the direction of our carrier strike group or one of our bases, then we have no choice but to put it on the bottom of the Atlantic. I'm not going to start this war, but I'll be damned if I let them cripple us without a fight."

"Yes, sir, Mr. President," Kent said. "Understood."

The team rose, gathered their things, and headed for the door. Ryan watched the video loop on the screen as they shuffled out. Mary Pat stayed seated beside him. When the door closed, he turned to her, raising an eyebrow.

"I want you to know I heard what you said and I understand why you said it," she said, "but you know better than anyone that in the espionage business there are always missing pieces of the puzzle. The team is trying, but there's no guarantees they will get you the answers you need in time."

"I understand," Ryan said. That wasn't the real reason she still sat here, he thought. He knew that already. "What is their OPORD?" he asked, inquiring about the team's operational orders.

"It's a mission of opportunity, Jack," she said with a smile. "You remember what that's like. Thanks to VICAR and Popov, we have names and connections established, but what we don't have are specifics. We don't know the cabal's motives or how deeply they may be entrenched in the Russian government and military. And we don't know their endgame."

Ryan sighed and watched her closely. He knew full well that Mary Pat protected him from too much knowledge when it came to these things. He knew damn well who the "team" inside Russia was likely to be—hell, he'd been involved in their charter. They were good at both intelligence collection and asset management, but they were also skilled at doing the unpleasant "wet" work sometimes necessary to protect a nation.

Does Mary Pat know more than she's letting on? Is there a hit list I don't know about?

"What are *his* rules of engagement, Mary Pat?" Ryan asked, suddenly worried about the unintended consequences of potentially eliminating the wrong Russian power broker. "What are his orders?"

She shrugged, a clear signal she wouldn't be baited—and that she knew she had the President's trust.

"To learn what he can, and then react accordingly based on his instincts."

She held his stare and he nodded again, ending the line of discussion and letting her off the hook, for now.

"I want to be in the loop."

"Yes, Mr. President," she said.

"I'm serious, Mary Pat."

"I know, Jack," she said without a blink. "I promise."

"Anything else?" he asked.

She shifted uncomfortably. "Katie is doing good work, Jack. She has incredible instincts and is really gifted at this job. Gets it from her dad, I hear."

He snorted at this, but smiled.

"Thanks for that, Mary Pat. But I'm . . ."

She raised an eyebrow. "You're what?"

He sighed. "I'm worried about her."

She rose, squeezed his shoulder, and headed out the door. He took a moment, enjoying the rare silence and solitude.

Instead of bringing peace and tranquility, the moment filled his mind with images of the USS *Gerald R. Ford* disappearing in a mushroom cloud, his little girl somewhere aboard.

"Son of a bitch," he mumbled and rose, heading for the door. "One more Ryan I have to worry about."

PART III

Danger, confronted properly, is not something a man must fear.

—Marko Ramius

40

S tanding in the middle of the control room, Konstantin surveyed the watch section team with no small amount of pride
as the final preparations for Operation Guillotine were made.
The *Belgorod* had completed its seven-thousand-plus-kilometer infiltration trek—traveling from north of the Arctic Circle in the
Barents Sea all the way south to a latitude in line with Washington,
D.C.—without being detected by the Americans. The next forty-
eight hours would be dangerous, and there was a possibility the
ship and crew might not survive the aftermath, but Konstantin felt
confident they would complete the mission before that happened.

"Captain, the ship is in position. I completed a sonar sweep of
the area and hold no submerged contacts or surface ships within
twenty nautical miles. Request permission to bring the main engines to all stop and engage the hovering system at a depth of three
hundred and fifty meters," the conning officer said.

The captain walked to the sonar repeater and scanned the display. The Americans were undoubtedly looking for them, but Konstantin saw nothing of concern in their immediate vicinity. The

data hub was two nautical miles west of the coordinates where the *Finitor* had been seized, giving them only a hair's separation from the Americans.

"Very well, conning officer," he said. "Order all stop and engage the hovering system."

"Aye, Captain," Blok said. "Helm, all stop."

"All stop, Helm, aye," the helm said. "Conning officer, the engines are stopped."

"Very well, Helm. Diving officer of the watch, engage the hovering system. Maintain depth of three hundred and fifty meters and coordinate with the quartermaster to maintain position over the target coordinates."

The DOOW repeated back the order, then engaged the *Belgorod's* special automated hovering system, which had been designed by Rubin and installed during the submarine's conversion to a special missions boat. The computer-controlled system used the ship's trim and drain system and a series of small auxiliary pumps to maintain a state of neutral buoyancy, allowing the sub to "hover" at the order depth. It also maintained the sub's angle of attack, or "bubble," at zero degrees, and prevented listing to the port or starboard side. Lastly, it utilized special water-jet "thrusters" located near the bow and the stern for low-speed maneuvering and station keeping. Without the thrusters, ocean currents would quickly push the massive submarine off the target—a phenomenon known as set and drift.

What most people didn't realize was that submarines, like sharks, generated lift as they moved through the water, much like an airplane wing. Bring a submarine's speed to zero while submerged, and there was a tendency for it to sink. A moving submarine could carry thousands of kilograms of "hidden" weight at speed—weight that only made itself known upon slowing. The next few moments would tell how good of a job the diving officer of the watch had done preparing for hovering by trying to estimate the trim needed to achieve neutral buoyancy at zero speed. The automated system was good, but it could only pump so fast. If the *Belgorod* started to "sink out," the conning officer might be forced to restore propulsion and try again after pumping off water weight.

Like everyone else in control, Konstantin kept his eyes fixed on the main depth gauge at the top of the diving control panel. The current depth read 356 meters and was drifting in the wrong direction. When the display changed to 357, the conning officer started to speak, but Konstantin cut him off.

"Give it a moment," he said.

"Aye, Captain."

The digital display changed to 358, then flickered back and forth between 357 and 358 for several seconds, before settling back on 357. A long moment later, it came up to 356, then 355.

"Good job, diving officer," Konstantin said. "You got us damn close. Looks like the system has everything under control."

"Thank you, sir," the dive said.

"Quartermaster, report position."

"Captain, ship is four hundred and twenty meters south-southeast of the target location," the quartermaster reported.

"Very well," he said and turned to Blok. "Conning officer, I'm going aft to the UUV hangar control room. I will have the control room supervisor notify you when we are ready to open the bay doors and launch the submersible."

"Aye, Captain."

He turned to First Officer Stepanov, who'd just arrived on the conn. "Your timing is perfect. I'm heading aft to supervise the launch and operation of the drone. Stay here and keep an eye on things."

"Yes, sir," Stepanov said.

Konstantin left the ship's control room and made his way to the wet hangar control room, which was located on deck five aft of the sail. Where a regular-build Oscar II submarine had an ICBM missile compartment in the middle section of the ship, the *Belgorod* did not. Instead of a missile bay, K-329 had been outfitted with a unique module that facilitated a variety of covert, deep-ocean missions that could be conducted by different submersible platforms— some manned like the deep-diving, nuclear-powered, top secret *Losharik* (AS-31), and others like the unmanned Klavesin-3P-PM they carried aboard in the wet hangar. These special "research" vessels fell under the purview of the Main Directorate of Deep-Sea Research, or GUGI, as did this mission. The *Belgorod*, for its part, was "on loan" to the GUGI from the Northern Fleet for this operation.

From an organizational perspective, deep submersible and UUV operations fell under the weapons department, which meant that Captain Lieutenant Morozov was the man in charge. When Konstantin arrived at the hangar control room, he found Morozov pacing.

"Captain, the preoperational checklist is complete. We have a good connection with the drone. Batteries have ninety-seven percent charge and the pilot is ready to commence the operation," Morozov reported the instant Konstantin entered.

Konstantin walked to stand in front of the man, placed his hand on Morozov's shoulder, and said, "Can you guarantee me that the bay doors will operate silently?"

Despite looking visibly nervous, Morozov answered without hesitation. "No, Captain. I cannot."

This was the response Konstantin had hoped to hear. Not because it was the news he wanted, but because it was the truth. The wet hangar bay doors sometimes made a "clank" sound during the last ten degrees of travel when opening. Frustratingly, this anomaly did not occur every time the doors were cycled. While the *Belgorod* had been in dry dock at Sevmash, correcting this problem had been a priority for Konstantin. The previous weapons officer had assigned a maintenance team to identify the root cause of the problem and fix it, but according to Morozov, the sound could not be reliably replicated and thus was never corrected.

Konstantin exhaled. "You understand that there is certainly an American hunter-killer submarine patrolling this area. That the American carrier strike group is operating in this area at this very moment. If the doors clank, it is an advertisement to every pair of sonar tech ears listening for hundreds of kilometers that we are here. It is like standing up on the battlefield, waving your hands, and shouting, 'Here I am, shoot me.'"

"Yes, Captain, I understand this all too well," the weapons officer answered. "All I can tell you is that before getting underway, I ordered the hinges and operating mechanisms thoroughly lubricated with fresh grease and cycled five times. The noise occurred on the first cycle, but not the next four. In reviewing the logs, it seems this noise happens most frequently upon the initial cycling after periods of inactivity. The bay doors have not been operated since leaving the shipyard. I'm sorry to say, but if it is going to happen, it will probably happen now."

Konstantin nodded. He'd read the report as well and had come to the same conclusion. "Let me ask you a question, Captain Lieutenant. What if we only open the doors eighty-five percent—stopping them before the point of travel where the noise occurs—can we still attempt to launch the submersible?"

Morozov thought a moment and said, "I considered this option myself and took measurements of the clearance with the doors at eighty-seven degrees open before departing dry dock. What you suggest is possible, *but* the clearance is small. The pilot will have to ascend perfectly. Ocean currents could easily push the Klavesin's hull into the doors and that will also make noise."

"So, it's a roll of the dice either way."

"*Da*, Captain."

Konstantin looked at the submersible drone pilot sitting at the console nearby. The young man had clearly been listening to the conversation while trying to appear otherwise. "Pilot, what is your opinion on the matter?"

"Sir, I default to Captain Lieutenant Morozov's decision," the man said.

He walked to stand beside the console, towering over the seated pilot. "I know you do, just like you have been trained, but that was not my question."

"Uh . . . I think we should open the bay doors all the way, Captain."

Konstantin gave a snort. "So you are not confident with your abilities. You would prefer that the captain lieutenant receive my wrath if the doors clank rather than take the risk yourself."

The drone pilot's cheeks flushed and he burbled something, but it mattered not. Konstantin had his answer. "We will fully open the bay doors. I am the ship's captain, and I take responsibility for the outcome of the decision. Captain Lieutenant Morozov, inform the control room that we are opening the hangar bay doors and commencing the operation."

"Yes, sir," Morozov said and nodded at their phone talker, who was already in direct communication with a phone talker in the ship's control room.

The young man passed the information to the conn and a beat later announced, "Captain, control acknowledges and reports that the ship is five hundred and forty-seven meters south-southeast of the target location. The thrusters are struggling to overcome the current."

"What is the last sounding?"

"Eleven hundred nineteen meters, Captain," Morozov answered.

"How long is the control wire?" Konstantin asked Morozov.

"Five thousand meters, sir."

"What is the maximum speed of the drone?"

"Twelve knots, Captain," the drone pilot and Morozov said at the same time.

"Then we're fine. We have plenty of cable, and the submersible can overcome the ocean currents. Proceed with the operation."

"Aye, Captain," Morozov said. "Pilot, open the wet hangar bay doors."

The pilot acknowledged the order, silently crossed himself, and pressed the button on his terminal to open the drone hangar doors.

41

Sorry, Juice," Knepper said to Lieutenant Junior Grade Mike Majewski, his voice ripe with sarcastic pity, "this is going to sting—I gotta seven, two eights, and a nine, so with the six on the flip that's fifteen-two, fifteen-four, fifteen-six, double long runs for eight more, and a pair for two, which makes sixteen points. And the crib is mine . . . So let's take a look. Ooh, what do we have here: two sixes, a nine, and a jack—that's fifteen two, fifteen four, a pair for six and nobs makes seven, *aaaaaand* with the six on the cut I've got trips for six more for a total of thirteen. Ouch, that's gotta sting."

With a victorious smirk, Knepper jumped his trailing peg on the cribbage board sixteen, then leapfrogged the other peg another thirteen, moving way around the bend and leaving Juice in the dust. Two sevens instead of two eights would have given him a bonus three points as a "blackfish" under the house rules, a nod to their hull number of seven-eight-seven. But he'd take the big win without it.

"Bastard," Juice muttered as he scooped up the cards to deal the next hand. "But I mean that with all due respect, sir."

"I'm trying to think, Juice, have you ever beaten me at cribbage?" Knepper said and took a sip of coffee from the *Blackfish* mug with XO printed on the back.

"Uh, yes, sir, I skunked you last underway," the JO said as he dealt them each six new cards.

"It wasn't a skunk. I would definitely remember that."

"Oh, it was definitely a skunk. In fact, it was almost a double skunk."

"If it was a skunk, I would have had to sign the back of the board," Knepper said, trying not to laugh. "And since I didn't sign, it didn't happen."

"No, sir. Remember I graciously exempted you from having to sign the board to spare you the embarrassment in front of the rest of the wardroom?"

"You know, Mike, I have control over the watch bill . . ."

"I think that was the same threat you used last time, sir, which is why I let you off the hook."

At this, both men burst into laughter, which was promptly interrupted by Knepper's MOMCOM, aka his Man on the Move underway personal radio, which rang against his chest, where he wore it clipped to his coveralls.

"CDO," he said, taking the call.

"CDO, Conn, the officer of the deck requests you come to the conn," the voice said.

"On my way." He scooted his chair back from the wardroom table and looked at Juice. "If you stack the deck while I'm gone, I'll know."

"No self-respecting submariner stacks the cribbage deck. That's sacrilege."

"Damn right it is. I knew there was a reason we gave you your dolphins," Knepper said and gave the big JO's back a pat on the way out.

Everybody on the *Blackfish* liked Juice, and for good reason— the guy was both competent and had a helluva sense of humor— which were the two currencies necessary for surviving and thriving in the submarine force. Knepper liked to think that he also possessed both attributes, which was why he'd advanced successfully through the ranks and screened for XO. But as the ship's executive officer, he'd had to modify his style from the persona he'd developed as a JO and department head. As the ship's XO, he didn't have the luxury of being everybody's buddy. He was responsible for maintaining order and discipline, and sometimes that meant playing bad cop so the CO didn't have to. True leadership wasn't about being liked. And it wasn't about being feared.

True leaders are respected.

Because even commanding officers needed sleep, the Navy created a position known as the command duty officer, or CDO. During the midwatch, which lasted from midnight to 0800, Knepper stood CDO, a period during which he acted in the captain's stead, only waking the CO in case of emergency or a tactical development of consequence. Knepper's goal for the deployment was to have none of the former and hopefully lots of the latter. Not because he secretly delighted in sleep-depriving his boss, but because the *Blackfish* was deployed as a tip of the spear asset and that meant sneaking its way into the enemy's business as aggressively as possible. They had high hopes for this deployment that they'd locate and track foreign submarines and that meant working the problem twenty-four seven.

And with the *Belgorod* out there somewhere, that mission was more important than perhaps any in his entire career.

"CDO in control," the messenger announced when Knepper stepped onto the conn.

"What have you got, OOD?" he said as Juggernaut—who was standing midwatch officer of the deck—met him at the OOD workstation.

She gestured with her head to the port side of the control room, where ST1 Boone was holding up a pair of headphones. "Boone picked up something. It's worth taking a listen to."

"What do you think it is?"

"We don't want to bias you," she said. "Would rather you take a listen and then discuss."

"Sure," Knepper said and made his way over to the row of sonar terminals where Boone was waiting. "Let me guess—you've got some whales getting busy? A little humpback action going on, huh?"

"No ocean porn tonight, sir," Boone said with a grin and handed Knepper a headset. "Now, keep in mind, we only heard it once, but I've got the recording on a loop so you can hear it several times."

"Gotcha," he said and slipped on the cushy over-the-ear headphones.

Boone tapped a button on the keyboard and the recording played—static followed by a distinct clank, then static again. Knepper closed his eyes and listened to the event three more times before opening his lids and taking off the headphones. "Definitely metallic and mechanical. That's no fish."

"My sentiments exactly," Boone said.

"And you say it only happened once?"

"Yes, sir," the sonar supervisor said.

"Bearing?"

Boone sniffed. "Bearing two-five-four."

Knepper glanced at the ship's heading displayed on the upper right corner of the sonar terminal screen that read two-eight-four. He turned to Juggernaut. "Is this the course you were on when you heard it?"

"No, I was on one-eight-five. I turned to close, but I wanted to have some aspect for narrowband," she said, referring to the *Blackfish*'s TB-29 thin line array, which was towed behind the boat and could not listen effectively in the three-three-zero to zero-three-zero relative bearing cone.

"Good call," he said. "So the clank is all you've got—no broadband or narrowband?"

"Yup," she said. "One ping . . . One ping only."

He chuckled at the inside joke and was about to tell her to keep him posted, when a thought occurred to him and he whirled to face the nav plot. "Quartermaster, show me the original line of bearing from the ship's position when we first detected the anomaly."

"Sure thing, XO," the quartermaster said, hovering over the horizontal digital workstation that functioned like an oversized Microsoft Surface.

Using a trackball, the sailor selected a point on the ship's track that corresponded with the time of detection and extended a line of bearing to the east. Knepper leaned in and squinted, following the bearing line over the bathymetry curves and annotations on the digital chart. Not seeing what he was looking for, he said, "Where's the mid-Atlantic DASH data node and cable? Shouldn't it be on here?"

"Oh my God, I can't believe I brain farted on that," the quartermaster said as he clicked a drop-down menu. "It's a top secret overlay, and this is the first time I've imported one. It times out every hour and you have to click 'show layer' and reenter your login and password for it to reappear. I'm so sorry."

"That's all right, that's why we're a watch section team," Knepper said, "so we can back each other up."

A heartbeat later the overlay was up and a mid-Atlantic DASH data node and cable appeared as a green square with a line snaking across the chart—the very system that the Russian surface ship the *Finitor* had been intercepted for loitering over. The black bearing line crossed the cable to the west.

"How far is that point?" Knepper asked, tapping the glass at the point of intersection.

The quartermaster used the trackball to measure the distance and said, "Nineteen thousand two hundred yards."

Knepper turned to Juggernaut. "Are you thinking what I'm thinking?"

"That we might've just caught somebody with their hand in the cookie jar?" she said.

"Precisely." With a snarky smile, Knepper turned and headed for the command passageway to knock on the CO's stateroom door.

Sorry, Skipper, looks like you don't get your beauty rest tonight.

42

Morozov's heart momentarily stopped beating when the hangar bay doors clanked during the opening sequence, just as he had predicted they would. The noise was so loud that it seemed to make the entire hull reverberate. Everyone in the submersible control room cringed, but nobody said a word. The captain also said nothing, but the crimson color his face turned made his feelings on the matter perfectly clear.

Gorov decided to roll the dice, and they came up crab's eyes.

Despite the clank being a brief and singular event, the sound would travel for kilometers in the ocean. If there was an American submarine nearby, they would undoubtedly have heard it. Whether the Americans acted on the anomaly and could find the *Belgorod* in hovering mode was another matter altogether. The world's biggest submarine had proven to be quieter than anyone had anticipated, including Morozov.

Which means I must find an opportunity to slip away to make certain the Americans find us, he thought, looking down at his feet.

"Captain, the conning officer reports that sonar has detected a noise event from our own ship," the phone talker seated next to the submersible pilot reported.

"*Da*, we all heard it," Gorov said in a surprisingly even tone.

"Tell the conning officer to closely monitor our sonar for submerged contacts or changes in the posture of the American fleet."

"Aye, Captain," the phone talker said.

Morozov knew the captain's order was more theater than anything else. The *Belgorod* had been forced to retrieve their towed array in preparation for Operation Guillotine. Without forward movement to keep the towed sonar array stretched out behind the submarine, it would droop and drift and could become tangled in the ship's propellers or the drone's control wire. Detecting an American submarine with the towed array was already a herculean task. Finding one with only the *Belgorod*'s bow broadband would take a miracle.

Gorov straightened his uniform, then clasped his hands behind his back, presenting the very model of Russian naval command dignity. "Pilot, deploy the drone."

"Deploy the drone, aye, Captain," the submersible pilot said.

Using what looked like a video game joystick, the pilot conducted a quick check of the drone's control surfaces, then "floated" the Klavesin-3 UUV out of the wet hangar. The Klavesin submersible—which translated to "Harpsichord" in English—was designed by Russia's premier maritime robotics engineers at the Rubin Design Bureau. The variant the *Belgorod* carried was the third iteration of the machine and had been specifically created for this mission. In addition to the lights, cameras, magnetometers, and advanced mapping sonar built into the previous variants, this UUV also had two robotic arms equipped with multifunction tool heads. While advertised as an "autonomous" drone, this claim was a gross exaggeration. To conduct complex interventions like the one they had planned in Operation Guillotine, the drone required a human pilot to guide it to the seabed floor and manipulate the mechanical arms. Since two-way data flow was necessary, the Klavesin-3 utilized a guide wire that unspooled from an internal cable drum not unlike the wire-guided Mark 48 ADCAP torpe-does used by the Americans.

Morozov watched as the pilot cleared the hangar doors without incident and started the Klavesin's propellers. While certainly smaller than the Status-6 torpedo, the Klavesin was not a small machine. At seven meters long with a mass of four tons, the Klavesin looked more like a midget submarine than a drone. With a maximum diving depth of six thousand meters and a range of fifty kilometers on its sealed lithium-ion battery pack, the Klavesin should have no trouble descending to the bottom there, where the depth was only a fraction of the machine's limit. But reaching the target depth and completing the mission were two entirely different things. Morozov put the odds of the pilot completing the mission at fifty percent. Russian engineers were some of the brightest and most creative thinkers in the world. Russian mechanics, on the other hand, often struggled to turn these fantastic ideas into a working reality.

"Passing four hundred meters, Captain," the pilot said as he dived the drone. "Data transmission rate on the wire is good at one megabit per second."

"Very well," Gorov said, his eyes glued to the pilot's instrument panel.

As he watched the UUV descend, Morozov's mind drifted to the other task on his mind. Morozov knew where Tarasov stowed the noise augmentation device when not in use. He also knew how to operate the machine. It wasn't complicated. Plug it in, set the desired frequency, and connect it to any welded connection on the hull or hull valve and it would create a sound short by sending acoustic energy directly into the ocean. Taking great care not to be seen, he'd retrieved the device from the stowage locker in the engine room and installed it in a place where it was extremely unlikely to be found—inside the lower lock-in/lock-out chamber located on the keel, where the *Losharik* submersible mated up to the *Belgorod*. The *Losharik* was presently in Olenya Guba, undergoing repairs and recertification in the wake of a tragic battery fire that had killed sixteen and severely damaged the deep-diving submarine. Operation Guillotine was ideally suited for the deep-diving, manned *Losharik*, but with that platform out of commission, the only option was using the Klavesin.

This made the docking chamber where the *Losharik* mated up to the *Belgorod* the ideal location to install the device, as the chamber would not be used or even accessed during this entire underway. Morozov had snuck down to the bowels of the ship during the last night watch and accessed the chamber. As an electrical engineer by training, he'd had no trouble splicing the device's power cable into a wire feeding a dome light *inside* the chamber. The plan had been brilliant, in his opinion, because with the access hatch shut, the device could not be seen. Also, to turn it on, all he had to do was flip the dome light switch, which was located on the bulkhead outside the chamber. The whole nerve-racking evolution had taken him less than ten minutes, and he'd completed it in between watch stander rounds. He estimated it would take hours, if not days, to locate the device. So long as he wasn't seen turning it on, it would be impossible to prove he was the culprit.

I need to be patient and bide my time, he told himself. *When the opportunity presents itself, I will take it.*

At one hundred meters from the ocean floor, the pilot requested permission to turn on the bottom-sounding sonar.

"Very well," Gorov said. "Now is a good time to turn on the lights and video camera as well."

"*Da,*" the pilot said and flipped three switches in succession, energizing the drone's sonar, lights, and camera in that order.

Two previously dark windows on the monitor energized to show the view from the Klavesin's forward- and downward-looking cameras. Despite the powerful halogen light bulbs, the field of view seemed surprisingly limited to Morozov. He mentioned this as he watched bubbles and floating particulate zoom past the lens in a field of gray.

The pilot shrugged. "It is very dark at the bottom of the ocean. There is no sunlight at these depths."

"I wonder what strange creatures we will see," he said.

"Maybe we will see a giant squid," the phone talker said, sounding hopeful. "Captain, what do you think we will see?"

Gorov smiled, surprising Morozov. "Maybe sleeping sharks or bioluminescent shrimp and crabs."

"Probably we will see nothing but silt and rock. In my experience, it is not like the nature shows," the pilot said, and he turned out to be right.

To their collective disappointment, the bottom of the ocean was like a barren desert of nothingness—just grayish-brown sediment and rocks. The pilot maintained the Klavesin UUV about two meters off the bottom as he searched for the cable, which, according to the UUV's estimated position on the nav screen, should be somewhere within a fifty-meter radius.

"There," Morozov said, pointing to a hump on the seabed as it came into the frame on the upper right corner of the monitor.

"You have good eyes, WEPS," the captain said. "It is completely covered in sediment and would be easy to miss."

"Yes, I think that is it," the pilot said, using the joystick to bring the drone into a hovering position over the mound.

In an impressive show of skill, he used the drone's forward and aft horizontal thrusters to spin the Klavesin on its central axis while goosing the propellers, which acted like a blower to clear the sediment off the data hub. The maneuver kicked up a massive underwater cloud of silt, completely whiting out the image, but after thirty seconds the cloud drifted off. When the water clarity returned, the display showed a domed junction box with one black cable entering from the west and two cables leaving to the east.

Gorov gave his affirmation with a curt nod. "That's it. Good job, team."

The pilot hovered the drone and flipped another switch.

"What does this switch do?" the phone talker asked.

"Energizes the magnetometer. I want to confirm this hub is actively transmitting data," he said and pointed to a data box, where the reading shot up from 0 to 3.4. "It is active. Captain, how shall I proceed?"

During the pre-evolution brief, a debate had erupted in the wardroom about how to optimally sabotage this critical American undersea communications relay. Some officers had lobbied to set charges and destroy the hub, while others including Morozov had argued that cutting the incoming cable would be just as effective, but also minimize the risk of counter-detection. The captain had decided on the latter.

"Cut the incoming cable," Gorov said.

"Cut the cable, aye, sir."

The pilot bent at the waist and retrieved a twin handle controller from a small black bag on the floor at his feet. He plugged the end of the cable into a USB port on the control panel and set the previous controller he'd been using aside. He then set the new controller on the desk surface and began using both joysticks simultaneously. Morozov watched as the pilot deployed the UUV's two robotic arms, which entered the field of view of the bottom-facing camera. He then released the joysticks and grabbed the previous controller and used it to descend the drone to within a half meter of the cable. Morozov watched in awe as the pilot switched back to the joysticks controlling the arms and tried to maneuver the left arm claw to latch on to the cable. The current pushed the drone off the mark and the pilot had to once again switch controllers to reposition.

"It seems a pilot and copilot arrangement would be ideal so one could hover while the other controls the arms," Gorov said.

"*Da*, a point I have made on numerous occasions," the pilot said, the tone in the man's voice implying this was an ongoing point of contention in his job.

Morozov was just about to offer to try to help, when the pilot latched on successfully with the claw. Next, he maneuvered the right arm's cutting head into position and fired up the electric saw, which resembled a chain saw. The saw bit into the jacket and sent debris spewing in all directions. The cutting tool seemed to make quick work of the cable, but then abruptly froze and an alarm flashed amber on the screen: CUTTING HEAD OVER TORQUE.

The pilot cursed and squeezed the trigger on the right joystick, but nothing happened.

"It's jammed," Gorov said. "Try to reverse it."

The pilot toggled a switch on the joystick and squeezed the trigger. The alarm momentarily went dark, then returned.

CUTTING HEAD OVER TORQUE.

"Shit, what do we do?" the pilot said, looking up at Morozov.

"What does the manual say?"

"The manual is in my stateroom."

"Where? I'll fetch it," Morozov said.

"In the locker over my desk."

Morozov rushed out of the hangar control room before the captain could assign the task to someone else. He would have to be quick, but this was the opportunity he'd been waiting for.

43

C ommotion at the sonar stacks drew Knepper's attention. *They've got something,* he thought with a satisfied smile. The report from the sonar supervisor came a beat later.

"Conn, Sonar, sonar holds new narrowband contact, designated Sierra Two-Seven, bearing two-three-seven," the sonar supervisor said. "Officer of the deck, Sierra Two-Seven is classified as a possible submerged contact."

"Gimme the deets, Boone," Juggernaut said, walking over with Knepper to take a look.

"151.7 hertz just fired up out of nowhere. Signal-to-noise ratio is solid," Boone said, pointing at the bright trace on the waterfall display.

The OOD put her hands on the back of Boone's seat and leaned in for a look. "Yeah, it is, and the bearing lines up with the clank we heard earlier . . . XO, I think Boone found us a Russian submarine."

"Looks that way," Knepper agreed. Why don't we stay on this course for another five minutes and collect some data, then come to heading 200."

"I was just going to propose something similar," she said.

"Great minds think alike."

"Do you want me to inform the captain?"

"I already woke him up once. Might as well be me this time, too," he said and headed out of the conn to command passageway to knock on the skipper's door.

"Come," Commander Clint Houston said through the door before Knepper could even tap his knuckles on the wood.

Knepper cracked the door open and wasn't surprised to find the CO sitting up in his rack with a book on his lap and his reading lamp on. No way he was falling back asleep with the possibility of a Russian sub poking around the data hub.

"Captain, we just picked up a narrowband trace on the twenty-nine in the same location as the clank."

Houston scrubbed his face with his hands, tossed the *Tier One* novel he'd been reading onto his desk, and swung his legs off the side of the mattress. He slipped his sockless feet into a pair of Olu-Kai Holos and headed out of his stateroom wearing the FEAR THE BLACKFISH T-shirt and gym shorts he'd been sleeping in earlier.

"How long ago did you pick it up?" the skipper asked as he shut the door behind him.

"Just now," Knepper said.

"Captain in control," the control room messenger announced as they walked onto the conn together.

"So Juggernaut decided to go fishing. What did you catch me, Jackie?" the captain said.

"I caught you a shark, Captain," Juggernaut said, crossing her arms on her chest. "*Literally.*"

Knepper cocked an eyebrow. "It's an Akula?"

"Yep. Boone just did a lookup in ASD and here's what popped," she said and gestured to the monitor on terminal two.

NAME: K-335 *Gepard*

TYPE: Akula III–class submarine

PENNANT #: 895

STATUS: Active

FLEET: North / Arctic

PORT OF RECORD: Polyarnyy

PROPULSION: Single 7-bladed propeller

SOUND OFFENDERS: 151.7 Hz on port aft quadrant

"Interesting," Houston said and stared at the middle distance for a moment while the man's formidable intellect churned through multiple scenarios. He did that from time to time, Knepper had noticed. Finally, the captain spoke. "It's possible it's been here the entire time. A silent escort for the *Finitor*, keeping tabs on the surface activity."

The theory got a collective nod from everyone in control, because it made perfect sense.

"What do you want me to do, Captain?" Juggernaut said, hands on hips. "Keep tabs from a distance?"

The corners of the CO's lips curled up into a mischievous grin. "Nope, I want you to get close."

Juggernaut smiled back. "How close?"

"Really fucking close, Jackie. I want to vacuum up every sound offender we can get on this guy. Also, I want a dead nuts firing solution locked in at all times. The *Ford* is up there right now, completely vulnerable. And based on the traffic we pulled down on the last broadcast, things are starting to heat up with the Russians. If the CO of the *Gepard* so much as thinks about engaging the carrier, we need to be ready." He tapped the *Blackfish* logo on the middle of his chest and uttered the boat's battle cry. "Fear the *Blackfish*."

Gooseflesh stood up on Knepper's forearms as he, and everyone on the conn, answered in unison: "Prepared for war!"

44

Konstantin watched the submersible pilot battling the controls, and his composure, as he tried to free the Klavesin's cutting head from the cable. On the video screen, the saw blade appeared to be about fifty percent through the cable when it became jammed. This did not surprise him. As someone who had used all kinds of saws to cut all kinds of materials *above* the water, he knew that upon reaching the midpoint of the cut, the cutting channel usually compressed and squeezed the blade, increasing friction and resistance. This was exactly what appeared to have happened here. The Klavesin's cutter was electric, not hydraulic, which probably meant it was underpowered for an evolution like this. Had this been a commercial rig, it most certainly would be powered by hydraulics, but such a system was impractical inside a one-meter-diameter deep-diving submersible.

"Read the passage again," the pilot snapped at Morozov, who was holding the Klavesin's operations and maintenance manual.

"It says, in the event of an over-torque alarm on the cutting head: One—release the trigger to stop power to the motor. Two—secure from cutting operations. Three—inspect the cutting head chain and track for obstructions or derailment. Four—if no signs of obstruction or derailment can be found, attempt to operate the cutting head under zero load—"

"As expected, the manual is useless," the pilot said, cutting Morozov off. "This is common sense. What does it say when the cutting head is stuck in the middle of the cut?"

Konstantin watched Morozov flip pages with a helpless look on his face.

"This condition . . . does not appear to be listed specifically," the weapons officer said.

"Of course not, why would the engineers put something that's useful in the manual? This is why the engineers need to come on the underway with us instead of staying behind in their office drinking coffee and getting fat!"

"Enough," Konstantin said. "Complaining does not solve the problem. We need to be systematic in our approach. I think it is time to call the engineer and put his mechanical mind to work on this problem."

"Captain, the conning officer requests your presence in control," the phone talker said, interrupting them.

"What is the reason?"

"They did not say . . . Would you like me to ask, sir?"

"*Nyet*, I'll go. In the meantime, find Tarasov and tell him to report to the wet hangar control room."

"Yes, Captain."

"Keep your cool, Galkin," Konstantin said to the pilot, whose attitude was starting to grate on his nerves.

"Yes, sir. I apologize for my unprofessional comments, sir," Galkin said, cowed.

Konstantin checked his watch, sighed, and left to confront the conning officer and the next problem that he'd have to manage. He was halfway there when it felt like someone had run him through with a flaming sword. For a moment, he was certain he'd been impaled, but a glance down at his abdomen showed that from the outside he was perfectly fine.

His real adversary was on the *inside*.

"Captain, are you okay?" a crewman in the passageway said as he rushed to Konstantin's side.

"Fine," he said through gritted teeth. "Just a very bad case of indigestion."

"Can I get you anything, sir?"

"*Nyet*. Thank you for your concern, but return to your business."

"Yes, Captain," the sailor said and left him alone, bent over and gritting his teeth in agony in the corridor.

It will pass . . . It always does.

And it did, after what felt like an eternity.

He wiped the sweat from his brow with his sleeve, straightened his uniform, and put on his command face. These "incidents" were growing more frequent and getting worse. If the trajectory continued at the current pace, he'd soon need narcotics to function or he'd be bedridden.

Possibly both, he thought, shaking his head. *I just need to hang on for a little longer, then it won't matter anymore.*

Forcing himself to stand tall, he strode into the control room.

"Captain on the conn," the control room messenger announced.

"What is the problem, conning officer?" he said, walking up to Blok, who was wearing a nervous, guilty look on his face.

Blok swallowed hard and said, "Sonar detected a 151-hertz signal. At first, we thought it was an American—"

"151 hertz?" he said, cutting Blok off.

"Yes, Captain."

"That's the frequency of the noise augmentation device. The signal is not coming from an American submarine, you bloody fool. It's coming from us!"

"*Da*, that's why I summoned you, Captain. Sonar is trying to isolate the source, but they are having difficulty localizing it."

"Idiots. We know exactly where the device is installed. Tell the engineer to meet me in the engine room." He whirled on a heel to head to aft. Over his shoulder, he shouted, "Tarasov should be in the wet hangar control room."

Rage fueling his steps, Konstantin ran through the passageways of the nearly six-hundred-meter-long submarine, shouting at everyone in his path to get out of his way. How could this happen? He'd seen Tarasov remove the device. Or . . . had he? For a moment, he wasn't sure if the conversation he remembered with the engineer was an actual memory or his imagination.

I must be losing my mind.

"Move!" he barked at a gaggle of sailors in the crew's mess passageway.

They scrambled, tripping and falling over each other, to make room for him to pass. When he reached the watertight door that controlled access to the shielded passageway, which cut through the reactor compartment to reach the engine room, he had to pause to catch his breath. For obvious reasons, he was not as physically fit as he'd been only one year ago. Wheezing, he cranked the handwheel to undog the hatch and pushed the heavy slab open. He ducked and stepped through the opening.

"I've got the door, Captain," a familiar voice said from behind.

He glanced over his shoulder to see Tarasov stepping through after him.

"I thought you removed the noise augmentation device?"

"I did, Captain."

"Then what the hell is going on?"

"I don't know, sir," the engineer said as he dogged the watertight door. "But I'm going to find out."

They jogged through the tunnel and into engine room, level 3, where the temperature was ten degrees hotter than the forward compartment. Konstantin let the younger and fitter Tarasov sprint ahead to the location at the port-aft quadrant, where the device had been installed.

"It's not here, Captain," Tarasov said, nonplussed, when Konstantin arrived at the spot.

Huffing, the captain scanned all the supports welded to the inside of the hull in the area and didn't see the device or anything out of the ordinary. "Then what is going on?"

"I'm going to check the stowage locker where I put it," the engineer said and darted away.

Konstantin did not follow. Instead, he leaned against the catwalk safety railing while his pulse and respiration rates came down. Tarasov returned two minutes later with a look that could melt lead.

"It's gone. Someone has taken it from the locker."

The Russian sub captain looked up at the ceiling, scarcely able to believe this was happening. "You realize, comrade, what is going on."

Tarasov hesitated a moment before saying, "Someone has done this on purpose?"

Barely able to contain his fury, Konstantin said, "That's right, and every second that damn noisemaker is on, we are advertising our location to the American fleet!"

"I will find it and destroy the machine, Captain. You can count on me."

Konstantin stared at Tarasov with cold, hard eyes. "And after, we find the man responsible. Then we destroy *him*."

45

K atie stared at the picture of Konstantin Gorov on her laptop screen. In the photograph, he wore his dress uniform—an immaculate black jacket with shoulder boards, a stack of ribbons on his chest, and gold stripes on his sleeves. He held his cover tucked under his right arm and stared at the camera with what she decided was his "command face."

He looked stoic and serious.

And very Russian.

He was not an unattractive man, she decided. The submarine captain projected a certain certitude and confidence in the picture that, strangely, reminded her of her big brother. Jack wasn't afraid of anything, even death, and she had the feeling the same was true for this man. The photograph was Gorov's official command photo, probably taken shortly after he'd been given command of the *Belgorod* . . . a happier time for him. She recalled her conversation with retired CIA case officer Reilly in his lonely sunroom surrounded by orchids, and she pondered the life and tragedies of Konstantin Gorov.

"Do you hate the world for what it's done to you?" she murmured. "Do you tell yourself that had America not reneged on its promise to your father, your future would have been different? *Better? Kinder?* Do you play the 'what if' game with yourself? Imagine that had you grown up in America, you would have married a different woman, who would have given birth in an American hospital, and that instead of being a widower you'd be a husband and father?"

Da, his eyes seemed to say, *and I blame your CIA for this.*

"Do you ever sleep, Ryan?" Captain Williams said from the doorway of the tiny office, snapping Katie from her trance.

"Only when there's time," she said with a weary smile.

"Ah, you're one of *those* types . . ."

"And what type is that?"

"The type of person who go-go-goes until your brain pulls the ejection handle and you pass out to avoid flatlining," Williams said, and she popped a piece of chewing gum into her mouth.

"As Ben Franklin once said, there will be plenty of time to sleep when I'm dead."

"I thought that was De Niro's line?"

"It is, but I'm pretty sure Franklin said it first," Katie said with a grin. "How can I be of assistance, XO?"

"There's something on the latest traffic I have a feeling you and your new best friend Jonesy are going to be very interested in looking at."

Katie perked up. "Did the *Blackfish* get a hit?"

Williams smiled. "Just take a look and come find me when you're ready to discuss. I'll be in the CIC."

"Thank you, ma'am," she said, her fingers going to the keyboard of her laptop. "Will do."

The XO left the doorway, but Katie barely noticed because she was already digging into the latest update transmitted by the USS *Washington*. The report wasn't long—submarine message traffic was powered by an economy of words—but these words were significant.

"A 151.7-hertz signal detected . . . preliminary classification as Akula . . . K-335," she mumbled as she read. When she'd finished she leaned back in her chair to think. "That's the same Akula the *Indiana* was tracking up in the Barents. What's it doing all the way down here?"

She plotted the coordinates where the *Blackfish* had identified the Akula.

"Shit!" She popped out of her chair and made a beeline to the stateroom where Jonesy had been put up.

Pulse racing, she knocked on the door. When no response came, she rapped on the door again, this time harder. She was just about to knock even harder when she heard movement inside. A beat later, the door opened a crack and a bleary-eyed Jones appeared in the gap, squinting at her.

Whoa, he looks different without his eyeglasses, she thought.

"Don't you ever sleep, Ryan?" he said, rubbing his eyes.

"Yeah, I get that a lot." The words spilled out of her mouth a mile a minute. "Hurry up and get dressed, there's something important I need to show you."

"Gimme sixty seconds," he said and shut the door.

The annoying part of her personality wanted to check her watch and confirm it had been *way* longer than sixty seconds when he finally reopened the door, but she reined that girl in.

"So, whatcha got for me?" he said.

"Thank you," she said with a smile.

"You're welcome?" he said with a confused smile. "But I'm not catching the non sequitur."

"Thank you for not getting your nose all bent out of shape and saying something like 'This better be important, Ryan,'" she said, dropping her voice an octave for the last bit.

"Yeah, well, we're both pros here. If it wasn't important, you wouldn't have woken me up in the middle of the night."

"Exactly," she said and set off to the N2 shop, where they could talk freely.

He followed her as she made the twisty-turny trek through the warren of passageways that was the USS *Ford*.

"How do you know where you're going?" he said behind her as they descended a ladder. "Didn't you arrive less than a day before me?"

"Quick orienting is just one of those useless skills I happen to have been born with, I guess."

"I wouldn't call not getting lost a useless skill," he said. "On a Los Angeles–class sub, there are only three levels with one central passage. You almost have to try to get lost, but not here."

"Your tour was on the *Dallas*, right?" she asked, but she already knew the answer because she'd memorized his CV.

"Sure was . . . She had a long run, the *Dallas*. Almost forty years at sea. Decommissioned in 2018," he said with a nostalgic tone. "They invited me to the ceremony. Got to catch up with my old skipper, Admiral Mancuso, while I was there."

"That must have been nice for you."

"It was . . . Anyway, enough with that stuff. What do you have for me?" he said as he took a seat at the conference table.

"The *Blackfish* just picked up the same 151.7-hertz signal that the *Indiana* tracked in the Barents."

"The *Indiana* identified the contact as K-335—the *Gepard*—if memory serves," he said, grabbing a tablet computer and pulling up an interactive map.

"That's right, the *Gepard* is an Akula based out of Polyarnyy. So my question is, what is it doing down here?"

"I think it's obvious," Jones said. "When we seized the *Finitor*—"

"We did not *seize* the *Finitor*," she said, cutting him off. "We conducted an inspection of the vessel."

He screwed up his face at her.

"Look, in my line of work, the words we use matter," she said. "We have to be precise and intentional about how we describe things so that the narrative doesn't mutate on us."

"Fine, but you get my point," he said. "The *Gepard* is both an expedient and convenient option. She was already at sea, so the Kremlin canceled her training exercise with the *Belgorod* and directed her down here so they could keep tabs on things and have firepower in place to protect their carrier in the event the situation spiraled out of control . . . Something that seems increasingly likely after yesterday."

"Makes sense," Katie said, but a different idea had already begun to take root in her mind. And the more she tried to discount it, the more right it felt.

"What's that look mean?" he said.

"What look?"

He fixed her with a face that looked like a squinty-eyed chipmunk. "This look."

"I don't make that face," she said.

"Yes, you do. You make it every time you're thinking hard about something."

She tilted her head at him. "You just met me, how can you say that?"

"Because you do it all the time."

"That's because I'm thinking hard all the time, Dr. Jones. I'm a hard thinker."

"Thank goodness, because you're an intelligence analyst. Now, spill it, LT."

She let out a long sigh. "Okay, here goes—I don't think that 151.7-hertz signal is the *Gepard*."

"Of course it's the *Gepard*. It's a documented sound vulnerability that multiple assets have tied to K-335."

"I know, but I think the Russians know that and they're trying to dupe us into thinking it's K-335 when it's actually not."

Jones gave her the squinty-eyed chipmunk face again. "If it's not the *Gepard*, what boat is it?"

"The *Belgorod*," she said, and just saying it aloud felt right and affirmational.

Jones laughed out loud.

"I'm serious."

He stifled his amusement. "Okay, then walk me through your logic."

"Okay, so the *Belgorod* gets out of the Sevmash dry dock in Severodvinsk and puts to sea two days later, unannounced and unscheduled, according to our intelligence. But Severodvinsk is on the White Sea, which means a long surface transit to the Barents before the *Belgorod* can dive and disappear. No matter how hard the Russians try, they can't hide the fact that K-329 went to sea from our satellites. And because of the long surface transit, we had time to get the *Indiana* into position in the Barents to try to shadow her . . . Are you with me?"

"Absolutely," he said. "This is all standard stuff."

"I know, and so do the Russians. They know we'll have an asset in position. They also know we're jonesing—no pun intended—to exploit the opportunity to get an acoustic fingerprint on K-329."

"You have my attention, Ryan. Go on."

"They don't want us to surveil the *Belgorod* and build an acoustic file on her, so my theory is they cooked up a shell game with us.

Don't you see? The *Indiana* wasn't tracking the *Gepard*. They were tracking the *Belgorod*, pretending to be the *Gepard*."

"You're talking about acoustic subterfuge—a frequency generator?"

"Precisely," she said and sat back in her chair.

Jones sighed, took off his glasses to rub his eyes, and then put them back on.

"From your silence, I take it that you're not buying it?" she said after a long pause.

"Here's the thing, Ryan. According to satellite imagery, K-335 put to sea two days before K-329. We know from historical data that this area of the Barents is a Russian submarine exercise area. They've practically blanketed the Barents seafloor with hydrophones."

"To listen for our assets?"

"Yes, but also to support their own training exercises. They can monitor their sub-on-sub exercises in real time. It's not surprising at all that the *Belgorod* would head north into this area for some red-on-blue practice with the *Gepard*."

"Okay, but according to the message traffic, the *Indiana* never reacquired the *Gepard* after losing that 151.7-hertz signal, nor do we have any reports that they tracked the *Belgorod*."

"That's not uncommon," Jones said. "Submarines are hard to find. The *Indiana* could spend weeks on station, and if they collected a few hours of data, it would be considered a huge success. Most submarine contact is fleeting and intermittent, especially when you're talking about trying to find and track the latest generation of Russian subs."

"Look, I'm telling you, the reason the *Indiana* can't find the *Belgorod* is because it's not in the Barents anymore. Remember, the *Belgorod* is technically a special projects boat. Its mission is to support deep submersible operations and serve as a platform to launch the Status-6 torpedo. The *Finitor* was mapping our transatlantic data cable and nodes in advance of the *Belgorod*'s arrival. The signal the *Blackfish* detected plots within a quarter mile of the data node. Can't you see, it's not the *Gepard* here on patrol—it's the *Belgorod* conducting its real tasking."

"Which is?"

"I can't say for certain, but my money is on physically hacking into the DASH data node the *Finitor* successfully located."

"Let's say for a moment that your theory is right," he said, leaning in and putting his elbows on the table. "Why in God's name would the *Belgorod* turn on its frequency generator at the exact geographic location and time when the mission demands absolute stealth? I call that self-sabotage, Ryan, and it doesn't make any sense."

"I know, I know," she said and ran her fingers through her hair with a sigh.

"Your theory is definitely creative and outside the box, kid, but—"

"Excuse the intrusion," Lieutenant Commander Kumari interrupted, striding into the room. "There's been a development, and the CO just summoned all senior staff for a briefing."

"What happened?" Katie asked, hoping Kumari wouldn't make them wait for the punch line.

"Someone just knocked out our DASH mid-Atlantic adaptive sonar array."

Jones's eyes went wide and he turned to Katie.

Despite her best attempt at self-restraint, she smiled grimly and said, "What do you think about me now?"

46

C lark paced the living room, feeling very much like a caged tiger in a zoo.

The days of sunglasses, ball caps, and hiding behind newspapers were long, long gone. Conducting surveillance operations in Moscow had always been dangerous, but these days it was practically a suicide mission. If the Russians had his face—or Ding's or Midas's or Adara's—in their database, they were at risk of being identified by one of the thousand CCTV cameras in the city. If the SVR had flagged any of them as a person of interest, then the Spetssviaz—the successor to FAPSI and the Russian equivalent of the NSA—would use its facial recognition surveillance system to scour the feeds and find them. And if that happened, the interrogation and torture that would follow their capture would be a fate worse than death.

"Hey, boss, why don't you take a seat," Ding said. "You're making me nervous."

Clark was a man of action, a problem solver, a *doer* . . . So sitting around and waiting wasn't in his vocabulary.

"I can't," he said. "Doing nothing is driving me crazy."

"I get it, but this ain't Severodvinsk," Ding said, "This is Moscow. And our marks aren't some mid-level weapons engineer like Popov. The guys we need to surveil are sharks, not minnows. Boldyrev is the head of the Russian Navy. Rodionov is second-in-command of the GRU. Aralovich leads the FSB."

"And Ilyin is the retired defense minister," Midas said.

"Exactly my point. These men are the untouchables of the Russian upper echelon. They all have security details watching their private residences. They all work in the most secure buildings in Moscow. We wouldn't get within a hundred yards of them without being made. And, boss, I'm worried about you getting made most of all. You met with VICAR twice in person. You were sitting across from him in Warsaw when the hit squad came. What are the odds you *weren't* photographed?"

"I know, I know," Clark grumbled. "But the President needs to understand what these sons of bitches are up to. How can he make tactical decisions if he doesn't know who the enemy is and what their objectives are? He needs us to figure out what the hell is going on."

"Okay, I hear you. So let's work the problem," Ding said, turning his attention from his open notebook computer to Clark. "Talk us through what's in your head."

Clark took a moment and gathered his thoughts, and then did just that.

"Popov said that Boldyrev personally paid a visit to the shipyard and ordered everyone out while the Status-6 torpedoes were loaded. Can you imagine the chief of naval operations showing up at the Portsmouth Naval Shipyard to micromanage a weapons load? That would never happen."

"Popov also said that Rodionov had 'toured' the facility and conducted interviews. Why would the number two guy at GRU drop by the Sevmash Shipyard in Severodvinsk for a tour and interviews?"

"I think the answer is obvious," Adara said. "The GRU was conducting a security and loyalty survey in advance of Boldyrev's visit and the *Belgorod*'s weapons load and secret underway."

"It still doesn't confirm a coup. Yermilov could have directed all of this. He's known to be both paranoid and meticulous about security and compartmentalization," Midas said, playing the devil's advocate.

"Good point," Ding said, and they were back to conjecture.

Clark closed his eyes and tried to replay the conversation with VICAR in his head. There was something the Russian double agent had said—a little detail—that Clark's brain told him was important, but that he couldn't quite recall. He'd always had a good memory for details—not eidetic, but formidable. Except, with each passing year, he was finding it harder and harder to retrieve memories on demand. It would come to him eventually, but he needed it now.

"What's wrong?" Ding asked.

"Quiet, I'm trying to think," Clark said, squeezing his eyes closed and coaxing his mind's eye back to the table in that restaurant and VICAR's final conversation with him.

"I suspect Colonel General Nikolai Ilyin may be in charge. He was observed at Glavpivtorg in Moscow with Admiral Rodionov."

"Does the word 'Glavpivtorg' mean anything to you guys?" Clark asked, his eyes popping open. "Is it some secret GRU facility?"

"Say the word again?" Ding said.

"Glavpivtorg, I think. But it could have been Glavapitvorg . . . I can't remember exactly."

"Got it," Ding said, fingers working the keyboard. "Glavpivtorg, Moscow—it's a restaurant and bar located, get this, across from the old KGB headquarters . . . Known to be a place where KGB officers drank after work."

"What's the connection, boss?" Adara asked.

"It's one of the last things VICAR said to me. He mentioned almost as an aside that Colonel General Ilyin was seen with Rodionov at Glavpivtorg."

"Plotting their coup over beer and borscht," Midas said with a chuckle.

"You laugh, but I have a feeling that might be closer to the truth than you know, Midas," Clark said.

"I'm going to do a deep dive on the owner," Ding said. "If these guys are having meetings there, it's because they consider it a safe place. Hundred bucks says the owner is former KGB and goes way back with the cabal members."

"I say we stake it out tonight," Adara said. "Who knows, maybe we'll get lucky."

"Good idea. Let's do it," Clark said.

"Not you," she said. "Remember, your face is on the watch list."

"I'll wear glasses and a hat," Clark said.

"Won't matter," Ding said.

"Then I'll put on a fake mustache . . ."

"Nope," Adara said, enjoying the moment it seemed.

"What will it take for you guys to let me do my job?" he said.

Adara looked at Midas, who with a deadpan delivery said, "If you shave your head, get a face tattoo, knock out your two front teeth, *and* wear glasses, only then will you be safe."

Clark sighed his resignation. "Fine, you win . . . I'll stay here."

47

K nepper had always wanted to conduct the evolution the *Blackfish* was about to attempt, but the opportunity had not presented itself during either his JO or department head tours. A close aboard acoustic collection of an enemy submarine required three necessary criteria: First, the target submarine had to be completely blind to the hunter's presence. Second, the environmental and tactical conditions had to support the evolution. And third, it took a commanding officer with nerves of steel—someone willing to risk undersea collision for the reward of acoustic intelligence.

Check, check, and check, he thought as he glanced at Commander Houston, who stood next to the command workstation in the middle of the conn. *I can't believe we're actually going to do this.*

The control room was more crowded, tense, and quiet than he'd seen since the day he'd come aboard as XO. The captain had ordered battle stations manned for this evolution—not because they expected a shooting match, but rather for the sake of preparedness and optimization. On a warship, "Man battle stations" was the command given to rapidly transition to the highest level of readiness. During normal operations, at any given time, a third of the ship's crew was on watch, a third was asleep, and the remaining third was scattered about the ship. At battle stations, all personnel were awake, accounted for, and posted where they were the most capable. For this evolution, the normal section tracking party rotation watch bill didn't cut it. If something went wrong, the CO wanted the best of the best on watch and all hands ready to respond at a moment's notice.

For his part in this highly choreographed dance, Knepper assumed the role of fire control coordinator. His responsibility was to analyze and maintain a firing solution on Master One—the *Gepard* K-335. If everything went according to plan, no torpedoes would be exchanged, but that didn't mean the evolution held no danger.

Knepper looked right at the WEPS.

Juggernaut stood—hands on hips—at the attack center, looking over the shoulders of the seated fire control technicians manning their consoles configured for target management and weapons control. The XO took a mental snapshot of the scene and burned it into his brain. This was Jackie's moment. What she'd spent a decade training to do. She knew the system and her people better than anyone else on board, and her confidence and knowledge of this fact practically glowed around her like an aura. If he were to try to step in and do her job for her, the intervention would only diminish the outcome. The same was true of every watch stander on the boat at this very moment. Every crew member was posted at the station where they were optimized to excel the most.

His gaze indexed around the control room, jumping from shipmate to shipmate. The pilot, the copilot, the nav—who was OOD—the sonar techs, the sonar LCPO standing supe, the ACINT specialist, the quartermaster, the contact manager . . . Knepper's life was literally in their hands.

Gooseflesh stood up on his neck.

Damn . . . There ain't nothing in the world more badass than a Virginia-class submarine control room at battle stations.

The *Blackfish* had been tracking Master One for nearly forty minutes and during that time had determined two very important things. First, Master One was stationary, and second, the contact was operating submerged. They knew this because the CO had ordered the boat to PD to take a look after getting multiple legs on the contact and a rock-solid fire control solution. For a surface ship, station keeping was no big deal. For a submarine, however, static hovering was no small feat. After visually confirming there was no surface vessel at Master One's coordinates, the *Blackfish* went deep and prepared for the next step.

The CO had chosen seven hundred and thirty feet—the shallowest depth the sound velocity profile would permit to maintain optimal acoustic reception, while hopefully maximizing depth separation between the target and the *Blackfish*. Unlike the surface Navy, submarine cat-and-mouse games were played in three dimensions. That uncertainty—the not knowing—was an omnipresent, ulcer-inducing stress for the submariner.

"Captain, Quartermaster—stand by for the turn to course two-eight-five," the quartermaster said, alerting everyone that the ship was approaching the calculated track.

"Very well, Quartermaster," the CO said, then added, "All right, everybody, buckle up and let's do this."

"Stand by for the turn . . . In three, two, one, mark the turn."

"Pilot, come left, steer course two-eight-five," the captain announced in a loud, confident voice.

The pilot acknowledged the order and Knepper felt the *Blackfish* heel ever so slightly as the rudder came on. From the corner of his eye, he saw the quartermaster—who was standing at the nav plot—cross himself. In theory, the plan was simple. The *Blackfish* would make two passes at a range of two hundred yards: the first pass, to the north on a westwardly course, the second, to the south on a reciprocal course to the east. The pucker factor at that range, however, was off the chart. Any unexpected movement of the target or change of depth could result in collision. And a collision between two submarines could result in the loss of both vessels. A pressure hull breach at depth would be a catastrophic and unrecoverable casualty.

"Captain, the ship is on course two-eight-five," the pilot reported a few moments later, a course that had them driving head-on into the ocean current to minimize the impact of set and drift while trying to maintain track.

"Very well," the CO said.

"Crossing two thousand yards to target," the quartermaster announced.

As per their pre-evolution brief, the quartermaster would be announcing range to target in increments as the *Blackfish* closed on Master One for all the watch standers in control.

"Very well."

The ship was also rigged for "ultra-quiet," which meant using the quietest propulsion plant and auxiliary equipment lineup. Routine maintenance, housekeeping, and activities that could generate transient noise were all prohibited. No toilet flushing. No cooking in the galley. No announcements on the ship's PA system. No movement of tools or stowed materials that could possibly drop. Even the crew spoke in hushed tones, although this was psychological rather than procedural. The *Blackfish* became a black hole of sound in the water so the target would never know what happened.

Knepper glanced at the closest stack and checked the fire control solution for Master One on the geoplot—a downward-looking, bird's-eye view of the patch of ocean they were operating in. "Own ship," as submariners referred to themselves, was represented as an icon centered in the very middle of the display and contacts being tracked were represented by triangular icons in relative space around it. In this case, the *Blackfish* held only one contact and that was Master One off their port bow.

Range: 1835 yds Bearing: 279 T AOB: S174 Course: 285 Speed: 0 kts

The FT had chosen to orient Master One facing into the current for the same reason the CO had chosen this course. The target's true orientation was unknown because Master One was hovering, but the FT's assumption was grounded in logic and certainty. Knepper watched the triangular icon for a beat, willing it to stay put. Somewhere in the back of his mind, he felt Mr. Murphy—the architect of entropy and chaos and every submariner's sworn enemy—loitering, waiting for the perfect moment to crash the party and ruin everyone's day by evoking his law.

If something can go wrong, it will go wrong, a voice in his head whispered.

Why did *that* have to be the submariner's aphorism?

He glanced over at the narrowband display on the upper monitor. The bright 151.7-hertz trace was nearly perfectly straight and smooth following the slow, leftward-predicted bearing drift he expected to see as they closed. The closer they got, the faster the bearing rate would change, reaching the maximum delta as the *Blackfish* passed Master One close aboard off her port beam. He loved the fact that he could see both sonar and fire control data at the same time on the same stack. Unlike the fire control systems on previous classes of U.S. submarines, on Virginia-class boats, the fire control technicians could access the same raw sonar data and displays as the sonar techs, seated at identical consoles laid out in a mirror image on the port side of control. This integration allowed the FTs to recognize any change in sonar bearings instantly, which would indicate a change in aspect, course, or speed of the target. The converse was also true, in that a sonar tech could pull up a fire control geoplot on their stack. This flexible approach to data management was called ADAW, or any display anywhere, and meant that any of the numerous flat-panel screens inside the *Blackfish's* control room could be configured to display any of the dozens of different tactical or operational interfaces used for piloting, navigation, sonar, fire control, system management, and weapons configuration.

"Fifteen hundred yards to target," the quartermaster announced as they closed range.

"Very well," the CO said.

A tense silence hung in the control room, so pronounced it almost felt suffocating. Instead of trying to pretend it wasn't there, Knepper acknowledged and embraced it. Like their namesake, the orca, they were an apex predator, fueled by adrenaline and gliding silently toward their quarry. But instead of capturing prey with serrated teeth, the *Blackfish* would be capturing sound using their TB-34 and TB-29—twin towed arrays consisting of hundreds of hydrophones arranged linearly on a cable. Unlike the hull-mounted sonar systems, which were the workhorses of the submarine for daily navigation and contact tracking, towed arrays were literally towed several hundred yards behind the submarine in a zone of quiet behind the propulsor wash and away from the submarine's hull noise. The real data collection would happen when the submarine was already beyond the target and the towed arrays were passing directly abeam of K-335.

"One thousand yards to target," the quartermaster announced.

"Very well, quartermaster," the CO said.

"Observed bearing rate matches fire control solution for Master One. Target is still static. Recommend maintaining course and speed," Knepper said, more a statement of reassurance than anything else.

"Very well, coordinator."

"Passing nine hundred yards."

"Very well."

Someone dropped a pen, a gentle sound that shattered the heavy silence in the conn, and Knepper saw one of his FTs jump slightly.

Knepper's heart rate ticked up as the range closed quickly. The call-and-response between the captain and the quartermaster developed into a cadence that was impossibly both unnerving and assuring at the same time—unnerving because the range was shrinking with each announcement, but assuring because of the calm certitude in the skipper's voice.

"Passing five hundred yards."

"Very well, quartermaster," Houston said. "Report distance to track."

"Ring laser one and two, hold ship on track, plus or minus twenty yards," the quartermaster answered, referring to the sub's two inertial navigation systems that continuously measured three-axis acceleration while submerged to calculate the ship's velocity, direction, and estimated position.

"Coordinator, how are we looking?" the captain asked, his voice soft and just above a whisper, glancing at Knepper.

The CO watched the same geoplot on the command workstation that Knepper had over at the attack center, but that wasn't the point. The captain was giving him one final chance to call an abort before they reached the point of no return.

"Fire control solution is still tracking. Recommend maintaining course and speed," he said, his voice equally as soft, seeing no signs at all of trouble.

"Very well, coordinator. Sonar, sitrep?" the CO said, covering all his bases.

"Still hold strong narrowband contact on the 151.7-hertz signal," the sonar supervisor said, "but we're starting to pick up some other transients from Master One. Analyzing . . ."

"Very well, keep after it."

"Passing four hundred yards."

Knepper watched the bearing rate accelerate and the sonar trace begin to curve left as the *Blackfish* approached CPA, or closest point of approach, on the target.

"Three hundred and fifty yards to target."

"Very well, quartermaster."

"Passing three hundred yards."

Knepper could feel his pulse throbbing in his ears as the icon for K-335 on the geoplot drifted closer and closer. His engineer's mind started integrating all the margins of uncertainty for this evolution, and he didn't like the output. Contact management when submerged was nothing more than a geometry problem consisting of lines of bearing, angles of offset, and ever-changing vectors . . . All calculated from sound waves that were constantly bending, bouncing, reflecting, and Doppler-shifting in the water, thanks to variability in temperature, salinity, and bottom topography.

God, I hope what I'm looking at on the screen reflects reality.

He didn't dare vocalize the crazy thought, but he suspected he wasn't the only one having it. Driving a submarine was like asking a blindfolded person to navigate a shopping mall without a cane— a crazy proposition. The "picture" they used on the geoplot was nothing more than an approximation of reality, based on imperfect sound data.

"Passing two hundred and fifty yards . . . two forty . . . two thirty . . . two twenty . . . two ten . . . mark closest point of approach."

"Coordinator concurs," Knepper said, his eyes on the sonar trace whipping across the display as they passed abeam of the Russian submarine.

"Sonar concurs," the sonar supe announced.

"Very well," Houston said, acknowledging them all.

"Two hundred twenty yards and opening," the quartermaster said with a notable tenor of relief in his voice as the *Blackfish* slipped silently and unmolested past the target.

So friggin' cool.

Knepper smiled as he watched the range to K-335 opening on the fire control screen.

Beside him, in a voice barely audible, Juggernaut said, "Hell yeah, fear the *Blackfish*."

48

Konstantin battled to maintain his composure, pacing the auxiliary control room as the two crises unfolded simultaneously. On a submarine, everyone cued off the captain. If he appeared flustered and worried, then the watch standers were more likely to become flustered and worried. If he projected confidence and certitude, then the crew would react in kind. He'd spent years honing his command presence for situations like this.

He had two options, and both were terrible. Abort Operation Guillotine, abandon the Klavesin at the bottom of the ocean, and flee, or continue hovering and try to salvage the mission. Fatalistic pragmatism served as his lodestar. So long as the noise augmenter was transmitting, the *Belgorod* was compromised and without stealth wherever it went. The 151.7-hertz signal they were broadcasting might as well have been a homing beacon for the Americans. However, there was a big difference between *finding* the *Belgorod* and *firing* on the *Belgorod*. Even the most cavalier American submarine captain understood that the latter would constitute an act of war. Being in the vicinity of the transatlantic data cable node when the signal went down was not enough. Without ironclad proof, the Americans would not engage. And even with proof, odds were good they would not use lethal force. Sinking the nuclear-powered flagship of the Russian submarine fleet was a surefire way to start World War III. Konstantin knew his adversary, and so the decision to stay and finish the job did not feel so fraught and ominous when viewed through the lens of logic.

Nevertheless, he needed to prepare for the worst.

"Phone talker, get me a status report on isolating the sound offender," he said to the young man wearing the communications headset.

The phone talker queried the control room, then reported: "Captain, the conning officer apologizes and reports that sonar has been unsuccessful narrowing down the location of the sound offender with any certainty."

"Very well," Konstantin said. "Tell the conning officer to man battle stations, but do it silently. Do not sound the alarm, do not broadcast over the main intercom. We're already making enough noise as it is."

The phone talker relayed the order. "Captain, the conning officer acknowledged the order to man silent battle stations."

Konstantin had no contact with any submerged contacts, but he knew the Americans were out there, hunting for them. The Americans were always hunting for them and now their saboteur had made their detection a certainty. He did not know if there was an American sub nearby, but a prudent captain planned for the worst. He needed his crew ready for battle or to respond to emergencies such as fire or flooding at a moment's notice. But manning battle stations did something else for him as well. By mustering the entire crew, he would have the maximum number of eyeballs distributed throughout the ship, and he would put those eyeballs to use looking for the noise augmenter. If they could find and silence it, then perhaps he could still slip away.

If sonar can't locate it, I will have to find it the old-fashioned way.

While a small army of junior personnel conducted wake-ups,

the drone pilot struggled to free the Klavesin's jammed cutting head. While not being a man who tolerated excuses, Konstantin had personally paged through the operation and maintenance manual for the submersible and found the guidance sorely lacking. As infuriating as this was, it made sense. Just like the *Belgorod*, the Klavesin UUV was a one-of-a-kind asset with limited operating history. What they were attempting to do now had never been done before. There was no procedure for this situation because they were writing it in real time.

"Captain, shall I proceed to control for battle stations or remain here?" the weapons officer asked.

Konstantin eyed the man. Morozov looked nervous, despite trying his best to hide it.

"I need you on the conn. Be ready to launch countermeasures and torpedoes at a moment's notice."

"Aye, Captain," Morozov said, turned a heel, and left.

The sub captain returned his attention to the drone pilot. "Enough of playing it safe. Take the drone's thrusters and main propeller to full power. Either we get the damn thing dislodged or we cut the tether."

"Aye, Captain," the pilot said.

As ordered, he applied maximum power and the UUV lurched forward and immediately pitched downward. The pilot jerked the control stick back to change the angle of attack with the control surfaces so the nose didn't arc down and ram into the seabed. The CUTTING HEAD OVER TORQUE alarm flashed on the control panel as the pilot applied full power to try to free it.

"Come on, you son of a bitch!" the pilot shouted, the ligaments in his neck straining as if he were physically battling to free the drone and not just using a joystick.

"Reverse thrust now," Konstantin ordered.

The pilot hesitated, his face a contortion of fury, before snapping out of it and acknowledging the order. Gritting his teeth, he reversed both the propeller and the thrusters. The Klavesin lurched backward, popped, and went spinning, the camera view whirling in a churning cloud of silt and sand.

Both the pilot and the phone talker cheered, but Konstantin's expression didn't change. If only he knew whether the damage to the cable had been sufficient to compromise the data node or not. Maybe he should attempt to cut into the housing of the data hub itself. That would be even louder than cutting the cable, but this opportunity would not present itself again and the drone was in position. He'd already made the decision to abandon the Klavesin in place. Recovery would be time-consuming and prolong their static loiter time.

Besides, it doesn't matter in the grand scheme of things. All that matters is completing the mission.

"Cut into the data node housing," he said to the pilot, who'd regained control of the UUV.

The man looked at him with a dubious expression. "But we are halfway through the cable. Are you sure you don't want me to finish the job?"

Konstantin considered a moment. It was no longer a noise issue. They were making plenty of noise, so why not attack the problem definitively while noise was not the issue?

"It will probably get stuck again. The compression in the cut channel is still present."

The pilot seemed to balk, but held his tongue.

"What is the problem?" Konstantin said.

"If the data node housing is made of titanium or very strong stainless steel, the cutting head will not be able to penetrate it. Otherwise, the cut could take hours."

"I understand. And if the housing is composite, the job will proceed quickly. We will know the answer in a moment. Make the cut."

"Aye, Captain," the pilot said and moved the Klavesin into position to try again.

49

K atie felt color creep into her cheeks.
Everyone in the room was staring at her like she had a unicorn horn growing out of her forehead, but she supposed she couldn't blame them. She certainly hadn't planned to say it. As soon as the CO confirmed her worst fear, that the advanced DASH sonar system was down for the mid-Atlantic corridor, dread hit her like a wrecking ball. She felt like the entire world was barreling toward oblivion and she was the only one who could stop it. Then an idea popped into her head out of nowhere, and a catastrophic failure of her brain-to-mouth filter resulted in her vocalizing it.

"Lieutenant Ryan, did I hear you correctly?" the CO of the *Ford* said, squinting at her like she had just declared her intention to ask NASA to drop her off on the moon. "You want us to shuttle you to the USS *Washington* right now?"

She swallowed.

Don't cave . . . Whatever you do, don't cave.

"Yes, sir, that's correct. Both me and Dr. Jones," she said.

"Whoa, whoa, whoa," Jones said, his eyes going wide behind his glasses. "Uh-uh, there is no *us* in this crazy plan of yours."

She turned and gave him the stink eye.

Come on, Jones. Back me up here.

"Katie, we did not discuss this in advance. I served on a submarine, remember. Getting on and off one at sea is really dangerous. That's why the only people who regularly do it are Navy SEALs."

"I apologize, I shouldn't have spoken for you," she said, regretting her overstep. What she was proposing was certainly dangerous. She turned back to look at the skipper. "Sir, I need to get aboard that boat, ASAP."

The strike group commander, Admiral Kiplinger, shook his head. "Lieutenant Ryan, I for one will go out on a limb and say you have me convinced that the Russian submarine down there sabotaging our sonar array is the *Belgorod*, but why do you need to deliver this message in person to the *Washington* when we can simply send them a message? Help me understand the logic here."

She heard the CAG mumble something under his breath, catching the word "insane," but she resisted the compulsion to glare at him.

"Because, Admiral, I believe that sometime in the next twelve hours, the CO of the *Washington* is going to find himself in the unenviable position of having to make a decision that will either start or prevent World War Three, and in that moment, he will not have the luxury of being able to communicate with us via message. He will be alone and forced to rely on only his instincts and judgment, and in that moment, he will need a sounding board," she said, surprised by the conviction in her voice.

The admiral leaned in and fixed her with a critical stare. "That's true, but why does that person need to be you?"

She was so close to winning the room that she could taste it. It felt as if her mind were attuned to some unspoken frequency of tenuous consensus. She suddenly wondered if this was how a trial attorney felt when making their closing statement to a jury.

I have to go for it, she decided. *I have to say it, even if it does make me sound insane.*

"Because I know Konstantin Gorov," she said with brazen certitude. "I know his history. I've studied his career. I know how he thinks. He's going to go off script, and when he does, I need to be on the conn, with Captain Houston."

Had she stretched the truth? *Definitely.* Did she care in this moment? *Absolutely not.*

The admiral looked at the CO of the *Ford* and a silent accord was reached.

Captain Mackenzie turned to the DCAG. "The *Washington* is too far to deliver Ryan by Seahawk. What do you think about sending her on an Osprey?"

The CAG gave a derisive snort for the whole room to hear, but he allowed his DCAG to answer.

"We've got a bird from VRM-30 aboard. I could have it ready to go in an hour," Captain Huddleston said, shooting a look at the CAG, who shrugged.

"We've never done this before," the DCAG said, speaking his mind now, but with a sympathetic glance at Katie. "It'll be pretty dicey, Lieutenant Ryan."

"This is not some evolution you do off the cuff," the CAG said. "I mean, what's the plan, surface the sub, hover over the sail, and drop her down the hatch?"

"Yeah, that's pretty much the evolution here," the DCAG said and then turned to flash Katie a shit-eating grin. "Except for the 'dropping you' part, of course."

"I should hope not," she said, while her stomach went preemptively queasy at the preposterous transfer operation she'd somehow, miraculously convinced a one-star admiral to support.

"The CAG and Spacecamp are right about the risk," the *Ford* skipper said, and Katie was afraid he was about to throw cold water on the idea. "We need to put some thought into this. I want to muster the Osprey crew and talk through the mechanics and safety factors of this evolution. We also need to get a message to the *Blackfish* and get positive confirmation they're in a position to support the evolution."

"I'll draft a message and get it out on the next broadcast," Kumari said. "Although I don't know off the top of my head when the *Washington* is due to come to PD next. It could be hours."

"All right, well, find that out and we'll adjust accordingly. Any other comments or concerns?" the CO said, scanning the room.

Katie did not give the CAG the satisfaction of looking in his direction during the pause. When nobody said anything, she raised her hand.

"Sorry, Ryan, we're *not* going to let you fly the Osprey," Captain Huddleston, the affable DCAG fighter pilot, said, which earned a round of laughter from everyone, breaking the tension.

"Oh, definitely not interested in that," she said. "Actually, I was just wondering about the USS *Indiana*."

"What about it? Is that your next stop after the *Washington*?" he said, still pulling her chain.

"I was just thinking that it might not be a bad idea to have another sub in theater in case things take a turn for the worse."

"Who does this woman think she is . . . SUBLANT?" the CAG said under his breath, just loud enough for her to hear.

The admiral must have heard it, too, however, because he said, "She's not SUBLANT, Marty, but she sure thinks like a three star."

"I'm sorry, sir, I'm not sure I catch your meaning," the CAG said, his cheeks turning red.

"As it turns out, the top brass happens to share Ryan's thinking, and that order has already been given. The *Indiana* is en route south at flank speed as we speak."

Thank God, she thought. *Finally, some good news.*

"All right, everyone, we've got a personnel transfer to plan. I'm going to want a fighter escort for this, since tensions are high."

"Roger that, sir," the DCAG said. "I'll get a brief going in the ready room with the pilots."

The CO ended the meeting and dismissed everyone.

Kumari made a beeline to Katie and pulled her aside into a corner to talk. "What the hell just happened back there? How could you spring this on me out of nowhere?"

"I don't know, I guess when I heard that the mid-Atlantic DASH is down, my mind war-gamed out the scenario and I couldn't help myself. Our legacy SOSUS system isn't capable of tracking a Status-6 nuclear-armed torpedo. Gorov knows this. He also knows that DASH can, which is why he was willing to risk disabling it. He knows we can't prove it's the *Belgorod* down there. And even if we could, he knows we won't engage him. Sinking a Russian submarine over sabotaging a data node is something my father would never authorize. Not only is it an asymmetrical escalation, but that's not how his moral compass works. He won't throw the first punch, but he will punch back."

"Then why are you so hell-bent on getting aboard the *Blackfish?*"

"Because I believe Gorov has gone rogue. I believe he intends to launch a first strike on the U.S."

"Ryan, listen to yourself. Do you know how insane that sounds? You realize that you've just staked your career on this wild-ass theory?"

"I know," she said.

"What if you're wrong?"

"Then the world goes on and I'll be grateful for it. The question you need to ask yourself is, what if I'm right?"

Kumari sighed and looked up at the overhead. "Then we're screwed."

"Exactly. We don't understand the true capabilities of the Status-6. How quiet is it? What is its maximum range? How fast can it go? What sort of autonomous navigation and countermeasures evasion capability does it have? We need a plan to stop this thing and we're running out of time and options. Which is why I need to be on the *Blackfish* in trail of the *Belgorod*, ready to react at a moment's notice."

"Okay, let's assume you're right. And let's assume the *Belgorod* gets the shot off, but you miss it happening. How do we find this weapon? There's no time to fix the DASH mid-Atlantic array."

"I might have an idea about that," she said and prayed her hunch was right. "Have you heard of Task Force 59?"

"You mean that new group working out of Bahrain for the Fifth Fleet? It's, like, a mesh sensor network or something they're piloting?"

"Yeah, that's the one. Their mandate is maritime domain awareness over five thousand miles of coastline encompassing the Middle East and Africa. They're using 'edge intelligence,' with hundreds of collectors streaming data back to a command center that uses AI to suss out patterns in the data. My brother is in Bahrain, working with the task force in some capacity, but his role there is a little unclear to me. I think we need to get him on the horn and see if he can help us, or at least connect us to the right people. They have an inventory of UAVs, USVs, and UUVs they use to survey the entire air-ocean interface. Maybe we can replicate from the top looking down what the DASH network was trying to do from the bottom looking up."

"That's a great idea. I'll go to CIC and see if I can open a channel with the command. Task Force 59, you said?"

"That's right."

"Okay," Kumari said and turned to leave, but then swiveled back. "Oh, Ryan, I'm going to confirm this, but I'm pretty sure the

Washington is not due back to PD for at least another four or five hours. Just sayin' it could be a while before we can get you out there."

Her stomach sank. "That's too long. I need to get out there ASAP. There must be some other way to contact them?"

"They're deep, and the *Blackfish* is an SSN. They don't have a VLF comms buoy like the boomers do to receive transmissions while they're deep."

"Damn," she muttered, feeling the crush of time.

What if I'm too late?

"Actually, I might be able to help with that," Jones said, stepping up from where he'd been nonchalantly eavesdropping a couple of yards away. "Next-generation UAC is a pet project I've been playing around with in my spare time."

"UAC?" she said, cocking an eyebrow at Jones. "What's that?"

"Sorry, underwater acoustic communication," he said. "You know, sending and receiving messages underwater using sound. Like what whales do, only with technology."

"The *Blackfish* is only the *Washington*'s call sign. It's not an actual whale," Katie said, teasing him.

"You're hysterical, Ryan," he fired back, "but what I'm talking about is frequency-shift keying and uses the same basic principle as whale song, except we'll be using technology to do it."

"Okay, you have my attention."

"We choose two distinct active sonar frequencies that the *Blackfish* will detect as narrowband signals on their TB-29, and then we modulate them to send a message. Frequency one will indicate zero bits and frequency two will indicate ones. We send them instructions in binary that they can decode."

She stared at him for a beat, before saying, "Precisely what I was going to suggest."

"Obviously," Kumari chimed in.

The three of them burst into laughter.

"Jonesy, I could hug you right now," she said, flashing him her pearly whites.

"Don't hug me yet," he said. "I can't guarantee it will work."

She narrowed her eyes playfully at him. "Well, if it doesn't, I'll have the admiral order you to come with me on the Osprey to the *Washington* as your penance."

50

K nepper noticed the new narrowband trace on the sonar display a split second before the sonar supervisor announced it to control.

"Conn, Sonar, we have a new narrowband contact designated Sierra Two-Nine, bearing zero-four-nine, possible submerged contact based on frequency range," the sonar chief said.

"Very well, Sonar," Houston said, stepping from the command workstation to stand by the sonar supe at the stacks.

"Captain, that bearing puts Sierra Two-Nine in the vicinity of the carrier strike group," Juggernaut said, quickly correlating this new development. "Recommend designating Sierra Two-Nine as Master Two and developing a firing solution."

"Very well, WEPS. Attention control room, designate Sierra Two-Nine as Master Two. Master Two is a possible submerged contact and a potential threat. Track Master Two."

All stations acknowledged the captain's pronouncement in turn.

"Conn, Quartermaster, two minutes until the turn to be on track for our second pass of Master One," the quartermaster said.

"Very well," the captain said absently, but his attention was fully devoted to the hushed conversation he was having with the sonar supe.

Knepper watched as the FT sitting in front of him entered a preliminary fire control solution into the system for the new contact. The timing could not be worse, as the *Blackfish* had just finished regrouping and was preparing for a second acoustic collection pass on the south side of Master One. If this new narrowband contact meant that a second Russian sub had arrived on the scene and was circling beneath the carrier, then the threat level had just gone up considerably.

"XO," the captain said. When Knepper made eye contact, Houston curled a finger, summoning Knepper to the very crowded port side of the conn.

Knepper squeezed through the gap between the navigator, who was standing behind the command workstation, and the quartermaster, who was at the plot to take his place at the CO's side.

"Notice anything odd about that signal?" Houston asked.

Knepper leaned in to study the trace, looking over the head of the seated narrowband console operator. It took him a second, but he saw it. "It's a 151.7-hertz signal."

"Exactly the same frequency as Master One," the CO said.

Knepper retrieved the little cylinder of toothpicks he kept in his coverall's chest pocket, shook one free, and popped it into the corner of his mouth. He worked it side to side with his tongue—an old habit from his Power School days—while he thought about this new wrinkle. "Seems a little odd that two Russian boats would have the exact same sound show up here at the same time."

"My thinking exactly."

ST2 Meadows, who was sitting narrowband, pulled the left cup of his headset off his ear and said, "Supe, I just got frequency shift on that signal. Jumped to 152.7 hertz . . . Oh wait, it just shifted back."

"I see it," Chief Adkins said and slipped a headset onto one ear so he could listen to the signal.

Knepper glanced at Houston, who had his middle-distance stare thing going on.

A beat later, having reached some silent conclusion, the CO said, "Quartermaster, plot a new course that will keep us outside two thousand yards from Master One, while keeping our own ship from blocking the line of sight between the towed array and Master Two."

The quartermaster acknowledged the order and repeated it back.

"Supe, just lost the signal," ST2 Meadows said.

Knepper's eyes flicked from the plot, where the quartermaster was adjusting their track, to the sonar display. Sure enough, the bright green trace on the waterfall display had stopped at the top of the gram and static filled the band as the interrupted trace drifted down the screen. Then a new trace appeared on the same bearing.

"Supe, it's back," the ST2 said.

The chief shook his head. "Nope, that's a different frequency."

"You're right, it's . . . 161.7 hertz. Exactly ten hertz higher."

The four of them stared at the new narrowband trace that was drifting down on the same bearing as the previous one.

"We've got a frequency shift on the new signal," the ST2 said. "It jumped to 162.7 hertz . . . Hold on, it just shifted back."

"Same pattern as before," Knepper murmured. "What the hell are they doing?"

"What bearing do we hold the *Ford* on?" Houston asked.

"Zero-five-one," the supe answered.

"What about the *Mason*?" Houston asked, referring to the carrier's Aegis-class destroyer escort, DDG 87.

"Zero-four-nine, sir."

"Frequency shift, Master Two," the ST2 said. "Same as before, a one-hertz upshift."

"That's no submarine. I think it's the *Mason*. They might be trying to signal us," Houston said to Knepper. He turned to the sonar supe. "Chief, shift the aux console operator to narrowband. I think we might have two narrowband signals we need to watch. And somebody get me a pen and pad of paper."

"Yes, sir," the chief said, but before he could pass the order to the aux console operator, the ST3 sitting at the stack had already made the switch.

"Ready, Chief," she said.

The control room messenger, who'd heard the CO's call for pen and paper, scrambled up to fulfill the request, handing the skipper a notepad and pen.

"Thank you," the captain said and got ready to write.

"Just lost the 161-hertz signal," ST2 Meadows announced.

"ST2, you track and report frequency shifts on 151 hertz, and ST3, you track and report frequency shifts on the 161-hertz signals," Houston said. "Got it?"

"Yes, sir," the sonar technicians replied in unison.

"Conn, Quartermaster, new track calculated. Recommend you come left to course zero-eight-one."

"Pilot, left five-degree rudder, steady course zero-eight-one," Houston announced.

The pilot acknowledged the order with a repeat back and added, "Captain, my rudder is left five."

"Very well."

A palpable tension hung in the air while the CO, XO, OOD, and sonar supe stared at the narrowband displays, waiting for something to happen. After a long moment, a fresh green trace appeared.

"Supe, regained 151.7-hertz signal bearing zero-four-nine," the ST2 said.

The sonar supe was about to announce as much, but Houston cut him off. "No need, I heard him."

"Frequency shift up to 152.7." After a three count, the ST2 said, "Just shifted back."

Knepper saw Houston put a dot on the paper.

"Frequency shift up . . . And back down again."

The CO put another dot on the paper.

"Signal lost."

"Regained 161.7-hertz signal," the ST3 said from the aux console. "Frequency shift up . . . Frequency shift down . . . Frequency shift up . . . Frequency shift down . . . Signal lost."

Knepper watched Houston put two dashes on the page beside the dots.

"Regained 151-hertz signal," ST2 Meadows said. "Frequency shift up . . . And back down again . . . Signal lost."

Houston put a dot down.

"You think it's Morse code?" Knepper asked.

"I do," Houston said. "I think they're using frequency-shift modulation to communicate."

"Regained 161-hertz signal," the ST3 said, and then she reported three up-down cycles.

Houston wrote three more dashes. Instead of the 151.7-hertz signal coming back right away, a pause of ten seconds unfolded before the trace returned.

"I think that was a break," Knepper said.

"Good call," Houston said and left a gap before he started recording the next sequence. The back-and-forth calls between the narrowband operators continued while the captain jotted down dots and dashes. After eleven sequences, both signals stopped.

"Somebody get me a Morse code translator," the CO said.

As it turned out, the OOD had thought ahead and had had one

of the radiomen bring a printed sheet to the conn already. Houston took it from the nav and started comparing his handiwork to the page.

After a few seconds, he threw up his hands in agitation. "Shit. I don't know what this is, but it sure as hell isn't Morse."

Knepper stared at the eleven clusters, eight marks per grouping, and an epiphany hit him.

"It's not Morse. It's binary," he said and extended his hand to the captain for the paper.

Houston handed him the pad and pen and Knepper went to work. Under each dot he wrote a zero, and under each dash he scribed a one, generating a binary code:

00110111 00111000 00110111 00100000 01100111 01101111
01110100 01101111 00100000 01110000 01100100

"What is that?" Houston said.

"I'm pretty sure it's eight-bit ASCII, also known as UTF-8," Knepper said and turned to the control room messenger. "Go to my stateroom and grab the iPad off my desk. It's in one of the cubbies."

"Yes, sir," the messenger said and took off out the back of control. He returned less than a minute later and handed the tablet to Knepper.

"Thanks," he said, took the iPad, and opened a coding conversion app.

"Hey, Supe," the ST2 said. "Just regained the 151-hertz signal."

"Captain, looks like it might be starting up again," the sonar chief said.

"Probably repeating the message. That's a good sign this is intentional. Chief, write it all down and we'll see if it matches. Zeroes for 151 hertz and ones for 161-hertz shifts."

"What if it's the other way around, sir?" the chief said. "I mean, maybe 161 is the zeroes?"

"We've got a fifty-fifty shot, but we'll run it both ways and see if one makes sense," Houston said.

"Yes, sir. On it."

Houston ripped the top page off the pad and handed it to the chief. Then he turned back to Knepper and said, "I'll read it to you while you type."

Knepper methodically entered the eighty-eight characters into a text window as the captain spoke the sequence aloud. Then he selected the "binary to text" translator from a drop-down menu and highlighted the character encoding option "ASCII/UTF-8."

He turned to the captain. "Here goes nothing," he said and pressed the convert icon on the screen. The translated message read:

787 GO TO PD

The captain let out a snort. "All that for this . . . You gotta be friggin' kidding me."

"I don't know, Captain," Knepper said with a smile. "I've gotta hand it to them. It's a pretty creative way to get our attention. We might have just pioneered a new communication protocol for SSNs who are deep."

"If we can translate it, so can the Russians," Houston said, "but in a pinch . . . pretty damn clever."

Houston was making no effort to hide his annoyance at being summoned to PD. Knepper could see the conflict on the captain's face as he undoubtedly tried to decide whether to make a second collection pass on Master One *before* going to PD, or to disengage now.

"If we go to PD now, there's a good chance we'll lose our shot to make a second collection pass on Master One," Knepper said.

"I know. The timing is terrible," the captain said and blew air through his teeth. "But if they went to all this trouble, it must be friggin' important."

"Agreed."

Houston gave Knepper a tight-lipped smile and, in his command voice, announced, "Pilot, make your depth one-five-five feet. All stations, Conn, make preparations to come to periscope depth."

51

I*f I was made, I'd already be in a concrete cell having my finger-nails ripped out.*

Clark allowed himself comfort at the thought, but knew it wasn't true. If Russian intelligence had identified him, they'd be in no hurry to black bag him. They had plenty of time for that, because once he was on their radar, there would be no escape from Moscow. The better move would be to leave him in play. Watch him, listen to him, determine who his teammates were and who he'd made connections with inside of the Russian military and intelligence communities. They would want to map his network of assets so they could round up all the traitors. They would also relentlessly hunt down Ding, Midas, and Adara.

But I'm not going to let that happen.

He strode into the lobby of the Boris Godunov Hotel, looking around and checking his watch. He couldn't loiter on the street any longer without looking out of place, waiting for his mark—Nadia Kraeva, wife of Anatoly Kraev and co-owner of Glavpivtorg. He'd taken a calculated risk leaving the safe house to take the lead on this op. Both Ding and Adara had argued strongly against it, but in his gut, he knew it had to be him who made the approach.

Only time would tell if he'd made the right call.

Using Campus uber-encrypted tech to access CIA data files, Ding had learned that Anatoly Kraev was former KGB and had worked in the same office as Colonel General Ilyin in the eighties. Midas was of the opinion that grabbing and questioning Anatoly— just like they had Popov—was the solution, and he'd lobbied hard for it. At first blush, it did seem like the perfect next move, because the odds were very good that Anatoly was read in on the cabal's plans and could answer all of the team's questions. But once again, VICAR's haunting words came back to guide Clark.

"In losing the Cold War, these men lost their identity. They lost their pride. They lost their purpose."

"Anatoly is a cold warrior and Ilyin's friend, which means he'll be an uncooperative mark," Clark had argued. "After interrogating him, if we let him go, he'd run to Ilyin and we'd be outed. Knowing that, we'd have to kill him, which also raises red flags. So either way, we put ourselves on the cabal's radar."

Fortunately, Ding had found them another option. Kraev's wife, Nadia, had been a CIA-managed asset for three short months in 1988, but she'd severed that relationship and never been caught. In Nadia's CIA case file, her handler had written many notes about the woman, but one observation had caught Clark's eye:

Nadia is proud, an idealist, but most of all, fiercely loves her husband.

With Nadia, Clark had an angle he could exploit. They'd caught a lucky break with her, or at least, Clark's gut told him they had. He had long ago made peace with the reality that luck mattered in the covert operations business. Preparation, tradecraft, discipline, staying one step ahead of one's adversary—these things all mattered more.

But luck . . . Luck put a thumb on the scales of every op.

"Got her," Adara said. "She's coming out of the Double B coffee bar and pouring vodka into her cup, just like yesterday."

Alcoholism was the number one public health crisis in Russia. Nadia Kraeva, it seemed, was battling her own demons.

Clark made a show of scanning around the empty lobby, glancing at his watch, and then shaking his head as if dealing with a no-show appointment. The woman at the reception desk gave him a smile and he shrugged, then headed back out the door.

He spied Nadia across the street and headed to the corner. She was heavyset and would have been a caricature of a Russian working-class woman, except she dressed a bit better. The jacket she wore against the mid-April chill was stylish and vibrant, unlike her gray hair, which she wore with heavy bangs and the rest tied up in a scarf. She crossed the street, and for a moment he thought she might continue east, but at the far corner she turned north.

He hustled to the corner and turned north, crossing to the east side of the street and then slowing to a stop as he watched her enter a cathedral on the north end of the block. He didn't need eyes on now because it was obvious what she was up to.

"She went inside," Adara said in his ear.

"Check," Clark whispered. "Moving in a minute."

He made a show of checking his phone, as if scrolling through text messages, and then pocketed it and headed up the small sidewalk between buildings, coming to the arched entrance of the Cathedral of the Nativity of the Blessed Virgin Mary. He resisted the urge to glance around and instead pulled open the tall wooden door with confidence, though he allowed himself the reassurance of pressing his forearm against the Vektor pistol inside the waistband of his pants beneath his suit coat.

The towering, dimly lit sanctuary was mostly empty. At the altar two young men dressed in the dark robes of acolytes tended to an arrangement of candles. The only other person inside was Nadia, kneeling in a pew on the left, halfway up the aisle. As he walked quietly up behind her, she took a sip of her spiked coffee, then bowed her head again.

He gave her a start when he knelt beside her.

In his peripheral vision, he watched her watching him as he crossed himself and bowed his head.

"Drinking in the sanctuary is prohibited," he said in Russian without looking up. He could hear her breathing quicken, but she didn't move or get up to leave.

She did, however, keep her stare fixed on him as she said, "I have an arrangement with Sister Ilga."

"*Da*," he said simply, then raised his head, staring at the illuminated crucifix behind the altar.

"What do you want?" she asked.

It wasn't lost on him that she didn't ask who he was.

"Don't you wish to know my name?" he asked.

She shrugged. "Whatever you say will be a lie."

"In that case, maybe you want to know who I work for."

"I know who you work for. You are here to question me about my husband and his dealings, but I have nothing to tell you. Anatoly is a good man, and he is retired. After years of serving Mother Russia, we now scrape out a meager living serving food and drink to the people. He is not in that business anymore."

Nadia is proud, an idealist, but most of all, fiercely loves her husband.

He smiled, relieved that she hadn't changed.

That was good.

He turned to her and when he did, she immediately shifted her gaze to the ceramic body of Christ hanging from the cross behind the dais ahead.

"I'm not here to ask questions about your husband. I'm here to help you save his life."

He saw her flinch at this. After a long pause, she said, "Your accent is terrible."

"*Da*, it is."

"You're American, an American spy . . . Not the first who has approached me over the years."

His gut told him this woman was more than she seemed. Her case file hadn't mentioned that she'd been KGB, but when you'd been in the business as long as Clark had, you just knew.

Maybe she'd been managing her handler and not the other way around.

"I know, Nadia. I also know that you and your husband were *both* KGB," he said, taking a gamble.

She smiled. "After all these years, you finally figured it out."

"I did . . . Why did you cut it off? You had the CIA fooled. You could have been the perfect double agent for the KGB."

She took another sip of her coffee and said, "I love my country . . . But I love my husband more. I couldn't handle the stress. It would have torn us apart."

"I can appreciate that," he said softly.

"Are you married?"

"*Da*," he said. Then, knowing he shouldn't, he went all in. "She's the love of my life, along with my grandkids . . . They're why I'm here."

She cocked an eyebrow at him. "Explain."

Clark let a beat pass, staring again at the figure of Jesus, then sighed and turned back to her. "The men that meet in your restaurant, Nadia. They're plotting something terrible. Something that, if it happens, will kick off a cascade of events from which there is no return."

"They were once great men. Sons of the Soviet Union," she snapped back.

"*Da*, great men indeed, but men from a bygone era. I am such a man myself, I think," he added with a soft smile. "But we can't turn back the clock. The Cold War is over."

"And we lost, I know," she said, her tone defensive.

"Now, that's where you're wrong. Russia didn't lose, Russia chose glasnost. Russia chose peace."

She answered with a derisive snort. "And look what we got for it. A kleptocracy run by a dictator who has surrounded himself with a corrupt oligarchy."

"That's true," Clark agreed, "but this is the same struggle every country on earth wrestles with. Democracy is hard. All governments are corrupt, even America."

This seemed to get her attention and she almost smiled. "What do you want, American spy? Why have you come here?"

"I want what every old idealist wants—to hold Armageddon at bay for another day. I'm here to lobby for the lesser of two evils, Nadia, which is keeping Yermilov in power. Because when you get to our age, you realize that the lesser of two evils is really the best you can hope for."

He saw her eyes rim with tears. "I'm so tired."

"I know . . . So am I."

"Do you really have grandchildren?"

"I do . . ."

She wiped her eyes and then proceeded to tell him everything she knew. When she'd finished, she said, "I've given you what you came for, and now I want something in return."

"Tell me," Clark said.

"I want you to guarantee my husband's safety as you try to ensure the lesser of two evils."

He reached out and gave her calloused hand a squeeze. "You have my word."

52

Ryan listened without interruption while Mary Pat reported everything the team in Moscow had learned and confirmed. Boldyrev, Rodionov, and Aralovich were indeed members of a cabal to oust Yermilov from power and Nikolai Ilyin was the ringleader and mastermind. The *Belgorod* was central to the plan, but the specifics were unknown. How much control Yermilov still retained over the military and intelligence apparatus was also unknown. Mary Pat assured him that they would be ramping up SIGINT and HUMINT collection efforts on the four principals, but there was no guarantee that effort would reap fresh actionable intelligence.

When she finished reporting, Ryan sat silent a moment, letting the details come together in his head, like a chemistry equation where new bonds were forming. It felt familiar and nostalgic—like the old days—as a new hypothesis about the maddeningly slow-moving coup began to crystallize.

"What if we're looking at this whole thing with the wrong paradigm?" he said, talking out loud as he worked out the details.

"In what way?" she asked.

"We're assuming the cabal is planning to slit Yermilov's throat when the opportunity presents itself, but what if what they're actually doing is laying the groundwork for Yermilov to slit his *own* throat?"

"Okay," Mary Pat said. "You have my attention."

Ryan felt a surge of adrenaline and excitement he'd not felt in ages as the analyst in him caught fire and worked the problem.

"I think we've been looking at this all wrong. We've all assumed that Ilyin used Boldyrev, Rodionov, and Aralovich to move chess pieces and mobilize assets behind Yermilov's back. But that's a tall order, Mary Pat. Ilyin is too smart for that. Because he knows the second Yermilov finds out, the gambit is up. So instead, he's done everything with Yermilov's blessing."

She screwed up her face. "I'm not following."

"What if Ilyin has sold Yermilov on the idea of making a big move to shift the balance of power, but he's not read Yermilov in on the *actual* endgame?"

"Okay, what's the big move?"

"The big move is to conduct a coordinated operation to make us think twice about deploying our carrier strike group and challenging Russian operations. It's classic military gamesmanship—the same thing we do when we have one of our SSGNs surface and make an unscheduled port of call near an adversary. It sends the message 'Hey, look what we can do, anytime we want, and you can't stop us.' Yermilov is trying to do the same thing with the *Belgorod* and the Status-6 by deploying it unannounced, but in conjuction with their big Arctic exercise. They know we're going to see it on satellite and try to track it. They use subterfuge to trick the *Indiana*, paving the way for the *Belgorod* to slip away, and they deploy the *Finitor* to send us a message."

"Which is?"

"That they know about the DASH network. That the *Belgorod* can evade detection and slip past our best subs. That Yermilov can launch a doomsday nuclear torpedo anytime he wants and sink our carrier or attack any city on the Eastern Seaboard and there's not a damn thing we can do about it."

"Okay, but why load actual nuclear-tipped Status-6 torpedoes aboard if he doesn't intend to strike?" Mary Pat said, playing the devil's advocate. "Why take that risk when it adds nothing to his show of force?"

"Because it's the threat of the nuclear-tipped Status-6 that creates the panic. Case in point, look at what it's done to us these past few days."

"Granted. So, what's Ilyin's actual endgame and how does he get Yermilov to slit his own throat?"

She looked laser-focused on what he was saying now.

"This is the part where Boldyrev, Rodionov, and Gorov come into the picture. As president and commander in chief, Yermilov has launch authority and control over the nuclear codes. The cabal has laid the groundwork to circumvent this authority and control. As far as Yermilov believes, the *Belgorod*'s mission is to prove to us that they defeat our defenses and launch a Status-6 whenever they want. But the cabal intends to actually launch a Status-6 and cripple our fleet."

"Jack, that doesn't make sense," Mary Pat said, "because that would start World War Three."

"Unless," Ryan said, snapping the final puzzle piece into place, "they initiate their coup—denouncing Yermilov as a madman, framing him for the attack, and remove him from power. The cabal members leverage their positions of authority and take control of the government, stand down the military, and perhaps even offer aid to the U.S. in the wake of the attack. With Yermilov as a scapegoat, they make themselves safe from retaliation, avert a nuclear response, but prove to the world that America is vulnerable. In the aftermath, they rule Russia and kick off a new Cold War against a weakened United States."

Mary Pat sat a moment, digesting, then she shook her head.

"I think you're reaching, Jack, based on what we actually have evidence for."

"But possible," Ryan pressed.

"Yes," she conceded. "Certainly possible."

A knock came on the conference room door. Mary Pat walked to the door, opened it a crack, and said, "Yes?"

"The President's guest has arrived and cleared security," the Marine said.

She turned to Ryan and smiled. "Looks like he's here . . . I'll leave you to it."

"Okay," he said. "But we'll continue this conversation later."

"Most definitely," she said and excused herself.

A moment later, Marko Ramius—or Mark Ramsey, as he was known these days—walked into the conference room, back straight, head high, hands clasped behind his back. Despite his advanced age, he did not use a cane, nor did he look feeble and unsteady on his feet. To the contrary, Ramius looked stately and strong. He was dressed in khakis and a simple blue chambray shirt, and wore a light gray jacket, but with his posture, bearing, and worn, chiseled face, he might as well have been wearing his iconic Soviet Navy captain's uniform. A wave of memories swept over Ryan, some touching and nostalgic and some terrifying.

"Thank you for coming," Ryan said with a smile, standing and reaching out a hand.

Ramius didn't scowl, not exactly, but he didn't look pleased, either, to be here. He took a step forward and firmly grasped Ryan's hand.

"It didn't feel as if I was given a choice," Ramius said, then took a seat at the table. "A military helicopter arrived at my ranch and the men aboard ordered me to D.C."

"I'm sorry about that," Ryan said and meant it. "I'm afraid the situation is rather urgent."

"Mmm," was all Ramius said. His eyes swept across the room where decisions affecting the fate of the world were often made. It was a room filled with power and energy, but Ramius seemed unimpressed. Then again, he'd once been the captain of a war machine with the firepower to destroy the United States twice over. "Impressive room, Ryan," he said, then with an impish sparkle in his eyes, added, "I apologize, I should be addressing you as Mr. President these days."

And there it was at last, the Ramius smile.

"After all we've done and been through, Captain, perhaps it's time you call me Jack," Ryan said, noting how he still felt a nostalgic reverence for the man.

"Ryan it is, then," Ramius said and smiled for real now. "What is it that's brought me to your Situation Room?"

Ryan gave the former captain of the *Red October* a detailed summary—holding back nothing. When he was finished, Ramius simply nodded.

"A very urgent situation indeed, Ryan," he said. "But what is it this old man can do to help you?"

But his eyes were not those of an old man and they both knew it.

"Insight, I suppose," Ryan said, then shared what he knew about both Konstantin Gorov and his father. At this, Ramius raised an eyebrow.

"Well, I suppose you never know," he said. "I'm quite surprised to learn the elder Gorov had planned to defect, but then again, who am I to say such a thing?"

"Do you think that the son, Captain Gorov, would go rogue and follow orders from Ilyin and Boldyrev to attack the United States?" Ryan asked.

"I don't know the man. And I'm afraid I know little more about the father. I only remember meeting him once. But speaking from personal experience, taking a Russian submarine rogue is no small feat and would require collaborators aboard the *Belgorod*." His eyes sparkled again at a memory they shared. "But to fire a nuclear-armed Status-6 torpedo would require far more planning and co-ordination. It would require support from the highest levels because they would have to steal the access codes to arm the war-head."

Ryan nodded. "That's where Ilyin's collaborators come into the picture."

Ramius sighed and looked unconvinced. "But why, Ryan? Why this act of defiance? Why launch a nuclear attack and start a nu-clear war they can't win?"

"Because nuclear war is not their objective. Turning back the clock and reestablishing the status quo is," Ryan said and summa-rized his new theory.

When the President finished, Ramius took a long deep breath, then rose from the chair. He paced toward the end of the table, back straight, hands clasped behind his back. He stared at the large screens above him with images of the *Belgorod* and Gorov on the right, but the center filled with pictures of the Russian coup mem-bers that Clark had confirmed. To the far right was a recent image of Yermilov. Ryan watched Ramius as the man studied the pictures—the faces.

Finally, he turned and faced him again.

"I know of these men—I knew Aralovich when he was young. They are Soviet-era thinkers . . . When it comes to war and politics, they view the zero-sum game, Ryan. To the Russian mind, and especially to the Soviet mind, there is no such thing as a win-win outcome. That is a uniquely American view of the world"—he closed his eyes and smiled—"and something we Americans so desperately seek. For these men, for Russia to rise, America must fall. You see?"

Yes," Ryan said. It was a concept he was intimate with already.

Ramius paced back toward him now, his brow furrowed in thought. "I fear that what you suggest is very possible, Ryan," he said finally. "And if that is what is happening, this situation is quite dangerous indeed."

"Could a decorated submarine officer like Gorov be convinced to go along with it?"

A strange look flashed across Ramius's face. Not regret—certainly not that, but something . . .

"Yes," Ramius said finally. "Because they would convince him that his mission *serves* Russia. Or they would capitalize on his hatred for America, which would be easy if he believed his father had been betrayed by the CIA. Being raised by a single mother in Soviet Russia would have been difficult." He turned to the photo of Gorov in his dress uniform on the screen. "You say the man's wife died?"

"Yes," Ryan said, and he felt Ramius's pain at the parallel. *That must be an anguish that never leaves.*

"Regret is a powerful motivator," Ramius said softly. "Given everything you've told me, I think Captain Gorov and his submarine are a clear and present danger to America."

Ryan felt himself deflate.

"What is that look, Ryan?" Ramius said.

Ryan sighed. "I was hoping that you would reassure me that Gorov was cut from the same cloth as you. That if the chain of command was circumvented and the order to fire was given by the cabal, he would have the conscience and the mettle to do the right and honorable thing."

Ramius pressed his lips into a hard, thin line, then said, "Unfortunately, the world isn't run by Boy Scouts."

"Yeah, something I've been reminded of repeatedly over the years," Ryan said and stared off into the distance as he tried to decide what his next move should be.

Ramius, who was patrolling—not pacing—the gap between the conference table and the north wall, said, "I want you to know I've reconsidered my position on Halsey."

The bizarre non sequitur snapped Ryan from his thoughts. "What?"

"Don't you remember? Your book about Halsey, we talked about it on the conn of the *Red October*."

"I remember," Ryan said. "You said my conclusions were all wrong. That Halsey acted stupidly."

"That's right, but I've reconsidered. There's no way Halsey could have known the true readiness condition of Ozawa's carriers, that their pilot ranks and aircraft inventory were decimated by that time. Halsey saw the opportunity to strike a devastating blow to the enemy and he pursued. He understood that danger, confronted properly, is not something a man must fear. My original judgment was based on hindsight. If Halsey had known what we know now, he never would have fallen into the trap and abandoned the straits."

Ryan was about to talk some well-earned smack when an epiphany struck him. He popped to his feet and said, "'If Halsey had known' . . . Marko, you're a genius."

"Well, I don't know if I'd go that far. It doesn't make me a genius to admit that I was wrong . . . Ryan, you seem very agitated suddenly."

"Not agitated, excited. I know what we need to do."

"You do?" Ramius said, one bushy eyebrow up with curiosity.

"We need to give Yermilov a gift," Ryan said, his next move crystallizing. "The gift of hindsight."

53

The phone on Yermilov's desk buzzed.

He pressed the intercom button and said, "What is it?"

"Mr. President, there is a Brown Fox transmission," his executive assistant said.

Yermilov felt a band tighten around his chest and his breath stuck in his throat. He glanced over his shoulder at Boris, who stood impassively by the large drapery, hands clasped in front of him. He was either not aware of the weight of this message on the intercom or, more likely, he was simply too professional to react.

"Thank you," Yermilov finally said, then pressed the button to break the intercom link with a trembling finger. "Leave me, Boris," he said without looking back at the man.

"Yes, sir," Boris said, and Yermilov felt the movement as the man retreated to the secret door beside the bookcase and disappeared, a metallic click signaling the door to the secret safe room and weapons depot had closed.

The Russian president opened his computer, then entered the

three-stage authentication that only he knew, and a message box opened. For more than a decade now, the only traffic on the top secret communications system that established a direct line between the Russian and American presidents had been the hourly, low-side messages between the operators, confirming the system to be operational. Twenty-four messages a day, twelve sent from each nation, and this was the first time he had received a message personally, despite the daily requirement to log in to confirm the system worked on the Kremlin's end.

The message box populated with a series of symbols and numbers at first, which instantly transformed to words, in Russian, as the program decrypted the message:

We must talk.

Yermilov leaned back in his chair, struggling to breathe. This was about more than the tensions between their fleets in the Atlantic. Ryan had communicated his position quite clearly in his national address—a message intended more for Yermilov than the American public, Yermilov suspected. It had contained the expected saber rattling and finger-pointing. After all, an American plane had been lost—but then, they had shot down a Russian jet in response. Yes, wars were started in such situations, but this must be more than that.

He knows. He knows, somehow, about the Belgorod *and the plan to place a weapon in Norfolk Harbor, to lie waiting should they escalate in the future.*

No. It was impossible. That operation was highly compartmentalized. This must be about the downed fighter. Nothing else made sense.

I must show strength.

He typed his reply.

Release the *Finitor*, return our sailors, withdraw
your carrier strike group . . . Then we can talk.

He watched the letters and symbols fill the screen again in real
time and could picture the American president, sitting at his desk
in the Oval Office, typing his reply.

We know about the *Belgorod* and its tasking.

Yermilov's heart skipped a beat.

But *how much* did Ryan know? That the Americans had a network of spies in Russia was known, and a constant source of pain
for him, not to mention cost. It seemed half the budget of FSB
operations these days was spent rooting out assets and closing
leaks. And with satellite technology, there were no secret movements or deployments. Of course, they had been watching from
overhead and had seen the *Belgorod* set to sea. He had leaked the
propaganda about the Status-6 torpedo capabilities for just this
reason, long before Ilyin had come to him with his plan. So what
this needed was bravado and saber rattling of his own.

K-329 is a deterrent to protect Russia from American aggression.

Before he'd even finished typing, a new message appeared.

**Intelligence indicates the *Belgorod* has orders to conduct a
Status-6 nuclear first strike against America.**

Yermilov felt instantly light-headed as all the blood drained
from his face. He'd interacted with Ryan long enough to know that

the American President was forthright to a fault. Ryan didn't lie. Ryan didn't bluff. Somehow, the man had managed to become and remain President with a policy of telling the truth even when it weakened his negotiating leverage. Yermilov didn't know what to type, so he stared at the screen and felt afraid.

Very afraid.

There would be no way for the Americans to distinguish between the attempt to sneak a Poseidon UUV into Norfolk Harbor and an actual first strike. And if Ryan knew about the mission, the Americans would be monitoring for it and much more likely to detect it.

I have to abort the mission. It's too dangerous.

He was still staring at the screen when more text came in.

Ilyin, Rodionov, Aralovich, and Boldyrev are plotting
against you.
We suspect Gorov is in league with these men.
The *Belgorod* attack will spark a war between our countries,
trigger a coup, and you will take the fall.

Thousands, if not millions, of innocent people will die.
This transmission is your last chance to remain in power
and save your country.

If you do not cooperate, our first Tomahawk salvo will
target your office and two dozen command and control
locations in twenty-eight minutes.

Yermilov stared at the screen, his head swimming. Ryan's transmission had confirmed his worst fears. The Russian president looked into the future and imagined with perfect clarity the sequence of events that would lead to his downfall and demise. Ilyin had manipulated him brilliantly, and in his gut, Yermilov understood that the old man meant to do it—detonate the nuke, cripple the American fleet and East Coast command, use it to justify a coup, and start a brand-new Cold War.

Let me help you stay in power, Mr. President.

He couldn't help but glance at his watch. *Twenty-seven minutes.* Then he placed trembling fingers on the keyboard.

What are your demands?

Pull the Northern Fleet out of the Atlantic and cease flight operations.

It will be done.

Terminate the *Belgorod*'s mission, order it to surface immediately and return to port.

Yermilov let out a long, hissing sigh through clenched teeth.

That might not be possible if Captain Gorov has gone rogue, as your intelligence suggests.

Ryan didn't reply for nearly a full minute.

Then our only choice is to hunt down K-329. Together.

First, cancel your missile attack.

Salvo suspended, but we will be watching.

Yermilov's fingers hovered above the keyboard. But to say anything further would be to cede any strength and dignity he had left.

So he said nothing.

He pressed the button on the intercom.

"Yes, Mr. President, sir?" came the strained voice. She must know that a direct message from the American President could not possibly be something good.

"Get Colonel General Andreyev on a secure line immediately."

"Yes, sir."

Yermilov dropped his head into his hands. His world was spiraling out of control. Should he move swiftly against Ilyin and the other traitors now? Or should he proceed methodically and dismantle their networks?

The FSO is still firmly under my control, as is the army, Wagner, and probably the GRU. Not everyone respects Rodionov.

The same was true of all the coup members. Certainly, they had a web of supporters, but Yermilov was still the president and commander in chief. Ninety-nine percent of the officers and rank and file would follow his commands . . . bend to his will. Institutions functioned because of *authority*, not loyalty. He wrangled his breathing under control and quelled the panic in his chest. Making decisions driven by fear and urgency rarely resulted in the optimal outcome. He'd risen to power by being calculating, methodical, and feared. He still had the upper hand. Coups were only successful when they had a catalyst and when they could capitalize on the element of surprise.

Ryan's Brown Fox transmission had robbed Ilyin of both.

One step at a time, he told himself. *De-escalate. Stop K-329. Then round up the traitors.*

The intercom light on his phone flashed and he pressed the button.

"General Andreyev is on the secure line, Mr. President," the secretary said.

"*Da*," he said and took the call. "Colonel General Andreyev, we have a problem. You are the only one I trust now, and I must have your complete loyalty."

"You have it, Mr. President," came Andreyev's proud and perhaps relieved voice.

"You must tell no one of this conversation, Oleg," he said, trying to sound intimate with his new confidant. "I've learned there is a conspiracy at the highest levels to undermine my authority and start a nuclear war with the United States."

"Nuclear war?" Andreyev said, the shock and dismay in his voice the proof Yermilov needed that the man was both unaware of the plot and properly terrified by the prospect.

"*Da*, comrade. The situation is both dangerous and delicate. It will require your leadership, discretion, and cooperation to identify the co-conspirators and stop the war. You will be my right-hand man putting down this dangerous cabal. Understood?"

"Completely, Mr. President. You have my unwavering allegiance."

"First, I need the Northern Fleet to pull back from the American strike group. Cease all flight operations at once and steam the fleet north back into the Arctic exercise area."

"It will be done immediately."

"There is more, Oleg," he said. "I have learned a most unsettling truth: submarine Captain First Rank Gorov has gone rogue. He is working with the conspirators. I fear we have lost control of K-329."

There was a long pause and he could imagine Andreyev trying to read between the lines.

"I am not surprised by this. Admiral Boldyrev has been working at odds with the NDMC and my staff. May I speak frankly, Mr. President?"

"*Da.*"

"Boldyrev is not loyal to us, sir."

"I know. What about Defense Minister Volkorov? Can we trust him? Or do you believe his loyalties lie with Ilyin?" Yermilov asked, giving Andreyev another nugget of trust.

"I think Volkorov is tired of trying to lead in Ilyin's shadow. Since Ilyin retired and you appointed Volkorov, he has struggled to win your confidence. Ilyin is constantly undermining him."

Yermilov nodded. "This is helpful information, Oleg. We need Volkorov in our corner."

"Show him favor and he will have the confidence to finally assert himself. He was afraid that working at odds with Ilyin would undermine your trust in him. He has been waiting for this moment."

By confiding in Andreyev, the man had reciprocated. This was exactly what Yermilov needed most.

"What is our best submarine in the Northern Fleet, Oleg?"

After a moment, Andreyev answered, "I assume you mean apart from Captain Gorov and the *Belgorod.*"

His head of military operations was piecing it together.

"*Da.*"

"Captain First Rank Denikin and K-560, the *Severodvinsk.* I would put the K-560 up against the American Seawolf without hesitation."

"What is K-560's status?" he asked. He thought he knew the position and readiness level of his most capable hunter-killer submarine, but that was before Ryan's transmission.

"It is patrolling the North Atlantic, ready to protect and defend our fleet at a moment's notice, Mr. President."

"And you are sure it is in theater?"

"I will confirm, but I'm highly confident that neither the asset nor its captain are compromised," Andreyev said, once again proving his loyalty, intuition, and worth. "What are your orders?"

How did I let it come to this?

He let out a long sigh, scarcely believing the order he was about to give.

"Transmit new orders to K-329 to abort its mission, surface immediately, and stand down. I want all communications routed through and monitored by your office at the NDMC. At the same time, send an encrypted flash message to Captain Denikin of the *Severodvinsk*. For the captain's eyes only," he said. "Presidential Order number 10522: K-560 shall hunt down and destroy the special missions submarine *Belgorod*, K-329."

"But, sir, this is dangerous to have both instructions out at the same time. What if K-329 complies and stands down? Do you still want me to sink it?"

"If Gorov complies, then we cancel Denikin's kill order, but I am afraid this is nothing but wishful thinking. I suspect we will not be hearing from Captain Gorov until it is too late and he has already started a war that will end us all."

54

Just when Konstantin thought his luck might be beginning to turn, the conning officer summoned him. As he made his way forward from the drone hangar control room to the conn, he could not help but notice the worried expressions and nervous stares of the crewmen who he'd ordered to battle stations.

A part of him resented them for their cowardice and doubt.

Do they not trust me? Do they not know that I, and I alone, am in command and my will should not be questioned?

Another part of him challenged this callous thinking. His standard operating practice was to make an announcement explaining the tactical situation to accompany changes in readiness or prior to commencing a new evolution. In this case, he had not.

They are young—very young—and they are operating in an information black hole. It is not mistrust you see in their faces, it is uncertainty.

He started nodding to his men and making eye contact to show them his confidence. Only then did he realize he was walking with his right palm pressed to his abdomen. Instead of the acute flashes of pain he'd been dealing with the past forty-eight hours, this steady burning gnaw he felt was new. And new was not a good sign. New was terrifying.

It's the cancer, a fatalistic voice reminded him, *consuming you from the inside out.*

As he reached the threshold of the control room, he forced both hands to his sides.

"Captain in control," Blok said, announcing the CO's arrival on the conn.

"As you were," he said and walked straight to Blok. "What is the problem?"

"Sonar picked up a series of powerful transmissions," Blok said.

"High-frequency active?"

"No, sir."

"An American submarine?"

"No, we don't think so."

"Stop with the guessing game, conning officer," Konstantin said, his irritation rising, "and just tell me."

"I think it is better, sir, if you take a look for yourself."

"Fine," Konstantin said and shoved past Blok, stomping toward sonar.

He opened the door and stepped into the dimly lit sonar suite without knocking.

"Captain," the sonar supervisor said, momentarily taken aback. "Would you like to see the recording?"

"Of course I want to see it," he snapped.

Collect yourself . . . Ignore the pain.

The sonar lead swallowed nervously and gestured to the nearest sonar terminal. "This is the signal. I will play the recording back for you."

The captain leaned in, placing his hands on the seat back of the chair in front of him. His heart skipped a beat when he saw the frequency. "This signal is 151.7 hertz?"

"*Da*, Captain."

"You're certain this is not the signal we are generating?"

"I'm certain," the sonar supervisor said. "The noise augmentation device is strongest on relative bearings one-four-zero and two-four-zero, which makes sense, as it is coming from own-ship aft of the bow sonar array. This signal was detected on bearing zero-four-nine true."

Konstantin's mind churned like a computer analyzing scenarios. "Where is the carrier now?"

"With our towed array stowed, we lost contact with the American fleet, but if we extrapolate the last known data, this signal would match the carrier's estimated position," the sonar lead said.

Then this is the Americans and it was intentional. It means they have identified this frequency, and they know we are here. But have they broken the riddle? Do they know we are not the Gepard? *Is this their way of gloating, telling us they see through my deception? Or are they trying to communicate?*

"There's something else you should know, Captain," Blok said and looked at the sonarman. "Tell him about the frequency-shift patterns you observed."

Konstantin listened as the sonar supervisor explained how the 151.7-hertz frequency underwent a series of small frequency shifts and then how a second 161.7-hertz signal had appeared and exhibited a similar pattern, with both signals taking turns alternating. When the sonarman was done with the explanation, the captain said, "It is a code. They are using frequency-shift keying to send a message."

"*Da*," the sonarman said. "This makes sense, but do you think the message is intended for us?"

"I don't know," Konstantin said truthfully. "But we need to find out, so get to work decoding it."

"Aye, Captain, but I am . . . not a code breaker. I am sorry. I will try of course, but—"

"I know this, comrade," the captain said and put a hand on the man's shoulder, "but we have men on board who are. I will send Gustanov to help you. He is a cryptological and signals expert. Send for me the instant you have something."

"Aye, Captain."

Konstantin turned to Blok. "Is that all, conning officer?"

"Sir, the ship is manned for battle stations and I have given orders to the section leaders to search every crevice and corner of the ship for the device," Blok said.

"Very well. I'm returning to the drone hangar control room. We will hover here until the device is found and destroyed."

"But, Captain—"

"*Nyet*," Konstantin said sharply. "When we run, we run in silence. They will not fire on us without provocation. I know the American President. I have studied him for years. He is logical and cautious. That is why we will win, comrade."

"Yes, sir."

Konstantin turned to leave, but then a new thought occurred to him, a tactic he'd not considered before when he'd been the hunter instead of the hunted.

"Conning officer, flood and make ready torpedo tubes three and four in all respects."

Blok balked for a second before repeating the order back, upspeak at the end making it sound like a question.

"*Da*, you heard me. Tubes three and four—make ready in all respects."

55

K atie huddled against the side of the island, trying to stay out of the bone-chilling wind whipping across the flight deck as she waited for the Osprey to conduct preflights. She watched with no small amount of wonder as the massive tilt-rotors began to spin up. A hand on her shoulder from behind gave her a start.

"Oh, you scared the crap out of me," she said, turning to find Jones hunching behind her.

"I'm glad I caught you in time," he said, huffing. He'd clearly been rushing, if not running, to find her.

"I'm so glad you changed your mind," she said with a wry grin. "I knew you wouldn't pass up this opportunity."

"Hell, no, I didn't change my mind," he said, shaking his head emphatically. "Now, hold out your hand."

"Okay," she said and stuck out her right hand, palm up, into which he slapped a double bag Ziploc with a USB memory stick inside.

"I gotta give props where props are due. You were right, Ryan."

"Right about what?"

"The *Gepard* and the *Belgorod*," he said with an ear-to-ear smile. "I couldn't help myself, and I had Kumari message SUBLANT with your acoustic camouflage idea. Turns out the *Indiana* had the same working theory as you."

"Really?"

"Yeah, they just transmitted the data package that proves it," he said and proceeded to ramble for the next minute about acoustic fingerprints and a sonar tech named Harris and how he'd used some analyzer program to figure out that the *Gepard* was actually the *Belgorod*.

"Wow, okay, that's a lot. I don't know if I will remember all that. Did you get a chance to look at the data and confirm it?"

"No, I downloaded it as soon as I got it, put it on a thumb drive, and ran to find you."

"What do I do with this?" she asked as she slipped the bagged memory stick into the left breast pocket of her cammie blouse.

"Give it to the lead ACINT rider on the *Blackfish* or the sonar LCPO. They'll know what to do."

"Thank you, Dr. Jones," she said.

So, this is what it feels like to be my dad.

"Strong work, Ryan," he said and gave her shoulder a squeeze. "Good luck out there."

"Are you sure you don't want to come? We could certainly use you."

"Nah, I'm a dinosaur," he said with a wane smile. "It's time to pass the torch to the ST2 Harrises of the world. The kids out in the fleet today can do anything I can do."

"Lieutenant, they're ready for you," a female white shirt from the deck crew said, jogging up to them.

"Go get 'em, Ryan," Jones said, stepping back and waving.

"See you on the other side when this is over," she called to him over the wind.

"Wouldn't miss it for the world," he said and, despite being retired all these years, popped her a parting salute.

56

USS *WASHINGTON*, SSN 787, "THE BLACKFISH"

Six-four feet . . . six-three . . . six-two . . . officer of the deck, ship is on depth six-one feet," the copilot announced as the number one photonics mast broke the surface of the water and the *Blackfish* reached periscope depth.

Knepper watched gray-black swells undulating on a large monitor while the CO made a controlled scan of the air-water interface. The initial periscope sweep after breaking the surface of the water was conducted in absolute silence. A ship's safety evolution, the twenty-four-second scan looked for counter-detection threats, ships inside five hundred yards, and silent navigation hazards that could endanger their sub. Unlike older submarine classes with optical periscopes, the *Blackfish*'s photonics mast had a camera that sent high-def imagery to the ASAW network. Knepper, along with everyone else in control, had the same view as the scope operator.

"No close contacts," Houston announced, breaking both the silence and the tension in the room.

The captain taking the ship to PD was a highly anomalous event. Most people didn't realize that the department heads and junior officers were the ones driving the submarine, standing watch as the officer of the deck, and thereby acting in the captain's stead.

But since the *Blackfish* was still at battle stations, the CO was literally driving the bus today.

"Conn, Sonar, no close contacts," the sonar supe reported.

"Conn, ESM, hold no close contacts," the electronic warfare supervisor reported over the open mic.

"Very well," Houston said, handing the Xbox controller they used for operating the photonics mast to the nav.

"Conn, Radio, receiving the broadcast on number one photonics mast," the radio supervisor reported on the open mic.

"Radio, Conn, aye," Houston replied, then to the nav added, "I'm ready to be relieved."

"Yes, sir," the nav said, and they conducted a quick turnover, which was purely procedural, since the nav had had the deck and been on the conn for the past hour and a half.

"Attention in control," the nav announced. "This is the nav. I have the deck and the conn."

"XO, go to radio and see what's taking so long," Houston said when several minutes had passed bobbing at PD with no report.

"Yes, sir," Knepper said, and he stepped out the back of the control room and entered the cramped cubby of a space that was the radio room after punching in the code for the controlled-access door.

"Hey, XO," the lead radioman said, looking up from his terminal for a split second before turning back to his workstation.

"Whatcha got, Felix?" Knepper said.

"Um . . . Yeah," was all the information systems technician first class replied as he grabbed a page from the printer and handed it to Knepper.

Knepper had to read it twice to make sure he hadn't misread the instructions.

"You've gotta be fucking kidding me," he murmured, looking up at the IST1.

"I know, right?" Felix said. "The old man ain't gonna like this one bit."

"No . . . He most certainly is not."

Felix flashed Knepper a Cheshire cat grin. "Thanks for stopping by, XO, and offering to give that to the captain."

"You dawg . . . You waited for me to come in here and get it, didn't you?" Knepper said.

"Who, me? Drag my feet? Sir, I would never," Felix said and extended his fist for a bump.

God, I love this crew, Knepper thought as he left Felix, the kid's fist hanging in midair, and turned to give the CO the bad news.

57

On the one hand, traveling by Osprey was a step up from the COD flight she'd taken when embarking on the *Ford*. While the C-2 Greyhound required a catapult launch to get airborne, the Osprey's vertical takeoff was totally smooth and the cargo hold was not so grungy and loud. On the other hand, something about the tilt-rotor aircraft didn't sit right with Katie. The Osprey wasn't quite a plane, nor was it a helicopter. It was the type of machine that probably had the words "Just Trust Me" stenciled on the side of it when it left the factory, which the Navy promptly painted over on delivery.

Her insides felt suddenly light, then instantly heavy, as a pocket of turbulence bounced the fuselage.

"You look nervous," said the air crewman, AW1 Castro, sitting in the fold-down jump seat beside her.

"I am," Katie said, heart pounding and fear quotient off the charts.

"Listen, you'll be fine," he said with a salty, reassuring smile. "We've done transfers to subs before."

The comment might have buoyed her spirits, but she sensed an important omission.

"With people?" she said over the din.

"No . . . With cargo. But it went fine."

"Uh-huh."

Just like on the C-2 flight, she was wearing a cranial safety vest with floatation, hearing protection, and goggles. Instead of muffs, however, they'd issued her headphones with noise-canceling and comms, the latter complements of the radio clipped to her harness. During the transfer, she would be in communication with the Osprey and the sub the entire time.

That way, everyone can hear me screaming all the way down.

On the C-2, the seating faced backward, but here on the Osprey it ran along the port and starboard sides of the fuselage. The fold-down jump seats faced centerline, and could hold sixteen, but for today's flight she was the lone passenger. No chill fighter pilots this time to soothe her nerves. She looked aft at the winch mounted in the overhead above the rear cargo ramp. A series of nonproductive "what if" questions ran through her mind:

What if they can't keep me steady and I slam repeatedly into the side of the sail?

What if the winch fails and I drop into the ocean?

Worse, what if the cable snaps and I hit the deck?

Oh God . . . I'm an idiot for demanding this.

Katie practiced a slow round of four-count breathing to try to tamp down her fear—just like her big bro, Jack, had taught her—but it didn't seem to help.

"Five minutes out," a voice said in her headset.

Castro held up five fingers and she nodded.

"Ma'am, if you could stand up for me," he said, getting to his feet. "I'd like to double-check your harness."

She did as requested, unfastening her lap belt and standing. The fuselage immediately wobbled and she had to steady herself against the bulkhead with a hand as a fresh pocket of turbulence shook the plane.

"Feels like it's getting rougher out there," she said as he checked her thigh buckles, shoulder buckles, keeper strap, and her safety lanyard.

"This is nothing," he said, tugging on her front D ring to get it centered mid-chest. "I've been through much worse."

"You probably say that to all the girls."

He flashed her a crooked grin, but didn't answer.

Busted.

The second crew member, a lanky guy who'd not said two words since she boarded the aircraft, made his way aft to the winch station. His name tape read ROBERTS, so she'd dubbed him "Silent Bob" in her mind. Silent Bob clipped his own safety harness to the port bulkhead and lowered the winch cable, which had a metal clip thingy attached to the end that kind of reminded her of a heavy-duty carabiner.

"Your harness looks sat. Let's get you clipped in," Castro said.

She nodded and he escorted her back, holding her arm to steady her as turbulence shook the deck. At the ramp, which was still fully raised, he clipped himself to the starboard bulkhead while Silent Bob connected a line with two heavy-duty safety hooks—one to the winch and one to the D ring on her harness. Next, he connected her safety lanyard hook to the same bow-shaped metal piece on the end of the winch cable.

"You're looking a little peaked, ma'am," Castro said. "You're not going to faint on me, are you?"

"Nope, I'm good," she said, forcing a brave expression onto her face.

"One minute out," said the pilot's voice in her headset. "Stand by."

"All right, LT, listen up. The pilots are going to settle into a static hover over the *Washington*'s sail. The captain has elected to broach the sub instead of surfacing it. I don't know what that means, but I'm supposed to tell you that. Nod if you understand."

She nodded and felt her knees starting to knock.

"Once we're in position, we're going to lower the cargo ramp. You're going to sit down on the end of the ramp below the winch. When the sub gives us the all clear from below, you're going to lower yourself off the edge like you're climbing into a swimming pool, okay? Matt will be working the winch, lowering you slowly, and the pilot will hold us as steady as possible during that part. Use your arms to keep your chest and head away from the lip of the ramp. As soon as your head is below the ramp, all you have to do is hang. We'll do the rest."

She looked down at her gloved hands, then up to meet his stare.

"Sounds like a plan," was all she could manage.

"Hovering over the asset," the pilot said on the party line. "Have comms with the bridge. Lower the ramp and proceed with transfer."

"Copy all," AW1 Castro said into his mic, then looked at Katie. "You ready, ma'am?"

She nodded.

He pressed a button on a control panel mounted on the bulkhead. Servos whirred and the hydraulic-powered cargo ramp slowly descended, revealing an ominous-looking predawn steel-gray sky and turbulent ocean below.

"It's rougher than I thought," she said, looking at the whitecaps and then at the swaying sail of the Virginia-class submarine below.

"You got this, LT," he said.

She lowered herself to the deck, and scooted on her ass to the end of the cargo ramp, Silent Bob working the winch to give her slack the whole time. When she got to the edge, she swung her booted feet off and clutched the aluminum lip with a death grip. A wave of vertigo washed over her as she looked down. The Osprey was much higher than she'd imagined for the transfer. It *felt* like they were lowering her from the top of the Empire State Building. She tried to do what Castro had said, but her limbs ignored the commands from her brain as she sat there frozen, staring down at the *Washington* getting battered by whitecaps.

"You've got the green light, ma'am, whenever you're ready," he said in her ear.

She looked back at him, her eyes saying, *I can't . . .*

"Take all the time you need," Castro said with patient and empathetic eyes. "This bird has plenty of fuel. If it doesn't work, we'll just pull you up. Hell, I might even give it a go when your turn is over."

None of that was true, of course, but she adored the guy for saying it and making her laugh, which took the edge off and momentarily unlocked her fear-induced paralysis. With a heavy exhale, she turned and lowered herself off the ramp, using her gloved hands to press herself clear from the edge, while Silent Bob expertly managed her weight with the winch. A split second later she was clear of the ramp and descending toward the sub.

"Clear," she said belatedly in her boom mic.

"Roger that, ma'am, you're doing great," Castro said.

Below she could see three people in bright orange jackets on the sub getting ready for her arrival. One person stood precariously on top of a little square platform on the sail in a surfer's wide-legged stance. He appeared to be tethered to the base of the lone mast and held a long pole with a hook on the end. The other two were only partially visible, standing in what she seemed to remember was called the bridge cockpit. A buffeting gust of wind sent her swaying and spinning simultaneously. She heard herself curse as she tried to counter the effects, but it was pointless. Her body was at the mercy of the elements.

"Lieutenant Ryan, this is Lieutenant Commander Knepper on the *Washington*," a male voice said in her ear. "Great to see you again. How's it *hanging?*"

The question made her roll her eyes, but just like with Castro, Knepper's joke was exactly what she needed in the moment.

This is why I love the Navy, she thought.

"A little bird said someone stole your peanut butter, so they sent me with an emergency supply," she said, looking down at the slowly spinning submarine.

"I'll be sure to tell Roth," he said with a chuckle. "In all seriousness, Ryan, the plan is to snag the drop line just above your head with a gaff pole and pull you into the bridge cockpit. The pole is grounded just in case there's any static electricity on the line, so let us grab you first. Do you copy?"

"Copy all," she said, suddenly more worried about the dude trying to balance on top of the sail falling off than she was for herself.

As the vertical separation shrank to less than twenty-five feet, she could see the concentration on the guy's face as he worked to maintain his balance and readied himself to grab her. Her gaze shifted to Knepper, who stood in the cockpit with another crew member, who held a microphone, talking, she presumed, to the sub's control room below. Despite the early hour and overcast skies, Knepper wore sunglasses and smiled large. He reminded her very much of a submariner version of Tom Cruise.

"Get ready," Knepper said when the gap had closed to within ten feet.

As the gap closed to mere feet, she relaxed, as it seemed like they were going to successfully pull off this crazy transfer. But just as the sail surfer reached out with the pole hook for her drop line, she felt herself yanked violently up and away. She gasped, and a split second later she was falling, the Osprey buffeted by a massive gust of wind that sent her swinging. Like the weight on the end of a pendulum, Katie suddenly found herself careening straight toward the side of the submarine's towering metal sail.

58

K atie didn't have time to think, only react.

With athleticism she didn't know she possessed, she somehow managed to turn a quarter revolution in the air and get the soles of her boots up. Using her legs as shock absorbers, she redirected the impact. Sea spray soaked her from bottom to top as an angry North Atlantic roller slammed into the sail below her and blasted upward like a geyser. The freezing cold made her breath catch in her throat and stole her attention as she swung back for a second collision.

"Markowski, grab the line," Knepper, who was now above her, yelled on the radio.

This time Katie wasn't able to orient properly and her left shoulder and hip slammed into the side of the sail. The impact knocked the wind out of her lungs and filled her vision with stars.

"Got it," someone shouted.

"Get her up, damn it, before she gets beat to death," someone else yelled.

She felt her stomach go heavy and the side of the sail blur as either the pilot or the winch operator—or maybe both of them together—raised her elevation. This time, when she swung in for a third collision, she tucked her legs to her chest. The instant she cleared the top of the sail, she extended them into a V and scissor-wrapped around Knepper, who was primed and ready to catch her. She felt him lock his arms around her hips, his face smashed into her lower abdomen, as the other pumpkin-suited sailor struggled to unclip her harness from the drop line.

"Fuck. I need slack!" he shouted.

She felt an upward tug, and both she and Knepper—who were clinging to each other for dear life—lifted into the air.

"I said slack, damn it!"

A heartbeat later, they dropped, gravity back in play. The deck grate reverberated with a metallic clank as Knepper took the full brunt of their combined weight. She heard him grunt, but he didn't drop her or let go.

"Both hooks are free," the guy who'd been manhandling her harness shouted.

"Angel, *Blackfish*, we've got the package. The drop line is clear, you're free to bug out," Knepper said as he gave Katie's back a comforting *I got you* pat.

Mind and body still flooded with adrenaline, it took her a long second to register this detail, but when she did she finally unclenched her death grip on his torso and lowered her booted feet onto the grate below.

He held her for a second to make sure she had her sea legs, then stepped back a foot to smile at her and say, "Welcome aboard the USS *Washington*, your underwater Uber. I'll be your driver, Dennis."

Despite the throbbing in both her left shoulder and ribs, she managed a smile.

"I deserve that," she said and let out a heavy exhale. "But thank you for accommodating."

"Accommodating" was an understatement.

A pair of booted feet and legs in orange foul-weather trousers now dangled in the bridge cockpit beside her. She followed Knepper's gaze up to look at the guy with the pole hook, who now sat, rather than surfed, on top of the sail.

"Quite the balancing act you did up there," she said.

"Petty Officer Markowski's previous tour was in Pearl Harbor," Knepper said. "They say he spent a lot of time at the North Shore, so I decided to put that rumor to the test."

"Well, I'm glad you did," she said to Knepper, then looking up again, added, "Thanks for risking your life to haul me in."

Markowski flashed her the *Hang loose* sign with his free hand, his other clutching the pole hook. "My pleasure, ma'am."

"All right, OOD," Knepper said, looking behind her at the only person she'd not met in the cramped bridge cockpit. "Transfer the watch below and get the bridge rigged for dive with Markowski. We need to get deep ASAFP."

"Yes, sir," the officer said and immediately hoisted himself up to sit beside Markowski to make room for Knepper to lift the deck grating they all stood on.

"The ladder rungs are wet and slick and it's a long way down," the XO said as he raised the grating to reveal a narrow vertical tunnel with a ladder in three sections that extended down into the belly of the submarine. "Take it slow and hold on with both hands at all times."

"Roger that," she said and did exactly as he said, working her way down methodically and carefully, her legs trembling the whole way down as her body burned off the adrenaline dump from her transfer.

Her ribs and left shoulder flared with each extension, but she gritted her teeth and concentrated on the climb. When she reached the bottom, she was greeted by the sub's captain, dressed in the iconic dark blue coveralls that she guessed represented the underway uniform of submariners around the world. Unlike Knepper, he did not look pleased to see her.

"Lieutenant Ryan, I'm Commander Houston, CO of the *Black-fish*," he said with a narrow-eyed stare. He paused a moment before sticking out his hand to her.

She shook it, making sure to return his firm grip despite feeling completely spent. Knepper stepped off the ladder and joined them in a closed circle of three in the narrow corridor.

"She, uh, took a pretty good shot against the side of the sail," Knepper said to the captain, then turned to her. "Ryan, do you want to get checked out by the doc?"

"I'm okay," she said, noticing that Houston's expression shifted from agitation to concern with this new information.

"Are you sure, Ryan?" the CO asked. "I didn't realize there was an incident up there."

"Not an incident . . . Just a hard landing, is all," she said.

"Okay, in that case, let's talk turkey. Why are you here, Ryan?" he said. "What was so important that you had to pull us off mission, force us to disengage while tracking an enemy submarine, and broach this ship in rough seas, putting multiple lives at risk, including your own?"

"Maybe we should talk in a SCIF," she proposed.

"No, you're gonna tell me right here, right now." He gestured around the small space. "You're in my SCIF."

For a moment, she said nothing. Then, in an exhausted, emotion-laden torrent, it all came out. He listened without interruption all the way until the end.

"I needed to look you in the eye and tell you that sometime in the next twenty-four hours the *Blackfish* is going to be the only thing that stands between Konstantin Gorov and World War Three. I believe that the *Belgorod* has gone rogue and intends an attack on the United States—a nuclear attack with a salted warhead delivered by a Status-6 torpedo, which we have confirmed he has on board. Captain Houston, how you decide to act on this information will determine the fate of the entire world."

He didn't say anything, just stared at her blankly, and for a moment she wondered if she'd hallucinated the conversation. Then he checked his watch and shot a look at Knepper. "XO, I want the bridge rigged for dive in the next three minutes. Then take us deep and get the thin line back out. Every second counts."

"Yes, sir," Knepper said. "Do you want me to secure from battle stations?"

"No," he said, then turned to Katie. "Ryan, follow me."

The CO turned on a heel and headed aft—at least she thought it was aft—but she'd not spent enough time aboard during her last visit to make a mental map of the sub. She followed him around a dogleg, down a ladder, then forward into the command passageway. He opened a door with a placard that read COMMANDING OFFICER and gestured for her to step into his stateroom, which was way less than half the size of the stateroom they'd put her up in on the *Ford*. He shut the door behind him and gestured to the lone chair for her to take a seat. She did as ordered and he squeezed past her to sit on a little bench seat in a cutout on the aft bulkhead.

She decided it best to wait for him to start the conversation.

He sighed heavily, then bowed his head to massage his temples. "Does the President know you're here?" he asked, going straight to the place where few dared to tread.

"Honestly, sir, I don't know," she said. "I haven't spoken directly with him or his staff in quite some time."

"Hmm . . . That's what I was afraid of," he murmured, still rubbing his temples and looking down at the floor.

"What's that supposed to mean?" she said with a defensive edge to her voice.

"It means that not only have you apparently dumped the fate of humanity on my shoulders, Lieutenant, but you've also made me responsible for safeguarding someone the President of the United States holds most precious." He looked up at her. "I assume you've heard the term 'burden of command,' Lieutenant Ryan?"

She smiled. "Yes, sir. It just happens to be a Ryan family dinner conversation greatest hit."

The corners of his mouth curled up, his eyes softening only slightly. "Yeah . . . I imagine it is."

She contemplated for a moment how to respond, before saying, "Look, I know I just dropped a two-ton ox yoke on your back, but I'm not going to apologize. The truth is, this is the last place on earth that I want to be right now. I would love nothing more than to be at home, curled up with a Jessica Strawser novel, blissfully unaware that there's a Russian submarine preparing to fire a nuclear-armed torpedo at the Eastern Seaboard. But a life of safety and comfort is not the life I chose . . . Which is why I'm here, at the vanguard of our national defense with you and this crew."

He stared at her, then glanced away, thinking perhaps. "I heard what you said about the *Belgorod* being loaded with nuclear Status-6 torpedoes, masking its acoustic signature, and sabotaging the mid-Atlantic DASH network. I also believe what you told me about Gorov's history and losing his wife and child, but—" A knock on his stateroom door stopped Houston midsentence. He stood and said, "Come."

The door opened and a handsome sailor dressed in coveralls and wearing a FEAR THE BLACKFISH ball cap stuck his head out. "Captain, we just got a P4 message on board," he said, referring to a "personal for" message.

Houston stuck out his hand for the printed page, but the radioman hesitated. "Actually, sir, it's for Lieutenant Ryan."

For a split second Houston looked taken aback, but then he said, "All right, then give it to her."

The sailor did, and Katie took the printed page and read the message from former CIA intelligence officer Matthew Reilly, sent via the Office of the Director of National Intelligence, implying it had been both seen and approved by the director herself, Mary Pat Foley. Instead of the typical intel message written to be concise, to the point, and sterilized of opinion or conjecture, below the header the body appeared to be a word-for-word transcription of a personalized note addressed to her, penned by Reilly. The body text read:

Katie, after we spoke I did some digging and pursued a nagging hunch based on our conversation. One of my contacts in Moscow discovered that Gorov has pancreatic cancer. He's kept it quiet by seeking treatment in the private sector outside the Main Military Medical Directorate health system. He is terminal.—M.R.

The final sentence reverberated in her mind like an echo after a rifle report.

He is terminal . . .

She handed the paper to Houston.

He scanned it, looked up at the radioman standing in the doorway, and said, "Thank you, Castaneda."

"Sir," Castaneda said, left, and shut the door behind him.

"Now do you believe me?" she said, meeting his hazel-green eyes.

"It's not a matter of believing you, Ryan. This message doesn't contain any orders," he said, shaking the page in the air. "This is not tasking. It's information. Important information, disturbing information, but that's all it is."

"But—" she tried to interject, but he stopped her with a solemn shake of his head.

"Ryan, you might be the daughter of POTUS, but you do not speak for POTUS. Your logic, your data, your gut instincts . . . they might all be spot-on, but when it comes to me ordering firing-point procedures on a foreign Navy's submarine, it's irrelevant. My mandate as a submarine captain is to execute this platform's tasking to the letter. Until we receive a message from my chain of command changing my rules of engagement, our tasking is to protect the carrier strike group and track this submarine. I can play defensive, but I can't shoot first."

"I'm an Academy graduate and a naval officer, sir," she said. "Believe me, I understand the chain of command. And if I gave you the impression that I'm here in my father's stead, speaking on his behalf, then let me say unequivocally that I am not."

"That's good, because from where I'm standing, it sounded like you came here to try to convince me to go rogue and take unsanctioned, preemptive action against a foreign nation's submarine."

"No, sir. One rogue submarine captain is already more than I can handle."

"Then why are you here, Ryan? Help me understand."

She let out a shaky exhale. This wasn't going like she'd scripted it in her head.

"I'm here, Captain, to make sure you are fully briefed on the mental and emotional state of your counterpart on K-329. To inform you that his submarine is carrying two nuclear-armed Status-6 long-range autonomous torpedoes. To help you connect the dots in advance for an enemy's future action that would defy all logic to a submarine captain and crew operating in a relative information vacuum. And finally, and most importantly, I'm here because I know, with absolute certainty, what is coming. And I know that you will likely be faced with a command decision to react, at a time when communications will be difficult and impossible, and you will have to make that command decision before it will be too late."

He thought for a moment, then said, "And while I appreciate

your efforts and concern, none of what you just said changes anything. I cannot and will not take firing orders from you."

"I know that, sir, and I'm not asking you to. I'm asking—"

The radio phone clipped to his coveralls rang and Katie felt the floor tilt aggressively in what her brain told her was the forward direction. The *Blackfish* was going deep.

"CO," Houston said, staring daggers at her while he took the call. "Very well, stream the TB-29 and reacquire Master One." He clipped the device back on his chest. "What, exactly, are you asking me to do, Ryan? Be specific in your word choice, because I have a submarine to command and I'm running out of patience."

"I'm asking you," she said, knitting her fingers together almost as if in prayer, "to prepare yourself now for the terrible decision Captain Gorov is going to force you to make when you don't have the chain of command to back you up."

Houston stared at her and then let out a long sigh.

"Well, Ryan," he said, rising, "it's not gonna matter much if we can't reacquire the contact that you believe is trying to start World War Three." His look softened, but again only barely, and he added, "So let's get to work."

59

What on earth are you talking about?" Ryan asked, failing to resist the need to rise from his seat at the Resolute desk. "Why is she aboard the *Washington* and why am I hearing about it after the fact?"

He was angry, but he knew he wasn't angry with Mary Pat. She knew it, too—he could tell from her eyes.

What in the hell is Katie thinking?

"You're hearing about it now, Mr. President, because I just heard about it myself," she said calmly, just the cadence of her voice actually helping Ryan center himself. "And I'm afraid I can't tell you why Lieutenant Ryan felt she needed to be aboard the submarine hunting the *Belgorod*. Maybe it's simple genetics."

He cut her a look.

"That's not fair. When we were hunting for the *Red October*, I had insight that the skipper of the *Dallas* needed to hear from me. It was essential . . ."

"Jack," she said gently and put a hand on his shoulder. "You raised four amazing kids, who, like you, are completely dedicated to this country. Katie is smart as hell. And, just like all your kids, she is dedicated to her duty and will execute what she sees as her mission to the best of her ability. And, more than any of them, she's, well, *you*, Jack."

"What is that supposed to mean?"

"Just that she sees things, details, that others miss—just like a young analyst named Jack Ryan did, more than once. And when she knows she's right, she's a dog with a bone. Again, just like her dad."

Ryan let out a long sigh and headed to the twin couches across from the desk, dropping heavily onto the one to his right. Mary Pat took a seat on the other, facing him across the low coffee table.

"She's not a submarine officer, Mary Pat. She's an intelligence analyst."

"Again, that sounds familiar."

He opened his mouth to speak, but had nothing.

"The good news, Jack, is that like you, she's probably right about whatever made her believe she needed to be aboard the *Washington*. I say we trust her."

Ryan nodded.

"And, just as good, our analysis of the data dump from the USS *Washington* that we received while she was on the surface has been analyzed. A lot of smart people, including Dr. Jones, who is still hard at work aboard the *Ford*, believe that Commander Houston's crew has done the impossible. It appears the *Washington* has found the *Belgorod*, but we still need to rule out acoustic subterfuge."

"Well, let's pray that's the case," Ryan said, "and also that Houston will do the right thing when the time comes, since we have no way to communicate with him unless they break off the hunt."

"Agreed," Mary Pat said. "I think that may well be why Katie felt she needed to be aboard."

Ryan looked at his closest adviser and friend. She was right.

Katie wasn't his little girl anymore. She was an Academy grad, a top naval intelligence officer, and one of the smartest, most capable people he knew. She'd been promoted early and made lead for a reason, and it had nothing to do with who her dad was.

And Mary Pat was right about something else. His daughter was doing exactly what he would do—what he *had* done.

The problem was, he didn't know if that made him proud or terrified.

"We need to stop them, Mary Pat. This crazy son of a bitch is going to start World War Three whether Yermilov wants him to or not. We're running out of time."

60

C aptain, the work is complete," the drone pilot said, looking up at Konstantin with a smile on his face. "The data node is destroyed. Using the onboard electromagnetic sensors, I can detect no signal transmission at all."

"Very well," Konstantin said, stopping short of complimenting the officer, who he felt did not deserve praise.

"Shall I recover the Klavesin, sir?"

"*Nyet*. I want you to program the drone to drive in circles over this location until it runs out of battery. I also want the cutting tool to be running, making noise, the entire time."

"But, Captain, the drone is very expensive and the only operational unit. The admiral will be very upset if we—"

"Let me worry about the admiral, Captain Lieutenant, and you worry about doing as you're told."

"Aye, Captain," the pilot said and, red-faced, returned to his console.

"Captain," the phone talker said, getting the captain's attention. "From control, torpedo tubes three and four are flooded and ready in all respects."

"Very well, tell the conning officer to open the shutter doors on torpedo tubes one through four."

The phone talker repeated back the order verbatim, his voice catching as he did. Then, after a moment, he turned and said, "Captain, the weapons officer is on the line and would like to speak with you."

Anger flared in Konstantin's chest as he picked up a handset and pressed it to his ear. "Captain on the line."

"Captain, this is the weapons officer. Why are we opening the shutter doors, sir?"

"Because I said so, Captain Lieutenant. It is not a conversation, it is an order."

"Captain, our established protocol is that we do not open the shutter doors unless conditions are present and satisfied to warrant firing weapons."

"That is correct, and such conditions are present and satisfied."

"But, Captain—"

"Captain Lieutenant Morozov, either open the shutter doors for torpedo tubes one through four, or you are relieved as weapons officer," Konstantin said, using his command voice.

Silence lingered on the line for so long that the sub captain was convinced that Morozov had hung up the phone, but then in a barely audible voice—ripe with barely veiled vitriol—Morozov said, "Aye, Captain."

Konstantin returned the handset to the cradle with a definitive *thwack.*

"Is the programming done?" the sub captain said, shifting his attention and ire to the pilot.

"Almost, sir . . . I just need another minute."

Konstantin resisted the urge to criticize the man under his breath, but he did not prevent himself from pacing in the tiny control room for submerged drone operations.

"Captain, control room reports that the shutter doors for torpedo tubes one through four are open," the phone talker said.

"Very well."

"Captain, the Klavesin is circling anticlockwise at thirty meters above the bottom and the cutting head is running. Remaining battery is twenty-seven percent," the pilot said.

"Very well, pilot. Eject the data link cable from the hangar bay plug."

The pilot acknowledged the order and after a pause—undoubtedly hoping Konstantin would change his mind—he pressed a button to eject the data cable plug from the connection point inside the wet hangar. "Data cable ejected. Communications lost with the drone."

"Very well. Close the hangar bay doors, pilot."

"Be advised, Captain, that closing the hangar bay doors will likely cause a sound transient that could compromise our position."

Konstantin couldn't help but laugh at this. "Have you not been paying attention, you idiot? We already have a massive sound transient compromising our position, broadcasting to the entire ocean. This is the very best time to open the torpedo shutters and shut the hangar bay doors. Let's get all the noisy things done at once!"

The pilot's cheeks flamed crimson at being talked down to, but Konstantin didn't care. His patience for the foolish and the meek had run out. Jaw clenched, the pilot flipped the switch to close the wet hangar doors. As Konstantin knew would happen, the mechanism clanked loudly as they passed the position in travel that had been causing trouble. However, after that point, the doors completed closing without further incident.

"Captain, wet hangar bay doors indicate shut," the pilot said.

"Very well."

"Captain, sonar reports sound transient from own ship," the phone talker reported.

"Very well," Konstantin said and gave the young phone talker's shoulder a squeeze. "Good work, shipmate. Secure your headset and muster at your assigned battle stration's watch position. Submerged drone operations are complete."

"Aye, Captain," the phone talker said and removed his headset.

Without a parting word to the pilot, Konstantin left the small drone control center and headed forward. First he would stop by his stateroom to relieve himself and take a handful of pain pills. Then he would proceed to the conn, where he intended to spend the remainder of his waking hours. He didn't make it to his stateroom, however, because he was intercepted in the command passageway by the ship's engineer. The most serious and reliable of his department heads, Tarasov rarely smiled, but he was smiling now.

"Captain. I found . . . the noise . . . augmenter," Tarasov said, his words punctuated by heavy breaths.

"Good job, Eng," Konstantin said, elated, as he patted the winded engineer, who'd clearly run some distance to make the report in person. "Where did you find it?"

"Inside the *Losharik* docking chamber on deck one."

"Ahhh, no wonder it took so long. It was the perfect hiding place. Our saboteur is very clever."

"Aye, Captain. In fact, whoever did this had electrical knowledge and skills. He wired into the lighting circuit *inside* the lockout chamber."

Konstantin considered this piece of information, his brain automatically dividing his crew into those capable of such a thing and those not. Unfortunately, the capable list included dozens of electrician mates, electronics technicians, and his entire officer corps. Submarine personnel were technically trained and industrious by nature. Discovering the saboteur would not be easy.

"Where is the device now?" he asked.

"I destroyed it. It's in pieces and beyond repair," Tarasov said, having regained breath.

"I knew I could count on you," he said and clapped a hand on the engineer's shoulder. "You're most trusted and competent, comrade. If something happens to me, I will need you to make sure my orders are carried out."

The smile on Tarasov's face evaporated. "Captain, how bad are you suffering?"

Konstantin ignored the question and said, "You are the only one who knows the truth about my condition. Stepanov suspects, of course, but I have not confided in him. I only trust you, Ivan, only you."

"I understand and you can count on me, sir," Tarasov said, and his face showed his loyalty. "What is your plan, Captain?"

"Now that we've regained our stealth, we set a course for the launch coordinates and deliver the payload."

61

Katie had the distinct sense that her presence on the busy, crowded conn of the *Blackfish* was neither required nor desired, but she refused to slink away to the wardroom and twiddle her thumbs. The control room of the submarine at battle stations tracking a Russian submarine was one of the most intense, coordinated evolutions she'd ever seen, and there was no way in hell she was going to miss a minute of it.

I just wish I knew where to stand.

As if reading her mind, the XO sidled up next to her and whispered, "If you take three steps back and one step to the right, you'll be out of everyone's way, but still able to see."

"Oh, sorry," she said and repositioned.

"Yeah, that spot where you were between the plot and the command workstation is coveted real estate. You were kinda standing in the skipper's spot."

She flashed him her cringy *Yikes* face, which made him chuckle. Their eyes met, and out of nowhere she found herself, inappropriately under the circumstances, wondering if Knepper was married. Silently mortified, she shifted her look away and over to one of the screens behind him and tried to look like she followed what was happening.

Not the time or the place, Katie.

"Conn, Sonar, metallic transient from Master One," the sonar supervisor said.

"Very well," the officer of the deck said.

"What did it sound like, Supe?" Houston said.

"A loud clank, Captain. Like somebody hitting a monkey wrench against an I beam," the sonar supe said.

After Katie had briefed the CO, who seemed to believe her that Master One was the *Belgorod* and not the *Gepard*, he'd briefed the watch team in control. But the one thing she couldn't figure out was why in God's name Gorov still transmitted the noisy 151.7-hertz signal. It was like a beacon and made monitoring the *Belgorod* child's play for the *Blackfish.*

"Conn, Sonar, we've got separation bearing on the secondary emitter and Master One," the sonar supe reported.

In her peripheral vision, Katie saw Knepper silently pump his fist in the air. Then he leaned in and, in a hushed voice, said, "You called it, Ryan."

She'd informed the watch team of her theory that the *Belgorod* was sabotaging the DASH data node with a battery-powered deep-diving UUV, but until this moment all the noise had been coming from the same static location. Before being able to classify one cluster of frequencies originating from a different transmitter than the others, Knepper had explained they needed bearing separation.

She saw the CO talking to the officer of the deck.

A moment later, the OOD said, "Very well, Sonar, designate second emitter Master Two. Track Master Two."

"Sonar, aye."

"Coordinator, aye," Knepper said, then leaned over the chair of the nearest fire control technician. "All right, Kearns, let's get solution in the system on Master Two, I don't care if it's quick and dirty."

"Working on it, sir," the young man said, "but bearings keep changing. I don't understand."

Juggernaut, whom Katie had only five seconds to exchange a smile and a nod with, leaned over and said, "That's because it's making donuts."

The FT looked up with a quizzical expression on his face.

"Driving in circles, Kearns," she said.

"Oh," he said, turning back to his console. "I'll try to make that work."

"Conn, Sonar, just lost the 151.7-hertz signal," the sonar supe said with urgency.

"Well, try to get it back," the officer of the deck said. "Do you need me to turn?"

"No, sir. It wasn't a fade or signal degradation. It just *stopped*, like somebody turned off a switch."

An epiphany hit Katie like a lightning bolt, and it all made sense. "That's because somebody did turn off the switch," she said, a little louder and brasher than she meant to.

Everyone in control, including Captain Houston, turned to look at her. "Go on, Ryan," he said, but from the look on his face she guessed he'd jumped to the same conclusion as her already.

"The *Belgorod* has completed their sabotage tasking, so Captain Gorov has turned off the noisemaker and he and his submarine are going to attempt to sneak away now," she said.

"And leave the UUV behind turning donuts as noisy, confusing distraction," Knepper said.

"Exactly," she said, her heart rate feeling like it practically doubled in her chest.

"But when you came aboard you said the DASH node was already degraded," Houston said.

"Yes, sir, but knowing Gorov, I'm sure he decided to take a belt-and-suspenders approach and make sure it was thoroughly destroyed before calling it quits. He's making noise on purpose. He knows we know he's here. If we didn't fire on him in the first fifteen minutes, he would logically conclude that we're not going to fire. So what's the rush? Do the job right the first time, because he's not planning on coming back."

Houston stared at her a long moment, then said, "Attention in control, Master One is bugging out. Tracking Master One is the priority."

"Coordinator, aye."

"Sonar, aye."

Katie's attention shifted to the conversation happening between the sonar supe and Houston, and despite herself, she wandered over close to the "the spot" where she'd been standing before and in the way.

"Captain, we don't have anything else on Master One. That loud narrowband trace and their hovering system transients was all we got," the supe said, his expression a mix of helplessness and panic.

"What about broadband?" the officer of the deck said.

"He wasn't moving, sir," the supe said. "Master One has been static since we first made contact. No hydrodynamic-flow noise. No screw action or blade rate. Nothing."

"I might be able to help with this problem," Katie said, and all eyes turned to her once again.

"Well, don't keep us in suspense, Ryan. The clock's ticking," Houston said.

She pulled the snack-size Ziploc bag with the memory stick Jonesy had given her from her left chest pocket and handed it to the sonar supe. She quickly recounted what Jones had told her about ST2 Harris on the *Indiana* and acoustic fingerprints and some sort of analyzer. "I can't tell you what to do with the data, but here it is."

"Well, you're just one surprise after another, aren't you, Ryan?" Houston said with a pursed-lip expression that morphed into something resembling a smile.

"I try, sir."

"Crider!" the sonar supe snapped.

A thirty-something dude with a mustache sitting at the port rear corner of the conn popped to his feet and said, "Yes, Chief?"

The supe tossed Crider the baggie with the drive. "Did you hear what the lieutenant here just said?"

"I did, Chief."

"Plug in that thumb drive and get me a profile on Master One."

"On it!"

"I'm not letting that sonuvabitch sneak away on my watch, Captain," the supe said with suddenly renewed swagger.

Houston turned to Katie. "Well, Ryan, if Gorov is bugging out, which way is he heading?"

"West, Captain," she said without a moment's hesitation. "He's heading west."

62

THE *SEVERODVINSK* (K-560), LEAD BOAT OF
THE YASEN-CLASS SSGN NORTH ATLANTIC

Captain First Rank Lev Denikin stood like a statue on the conn of the *Severodvinsk*, the fastest, stealthiest, and most capable submarine in the Northern Fleet. When the encrypted ORDMOD had come in directly from Colonel General Andreyev to proceed at flank speed toward coordinates off the American Eastern Seaboard and sink the *Belgorod*, Denikin had almost spit his coffee all over the printed paper. Heart palpitations had followed, and he'd ordered his radioman to send a reply requesting confirmation.

Confirmation had come . . . directly from President Yermilov himself.

In the hours since, Denikin had been forced to rewrite the narrative in his head. He was not going to battle with his fellow countrymen, he was tasked with eliminating a rogue submarine captain. To swallow this bitter pill, he'd stoked a fire of resentment in his heart about the vessel and its captain. As the crown jewel of the Northern Submarine Fleet, the *Belgorod* got all of the attention, but it was—*let's be honest*—just a bloated Oscar II with an unproven propaganda weapon. As for Gorov, was his reputation as a tactician and legendary submarine captain even deserved? He'd spent the last three years in the Sevmash Shipyard, while Denikin was at sea going toe-to-toe with the American Virginia-class submarines in the Arctic and Atlantic.

And then there was that odd night six months ago at Viking . . .

Denikin had arrived at Severodvinsk's best restaurant and been seated at the table next to Gorov and another officer, who were dining at the corner table. Their tongues were loose with alcohol. The host had sat Denikin with his back to Gorov, who Denikin recognized, of course, but had never actually met. At the time, the conversation he'd eavesdropped on had not registered as particularly troubling. Gorov and the other officer, who Denikin quickly deduced was a department head on the *Belgorod*, were complaining about the Americans and American foreign policy. This was nothing new or surprising. Bad-mouthing and complaining about the adversary was something Russian submarine officers did in solidarity regularly. It was a symptom of the overmatch—an underdog's bravado. Like professional athletes before a big match, the trash-talking helped motivate and dull the mind to the American advantage. But the conversation in the corner had been more than that, and the kill order from the Kremlin provided context for him to reevaluate the memory. But one particular thing Gorov had said now played over and over in Denikin's mind, like a lyric from a song stuck in his head:

"We've already lost, comrade. To move forward, we must knock them back. If Yermilov doesn't have the balls to throw the first punch, then maybe I will."

"We've already lost, comrade . . ." he murmured.

"What was that, Captain?" the conning officer asked.

"Nothing," he said, snapping out of his fugue. "How much longer until we reach the target coordinates?"

"About an hour, Captain."

"Status of the heavyweight torpedoes?"

"Last report from the torpedo room, they had loaded three and were working on number four," the conning officer said. "Would you like me to ask for an update?"

"*Nyet*, I'll walk down there and take a look for myself."

"Aye, Captain."

"Oh, and Captain Lieutenant . . ."

"Sir?"

"Pass the word to all compartments to rig the ship for angles and evasive maneuvers."

"Aye, Captain," the conning officer said with worried eyes.

Denikin had decided to compartmentalize the tasking and had not informed his crew about the engagement waiting ahead in the Atlantic.

It will be better that way, he told himself as he walked off the conn and headed toward the nearest down ladder. *This is one burden they are not equipped to bear.*

63

Ryan felt his anxiety and irritation rising in lockstep. That the *Washington* may well have found the *Belgorod* and was tracking her was good news, but the communication was one way. Commander Houston had risked floating a communications buoy to transmit the encrypted message, but they had no way to respond or give the ship orders unless she came back to periscope depth. The bad news was that the mid-Atlantic DASH node had gone dark. That the *Washington* had detected the *Belgorod* in the same coordinates was not a coincidence. The sequence of events was unfolding exactly as he'd both feared and predicted, and now a new, disturbing thought was tumbling around in his brain, making it impossible to concentrate.

What if Gorov had already launched one or both Status-6 nukes? Right after the DASH node went dark would be the ideal time to do it. And, of course, the people he needed to talk to the most about this he couldn't because the videoconference system in the Situation Room couldn't establish a secure damn video link with Task Force 59 in Bahrain.

"Just a few more moments, I'm told, Mr. President." The young woman and IT expert gave him a tight smile and her face flushed red. He wanted to let her off the hook, but a little wave was all he could muster. He let the men and women around the table continue their hushed conversations and leaned back, allowing himself the luxury of a few moments of rumination.

The fact that they couldn't get the videoconference feed to work was metaphorical for the helplessness he felt. He was sitting in the Situation Room—the most secure SCIF in the world—but he was powerless to interact in a hands-on capacity with the world outside these walls. He would give almost anything to swap places with his younger daughter, and not just because trading places would take her out of harm's way. As a father, that was his priority, but as a former CIA analyst who'd once stopped a war from the pointy tip of Neptune's trident, he was envious. Sure, as President he made the hard decisions that determined the fate of the world, but he did so with an arm's-length separation from the crisis. It was like watching a fireplace on a TV screen. The heat, the smell of ash wood smoke, the pop and crackle of the logs—all absent.

What Katie was experiencing on the *Blackfish, that* was authentic.

That was real.

He glanced up, but only a blue glow filled the screen. He ground his teeth and kept silent.

For a moment, he let himself be transported back in time—back to when he'd boarded the *Mystic* DSRV mini sub and docked with the *Red October* while it submerged. Ryan was no adrenaline junky. In fact, he often wondered where Jack Junior's hard edge had come from, genetically speaking. But despite the adrenaline of the chase, the uncertain danger, and the fear he'd experienced during the *Red October* defection, he knew the experience had forged him into a man who took control of his destiny. Yes, his life had been on the line, but he'd also been in a position to act.

He'd had skin in the game.

He'd been a piece on the board in the chess match, not lording over the game from above.

Here in the Situation Room, the only real skin in the game was that of the brave sailors out there on the pointy tip. Skin like that of Lieutenant Ashley Cannon, Commander Clint Houston and his crew, the sailors of the *Ford* strike group, and, of course, Mary Pat's covert ops team—deep behind enemy lines inside Russia.

And Katie—my little girl turned naval officer overnight.

"Here we are, sir," the woman said, relief so evident in her voice it must have been a struggle not to collapse into one of the chairs around the table.

"Thank you very much," he managed somehow.

The center screen flickered and then filled with the image of a twenty-something naval officer dressed in green Guacamoles.

"You are in the conference inside the Situation Room, Lieutenant, and you have the assembled defense team as well as the President and the director of national intelligence," General Kudryk, who was seated on Ryan's left, said.

"Thank you, sir," the young man said, the stress evident on his face. He stared at his computer camera and seemed unsure whether to jump right in or not. Ryan had hoped to see Kyle on the screen, but his youngest son was not in attendance for the brief. "My name is Lieutenant Tucker, and I'm project lead on the data collection team for Task Force 59."

"Before you give us your update, Lieutenant Tucker, let me give you ours," Kudryk said. "We have confirmed that the DASH network is down, and thus our detection capabilities are extremely degraded. We will be routing the raw data through the old SOSUS system, but that rerouting will take time. In the meantime, we have the patrol aircraft and ships dropping sonobuoys old-school all along the East Coast, and the USNS *Able* patrolling off the Virginia and Maryland coast with an escort. The *Able* is employing both her SURTASS towed array and low-frequency active sonar— but this is still a needle-in-the-haystack situation."

"I understood that the USS *Washington* is now tracking the *Belgorod*," Tucker said from the screen and in his own SCIF thousands of miles away in Bahrain. "Is that not the case?"

Kudryk shot a look at Admiral Kent.

"The *Blackfish* is tracking a submerged contact, Lieutenant," Kent said. "But the Russians have deployed acoustic subterfuge to make it difficult to confirm with certainty that the contact is, in fact, the *Belgorod*."

Tucker grimaced, but it was the truth. The argument made by Jonesy, based on the confirming assessment of the crew of the *Indiana*, was compelling indeed. But, as Kent said, it was far from certain. In fact, even using the word "certainty" in the assessment seemed hyperbolic.

"The other concern we have, Lieutenant," Ryan said, stepping in, "is what if the *Belgorod* has already launched a Status-6 weapon? The reason the Russians created a blind spot in our acoustic surveillance net is to exploit it. If the *Washington* missed the launch, or was not able to detect it, we could have a nuclear torpedo cruising toward the East Coast as we speak."

"I understand, Mr. President, and we share your concern, sir," Tucker said.

"At your recommendation, Lieutenant, we've deployed the entire shipment of USV and UUV ocean drones from inventory in Norfolk."

"All one hundred are deployed?" Tucker asked, clearly amazed that was the case.

"Nearly," Kent confirmed. "We have all but seven of the fifty

USVs dropped and all but eight of the UUVs. They are currently under the control of operators from Norfolk, but I understand you want control of the assets transferred to your team in Bahrain?"

"Yes, sir, Admiral Kent," the young officer said. He looked older as his comfort and confidence increased. "We have the tech here to more maximally employ the assets."

"Maybe you can explain, Lieutenant," Kudryk said, taking the helm again, "how in the hell a hundred surface and undersea drones are going to be of any value hunting for a single torpedo over thousands of square miles." He stopped short of actually snorting his disapproval. "The capabilities of these drones pale quite significantly from that of the towed array sonar systems. It seems hardly a substitution for the DASH system we lost."

"Individually, yes," Tucker said, seemingly unfazed by the cynical general. "The magic of the Task Force 59 project lies in the power of the system in aggregate. In fact, I would ask that you stream data from the patrol ships and planes involved, as well as from the USNS *Able*, directly to us in real time as well. Every additional data point helps. The key to our system is taking what would be an utterly unmanageable volume of data from multiple streams and whittling it down to the bits that are relevant. We are using very sophisticated AI technology—a self-learning and, more important, self-correcting program—to take seemingly unrelated bits of data and use them to paint a mind-blowing, highly accurate picture of what is happening in the Atlantic. This has proven far more successful in the Fifth Fleet than we had even hoped. We are already streaming satellite imagery and other existing fixed assets in the Atlantic into the system. We may not be replacing the DASH, General, but we can come pretty damn close."

This was met with a moment of silence as the senior members of the team exchanged glances.

"If the *Belgorod* has already launched a Poseidon, I can't promise we'll find it," Tucker added, perhaps hedging his bets from the hubris of his comment, "but we will significantly increase the chances."

"Very well, Lieutenant," Ryan said, the excitement of the technology diluted by the urgency of their situation. "Any request for data we can stream to you in real time will certainly be approved immediately. Spare no resource. The situation is urgent."

"Yes, sir, Mr. President. We understand and we won't let you down," Tucker said, and then the screen turned blue again.

"What else do we have, people?" Ryan growled. He already knew there would be nothing of substance, so he sat through the obligatory rehashing of what he already knew.

Yermilov had indeed turned the Russian Northern Fleet north and steamed away from the *Ford* strike group. The *Ford*'s air wing was still on a high-alert posture, flying constant combat air patrols around the strike group, but no encounters with the Russians had occurred since the pullback.

The door clicked and opened and a harried-looking Mary Pat Foley entered, her leather folder tucked under her arm.

"My apologies, but we were verifying new data just in to ODNI," she said, taking a seat and not seeming to flinch at having cut off General Bruce Kudryk, who had been speaking at that moment. The usually grumpy general actually seemed relieved by the interruption to his updates and stared at her expectantly. "Our British partners at GCHQ, working in a joint task force with the NSA, have intercepted and decrypted two relevant messages. The first was from the head of Russia's NDMC, Colonel General Andreyev, aborting the *Belgorod*'s tasking and ordering it to surface."

"What?" Kudryk's eyes were wide in surprise at the news.

Ryan was far less surprised and suppressed a satisfied smile.

"And the second message?" Kent asked.

"The second was to a Yasen-class SSGN submarine, the

Severodvinsk, to proceed to coordinates matching the mid-Atlantic DASH node, find the *Belgorod,* and destroy her."

Ryan leaned back in his chair in disbelief. That son of a bitch Yermilov had actually done it.

"That's both shocking and incredible news," Kudryk said, and his face suggested he was as happy as he might be capable of feeling.

"Yes and no," Kent said, and all eyes turned to the admiral. "If the *Washington* is trailing the *Belgorod,* there are certainly risks involved in having this other Russian submarine hunting down their comrade."

"So, do we pull the *Washington* off station?" Secretary of Defense Burgess asked, speaking for the first time. "If we let the Russians do the dirty work for us, it sure saves us problems later if there's a change in leadership."

Ryan felt a new uncertainty percolating inside him. The father in him wanted nothing more than to jump on this gift of an opportunity to pull his daughter out of harm's way. But . . . he couldn't let his personal feelings cloud his judgment.

"We could," Ryan said. "But that would mean we have to trust that, first, the order is legitimate and not subterfuge for our benefit." Yermilov was not someone he was ready to trust with the fate of his nation. "And, second, we would have to have complete confidence that the Russian submarine *Severodvinsk* is capable of finding and killing the *Belgorod* in time . . . Which I am not."

"I agree, Mr. President," Kudryk said. "I'm not willing to put our fate in the adversary's hands."

Others nodded their agreement.

"Then it's settled," Ryan said, a lump forming in his gut at the thought of Katie potentially being in the middle of a submarine torpedo battle. "For now, we trust that Captain Houston and the crew of the *Washington* will prevail if it comes to that. And we use the drone network managed by Task Force 59 to scan for anything that could be a Status-6 UUV headed for the East Coast or the *Ford*."

While his leadership team talked, Ryan glanced up to the map on the flat-screen monitor and he stared at all the green triangles of the ships and submarines at sea. His mind drifted back to his recent conversation with Ramius, which he'd had in this very room, and he could practically hear the old Russian sub captain's voice in his head.

"If Halsey had known what we know now, he never would have fallen into the trap."

As soon as the thought came to him, he blurted it out, interrupting and stopping the conversation instantly.

"What was that, Mr. President?" the SecDef said, staring at Ryan with a confused look on his face.

"I said, I want to initiate an evacuation protocol of all military assets in Norfolk, Admiral Kent," Ryan said. "Just like we would under hurricane protocol—hell, call it that if you want. Evacuate aircraft out of Langley, Oceana, and Norfolk. I want all ships put to sea. I want the East Coast–based SEAL teams redeployed to Naval Air Station Jacksonville."

"Yes, sir, Mr. President," Kent said with a look on his face that suggested he was disappointed for not having thought of that himself. "I'll make it happen immediately."

"And Admiral Kent?" Ryan said, another thought coming to him.

"Yes, sir?"

He picked up the laser pointer beside him and shone the light on a patch of Atlantic between the Virginia coast and the position of the USS *Washington*.

"Redeploy the USS *Indiana* to this position, just in case."

"In case the *Belgorod* sneaks away from the *Blackfish*?" the admiral asked.

"No," Ryan said grimly. "So we have an asset in position in case the *Belgorod* gets a shot off or, God forbid, already has."

64

THE *BELGOROD* (K-329)
NORTH ATLANTIC
759 KILOMETERS EAST OF NORFOLK
1531 LOCAL TIME

K onstantin vomited until he thought his insides might be coming out.

The nausea had been so acute and sudden he'd barely made it to the toilet. Had he not retired to his stateroom for a short rest, he certainly would not have made it off the conn before evacuating his stomach. He spit, wiped his mouth, and peered down into the commode. Crimson swirls colored the bowl and fresh blood stained the wad of white tissues in his hand. He tossed them in and flushed.

Sweat dappled his forehead.

Getting to his feet was a labor, and once upright he instantly felt as though he might black out. He shuffled to his rack and crawled in, curling into a ball on his side. The momentary relief he'd earned from vomiting was erased by a fresh solar flare of pain in his midsection—pain so intense he heard himself moan and tears rimmed his eyes.

Russian men don't cry, a voice chastised him in his head, but these were not tears borne of self-pity or sorrow. These tears were involuntary, a product of a biological mechanism over which he had no control.

Russian men don't cry, the voice said again, pitiless. *Get up.*

"I can't," he groaned from where he lay in a fetal position on his rack.

Get up and do your duty, Captain.

Gritting his teeth, he swung his legs off the side of the rack and let them dangle a moment. He could still taste blood in his mouth and his undershirt felt soaked with sweat. He forced himself to take three deep breaths and then pressed to his feet. The pain ebbed as he did but, as goes the tide, he knew the next surge was inevitable. He shuffled to the lone mirror in his stateroom and met his reflection with stoic resignation. The man staring back at him looked like the Grim Reaper's familiar visage—sunken cheeks, gray pallor, and weary eyes.

"*Don't do it, my love*," his dead wife's voice said behind him.

He whirled around, but she was not there.

When he turned back to the mirror, he saw her in the reflection, standing behind him, her thin, bone-white fingers resting on his shoulder and her sad, beautiful face staring at him. He knew he was hallucinating. He knew if he turned to look behind him again, she would not be there, and so he didn't, because he would not rob himself of this moment.

"Calina?"

"*Yes, my love. It's me.*"

"I've missed you," he said, choking on the words. "I'm lost without you."

"*I know you are . . . The man I married would never do such a thing as you are planning.*"

"But he has to pay."

"*Who has to pay?*"

"Jack Ryan," he said with a bloody-lipped sneer. "It's all his fault. He robbed me of the life I was *supposed* to have."

"I don't understand."

"I never told you, did I?"

"Told me what?"

"About the true fate of the *Red October* . . . I knew there was more to the story. I knew they were hiding something. And so I dug, and I dug, and I traded favors, and paid bribes until I finally learned the truth. Marko Ramius defected and handed the Americans the *Red October* on a silver platter. And the American CIA analyst who made it happen was Jack Ryan."

"So you blame this man for your father's death?"

"And my mother's, and yours, and our son's . . ."

She laid her head on his shoulder and fixed him with a pitying stare. *"And so you will punish this man by taking the lives of tens of thousands . . . perhaps millions? Robbing the innocent and the blameless of their mothers, and wives, and sons. You will trade a wrong for a wrong?"*

"*Da*, because their blood will be on Ryan's hands. His penance is to feel as I do."

A tear trickled down her cheek and he turned to embrace her . . .

"Calina?" he said, scanning his stateroom in a panic. He turned back to the mirror, but found himself alone. "Calina, don't go! Please don't go!"

A knock on his stateroom door snapped him from the mania.

"Who is it?" he barked.

"Tarasov."

Konstantin ran his fingers through his hair, stood up straight, and said, "Come."

The engineer opened the door, took one look at his captain, and quickly slammed it shut. He rushed to Konstantin and immediately put a hand to the sub captain's forehead. "You're burning with fever, Captain."

The idea had not occurred to him, but made sense now.

Tarasov took a step back and stared at Konstantin with the same dispassionate expression he used when assessing a broken piece of equipment in need of emergency maintenance. After a moment, he said, "In the next few minutes, the quartermaster will report that we have reached the launch coordinates you selected. Do you still want to carry out the plan?"

"Yes," Konstantin said firmly, but his voice was softer than he intended.

"Very well," Tarasov said, fulfilling the promise he'd made to take control if his captain faltered.

Like a squire dressing a knight, Konstantin let his most trusted lieutenant help him change out of his coveralls into his black dress uniform. He let Tarasov wipe the sweat from his face and brow and comb his hair. He let Tarasov straighten his medals and tie his shoes. And when the ritual dressing was complete, Tarasov put a hand on Konstantin's shoulder and met the captain's gaze.

"I have always considered you as both a brother and a father. In my darkest hours, in my lowest times, you never abandoned me, Captain. I have served with you and under you for over ten years . . ."

Konstantin pulled Tarasov in for a hug, the first and only time he'd embraced the man as a brother. As a son. "You honor me," he said.

The CO's stateroom phone buzzed.

"It's time," Tarasov said and turned toward the door to leave.

Konstantin nodded and picked up the handset. "*Da* . . ."

"Captain, we've reached the launch coordinates," the quartermaster said.

"Very well, I'm on my way."

Konstantin paused in front of the mirror, hoping to see Calina one last time. But he was alone. Alone in all his splendor and glory. Jaw set, he walked to his safe, turned the dial to enter the combination, and retrieved his captain's key, which hung on a steel-chain lanyard. He put the loop over his head and positioned the dangling launch key in the center of his chest. Then, chin high and shoulders back, Konstantin Gorov strode out of his stateroom for the last time and into control.

All eyes locked on him and he saw both reverence and confusion in their eyes. This was good. Tarasov's instincts had been sound. He walked to the nav plot, confirmed the sub's position, then checked the sonar repeater on the conn. Immediately after securing his boat from hovering and departing the data node coordinates, Konstantin had ordered the *Belgorod*'s towed array deployed. The kilometer-long string of highly tuned cylindrical hydrophones had allowed the sub to reacquire the USS *Ford* carrier strike group, despite the distant range, and also search for American hunter-killer submarines, of which he suspected at least one trailed them at this very moment.

Unfortunately, even though significant gains had been made over the past decade in Russian sonar hardware and software technology, the Americans had maintained an advantage with the Virginia-class submarine design improvements that made them virtually undetectable with passive sonar alone. Konstantin had ordered several course changes to search his baffles, but the American subs were black holes in the water and the sweeps had found nothing.

No matter, he decided. *I will have first mover advantage. There is nothing the Americans can do to stop me.*

He shifted his attention to the weapons control console, where Morozov should have been standing, but found the post vacant.

"Where is the weapons officer?" he asked, not addressing the question to anyone in particular.

"The torpedo room," the conning officer, Captain Lieutenant Blok, said.

"Firing-point procedures, conning officer. Ready salvo one—torpedo tubes one and two," Konstantin announced.

Blok hesitated a beat, then repeated the order back and announced, "All stations, Conn, firing-point procedures. Ready salvo one—torpedo tubes one and two."

Konstantin listened as all the stations acknowledged the order . . . all stations except for the torpedo room. "Conning officer, query the torpedo room," he said after thirty seconds of waiting.

"Aye, Captain," Blok said and nodded to the fire control watch stander at the weapons launch console, who was in direct communication with the phone talker in the torpedo room.

The fire control technician turned to Blok. "Conning officer, the torpedo room is not responding."

Konstantin marched over to the weapons launch console, removed the launch key lanyard from his neck, and inserted the key into the launch permissive selector switch. As with the SSBNs, which carry nuclear-tipped ICBMs, the designers of the *Belgorod* had carried forward the same design of redundant keyed interlocks at two locations—the weapons launch console in control and the torpedo launch console in the torpedo room. The captain carried one key and the weapons officer carried the other. That way no single key and no single man could independently launch a nuclear-armed Poseidon.

Konstantin turned his key from "locked" to "permissive."

Then he scanned the conn for Tarasov, who—having clearly anticipated this development—stood in the back starboard corner with his arms crossed.

"Engineer, you're with me," he said to his loyal officer.

The captain marched out of the control room, took two down ladders, and made his way into the torpedo room, with Tarasov in trail. Upon entering the massive weapons handling compartment, Konstantin was surprised to find it empty.

"Where is everyone?" he said, turning to Tarasov, who he now noticed clutched a large shiny spanner wrench in his left hand.

"I dismissed them," Morozov said, stepping around the corner of the torpedo launch console, behind which he'd apparently been waiting.

Konstantin met the man's eyes and, in the moment, he knew. "You turned on the noisemaker."

Morozov looked down at his feet, but nodded.

"Very clever, wiring it inside the lock-out chamber at the bottom of the hull. If not for Tarasov, I don't think we ever would have found it."

Morozov's eyes rose again and ticked from Konstantin to Tarasov to the spanner wrench in the engineer's hand.

"Why did you do it?" the captain asked.

"Because somebody had to try to stop you. And if I fail, maybe the Americans will succeed."

"Well, despite your best efforts you have failed. Captain Lieutenant Morozov, you are hereby relieved of duty. Captain Lieutenant Tarasov, you are now the acting weapons officer."

"Aye, Captain," Tarasov said behind him.

"Surrender your launch key," Konstantin said to Morozov.

"Nyet."

"I said, surrender your launch key!"

Morozov crossed his arms in defiance and did not move.

"Captain Lieutenant Tarasov, summon the ship's master-at-arms and place this man under arrest," Konstantin said.

"Aye, Captian," Tarasov said, but he didn't call the master-at-arms.

Instead, the engineer slipped past Konstantin and, in a blur of premeditated fury that took both the captain and the former WEPS by surprise, Tarasov slammed the spanner wrench into Morozov's temple. Konstantin heard a sickening crunch and watched the light leave the man's eyes. Morozov was dead before his limp body hit the floor.

Tarasov took a knee beside his murdered comrade and lifted the dead man's head via a fistful of hair with one hand while he removed the silver chain from his neck with the other. After retrieving the key, he let Morozov's head go, and the back of the dead man's skull hit the metal deck with a loud thump. The engineer, still kneeling, turned to show Konstantin the key . . . which was not a key, but a metal washer hanging from the chain.

Instead of fury and rage, ironic laughter consumed Konstantin.

"What is so funny?" Tarasov said, standing.

When he finally caught his breath, the captain said, "It appears by killing him, you made Morozov the victor. Without his key, we cannot launch."

The engineer's face twisted in anger as he stared at the washer in his palm, but then the scowl morphed into a self-satisfied grin.

"What?" Konstantin said, his curiosity piqued.

"I wonder," the engineer said and set off at a quick pace.

A fresh wave of pain buckled Konstantin at the waist before he could follow.

"I'll wait here," the captain said and took a seat on a toolbox strapped to the deck. While he waited, he stared at Morozov's unmoving body. The spanner blow had collapsed the side of the skull, deforming the right eye socket. "You had courage, comrade, I'll give you that."

A long moment later, he heard the pounding of boots on the deck as Tarasov returned, huffing. With a victorious smile he held up the missing launch key.

"Where?" Konstantin asked.

"The repair shop in the forward auxiliary mechanical room," Tarasov said proudly. "It is where I would go to find an M20 washer."

"You know your boat quite well," Konstantin said and then, with great effort, pressed to his feet. "Acting Weapons Officer Tarasov—insert the launch into the torpedo control panel launch selector switch and select 'permissive.'"

"Aye, Captain." Tarasov walked over to the torpedo launch control panel and used the key to override the nuclear safety interlock. "Launch selector switch is in permissive."

Konstantin exhaled.

The target data, detonation coordinates, and attack parameters had already been loaded into the onboard computers inside Poseidon One and Two. The torpedo tubes were flooded. The shutter doors were open. And there was nobody here to stop them. The system allowed the launch to be initiated from the control panel at either the weapons launch console or locally in the torpedo room from the torpedo control panel.

A wave of vertigo washed over Konstantin, and he stuck out a hand to steady himself.

Sweat ran from his brow in twin rivulets down his temples.

His vision began to blur.

He blinked. Where a moment ago, Tarasov had been the one standing at the control panel, now stood his dead wife. She was pregnant and holding her bulging stomach.

"Don't do this, my love . . . For us, please."

He reached for her. "Calina?"

"Captain, are you all right?" she said, but the voice was not hers.

Konstantin blinked hard and squinted at the person in front of him. "Tarasov? Is that you?"

"*Da*, Captain. It's me."

"I've changed my mind, Tarasov. Stand down and secure the weapons."

"I'm sorry, Captain. I made you a promise, and I am a man of my word," the engineer said with a cold, hard stare. He then turned and pressed the launch buttons for Poseidon torpedoes One and Two.

65

Katie saw dread ripple across Knepper's face and knew something was terribly wrong.

The announcement came a split second later.

"Torpedo in the water!" the sonar supe shouted. "Bearing two-four-two, designated Sierra One-Zero-One."

"Captain has the conn," Houston announced.

"Captain, Sierra One-Zero-One tracks with Master One," Knepper said.

"Second torpedo in the water, bearing two-four-zero," the sonar supe shouted. "Designate Sierra One-Zero-Two."

Katie looked at Knepper, eyes wide, wondering why Houston wasn't doing anything. Panic bloomed in her chest, and she suddenly found it difficult to breathe.

Doesn't every second matter? Shouldn't we be turning and trying to get away?

Knepper met her gaze. He looked tense, but she saw no fear in his eyes. As was becoming a pattern with this guy, he read her mind. "Ryan, we train for this. We assess first, then we react."

She nodded and tried to steel her nerves. Just like she'd put her faith in the pilots on the C-2 to make the carrier trap landing, the crew of the *Ford* to keep her from harm's way, and the team of aircrew aboard the Osprey to deliver her to the *Washington*, she needed to put her faith in this team of nuclear engineers and highly trained sonar and fire control technicians.

"Sonar, classify Sierra One-Zero-One and One-Zero-Two," Houston said, his voice perfectly calm and even. "Does the sound profile match Russian heavyweight torpedoes or sound like something else?"

In her peripheral vision she saw Knepper turn and shift into what looked like a quarterback stance between two fire control technicians' chairs.

"Kearns, you work torpedo one; Smallbrock, you work torpedo two," he said, then to Juggernaut he added, "WEPS, be ready to—"

"On it," she said, cutting him off as she worked with a third FT at a stack with a very different interface than the others.

"Captain, Sierra One-Zero-One, bears two-four-six, range is five thousand three hundred yards and opening, speed seventy knots, torpedo course is west," Knepper said.

"Very well, coordinator," Houston said.

"Conn, Sonar, Sierra One-Zero-One and One-Zero-Two do not—I repeat, do *not*—match the sound profiles of Russian Type 53 or 65 heavy torpedoes," the sonar supe said.

"Very well," Houston said.

"Captain, Sierra One-Zero-Two, bears two-two-eight, range four thousand eight hundred yards and closing, speed seventy-two knots, course zero-five-zero."

"Holy shit, that's coming straight toward *us*," someone said.

"Captain, recommend torpedo evasion," said the nav, who also had the deck.

"Attack center does not concur," Juggernaut said immediately, her voice loud and confident. "I don't think we're the target. Torpedo two's course has a seven-degree offset from own ship. Initial solution has it on an intercept course for the carrier strike group."

"Sonar report targeting status of Sierra One-Zero-Two," Houston said.

"Sierra One-Zero-Two is in passive search," the sonar supe replied.

Katie looked from Juggernaut to Houston, who stared into the distance, his expression blank. For a second she'd worried that he'd had an aneurysm or something, but when he spoke a moment later, she understood that he'd been conducting tactical calculations in his head.

"Quick reaction fire, tube two, Sierra One-Zero-Two. Quick reaction fire, tube one, Sierra One-Zero-One. Fire in that order."

"Sonar ready," the sonar supe announced.

"Are we trying to kill the torpedoes?" Juggernaut shouted.

"Yes," Houston said.

Juggernaut turned to the FT at the attack center and said, "One kills one. Two kills two. Use normal submerged presets."

The technician's fingers moved in a blur as he worked updating his console. After a beat, he said, "Ready."

"Solution ready," Juggernaut shouted.

"Shoot on generated bearing," Houston said.

A heartbeat later, Katie heard and felt a *vroooosh* sound. At the same time, a pressure transient made her ears pop and the deck shuddered beneath her feet.

"Torpedo one away."

A second *vroooosh*, a second pressure transient, and a second shutter followed a moment later. "Torpedo two away."

Katie grabbed Knepper by the upper arm and said, "Can you please tell me what the hell is going on, Dennis?"

He turned to face her. "If the captain's instincts are right, your buddy Gorov just shot his nuclear wad in a single salvo. One Status-6 is screaming due west toward the East Coast at seventy miles an hour, and the other is streaking toward the USS *Ford*."

"Oh, dear God," she said, still clutching his arm.

"Yeah, and Juggernaut just launched two ADCAP torpedoes to try to intercept and blow them up. Here, take a look," he said and pointed to the fire control geoplot. "That's the *Belgorod*, five thousand yards away to the southwest off our port quarter. He's heading due west. We're on a parallel course, shadowing him on the edge of his baffles. Sierra One-Zero-One is the first Poseidon he fired. See it there with the torpedo icon moving west away from us?"

"Yes," she said, her voice tinny and small.

"That other blip following it is the ADCAP we shot in pursuit." Next he pointed to a swooping green trace on the upper display of Smallbrock's console, which she knew was a sonar screen. "See that trace with lots of bearing rate?"

"Yes."

"That's the second Poseidon. The *Belgorod* fired that one using an 'over the shoulder' trajectory. At first, we thought it was meant for us, but Jackie's quick mental gymnastics determined that it is intended for the *Ford*."

"Are you positive?"

"We've got closing range, but high bearing rate, and no active homing," he said. "Two out of three indicators support that we are not the target."

"Is it possible for one torpedo to blow up another?" she asked.

"Theoretically," Juggernaut said. "But we've got a hundred and twenty knots of relative closing speed. The ADCAP is designed to hunt and kill big targets moving slower than it is, not other torpedoes moving faster. But because of the massive size of the Status-6, the ADCAP should get a decent active sonar return. Because of the geometery, we've got a chance to take out number two."

"What about number one?" Katie asked, not liking the subtext of Jackie's comment.

"Number one Status-6 is too fast. The ADCAP is chasing it from behind and unless the Status-6 slows down, the ADCAP is not going to catch it before it runs out of fuel."

A macabre mental image of a nuclear detonation and a mushroom cloud engulfing Virginia Beach played in her head.

Oh, no . . . We were too late.

"XO," the FT called Smallbrock said with urgency in his voice. "I calculate torpedo two will intercept Sierra One-Zero-Two inside sixteen hundred yards."

"Oh, shit," Knepper said. "Captain, the calculated—"

Houston cut him off. "I heard. Pilot, all ahead full."

"All ahead full, Pilot, aye," the pilot said.

Houston whirled to face her. "Ryan, I just had a terrible thought. When our ADCAP detonates, is it going to trigger the nuclear warhead?"

"Um . . . I don't know," she said, her stomach suddenly feeling like it was filled with molten lead.

"Wonderful," Houston said, with a *God help me* look up at the overhead.

"Loss of the wire, torpedo two," Smallbrock announced.

"Awesome," she heard someone else say in a voice ripe with sarcasm.

"What happened? What does 'loss of the wire' mean?" she asked Knepper.

"Our torpedoes are wire guided with a data link that allows for two-way communication with the weapon. The wire is really stout, but we're going this way at a full bell and the torpedo is going the other way at max speed," he said, using his hands as props. "The wire is not designed for that kind of force and so it snapped. Now we can't control the torpedo anymore remotely. Even if we wanted to stop it, we can't," he said.

"Conn, Sonar, torpedo two is range-gating on the target."

"Very well, Sonar."

"Coordinator, report predicted range to Sierra One-Oh-Two at detonation," Houston said.

"Predicted range at detonation is one-nine-three-nine yards," Knepper said.

"Very well, coordinator."

"That's inside two thousand yards. Is that bad?" Katie asked.

"It ain't great," someone said, she couldn't tell who.

"WEPS, make tubes three and four ready in all respects," Houston said in his command voice.

Juggernaut acknowledged the order.

"What's going on?" Katie asked. "Are we prepping another salvo in case we miss?"

"I don't think that's what the captain has in mind," Juggernaut said.

Having zero submarine combat experience, she'd been a little slow on the uptake so far, but her quick analyst's mind was beginning to wake up. "Captain, do you intend to engage the *Belgorod*?"

"When I consider the intelligence you risked your life to tell me face-to-face, and the empirical data we've just had the pleasure to collect, it is undeniable that the *Belgorod* has fired two weapons of mass destruction at American targets—one is heading for the Eastern Seaboard and the other the USS *Ford* carrier strike group. So, yes, Ms. Ryan, I *intend* to send K-329 to the bottom of the Atlantic and do so with extreme prejudice," Houston said, his jaw set. "That is a response that is clearly within my command authority in response to an overt act of war."

"Conn, Sonar, torpedo two is in terminal homing."

"Very well," Houston said, but his stare was locked on Katie.

A strange and disassociated uncertainty settled over her. She'd been the one screaming from the hilltop that Gorov had gone rogue. That preemptive action needed to be taken before he fired his WMDs. But now that it had happened, making a crew of innocent Russian conscripts pay for one man's madness seemed . . . well, wrong.

"Captain, thirty seconds until impact," Knepper said.

"Very well," Houston said and shifted his focus and apparent frustration from Katie to Juggernaut. "WEPS, sitrep on tubes three and four."

He wants to get a shot off before the ADCAP explodes, she realized, *in case the ship is damaged by the shock wave.*

"Twenty seconds until impact," Knepper called.

"Captain, tubes three and—" Juggernaut started to say, but her voice was eclipsed by a roar that rocked the *Blackfish*.

For a terrifying split second, Katie felt like she was on the back of a bucking bronco as she and everyone who stood in control lurched forward. Someone or something heavy slammed into her back, knocking her to her hands and knees.

The lights flickered in control.

A voice on a loudspeaker said, "Conn, Maneuvering, reactor scram. Loss of propulsion."

An alarm wailed.

A booted foot stepped on her left hand, and she yelped.

The alarm stopped, followed immediately by a loudspeaker report. "EMERGENCY REPORT, EMERGENCY REPORT! Fire in the machinery room. Fire from the trim pump motor controller. Class Charlie fire."

Time shifted into slow motion.

Katie let her eyes drift around the room as her mind attempted to decode the chaos. Houston barking orders. The pilot pulling back on his control stick. The depth gauge number getting bigger instead of smaller. The COB pulling gear from lockers . . .

A pungent, acrid stench—smoke and burning rubber—tickled her nostrils and throat.

Strong hands gripped her armpits and hoisted her to her feet.

She turned to see who it was, but before she could, someone slipped a rubber mask with a plexiglass visor over her face.

66

C aptain Denikin was raising his coffee mug to his lips when it happened.

"Torpedo salvo! Torpedo one bearing one-eight-five," the sonar operator shouted. "Torpedo two bearing one-seven-seven."

Denikin spilled the hot coffee down the front of his coveralls, cursed, and handed the mug to the closest sailor on the conn.

"Take this," he barked and popped out of his captain's chair to rush over to the sonar stacks.

Unlike surface ships with their wide, spacious bridges, submarines didn't typically have room for a "captain's chair" on the conn. But on the *Severodvinsk*, the sub's commissioning CO had ordered one installed and every succeeding captain had kept it.

"Talk to me, Pushkin," Denikin said to his leading sonarman.

"Two torpedoes . . . They do not sound like Fizik- or Futlyar-class torpedoes."

"What about Mark 48 ADCAPs?"

"*Nyet.* They are not using combustion engines. I hear no engine harmonics," Pushkin said, pressing the left earcup of his headset tight against his skull. "They sound turbine driven. They must be Poseidons."

"Good job, Pushkin," Denikin said and gave the man's back a pat. "What is the range?"

"Working on it, sir . . ."

Denikin's first officer, Mats Tamm, a Russian Estonian, arrived on the conn in a dead run. "Did we find K-329?"

"*Da*," the captain said. "He just fired a salvo of two."

Tamm, the most gifted young officer Denikin had ever seen, ran to a fire control station and immediately started coaching.

"Not like that," Tamm said to the *starshina* sitting at the terminal. "This one is going that way, and that one is going this way. Use the slider bar . . . Align it to the bearings . . . *Nyet*, they are going fast. Not like that . . . Better . . . *Da, da*, you got it. Okay, enter solution one. Enter solution two. Now we extend each torpedo track backward to where they intersect, and that, my friend, is where K-329 was when he fired three minutes ago. Do you understand now?"

Denikin watched with pride as his first officer both worked the problem and instructed the junior sailor simultaneously. The watch team on the conn was terrified. He could see it in their faces and feel it in their silence. Their fear was because they didn't understand what was happening. They assumed the torpedo salvo had been fired at *them*. Denikin knew otherwise, and now Tamm had proven this reality for the men in fire control.

"Aye, sir. Thank you, sir," said the *starshina*.

"Now make your report to the captain," Tamm said.

"Captain, torpedo one is on course two-seven-one, bearing one-eight-nine, range thirteen thousand meters and opening. Torpedo two is on course zero-five-five, bearing one-seven-one, range twelve thousand meters and closing," the fire control operator said.

"Based on your solutions, is either torpedo targeting our ship?" Denikin asked.

"No, Captain."

"Very well. Where is K-329?"

"K-329 bears one-eight-two, at a range of twelve thousand meters, Captain."

Denikin looked at Tamm and they had a silent meeting of the
minds. He and Tamm had talked privately and at great length
about both the importance and disturbing reality of their orders.
Neither man had fired a torpedo in battle. And neither man had,
in their wildest dreams, imagined that the first time they did, they
would be firing on one of their own. Every submariner on the
Severodvinsk knew comrades on the *Belgorod*. Sinking a Russian
submarine manned by their countrymen felt so . . . dystopian.

And shameful.

But orders are orders.

Tamm nodded, confirming his assent, and walked to the weapons launch console and directed the operator to upload targeting
data for the *Belgorod* into the two ready torpedoes.

"Attention in control," Denikin said. "We have just observed
K-329 firing two nuclear-armed Poseidon torpedoes at American
targets. This order did not come from Northern Fleet Joint Strategic Command. Nor did it come from the Kremlin. The commanding officer of K-329, Captain First Rank Gorov, and his senior
officers have gone rogue and are attempting to start World War
Three with the Americans. Our mandate, comrades, is to sink
K-329."

"We are with you, Captain," Tamm said, carrying out his part
of the script perfectly. "We will execute our orders from fleet command."

Denikin clasped his hands behind his lower back and puffed out
his chest. "Firing point procedures—target K-329."

"Captain, the firing solution has been entered. Torpedo tubes
one and two are flooded and ready in all respects," Tamm said.
"Standing by to open shutter doors."

"Very well. Open shutter doors for tubes one and two."

Tamm acknowledged the order while the seated operator pressed two buttons in rapid succession on the WLC. Upon getting the open-indication green lights on the console, Tamm said, "Captain, shutter doors for torpedo tubes one and two are open."

"Shoot tubes one and two," Denikin said quickly, not giving himself time to think and change his mind.

"Shoot tubes one and two," Tamm said to the console operator.

The port and starboard rams indexed simultaneously in the torpedo room, located two decks below amidships. The hull shuddered, his ears popped, and the captain of the *Severodvinsk* looked down at the wet brown stain on his coveralls that had gone cold against his chest.

God forgive me.

67

When all hell breaks loose on a submarine, it's the XO's job to tame the chaos. That's what the captain told Knepper during his one-on-one indoc brief with the skipper his first day aboard the *Blackfish*. With alarms blaring, people screaming, fires burning, and torpedoes exploding, how prescient those words had been. In casualty situations, systematic triage was the key to survival. Prioritize and act.

Never stop thinking, never stop moving.

After picking up Ryan, he turned her by the shoulders and slapped an emergency breathing apparatus (EBA) on her face. He clipped the regulator to her belt and double-checked that her air hose was properly plugged into a manifold. Next, he grabbed the shell-shocked intelligence officer by the sides of her face and shouted, "Look at me, Ryan—do *not* take this off. To breathe you must be plugged into a manifold or daisy-chained into someone else's EBA that's connected to a manifold. Nod if you understand."

She nodded.

He glanced at the command workstation and saw that the pilot had gotten control of their depth. They had a cushion of three hundred feet until they hit test depth. The boat was slowly ascending now, but their speed was rapidly falling off. On a sub, speed equals lift. If they didn't get propulsion restored quickly, they would sink again, and if they reached test depth, the CO would be forced to order an emergency blow, forcing high pressure into the main ballast tanks and the submarine emergently to the surface. An emergency blow, while saving the ship from sinking, would potentially kill them another way. The blow would steal their stealth, trap them on the surface, and make the *Blackfish* a sitting duck for the *Belgorod* to kill. The direness of the situation was compounded by the fact that the trim pump controller was on fire, and the trim pump was the high-capacity pump used to pump extra ballast overboard and make the ship lighter.

"Conn, Maneuvering, commencing fast reactor start-up," the EOOW reported on the 7MC.

Knepper checked that mental box.

Good.

"Recommend cross-connecting trim and drain," Knepper shouted.

"Agreed," Houston barked and then, grabbing the 7MC handset, said, "Maneuvering, Conn, cross-connect trim and drain."

"Cross-connect trim and drain systems, Conn, Maneuvering, aye," came the reply.

Knepper checked mental box two.

"Captain, I'm going to put out this fire. WEPS is your coordinator."

"Go," Houston said.

"WEPS, you're—"

"Got it!" Juggernaut said, her voice tinny through the mouthpiece of her EBA.

Knepper looked back at Ryan and said, "Stay here and do whatever Juggernaut tells you."

Ryan nodded.

Knepper coughed as smoke began to waft into control. He

ducked and sprinted out the back of the conn into the command passageway. He burst into his stateroom and retrieved his self-contained breathing apparatus, or SCBA—a mobile unit with a pressurized tank like the Scott Air-Paks that civilian firefighters used. As the designated scene leader, he needed mobility, so an EBA was his second choice.

Unlike surface Navy ships, submarines did not have a dedicated damage control division. On a submarine, every sailor with dolphins was a firefighter. Similarly, on a submarine there was no dedicated DC Central with gear lockers and status boards. On the *Blackfish*, the CO's stateroom became DC Central and the XO was the designated officer in charge of coordinating the effort to fight the fire casualty.

After shrugging on the bottle backpack, he donned the face mask and pulled the flash-guard flame-retardant hood over his neck and shoulders. Then he checked the seal and took his first breath. Good to go, he tuned his MOMCOM to the forward compartment common channel. Before leaving, he glanced at the tactical monitor in his stateroom, which he had set to quad-view, showing four different windows that were repeaters of screens in control. He checked the ship's speed, three knots, then depth. They were only a hundred and ten feet from test depth, and sinking. The captain had not yet ordered maneuvering to shift to the emergency propulsion motor, which in normal circumstances for such a casualty would be the likely course of action. Battery powered, the EPM was designed to provide limited propulsion—just enough to maintain nominal lift for depth control when the sub was overly heavy from too much ballast or a flooded compartment. But shifting to the EPM and back to main propulsion was time-consuming. The *Belgorod* had undoubtedly heard the *Blackfish*'s ADCAPs active sonar. And if not, it could not have missed the explosion. If K-329 fired a third Status-6 with a conventional warhead at the *Blackfish* and the *Blackfish* was stuck on the EPM, they were dead. Houston was gambling that the fast recovery start-up of the sub's nuclear reactor would be complete before they hit test depth and needed to emergency blow.

He shelved the concern and darted out of his stateroom. In the command passageway, he passed LTJG Walker, who moved forward as he moved aft. She was red-faced and holding her breath inside her EBA as she ran toward the CO's stateroom, where she would coordinate comms and track progress on a status board with markers.

"Power is secured to trim pump motor controller," reported the A-gang LCPO on the 4MC. Chief Cole Marxen was a man whose voice Knepper would recognize anywhere. "Hose team one is fighting the fire."

A gray-black layer of smoke had filled the top half of the command passageway, limiting visibility above waist height. Knepper relaxed a little knowing that Marxen had reacted so quickly and already had a hose team on the scene. As the auxiliary division chief, the machinery room was Marxen's domain and the trim pump was his piece of equipment. This type of casualty was one they trained on and Cole Marxen was a shit-hot chief who didn't back away from any challenge.

Knepper took the first down ladder he came to and made his way aft to the machinery room. The trim pump and trim pump motor controller were located in the forward starboard outboard section of the space. As he faced aft, the fire was on his left just inside the door—but this was something he could only visualize in his head because visibility was shit. Crouching low, taking care not to step on the hose or knock any of the first responders off balance, he moved forward. His regulator hissed and warbled with each labored breath as he scooted forward, feeling his way.

"XO is on the scene," he shouted. A beat later he was directly behind the crouching Marxen, who had his hand on the second hoseman's back.

A water jet from the nozzle disappeared into the haze and steam poured out in the passageway, mixing with the dense smoke.

Chief Marxen used a NIFTI—a Navy infrared thermal imager— to peer through the smoke and see the fire. "XO, the fire is contained to the motor controller," he shouted.

Knepper called the update to LTJG Walker, who would update control and all stations. "DC Central, XO, the fire is contained."

"Move your stream down and left," Marxen barked, guiding the hose team. "Too much . . . Yeah, right there."

Knepper conducted a mental inventory of the equipment around the trim pump that could also potentially catch fire and the tactical and engineering implications if they did.

"XO, the fire is out," Chief Marxen shouted.

"Check for hot spots and set the reflash watch," he shouted back. Then, on his MOMCOM, he reported, "DC Central, XO— the fire is out. Checking for hot spots. The reflash watch is set."

A split second later a 4 MC announcement was made: "The fire is out in the machinery room."

The hose team, which had secured their nozzle stream, stayed crouched and ready to reopen the spigot, while Marxen scooted past them into the machinery room to scan with the NIFTI for hot spots in the surrounding area that could reignite the fire. In the case of electrical fires, once the power was secured to the source, the fire was typically quick to put out. But the machinery room was home to the ship's diesel generator, which burned diesel fuel, adding a significant Bravo Class fire risk if things got out of control. Any lagging or other combustible materials that caught fire needed to be dealt with quickly.

"No hot spots," Marxen called.

"DC Central, XO, no hot spots in the machinery room," Knepper reported.

But no sooner had LTJG Walker acknowledged the good news than she came back with a report that made his breath catch in his throat.

"XO, Captain wants you in maneuvering to restore propulsion by any means necessary. We've got torpedoes in the water!"

68

Clutching a pipe in the overhead to steady herself, Katie watched helplessly as the crew of the *Blackfish* dealt with one problem after another. The air inside the EBA smelled funny and the rubber seal almost burned her skin everywhere it made contact. She wondered if it had been cleaned with some sort of astringent chemical after its last use that was seeping into her pores. It was a stupid thing to think about, considering there was an active fire and the sub was sinking, but that's where her brain went.

"The fire is out in the machinery room," someone announced on the loudspeaker.

"Oh, thank God," she heard herself murmur.

A few people cheered in control, which sounded funny because everyone was wearing EBAs. But then, as if Fate had been waiting for just the right moment to smite all hope, the sonar supervisor announced: "Torpedoes in the water, bearing three-five-eight. Designated Sierra One-Zero-Three and One-Zero-Four."

Katie's heart fluttered back-to-back palpitations.

Not again, she thought.

She looked at Houston. She couldn't read his expression because of his EBA, but his posture was defiant.

"Sonar, do we hold any contacts on that bearing?" Houston asked.

"Conn, Sonar, negative."

Houston turned to Juggernaut, and for a moment Katie thought he was going to order her to fire, but he said nothing.

"Standing by for a snapshot," Juggernaut said, as if prompting him.

Houston did not give the order to fire; instead, he shifted his gaze to Katie. "Ryan, do we have another asset in the area? Is it possible the President decided to hedge his bets?"

Her mind went to her last conversation with the leadership team on the *Ford*. *The* Indiana *is en route south at flank speed as we speak*, Admiral Kiplinger had said.

"It's possible," she said. "SUBLANT pulled the *Indiana* off station and ordered her south at flank speed."

Houston turned to face sonar. "Supe, you've got twenty seconds to classify those torpedoes."

"Aye, sir."

"Captain, DC Central reports no hot spots. The reflash watch is stationed," a young sailor with a headset reported.

"Very well."

"Captain, loss of steerage," the pilot announced.

"Very well, pilot."

"Captain, crossing test depth," the pilot said. "Recommend emergency blow."

"Are we pumping aux tanks down with the drain pump?" the CO snapped, his voice ripe with frustration and tension.

"Yes, sir, as fast as I can," the copilot, Petty Officer Campright, said.

Houston turned to the phone talker. "Inform the XO we have torpedoes in the water and tell him to get his ass to maneuvering and restore propulsion by any means necessary."

"Yes, sir," the phone talker said and spoke into her headset.

"Captain, torpedoes Sierra One-Zero-Three and One-Zero-Four are on parallel tracks. Traveling south and on course toward the plotted position for Master One was when it launched the Status-6 weapons," Juggernaut said. "I think they're intended for Master One. The problem is—"

"We moved into the way and onto the track when I ordered the full bell to get clear of the blast zone," Houston said, interrupting.

"Yes, sir," she said. "When they go active, they could acquire us instead of the *Belgorod,* and we're dead in the water."

"Literally," Smallbrock said under his breath at his fire control terminal beside Katie.

"WEPS, ready countermeasures," Houston said.

Juggernaut acknowledged and passed the order over comms.

"Passing one hundred feet below test depth. Four hundred feet until crush depth," the pilot announced. "Captain, recommend emergency blow."

"If we emergency blow with two torpedoes in the water heading our way, we die," Houston said for everyone in control to hear.

"Aye, sir," the pilot said.

No one had explained to Katie the precise definitions of test depth and crush depth, but the answers were pretty easy to infer. She assumed test depth was the depth to which the submarine had been tested. Which meant crush depth was the sub's design limit, below which *survival* was prohibited. As if confirming this for her, the *Blackfish's* hull reverberated with a sphincter-clenching metallic groan.

"Conn, Sonar, Sierra One-Zero-Three and One-Zero-Four are classified as Russian Type 65 heavyweight torpedoes," the sonar supe said.

"Russian torpedoes?" Houston said. "Are you sure?"

"Yes, sir."

"Chief, is there any plausible scenario where Master One repositioned north of us?"

"No, sir, we still hold Master One, bearing one-eight-eight."

"Shit. Two Russian subs . . . Maybe they *are* shooting at us," Houston said.

"Sir, I don't think so," Katie said, going with her gut. "If I know the President, he would have given the Russian president an opportunity to clean up their own mess before he gave the order to sink the *Belgorod*. I think that's exactly what's happening here. Juggernaut said it herself, those torpedoes were fired at the point in the ocean where the *Belgorod* was when it launched the Status-6s. That Russian sub captain probably shadowed her and waited just like us, waiting for Gorov to fire."

"Passing two hundred feet below test depth. Three hundred feet until crush depth," the pilot announced, but this time did not recommend emergency blow.

"Very well," Houston said. His eyes still fixed on her in an unreadable stare, he picked up a handset to speak, but before he could, the loudspeaker in control reverberated with Knepper's voice.

"Captain, XO, propulsion restored."

"Pilot, all ahead full," Houston said.

"All ahead full, Pilot, aye. Captain, maneuvering answers all ahead full."

"Swistak," Houston said, walking up to stand behind the pilot. "Sir?"

"Listen very carefully. We're going the wrong direction. We need to go east to get out of the way of two incoming torpedoes, but we also need speed and lift to get our fat ass above test depth. We can't afford to turn slow, to sink out, or to cavitate during the turn I'm about to order. Do you understand what I'm saying, son?"

"Yes, Captain," Swistak said, eyes straight ahead on his display. "You want me to do the impossible."

"That's right. You're the best damn pilot I've ever seen, but there's no shame if you want to punch in the heading and let the computer do the driving."

"No, sir. I got this," Swistak said, then looked at his copilot, Campright. "I mean, we got this."

Houston squeezed the young man's shoulder. "Pilot, make your depth five hundred feet, come left to course one-three-zero."

The pilot acknowledged the order and Katie watched as the sub's depth climbed and the heading began to change. She wasn't a submariner, but the past hour had been education by fire hose, and it was all beginning to click. The CO's plan was to sneak out of the path of the incoming Russian torpedoes meant for the *Belgorod* so that the *Blackfish* did not become the accidental target. Doing so was a difficult dance of trade-offs. Anything they did that made noise would register on the torpedoes' passive sonar, which could trigger the torpedo to turn on its active sonar. Being quiet wouldn't matter against active sonar. Being big and close was the problem. The *Belgorod* was bigger, but the *Blackfish* was closer.

To Katie, it began to feel like their fate was going to be decided by a cosmic coin flip . . . But with two torpedoes that meant two coin flips, and she didn't like those odds.

69

USS *WASHINGTON*, SSN 787, "THE *BLACKFISH*"

Knepper sprinted through the reactor compartment passageway toward the forward compartment. The EOOW had conducted the fast recovery start-up, and with a little bit of help from him speeding up the orders, had gotten propulsion restored. On reaching the bulkhead at the end of the tunnel, he undogged the watertight door, yanked it open, and stepped through the oval-shaped hatch.

"I got the door, sir," the battle stations watch stander on the forward compartment side said.

"Thanks, shipmate," he said and sprinted toward control, still wearing his SCBA.

The smoke levels were slightly improved, but it would take the ship's air filtration system hours to clear the particulate. Standard operating procedure after a fire was to snorkel or surface and emergency ventilate, but that option was out of the question given their tactical situation. The crew would be in EBAs at a minimum until this conflict was over.

He took the first down ladder to middle level and worked his way forward into control, where he made a beeline to the captain. "Sir, do you want me here or in the machinery room?"

"Here," Houston said, then in a loud voice, "Attention in control, the XO is the fire control coordinator."

The relevant watch standers acknowledged the report, while Knepper repositioned himself next to Juggernaut, who was standing at the attack center.

"Bring me up to speed," he said to the FTOW, scanning back and forth between the broadband sonar gram on Smallbrock's upper screen and the geoplot on the lower.

Smallbrock glanced over his shoulder and said, "Two torpedoes fired from an unidentified Russian submarine to the north, which we do not hold sonar contact on. Torpedoes are heading for Master One's location when he fired his Status-6 salvo."

"Oh shit, we're in the way," Knepper said, studying the icons on the geoplot.

"Yes, sir. We're trying to sneak clear. Coming left to course one-three-zero."

"Conn, Sonar, both torpedoes have slowed," the supe said, and after a moment added, "Torpedoes have transitioned from passive search to active search."

Knepper first checked the ship's heading, which was passing two-four-five, then he looked at the ship's depth, which had ascended above test depth. He shifted his gaze to the broadband display.

"Oh, no," he said under his breath, then in a loud voice, "Captain, looks like the bearing rate is coming off on Sierra One-Zero-Four. One-Zero-Three is on the right, drawing left rapidly across our bow, but One-Zero-Four is on the right, staying right. Recommend torpedo evasion."

The call for evasive action was possibly premature, but Knepper's gut told him they were in trouble. Since being fired, both weapons had been on parallel tracks, but bearing rate never lies.

Seeing one torpedo's relative bearings deviate dramatically from the other, along with its bearing rate going to zero, was a very bad sign—it indicated the second torpedo had changed course and was on a collision course with the *Washington*.

"Conn, Sonar, Sierra One-Zero-Four is range-gating own ship."

"Torpedo evasion, course two-zero-zero," Houston announced. "Launch internal countermeasures. Pilot, make your depth eight hundred feet."

"Torpedo evasion, course two-zero-zero, make my depth eight hundred feet, Pilot, aye . . . Captain, maneuvering answers all ahead flank," the pilot said.

"Two countermeasures away," FT1 Kearns announced after firing the internal countermeasures launcher in remote mode.

"Captain, course two-zero-zero puts us on intercept course with the *Belgorod*," the sonar supe said.

"I know that, Chief."

"But the other torpedo is targeting the *Belgorod*."

"Yes . . ." Houston said. "Coordinator, report when distance to Master One is one thousand yards."

Knepper repeated back the order. He could guess what the captain was trying to do—lead the torpedo that was homing on the *Blackfish* to a bigger target. If the torpedo was not fooled by the first set of countermeasures, he predicted that Houston would launch a second set at the last moment, then order a hard rudder—hoping the torpedo would detonate on those countermeasures or blow through them, and once on the other side acquire the *Belgorod* instead of reacquiring the *Blackfish*.

It's what I'd do.

He turned and looked at Ryan for the first time since he'd returned to control. Inside her EBA she was as pale as a ghost, but to his astonishment, she flashed him a tight-lipped smile.

We're going to be okay, he mouthed.

She gave him another tight smile, but looked hardly reassured.

"Conn, Sonar, both countermeasures are active and passing into our baffles."

"Very well," Houston said.

"Captain, steady on course two-zero-zero and on ordered depth eight hundred feet," the pilot said.

"Very well, pilot."

"Conn, Sonar, blade rate and change in bearing rate indicates Master One has started torpedo evasion maneuvers," the supe shouted, his voice a tight cord.

Houston whirled to face Knepper. "Coordinator, figure out their evasion course. Whether we live or die depends on it."

"Aye, Captain," Knepper said and leaned over Smallbrock's terminal as the FTOW went to work updating Master One's changing course and speed.

"Conn, Sonar, torpedo Sierra One-Zero-Four is through the countermeasures."

"XO, hurry!"

"I got this," Smallbrock said, and Knepper watched as the FT2 dialed in a solution that matched the exact course Knepper predicted the Russian sub captain would choose. "Master One turned south, course one-eight-zero!"

"Conn, Sonar, torpedo Sierra One-Zero-Four is terminal homing."

"Captain, past CPA on Master One," Knepper shouted, checking the computer's updated calculated closest point of approach given the *Belgorod*'s course change. "Twelve hundred yards and opening."

It's now or never, Captain, Knepper thought, clutching the back of Smallbrock's chair so tight his knuckles turned white.

"Right full rudder," Houston shouted, his voice firm, but in control. "Launch external countermeasures!"

"Right full rudder, aye," the pilot said.

"External countermeasures away," Kearns said.

"Maneuvering, Conn, go to one hundred ten percent reactor power," Houston ordered on the 7MC. "Propulsion Plant Operator, make maximum possible turns."

"Conn, Maneuvering, aye," came the EOOW's report.

Knepper knew that every submarine captain, prior to taking command, was given certain confidential information about the boats in extremis capabilities. In his twelve years in the Navy, this was the first time he'd ever seen or even heard of a Virginia-class SSN operating at one hundred ten percent power. But if there was ever a time to risk it, this was it.

He could feel Ryan's eyes on him, but he didn't have the heart to look at her, and kept his eyes locked on the broadband display, praying for the torpedo's bearing rate to break hard right. He exhaled slowly inside his SCBA mask.

This is going to be effing close.

70

Captain Second Rank Yuri Stepanov, first officer and second-in-command of K-329, stared at his friend, mentor, and captain and knew that the moment had come. Drenched in sweat, Gorov was delirious with fever. Blood ringed the inside of his lips. The captain could barely stand, was talking nonsense, and seemed to be hallucinating. Also, despite not having witnessed the act, Stepanov was certain Gorov had had the weapons officer murdered in the torpedo room before launching the two nuclear Poseidons and had done both without consulting Stepanov.

It's time, the voice said in his head, *or we all die.*

"Captain, I think it's time you retire to your quarters," Stepanov said, placing a hand on Gorov's shoulder. "I will stand conning officer in your stead while you rest."

The captain shrugged him off and, like a stage actor quoting Dostoyevsky, exclaimed, "Life is pain, life is fear, and man is unhappy. Man loves life because he loves pain and fear. But life is given in exchange for these things, and that is the whole deceit . . . But he who overcomes pain and fear will himself be God. And this God will not be!"

Stepanov turned to Tarasov. "Take him to his stateroom and lock the door. Stay with him until the ship's doctor arrives."

Tarasov hesitated.

"That's an order, Captain Lieutenant!"

The engineer nodded, hooked his arm under the stumbling Gorov's armpit, and led him off the conn.

"Attention in the control room, the captain is not well, and I am temporarily assuming command. Lieutenant Blok, I relieve you of the conn. You are my junior officer of the watch."

"I stand relieved of the conn, sir," Blok said.

"Messenger, find the ship's doctor and dispatch him to the captain's stateroom," Stepanov said.

"Aye, sir," the messenger said and scurried away.

No sooner had he exhaled with relief at ending the circus that had been the control room than the loudspeaker reverberated with a report: "Torpedo salvo in the water! Bearing zero-zero-five."

Stepanov knew that the American hunter-killer SSN 787 had been in trail, because the *Belgorod*'s cryptological specialist on board had decoded the coded sonar message. Unfortunately, the Virginia-class submarine was so quiet and its captain such a formidable tactician that they had not been able to detect, much less track, 787. The Americans had already fired two torpedoes in an attempt to destroy the *Belgorod*'s Poseidons, and now they obviously had circled around to finish the job.

"Sonar, Conn, how many torpedoes?"

"Conn, Sonar, two torpedoes, classified as . . . Russian Futlyar torpedoes."

Stepanov felt the blood drain from his face at the news. The Futlyar torpedo was new, the latest and most advanced wire-guided model in the fleet, but only available in limited numbers. Only one submarine in the Northern Fleet was carrying them, and it was the most capable and deadly killer in the Russian submarine ranks—the K-560 *Severodvinsk*.

"The president has sent reinforcements to help kill the Americans," someone in control shouted, and the rest of the watch standers cheered.

But Stepanov knew otherwise—he could feel it in his bones. The hopeful, celebratory mood in the control room immediately turned when he did not second the sentiment. The men could see from his expression that the torpedoes were not intended for their American adversary, but instead were meant for them.

"Fire control, track these torpedoes. Report their course, speed, and range, and tell me where they are headed."

"Aye, Captain," the senior fire control operator of the watch said.

He called me Captain, Stepanov thought with a prideful upturn of the corners of his mouth.

The *Belgorod* had two large, pressurized water reactors, two powerful propulsion turbines, and two screws. However, despite all this power, the ship was massive, with a displacement of thirty thousand tons, making it slow to accelerate and maneuver. Stepanov could not outrun or outturn one Futlyar torpedo, let alone two. Their best hope for survival was to be quiet and avoid detection. If the captain of K-560 had fired the salvo at the coordinates where the *Belgorod* had been when Gorov launched the Poseidons, there was a chance the torpedoes would search behind them and not detect them.

And if Fate is smiling on us, maybe the Futlyars will acquire the American SSN instead.

Unfortunately for the crew of the *Belgorod*, Stepanov quickly saw that Fate had other plans. The tactical picture deteriorated rapidly as his submarine and the American conducted torpedo evasion maneuvers and launched countermeasures at the same time. In an arena of swirling and churning ocean, noisemakers and bubble shields tried to distract and fool the hunters as two blind leviathans jockeyed for survival. In the end, both torpedoes chose the bigger target.

"Conn, Sonar, countermeasures have failed. Futlyar torpedoes one and two are in terminal homing on own ship. Impact in thirty seconds," the sonar supervisor reported.

Death seemed a foregone conclusion, but he had one more trick up his sleeve. Like its Oscar II brother subs, the *Belgorod* was built with a double-hull design—a robust inner-pressure hull, fully encapsulated by an outer hydrodynamic hull. The large gap between the two hulls gave the *Belgorod* tremendous reserve buoyancy and served as a shock absorber against torpedo concussive effects. Also, unlike its American counterparts, which had only two watertight compartments—forward and aft—the *Belgorod* had ten . . . Ten compartments to isolate and contain flooding to dramatically increase survivability in the event of a hull breach. Finally, because the ship had been designed as a special missions platform for deep submersible operations, the shipyard had used a more expensive steel with higher tensile strength for the hull. Special bracing and reinforcements were also required for the wet hangar and the docking chambers in the submarine's midsection. If any sub in the fleet could survive this attack, it was K-329.

"Diving officer of the watch," Stepanov said. "Twenty-degree up bubble and stand by for emergency blow on my mark."

"Twenty-degree up bubble, aye, sir," the dive said and ordered the planesmen to tilt the stern planes and bow planes to ascend rapidly. As the bow tipped upward and the floor began to tilt, the diving officer stood and placed his hands on the emergency blow activation levers in the overhead above his chair at the ship's control panel. "Standing by for emergency blow on your mark."

"Fifteen seconds until torpedo impact."

Getting shallow was their only chance for survival. At deep depths, the water pressure would fill a breached compartment in seconds and make escape impossible. But on the surface, he gave his crew a chance.

If I time it perfectly, I will create vertical separation between the torpedoes and the bottom of the hull.

He knew from his engineering studies that the force of an explosion decreased exponentially with increasing distance from the point of detonation. The shock wave might even help push the boat to the surface.

The up angle on the sub was at twenty now, the most severe angle permitted by procedure, and Stepanov's calves strained as he leaned forward while gripping the railing that encircled the periscope stand for support.

"Ten seconds until impact . . . Nine . . . Eight—"

"Emergency blow!" he shouted, praying he'd factored in the optimal amount of latency for both reaction time and the pressurized air system to force the hundreds of thousands of liters of water from the ballast tanks.

The diving officer activated the levers as he shouted, "Emergency blow, aye!"

The roar of compressed air reverberated through the ship, and Stepanov felt the massive submarine buoy upward. And somewhere that sounded very far away, he could hear the sonar supervisor's voice on the control room speaker.

"Detonation in three . . . Two . . . One . . ."

71

I t had happened to Katie only once before, when she was young and terrorists had tried to kidnap her. And now it was happening again. As chaos and impending death swirled around her, she took a step back. Not an actual step back, but a metaphysical one. She felt detached from her body—as if some cosmic fourth wall had been broken, allowing her to be an observer of the play that was her life. Her character was in imminent, mortal danger, but the fear that had gripped her moments ago suddenly felt very far away.

Time altered for her in this state. The measured predictable cadence, the universal drumbeat that marched the present into the future, changed in tempo. Like music . . . presto and lento.

Fast and slow, she thought.

Her attention jumped around the control room, like a film director ordering different camera captures.

Knepper: "Captain, Sierra One-Zero-Four is on the right, drawing right. High bearing rate."

Juggernaut: "It took the bait."

Sonar supervisor: "Conn, Sonar, both torpedoes terminal homing on Master One . . . Master One just launched countermeasures."

Pilot: "Captain, maneuvering reports making maximum turns at one hundred ten percent reactor power."

Houston: "Coordinator, report distance to Master One."

Knepper: "Passing two thousand yards and opening . . ."

She blinked and everything was still.

Lento . . .

And then came the storm.

The ship shook violently, buffeted as if by an ocean quake. An aftershock followed, almost as bad as the first.

She blinked again and was in the middle of the pandemonium.

Presto . . .

Alarms blared and orders were given, but this time the recovery was faster. No fires. No reactor scram. Damage and injury reports came pouring in, but the captain and the watch team managed them. A modified electric plant and propulsion lineup was reported—whatever the hell that was—with terms and configurations that meant nothing to her. But the submarine was not sinking. Not this time. The lights were still on and the ocean stayed on the outside of the pressure hull, where it belonged.

And during it all, the regulator on her emergency breathing mask hissed like Darth Vader . . .

"Ryan? Ryan!" a voice shouted.

Katie stepped back into herself, and the cadence of time reset to normal.

"What?" she said to Knepper, who stood in front of her.

"I said, are you okay?"

"I'm fine. Is the ship okay?"

"It's a boat."

"What?" she said, confused.

"Ships are the things on the surface—you know, targets. Submarines are boats," he said, grinning at her from inside his fireman's getup.

"Really? You're cracking jokes now? Just tell me if we're safe."

"Sorry. It was touch-and-go there for a minute, but we've got everything under control now. We're safe."

"Good," she said, closing her eyes slowly and then opening them again to meet his stare.

"Man, you kinda zoned out there for a minute," he said.

"Figured the best thing I could do was keep quiet and stay out of the way."

"Yeah, smart thinking, actually."

"What happened to the *Belgorod*?" she asked, turning to look at the fire control terminal behind her, like an actual submariner. What had been Greek to her before was starting to make sense now.

"We think she's on the surface. Sonar has indications she's badly damaged, but thinks she somehow survived the attack. The *Belgorod* is one badass bitch, it seems. We're making preparations to come to PD so the captain can take a look."

That comment was like CPR for her brain and she gasped. "Dennis, did we blow up the other Status-6 drone? The one heading west—the one you told me our ADCAP would probably not be able to catch?"

His expression fell. "Shit, in all the chaos and damage control, I don't think we confirmed—"

"We have to warn the White House," she blurted, cutting him off. "We have to tell them that it got through and is heading for the East Coast!"

Knepper turned to Houston. "Captain, we need to update SUB-LANT that the westbound Status-6 is likely intact and en route to its target."

"Radio, Conn, did you hear that?" Houston said loudly for the open mic.

"Conn, Radio, aye," came the immediate response over the control room's loudspeaker. "Prepping a message now."

Houston turned to Ryan and gave her a solemn nod of recognition.

"Thanks for the backup, Katie," Knepper said.

"If there's one thing I've learned from the past six hours on this boat, it's that the thing that makes a submarine crew so formidable is that everyone has each other's backs. No ego. Everyone always thinking, and working, and contributing."

"I think you're one of us now," he said and put a hand on her shoulder.

"Thanks," she said, but then another dreadful thought occurred to her.

"What?" he said.

"What happened to the other Russian submarine? The one that fired the torpedoes at the *Belgorod* that almost killed us?"

"It's still out there," Knepper said. "But the captain and I think that we're not its mission. The *Belgorod* was. We're going to keep a very wide berth from K-329 while we're at PD, just in case the other guy decides to take another shot."

"Great," she muttered.

"Listen, I gotta go to radio to make sure this message says everything we need it to and sign off on it. Are you going to be okay here?"

She flashed him a crooked smile and lifted the black rubber air hose that was keeping her alive. "Where else am I going to go?"

After he left, she turned to Captain Houston as he and the control room made preparations to go to periscope depth. She watched him with no small amount of awe as he prepared his battle-weary, but battle-hardened, boat and crew for yet another risky evolution. But that was the job they'd all signed up for, wasn't it? The

Blackfish truly was the apex predator at the tip of the spear. They had saved the carrier strike group, and now they were going to have to pass the torch to her father to save the country.

I did my best, Dad, she thought with a wan smile as the boat angled up to go to PD. *I hope it was enough.*

72

Ryan let the massive, combined intellect of the room storm for a bit. As a much younger man he had learned that chaos—properly channeled and contained—was nothing to fear.

He looked up at the analog clock on the wall and let fifteen more seconds tick by. The chaos had been kicked off by the relatively good news in the emergency message from the USS *Washington*. The *Belgorod* was on the surface and damaged. The *Washington* was fully operational and it appeared the Russians had, indeed, fired on their own submarine, as Yermilov had promised. The *Ford* strike group was safe, one Poseidon having been destroyed by Captain Houston's submarine.

That was the good news.

The bad news, however, was that a second nuclear-tipped Status-6 was screaming toward the East Coast of the United States.

"All right," he said firmly. "Where are we?"

"Mr. President, even though the *Belgorod* is damaged and on the surface," General Kudryk said, "I strongly urge that we finish her off before she shoots off any more Poseidons."

Ryan pursed his lips. "Do we have imagery?"

"Coming in now, Mr. President," Mary Pat announced and tapped away on a computer at her seat. "This is streaming live from NSA, sir."

The live stream video might have been from a plane circling just above the injured Russian submarine, the image crisp, clear, and filling the large-screen monitor on the wall. The massive Russian sub was on the surface, but listing nearly twenty degrees to port. Sailors filled the deck, all in brightly colored floatation vests, and were preparing large orange rafts.

"They're abandoning ship," Admiral Kent said, stating the obvious.

It could always be a ruse, Ryan knew. Hell, he'd participated in just such a ruse with Captain Marko Ramius a lifetime ago. But Mary Pat's team had told them only two nuclear-tipped Status-6 torpedoes had been aboard the *Belgorod*. Those had been fired. The threat had been neutered, in his assessment. Most of the sailors aboard the damaged sub were likely completely unaware of all that had transpired. They were, in many respects, victims.

These men didn't need to die.

"The *Belgorod* is combat ineffective, it would appear," he said. "And the *Washington* is there, ready to act. If they make any move to fire more torpedoes, tell them to blow the *Belgorod* to hell, but otherwise, we move into a rescue phase to save the crew abandoning the submarine."

"Yes, sir," Kudryk said, his face a mask and his tone hard to read. Was he relieved or disappointed?

Ryan didn't care.

"Our only priority now is to find the other Status-6," he announced. "How much time do we have?"

"Well," Kent said, doing the math in his head, "depending on the true speed of the Status-6, from the point where it was fired, if the target truly is Hampton Roads, we have somewhere between seven and twelve hours."

Ryan gritted his teeth. He knew that wasn't the biggest issue at hand. Finding it was no small feat—a large torpedo was still a tiny needle in the haystack of the Atlantic, even knowing the likely track the weapon would take. Stopping it might well be the bigger challenge.

"Sir, we have a video link from Bahrain," the aide to his SecDef said.

"Put it up," he ordered.

Lieutenant Tucker filled the screen, his face creased with worry lines, but his eyes unblinking.

"Mr. President, I know time is critical, so I'll cut to the chase," the young officer said. "We're playing catch-up, but we're not out of the fight yet. We believe we can find the Status-6 torpedo, sir."

A collective sigh of relief filled the room, but the relief was only temporary as each member of the team came to grips with the fact that finding the weapon wasn't the same thing as stopping it.

"We know the time and coordinates when the weapon was launched. If you provide us with a list of probable targets in rank order, our AI can easily calculate the projected course for each. We can then provide every surface and submerged drone—along with all other search assets in the theater—detection windows based on the projected track to each target," Tucker said, his voice suggesting that there might be more to the system than he'd previously briefed. "When and if alerts start coming in, our AI will match up the actual data with the predicted detection windows and perform a best fit analysis to identify the target. At that point in time, we can narrow the search area and focus all assets on tracking the target. The commander of undersea surveillance will be receiving all data we're generating via the Integrated Undersea Surveillance System in real time."

"Excellent work, Lieutenant," Kent said.

"What does your fancy computer suggest is the likelihood of finding the Status-6?" Kudryk asked, dampening the mood slightly.

"Seventy-eight percent, sir," Tucker said.

Kudryk glanced at the President, a scowl on his face.

Ryan got it. Seventy-eight percent was good, but there was still a twenty-two percent chance that the Poseidon made it past the network of assets hunting it. "Keep us updated in real time, Lieutenant."

"Yes, sir, Mr. President," the young officer on the other side of the world said, and the screen went blue.

"Assuming we find it, how do we kill it?" Ryan said.

"Sir," Kent said, "the *Washington* proved that an ADCAP can kill a Status-6, but even at top speed, an ADCAP can't catch a Status-6. To have a chance, the ADCAP needs to be fired in a closing geometry. The *Indiana* is in position to interdict the Status-6 if the target is Norfolk. If, however, Captain Gorov targeted New York or Charleston or some other port, then all bets are off."

Ryan's head was swimming now with contingencies, trying to anticipate the problems and conflicts and have solutions in place in real time. "Logic dictates that the target is Norfolk, but we need a backup plan in place in case we're wrong," he announced.

"Sir, I propose that the moment the torpedo is located, we take action. We shouldn't wait for the *Indiana*. We immediately deploy every available air or surface asset in range to drop Mark 46 and 54 torpedoes on the target," Kent said, his face suggesting his own sharp mind was calculating the math for a solution. "Seventy-five knots is fast as hell for a torpedo, but not so fast that we can't position assets."

"Do it," Ryan said.

"The 46s and 54s are lightweight torpedoes. Do they have the payload to destroy a Status-6?" Kudryk asked.

Kent gritted his teeth. "We'll check in with our SMEs, but I think they should have the punch to at least disable it. My concern, frankly, has less to do with payload and more to do with limitations such as range, maximum operating depth, and the onboard sonar and data-processing capabilities."

"What do you mean?" Ryan asked, not liking the sound of that.

"Well, sir, the advantage of the lightweight torpedoes is that they can be deployed from both surface ships and helos, but they're less capable in all respects compared to an ADCAP. Depth has me particularly concerned. We can get the 46 and 54 down to fifteen hundred feet, but it's very possible the Status-6 could be operating twice that, sir. If I was Gorov, I would program it to stay as deep as possible as long as possible. The truth is, we just don't know enough about the damn thing, other than the bullshit propaganda out of the Kremlin."

"Well," Ryan said, his voice tight, "we go to war with the Navy we have, not the Navy we wish we had. If we could fire ADCAPs from helos we would, but we can't. Hopefully, the *Indiana* is in the right place at the right time, but we cannot bank on that, people. Admiral, I want the fleet ready to rain a curtain of 46s and 54s ahead of the Status-6 once it is located."

"Yes, sir," Kent said.

"But be prepared to deliver a second salvo closer to shore, where depth will not be a constraint."

"That's pretty close to shore, sir. What if the warhead is triggered?"

Ryan sighed.

"We might not have a choice if it's transiting deep," he said, and the admiral nodded his understanding. "Our last line of defense should be at the maximum possible standoff distance from shore, but follow a line where the depth is no more than fifteen hundred feet."

"Yes, sir, Mr. President."

The bottom line seemed to be that the crew of the USS *Indiana*, armed with heavyweight ADCAP torpedoes, might well be the best last hope of stopping the inbound nuclear attack. And at the speed the torpedo was traveling, they would only get one shot at it.

If they could find the damn torpedo in time.

And if he could notify them in time.

And if they could get into position . . .

73

Konstantin heard them talking about him . . . Stepanov and the ship's doctor.

Although he'd refused to accept a morphine injection, the doctor had given it to him anyway. The writhing and wailing probably pushed him over the edge. But now that the drug was coursing through his veins, and his pain diminished, Konstantin was grateful for the relief.

"Thank you, Doctor. You've done everything you can," he heard Stepanov say. "Now, hurry topside, we have but minutes before the ship sinks."

"And what about . . . ?" the doctor said.

"I'll take care of the captain."

Gorov turned and watched the doctor leave his stateroom, while Stepanov, his loyal first officer and friend, dragged a chair over to sit at his bedside.

"We are on the surface?" he asked, feeling the hull gently rocking from side to side.

"*Da*, Captain."

"How bad is the damage?"

"Beyond repair. We have flooding in multiple compartments.

The reactors are scrammed. We cannot evacuate the water fast enough to stay afloat."

Gorov nodded, not surprised by this news. "And the crew?"

"Evacuating to life rafts as we speak."

"How many souls survived?"

"Eighty-eight of one hundred and fifteen are accounted for."

Gorov coughed and then swallowed a glob of bloody phlegm. "The Americans are to blame, *da*? They fired on us?"

"*Nyet*, it was K-560."

"What!" Gorov said, trying to sit up, the fog of morphine burning off at this. "Denikin killed us? How do you know this?"

"The torpedoes were Futlyar class."

"Ah, I see," he said, relaxing back into his pillow. "Only K-560 carries these weapons . . . Well, I suppose it is better that way."

Stepanov remained silent on this point.

"What about the mission? Did we succeed?"

Stepanov hesitated a moment, then said, "The Americans destroyed the Poseidon aimed at the carrier strike group. We think the other one outran their Mark 48 torpedo and is cruising toward the target."

"Good, this is good news . . ."

"Is it, Captain? I'm not so sure anymore. If it explodes, I don't think it will change the balance of power like we hoped. I think Morozov was right. This mission was a mistake."

"Calina certainly thought so," Gorov said, closing his eyes. "She tried to stop me, but it was too late."

"Calina?" Stepanov said with a pitying timbre. "Your wife is dead, my friend."

"I know," he said, his heart broken. He opened his eyes and moved his hand to clutch that of his first officer. "I give the *Belgorod* to you, Yuri. You are the captain now."

"Thank you, I will do my best." Stepanov turned over Konstantin's hand, placed something in his palm, then stood to leave. At the threshold, he paused and said, *"Poka my ne vstretimsya snova, Kapitan."*

Until we meet again . . .

Konstantin watched his stateroom door close. Then he lifted his hand, opened his fingers, and looked inside his palm to see a Soviet-era submarine captain's insignia—a brass U-boat with a red star in the center. A smile curled his lips as he closed his fingers tight around the pin, let his eyelids fall shut, and his mind drift off into a cold, dreamless sleep.

74

A W1 Levi Prescott arched his back and rolled his neck, letting out a little sigh and blinking a few times. The mission was nothing new to him—he'd been flying long patrols in the P8 since he'd graduated A School and had been with VP-5 through the block 2 upgrades. But today, the stakes of the mission changed everything. He'd been razzed by friends for years after being assigned a mission many thought antiquated. With twenty years of hunting terrorists in the Middle East, hunting submarines seemed like Grandad's Navy, and in fact his grandad had been a submarine sailor.

Prescott wasn't fully read in on all the details, but he knew today's op was different. The tension was high in the cabin of the Navy's most advanced maritime surveillance jet, and even the normally laid-back practical joker Lieutenant Commander Brenner seemed quiet and steely-eyed. The officer was even sitting at his own station, working as hard as the rest of them to find whatever it was they were hunting.

"What the hell kind of submarine goes seventy-five knots, bro?" the aviation warfare specialist to his right, a kid from Hoboken,

New Jersey, named Tony Gallo, said softly. He liked Tony, and not just because they were both from Jersey—they were "the Jersey Boys" among the rest of the crew.

"I don't know, bro," he answered, "but if we get close to it we should find it. I mean, it must be making a helluva lot of noise at that speed, right?"

"Yeah," was all Gallo said, then he looked with envy at Prescott's workstation. Gallo was working the active sonar buoys, which meant he received very little data this far out, mostly a school of fish or other biologics, and the contours of the ocean floor. Prescott worked the passive sonar. His job was to just listen to the ocean, and the ocean, it happened, made a lot of noise. Normally, he adjusted his filters pretty narrowly to remove any biologics and wave action. Today, he'd been ordered to broaden the filters, so he was receiving tons of data, which at least made the time go by. The military version of the Boeing 737-800 ERX could, with aerial refueling, which they had already done once, stay on mission almost indefinitely, but at least for a full twenty-four hours. It was good to have something to do . . .

"Hey, Prescott," LCDR Brenner said.

"Yeah, boss?" Prescott answered. He liked that he could be casual with this crew. He'd worked with a lot of officers who were uptight assholes. As long as the crew got the work done, Brenner liked to be one of the boys.

"You still have the pass seven data coming to you?"

He checked his screen and then moved his mouse to open up a dialogue box and bring the pass from a good while ago back into his dataset.

"I do now," he said.

"They want us to listen in that area."

"Who the hell is this 'they' we keep talking about?" Gallo grumbled.

"I don't know, Gallo. It all comes through UNSEA," Brenner said, using their slang for Commander, Undersea Surveillance or COMUNDERSEASURV in the aronym-laden Navy parlance, "but it definitely has a new vibe, like someone else is driving the boat. But this is a no-bullshit mission, boys, I can tell you . . ."

Prescott held up a hand and leaned in, and all chatter stopped. He pressed his hand to his headset, sealing it better from the cabin noise, and used the mouse to increase the gain. Then he drew a line to where sonobuoy-47 sat in the ocean below the surface, with its antenna poking out above the waves, sending him the data it was collecting.

"What in the hell?" he mumbled.

"Whaddya got, Jersey?" Brenner asked.

"Flight, turn left heading one-three-five and close on SB47."

"Flight," came the voice of the copilot, Lieutenant Derek Hines, from Florida.

The plane closed the distance on the sonobuoy to the east, and the intermittent signal became constant as he adjusted his gain and then his filters.

"Holy shit," he said and looked over at Brenner.

"What?"

He listened another moment, eyes closed, then opened them and smiled at his boss.

"Got 'em, boss," he said. "We have something moving fast and cavitating like hell, bearing rate indicates westbound."

He worked the mouse and added the contact to his screen, which shared immediately with the other stations.

"Get me something on active and triangulate," Brenner said.

"Damn," Gallo said. "It's screaming through my active line now and . . ." He squinted at the screen. "That ain't no great white shark, boss. This thing is moving at seventy-eight knots."

"Tracking," Lieutenant Sarah Beach said from the terminal beside Brenner. "This has to be what we're looking for."

Brenner smiled, but his smile seemed grim.

"I'm calling it in right now," he said. "Don't lose it, guys."

Prescott glanced at Gallo, who smiled.

"I don't think we gotta worry about that," Prescott said. "That thing is screaming. Now that we have the signature in the computer, we can track it wherever it's going."

"What do you think it is?" Gallo said. "Has to be some sort of experimental high-speed UUV? One of ours, right? A test?"

Prescott saw worry on his crewmate's face. He looked at the map, extending the track of the contact to the west as he zoomed out. The magenta line he created ended at Norfolk Naval Base. "I don't think so, dude," he said and felt his stomach tighten. "Stay on this shit, bro."

75

ST2 Harris concentrated on listening to the sounds of the ocean like the world depended on it because, well, it did.

The *Battle Bass* had flanked across the Atlantic, on orders from the President, to this one particular patch of water, where—based on data from a hundred water drones, scores of sonobuoys, and who knew what other assets—some kind of artificial intelligence on a server in Bahrain had predicted that some big-ass, nuclear-armed torpedo was going to pass through. Then they'd received flash traffic at PD that the target had been found and it was the *Indiana*'s job to kill it. According to the skipper, who'd briefed the entire watch section on the details, there was great irony in this development. The big-ass nuclear torpedo on course to blow up Norfolk had been fired by K-329 *Belgorod*, the same damn Russian submarine that had tricked them in the Barents.

The skipper had then done something that Harris had not expected, which was give him props in front of the entire crew, by saying that if Harris hadn't figured out the Russians' ruse, the carrier strike group would have been nuked and they wouldn't have this chance to stop the doomsday weapon speeding toward Norfolk.

It wasn't all me, Harris thought with a head shake. *The ACINT dude deserves credit, too.*

Since he and Jason Torvik had worked to figure that out, they'd become fast friends. Torvik had even tried to talk Harris into applying for the ACINT program. He told him that he was a gifted sonarman. Harris didn't know about that, but he appreciated the brother for saying so.

An emerging tonal, just barely audible, snapped him from his thoughts.

Harris closed his eyes and listened. Convinced it wasn't an imagined signal—which happened sometimes—he opened his eyes and scanned the broadband gram for a pattern in the static. Usually, he picked up frequencies by ear first, before the signal crossed the threshold for the computer to distinguish tonal from background noise. Ten seconds later, a line began to collate at the top of the gram.

"Hey, Supe," Harris said, waving his chief over. "I got something, bearing one-one-two. High-pitched whine."

Schonauer came over and so did Torvik, who'd been nervously pacing in the corner.

Schonauer took one look and said, "Conn, Sonar, new sonar contact, designated Sierra Seven, bearing one-one-two, possible inbound Status-6 drone."

"Sonar, Conn, aye," the officer of the deck, Lieutenant Yu, said and turned to the sub's skipper, Commander Bresnahan, who stood next to him at the command workstation. "Captain, I think this could be it. Bearing is to the east, matches expected track provided to us by COMUNDERSEASURV, and we're inside the time window."

"I agree, Lieutenant," the CO said. "Fire Control, let's get a firing solution on Sierra Seven."

"Aye, Captain," the XO, LCDR Pifer, who stood watch as fire control coordinator, said.

"ACINT, run that signal through the narrowband analyzer," Schonauer said.

"Aye, Chief," Torvik said. He dropped into the console next to Harris and went to work.

"Sounds like it's screaming through the water to me," Harris said and passed his headphones to the chief.

Schonauer took a quick listen, eyes closed. "I can hear the screw. The blade rate is off the charts." He opened his eyes and handed the headset back to Harris.

"But I don't hear a combustion engine like a typical torpedo," Harris said after slipping the muffs back on and listening.

"And you won't," Torvik said, "because the Status-6 has a small nuclear power plant inside it. It's turbine driven . . . Looking at the analyzer, I'd say the acoustic profile matches the expected one. Chief, I recommend classifying Sierra Seven as an inbound Status-6 drone torpedo."

Schonauer called it out. "Conn, Sonar, Sierra Seven is classified as a Status-6 nuclear torpedo."

"Very well," Yu said.

"Attention in control," the CO said. "It appears ST2 Harris has once again, thanks to his keen ears and insightful mind, found our bogie. Sierra Seven is now Master One."

All stations acknowledged the CO's announcement.

"Officer of the deck, Master One bearing one-one-five, range twenty-six thousand yards, is on course two-seven-one, making seventy-six knots," Pifer said, announcing the fire control solution they'd built for the target. "Recommend firing point procedures."

"Very well, Coordinator," Lieutenant Yu said, standing watch as the OOD. "Captain, do you want to take the conn?"

"I could," the CO said, "or you could take the shot. How'd you like to be the guy who saved a million people and stopped World War Three? That's the sort of thing that looks good on a FITREP. I imagine you'd probably screen for XO with that."

"Yeah, unless he misses," the JOOW, LTJG Rucker, piped up.

As first, Harris was baffled by the captain's words. By all normal protocols, letting Yu keep the conn for the shot was unprecedented. The captain was the most experienced ship driver and war fighter on the boat. But Bresnahan's command tour was winding down in two months. This wasn't the CO being cavalier or careless. It was mentorship. It was the passing of the torch to the next generation of submarine captains. The skipper would be standing right beside Yu, ready to intervene at a moment's notice if necessary.

Now, that's leadership.

Yu seemed to consider the question for a moment, then he said, "I'll take the shot, sir."

"All right, LT, let's sink this bastard," Bresnahan said.

"All stations, Conn, firing point procedures, Master One," Yu said. "Ready two torpedo salvos. Tubes one and two are salvo one, and tubes three and four are salvo two."

"Intelligence indicates that these things run fast and deep, so use submerged presets and search deep on salvo one," Bresnahan added.

"Coordinator, aye," the XO said.

Harris, despite desperately wanting to turn and watch the proceedings, had a job to do, so all he could do was wait and listen as the fire control team and torpedo room readied the salvo. Less than a minute later, he heard the XO report they were ready.

"Captain?" Lieutenant Yu asked.

"Do it," the CO said.

"Coordinator, shoot salvo one!" the OOD announced.

Tube one cycled and the boat shook. Tube two followed three seconds later. Harris forced a yawn and wiggled his jaw to pop his ears after the pressure transients while he watched the traces appear on his broadband display for two Mark 48 ADCAPs that now tore through the deep at over sixty knots toward the target.

"Conn, Coordinator, telemetry is good. Both torpedoes are in passive search," the XO reported.

"Torpedo one has slowed and is in active search," Harris reported. Three seconds later, he said, "Torpedo two has slowed and is in active search."

"Conn, Sonar, both torpedoes are active homing on the target."

Harris closed his eyes and listened, imagining the torpedo duel unfolding in the dark at over a thousand feet below the surface. He heard the characteristic change in the torpedo's active sonar profile, indicating that it had transitioned from scanning for the target to having acquired the target.

"Supe, torpedo one is range-gating," he said.

"Conn, Sonar, torpedo one is range-gating," Schonauer said.

"Very well."

"Supe, torpedo two is range-gating and torpedo one is in terminal homing," Harris reported.

The supe passed the report to the OOD.

"Thirty seconds to impact on torpedo one," the XO announced.

"Very well, Coordinator."

"Torpedo two is terminal homing," Harris said, and Schonauer announced it.

"Twenty seconds to impact . . . Fifteen seconds . . . Ten seconds . . . Five, four, three, two, one . . ."

Harris didn't hear a detonation. "Supe, torpedo one missed."

"Torpedo one missed the target," the XO announced.

"Sonar confirms, torpedo one missed the target."

"C'mon, number two, kick his ass," Harris murmured.

"Ten seconds to impact on torpedo two."

Harris crossed his fingers and closed his eyes.

"Five . . . Four . . . Three . . . Two . . . One—"

The explosion rocked Harris's ears, but he didn't care. "Detonation, torpedo two!" he shouted, but that didn't mean the Russian Status-6 was destroyed. He needed to confirm that its sonar signature and trace were gone.

"Supe, I got nothing on Sierra Seven—I mean Master One. No broadband, no blade rate, no narrowband. I think we sank it."

"Conn, Sonar, lost contact on Master One, believe Master One has been destroyed," the supe said.

The conn erupted into whoops and hollers and "hooyahs."

Harris watched the CO give the OOD a bear hug. He even saw victory tears in Schonauer's eyes. He felt a tap on his shoulder and turned to find Torvik looking at him. The ACINT dude raised his fist for a bump, but Harris popped to his feet and wrapped his brother sonarman up in a back-slapping hug.

"How does it feel to be the guy who saved the world?" Torvik said when Harris let him go.

"I gotta say, shipmate," he said, feeling tears of joy and relief rim his own eyes. "It feels pretty damn excellent."

76

Colonel General Nikolai Ilyin was fuming.

The failure of the *Belgorod* operation was a tragic blow—as was the loss of Captain Gorov—but that was not the only thing that had him agitated tonight. The fact that he had been *summoned* had gotten under his skin. It was not the place of Admiral Boldyrev to summon him, no matter the source. The message from the commander of the Russian Northern Fleet had been cryptic, simply implying he had news that must be shared with the entire group face-to-face. Boldyrev was a friend, but in this New Russia they were building, he was also a subordinate. It was simply not the way things were done. And on top of all that, he was irritated at being late. Colonel General Nikolai Ilyin was never, ever late. But the delay from the detour caused by the closure of Ulitsa Kuznetsky had been compounded by a traffic accident on Ulitsa Bol'shaya Lubyanka and would most certainly make him the last to arrive.

Upon reaching the front door, he paused, his hand literally frozen in midair as he stretched for the handle. Was it possible he was being betrayed? Might Boldyrev, shaken by the loss of Gorov and the *Belgorod*, have confessed their true plans to Yermilov?

No—impossible.

I am being paranoid.

He pushed open the door and shrugged out of his overcoat.

A figure appeared, an unexpected figure, and he started—but quickly recovered and summoned a placating smile.

"I am sorry, Nadia," he said to the wife of his lifelong KGB friend. "I didn't see you there. Where is Anatoly?"

She smiled back at him, but her smile seemed that of stone. She'd always been cold to him, but he'd written it off as her default state. Many women of her generation were cold and bitter. Nevertheless, she was loyal to her husband and indulged Anatoly's whims—such as closing the restaurant for secret meetings of the old guard club.

"He is in the kitchen," she said, but her voice sounded flat. Perhaps the others' negative emotions had set a dour mood. Perhaps she sensed that all was not well and wished her husband to no longer be a part of it. "He is preparing your usual meal. Our cook is ill, so he is doing it himself."

"Of course he is. Anatoly is a good man and a good friend."

"Yes," she said simply. "And sometimes a good husband." She turned and headed to the kitchen, calling over her shoulder, "You're the last to arrive. The others are upstairs waiting."

He nodded and then ascended the stairs, the creak of the old wood comforting. It was a sound of the old Russia and, he had to believe, a Russia that could still be brought back to life.

Darkness seemed to hang thick and suffocating on the second-story balcony. Bathed in shadow, his colleagues sat around their usual table, watching him expectantly as he approached.

"I know that this has been a disappointment . . ." he began, but his voice trailed off.

Something was wrong.

A lone figure emerged from the dark corner of the room, still in shadow, but the weapon in the killer's hand clearly visible in the smoky streams of light from below.

"Anatoly? What is this . . . ?" Ilyin said.

But the figure wasn't Anatoly. This man was too thin. Too fit.

Then everything became clear to him. The motionless bodies at the table came into focus as his eyes adapted to the dark. They were slumped in their seats, heads tilted back. They had been staged for him to see as he arrived, but they were all quite dead. He could see a rivulet of blood on Rodionov's face, black in the poor light, running from a hole above his left eye, along his nose, and ending in a clotting drop on his chin.

He turned to the thin man, recognizing the pistol leveled at him as an SR-1 Vektor—a favorite of both the FSB and GRU.

"*Prezident Yermilov bol'she ne nuzhdayetsya v vashikh uslugakh,*" the man growled.

"Impossible," he replied in Russian, though he was certain this man was not Russian. He switched to English on a hunch. "President Yermilov has neither the courage nor the audacity to send you here. Let us talk and come to an arrangement—one that will benefit us both."

Ilyin took a step forward, but the man raised the Vektor higher, aiming now at his face.

"In that case," the man said, "President Ryan sends his regards."

At those words, Ilyin's heart skipped a beat.

He tried to think of something clever to say, something that might buy him time while he contemplated a proposal to save his life, but the pistol flashed fire.

For a millisecond his head erupted with pain, and then he felt nothing as the world went completely and unforgivingly black.

77

Clark shuffled slowly along the sidewalk, glancing at the crowd waiting to get inside the busy hot spot across the street. He held his cell phone to his ear with his left hand, speaking in English, but to no one. A listener would see him as a foreigner, perhaps speaking to his wife or girlfriend, but then, Moscow was full of tourists these days. He laughed at something the fictitious person on his fictitious call said, his right hand inside his jacket pocket, still clutching the Vektor pistol wrapped in a brown sandwich bag he'd taken from the restaurant. Nadia had gone behind her husband's back to help Clark orchestrate the hit, and Clark suspected she had done it for herself as much as she had to save the world.

He vectored toward a trash can, still talking, and then pulled the brown bag from his pocket and dropped it in the can as he walked past. It landed with a dull thud, napkins packed around the gun inside the bag muting the sound.

"I'm having a great time, but I'm eager to be home," he said without breaking stride.

"I hope that's not supposed to be code, Viking One," Ding said into his earpiece. "'Cause if so, I missed it in the pre-op."

Clark glanced again at the crowd in front of the Atmosphere nightclub. It might as well have been a club in L.A. or New York or Miami. The young people out front laughed and shouted to one another, all on their iPhones, AirPods in their ears. This wasn't the Russia from his past—or the Russia inside of the dark-wood-paneled Glavpivtorg, where he'd left the dead bodies of men who were shackled to that past. Inside the restaurant he'd felt young. He had plenty of years left in him, but when he looked across the street at the young *new* Russians, he felt—not old, not yet—but tired.

"That's right," he said, still pretending to talk into his phone and heading off now to the west. "I promised my wife I'd spend a week at home with the grandkids."

Clark could picture Ding at a laptop, open on a desk in his hotel room at the Marriott Royal Aurora a few blocks away.

"We can make that happen. I assume Viking is Jackpot?" Ding said, prompting Clark for actual code-word confirmation that the mission was complete, which Clark had yet to give.

"Jackpot," he said softly.

He slipped his phone into his jacket pocket as he approached the corner. He was tired of the ruse. Whatever deal President Ryan had made with the feckless thug running things in Russia didn't apply to Clark and his team. This operation couldn't be avowed, not by either nation. And, more important, Clark had not sought approval for the assassinations. He liked and admired Jack Ryan and considered him one of the very few true friends he had. But it wasn't Ryan's nature—nor his job, he supposed—to operate in the amoral world of gray. Ryan was a black-and-white guy. There were only two buckets: right and wrong.

Clark didn't know what information the American President had passed to Yermilov through his back channels about the cabal members, but he did know that the world couldn't afford to give the Russian mastermind, Colonel General Ilyin, and the other cabal members a second chance. He knew in his heart they would try again, and he refused to risk Ilyin pulling the trigger on any contingency plans the man had in place. His job was to tie up the secret loose ends. His job was to give the White House cover and deniability. His job was to safeguard the President's conscience so Jack could save the world during the day, but be able to sleep at night.

Unless told otherwise, Ryan would assume the cabal members had been eliminated on Yermilov's order. Betrayal was an unforgivable sin, and Russian justice was what Yermilov did best.

He doubted Yermilov would thank him for doing the deed. In fact, the dictator would probably be incensed that he'd been robbed of the opportunity to mete vengeance himself. Russians were funny that way. Clark and his team wouldn't be safe until they were airborne and out of Russian airspace.

"Viking One is ready for exfil," he muttered softly.

"Roger, Viking. You coming back to the roost?"

He thought a moment.

"No," he said. "No sense risking the team if I'm being followed. Give me a few mintues to check for ticks, then I'll meet you outside the Bolshoi."

"Copy," Ding said. "Packing it up. We'll pull into the valet at the Ararat Park Hotel across the street from the Bolshoi to the east. Our jet is standing by with a flight plan filed and clearances ready to go."

"Copy," Clark said. "Fifteen mikes."

He didn't really need fifteen minutes. He was a block from the pickup location and had already checked for tails. He just needed . . . a moment.

A moment for himself.

He stepped out of the shadows of the buildings lining Pushech-naya Street and into the bright lights of the main thoroughfare heading south, toward the Bolshoi. He wanted to sit a minute and take in the sights and sounds of the beating heart of Moscow. He doubted the opportunity would come again. With a tight-lipped smile, he found an unoccupied bench and took a seat.

The world was changing fast.

But so long as he was in it, he'd make the hard choices, and do the hard things, to ensure that change was for the better.

78

USS *WASHINGTON*, SSN 787, "THE *BLACKFISH*"
INSIDE THE AMALFI-NAPOLI SHIPPING CHANNEL
   IN THE GULF OF NAPOLI
NINE NAUTICAL MILES SOUTH OF SUBMARINE GROUP 8
   FORWARD BASE
NAVAL SUPPORT ACTIVITY NAPLES
0610 LOCAL TIME

Katie was ready to go home.

The feeling had hit her hard and unexpectedly during breakfast. Probably because the *Blackfish* was pulling into Naples this morning, and by this afternoon she'd be on a plane heading back to D.C. It was difficult to articulate, but it reminded her of the feeling she had at the end of a long workday when she couldn't wait to strip off her uniform and change into comfy clothes. Her adventures on the *Ford* and the *Blackfish* had been incredible, but she was ready to get back to her regular life.

In the meantime, she wasn't sure what to do with herself.

As soon as they'd secured battle stations and the adrenaline had burned off, she'd slept hard—hell, she practically lapsed into a coma for twelve hours. Ever since, she'd been wrangling with a strange cognitive dissonance. Sometimes the traumatic torpedo battle with the *Belgorod* seemed like it had just happened five minutes ago, other times it felt like a different lifetime.

So weird . . .

After breakfast, she'd come to the conn, because that's where all the action was. But now she felt very much in the way. Transiting on the surface was more frenetic on a submarine than traveling submerged. She understood why submariners couldn't wait to "go deep" after leaving port.

Someone bumped into her and apologized.

A minute later it happened again.

Maybe I should just go sit in the wardroom, have a coffee, and stay out of the way . . .

"Lieutenant Ryan?" Commander Houston said.

She looked up to find the venerable captain of the *Washington* smiling at her from where he stood beside the OOD's workstation in the middle of the conn.

"Yes, sir?" she said.

"Commander Knepper is requesting your presence in the bridge cockpit."

She raised an eyebrow. "The bridge cockpit, sir?"

He chuckled. "Up on the sail, Ryan. Remember the way you came aboard?"

At the time, the transfer from the Osprey to the sail of the *Washington* had been the most terrifying evolution of her life. Of course, that was before everything else that had happened since she came aboard.

"Oh, I remember, sir," she said.

"This way, ma'am," a young sailor said from behind her and handed her a harness and a spray jacket. "Pretty calm seas today, but it might get a little wet up there."

"Thank you," she said and let him help her into the safety harness.

Then she shrugged on the waterproof jacket, grateful for the warmth. *Damn, they kept these submarines cold.* Knepper had explained why, but she didn't remember what he'd told her. She followed the sailor aft through the command passageway, up a ladder, then forward and around the lock-out chamber to the bridge trunk.

"Careful on the ladder, ma'am. It gets wet and slippery sometimes," he said, pointing up through the open hatch into the bridge trunk.

"Thanks," she said.

Methodically, she climbed the two-story ladder, holding on tight to the handrails as the sub rolled side to side with the waves. When she neared the top, someone raised the grate hatch and she emerged beside a pair of booted feet. When she looked up, Knepper offered her his hand, giving her something to hold on to as she took the last few rungs. With a relieved exhale, she stepped up into the cramped bridge cockpit, which felt ridiculously bare-bones. Another pair of boots hung behind her and she looked over her shoulder to find Juggernaut sitting on the top of the sail, feet dangling into the cockpit area. A third person, the lookout, stood behind Jackie, leaning against the railing of the flying bridge, binoculars up and scanning.

"I told you the day we met, Ryan," Knepper said, apparently reading her thoughts, "space is a commodity on a submarine." He lowered the grate back down so Katie had something to stand on.

"I remember."

He reached over, unclipped one end of her safety lanyard from the D ring on her shoulder strap, and attached it to a metal stanchion.

"Thanks," she said.

He nodded. "After all you did for us and our mission, I thought it only fair to let you come up and enjoy this. Being up here—cruising on the surface when the sun is shining and the breeze is blowing—this is my favorite part of driving submarines."

The XO of the deadliest war machine on the planet gestured with a hand and she took in the view.

Ahead, blue water slid across the sub's massive sonar dome, then frothed white as the impressive bow wave split into a V, before churning into a turbulent wake that rippled down the port and starboard sides of the hull. To her right, the horizon was a glowing ribbon of red and orange, the sky an infinite canvas for the rising sun to paint. The air had a chill and a smell of salt that reminded her of home—the Ryan family home back on the Chesapeake. She inhaled the fresh sea breeze, only to have the experience rudely interrupted by an unpleasant tang wafting up from the grate beneath her feet. Knepper had explained that the malodorous mélange was a mix of amine, lube oil, body odor, and garbage.

Nice, she thought with a *God help me* glance at heaven, and couldn't help but wonder if she, herself, now smelled like an authentic submariner.

She tipped up on her toes to watch the bow dip and rise in a soothing rhythm as they plowed the sea, silently propelled by nuclear power. Off to her right, an albatross skimmed the wave tops, cutting this way and that as if teaching a master class in precision flying.

Savoring the moment, she glanced at Knepper, who was squinting slightly against the sea breeze, the hint of a contented smile on his face.

Feeling her gaze, he looked over. "God, I love my job," he said.

"I can see why," she said and meant it.

"I just love blowing shit up," Jackie said from behind her, and they all laughed.

Knepper pulled a hand from his pocket and extended it to her. Katie reached out and shook it, feeling the cool metal of a command coin pressed between their palms as she did.

"Thanks for everything, Katie," he said.

She broke the handshake and took the coin, resisting the urge to look at it like some tourist, and slipped it into her pocket.

"And thank you for saving the world," she said.

"I've got something for you, too, Ryan," Juggernaut said.

Katie turned and the feisty genius of a weapons officer handed her a ball cap. Inside, she saw a Velcro patch just like the one the ship's crew wore—a multi-cam green flag with a cartoon orca grinning from the center. In the upper left corner *SSN 787* was stitched, and at the bottom, in cursive, *Fear the Blackfish*.

Katie slipped the patch into her pocket and the cap onto her head.

"One more thing, Ryan," Knepper said and dropped something else into her hand.

Katie stared at it in awe.

The submariner warfare pin—known in the submarine community as getting one's fish—depicted a surfaced O-class submarine flanked by two center-facing dolphins. But instead of a shiny silver finish for enlisted personnel or gold for officer corps, this insignia had been painted black.

Black . . . fish, she realized.

"Keep those somewhere special, Katie," Knepper said. "You'll always be a part of the *Blackfish* crew."

"I will," Katie said, then felt horrified at the realization that tears were rimming her eyes. Hopefully, they wouldn't notice.

"Who knows, Ryan," Juggernaut said, leaning over from her perch and slapping Katie on the back. "Maybe someday you'll have the balls to change your designator and join us for real."

"Who knows," she said with a glance back at the WEPS.

She stared out across the water, where the lights of Naples were growing larger in the distance. She had things to say, but the moment, she decided, called for silence. So she stood in the sail of the mighty USS *Washington*, beside her shipmates, and quietly watched the sun rise on the horizon of a new day.

EPILOGUE

Jack Ryan—husband, father, and President of the United States—sat quietly at the head of the table, watching his kids laugh, smile, tease each other, and break bread, as if time had stood still, lives had not changed, and the family still lived here in peace on the plot of land looking over the Chesapeake. Peace, despite the playful bickering, which had once seemed like noise and now warmed him like a blanket, was the exact, right word. Here there was the peace of a family who knew each other intimately. But out there—outside this house—each of them fought a battle that was anything but peace. Out there, they shouldered the burden of keeping three hundred forty million Americans safe, each Ryan in his or her own chosen way.

He was proud.

And a little sad. But mostly proud.

"I can't believe you came all the way home for dinner," Katie joked to her twin brother, who sat beside her, with a playful elbow to the ribs.

"Ow," Kyle said, smiling and rubbing his ribs. "And I didn't come home for dinner, I came home on leave. And you're welcome for introducing you to Lieutenant Tucker and Task Force 59 so they could make you look good."

"Make us all look good," Ryan said, smiling at his youngest son.

Kyle, always the one to take things a bit seriously, blushed.

"I was just kidding, Dad," he said.

"I know," Ryan said. "I wasn't."

"Thanks for the connection," Katie said. Then Ryan watched her study her twin brother quizzically. "By the way, I still don't know exactly what you do for the Navy in Bahrain."

"I could tell you, sis," Kyle said, his face quite serious, "but then I'd have to kill you."

He burst out laughing, and the whole table joined in.

"Well," Jack Junior said, folding his napkin and placing it on the table, "since I'm in the unusual situation of being the one *not* read in on what happened, I'll clear the table." He rose and began collecting plates and utensils.

"Since I'm *never* read in—and don't really even know what that means—I'll help you," Sally said, kissing her husband, Davi, on the cheek and then rising. She collected the drinking glasses and followed her brother into the kitchen.

It was the right moment, Ryan decided.

"How about everyone pitch in?" he said, seeing the knowing look and basking in the loving smile from Cathy at the other end of the table. "Except you, Katie. How about you come with me to my office for a minute?"

Katie raised a curious eyebrow, but rose to follow him.

"Uh-oh," Kyle said, followed by a childlike, singsong, "Someone's getting in trouble . . ."

She laughed, tossed her napkin at her twin, and followed Ryan through the foyer and the dayroom to his office. Given recent events, Katie seemed to be following most closely in his footsteps, though she probably had no idea that was true.

Something I intend to remedy in the next few minutes.

While it qualified as a SCIF, Ryan's office was more like the den of a business tycoon from the eighties—plush leather chairs and a matching sofa, a large walnut desk with a high-back chair, and even a small bar in the corner. The office had no windows, and hidden inside the walls was sound-absorbing material and technology that worked like a Faraday cage, blocking any and all physical and electronic eavesdropping.

Katie took a seat on the sofa, perpendicular to the desk, instead of across from him.

"Is this okay?" she said.

Her face suggested she wanted to be his Katie, but was prepared to sit across from him in the "hot seat," if that was where things were headed.

"Perfect," he said, and it was. This was a Daddy-daughter moment, not a conversation between the commander in chief and a senior ONI analyst.

Well, maybe a touch of both . . .

He grabbed an ornate wooden display box and opened the lid to reveal a polished brass depth gauge sitting in a velvet-lined cradle. He tapped his finger on the gauge's glass face while Katie looked on.

Her curiosity now piqued, she leaned in for a closer look, screwing her face up as she worked the problem.

"That thing has been on your desk my whole life. When I was a kid, I always thought it was a weird clock. But looking at it now . . ." Her voice trailed off, and he could see her mind racing. That big brain of hers just never stopped, did it? Analyzing, dissecting, solving, and, most important, questioning.

"It's definitely not a clock," he said with a wry grin.

"It has Cyrillic writing on it. How did I not notice that before?"

"We'll get to that," he said, remembering watching this very gauge with knots in his stomach from the helmsman's chair on the *Red October*. "Why I have this and how I came upon it is what I want to talk to you about, kid."

"Kid?" she said with a warm laugh. "I'll allow that, I guess, since you're my dad and my commander in chief."

"I want to tell you a story, Katie," he said.

"Okaaay," she said, drawing the word out, her face rife with curiosity.

"It's an old story, from my life before all this happened," he said, gesturing around the office. "And one I want to share with you not only because you're my daughter, but also because you're ready. And I want to tell it now, because you're the one person in the family who has both the personal experience, but also the clearance, needed to hear and appreciate it."

"Okay," she said. "You definitely have my attention."

"Katie, this story—*my* story—may seem like a tale from another generation, but it's time for the next generation of leaders to hear it, and stories like it."

"'Those who cannot remember the past are condemned to repeat it'—George Santayana," she said, her voice soft and reverent.

"Precisely," he said, feeling an upswelling of love and pride for his daughter.

She leaned in, elbows on knees, ready.

"What you're about to hear is the true story," he began, "of the hunt for the *Red October* . . ."